Pirates of the Relentless Desert

Pirates of the Relentless Desert

THE CLOUDED WORLD: BOOK TWO

Jay Amory

GOLLANCZ

LONDON

The right of Jay Amory to be identified as the
author of this work has been asserted by him in accordance
with the Copyright, Designs and Patents Act 1988.

First published in Great Britain in 2007 by
Gollancz
An imprint of the Orion Publishing Group
Orion House, 5 Upper St Martin's Lane, London WC2H 9EA

A CIP catalogue record for this book is available
from the British Library

ISBN-13 978 0 57507 880 2 (cased)
ISBN-10 0 57507 880 4 (cased)
ISBN-13 978 0 57508 032 4 (trade paperback)
ISBN-10 0 57508 032 9 (trade paperback)

1 3 5 7 9 10 8 6 4 2

Typeset by Input Data Services Ltd, Frome

Printed in Great Britain by Mackays of Chatham plc,
Chatham, Kent

www.orionbooks.co.uk

The Orion Publishing Group's policy is to use papers that
are natural, renewable and recyclable products and made from
wood grown in sustainable forests. The logging and manufacturing
processes are expected to conform to the environmental
regulations of the country of origin.

CHAPTER I

The Black Cloud

The night sky above the Relentless Desert gave birth to a new cloud.

At first there was just the usual inky swirl of the cloud cover, palely marbled with moonlight. Then a long, rounded shape appeared, pressing itself out from the underside of the clouds. Black against blackness, the shape broke free, then rotated around its own axis and moved northward at an unhurried pace, emitting a low, droning hum as it went. Gradually it began to lose height. The faint, cigar-like shadow it cast on the sand below grew larger.

On the ground a few kilometres ahead, a small man-made spark glinted in the midst of the desert emptiness. It was a cluster of lights which shone out from a maze of criss-crossing roads that ran between drilling towers, distillation columns, 'nodding donkey' pump units, storage tanks, pipelines, derricks, and one-storey concrete housing blocks.

The lights belonged to Westward Oil Enterprises extraction and refining installation number 137, popularly known as Desolation Wells, and they burned all night long even though everyone on the workforce was fast asleep in bed. They burned to keep the darkness at bay – the vast, terrible darkness of the desert at night, which was as pure and unending as oblivion and could drive a person mad.

The lights were like a beacon. They drew the black cloud to them. The cloud vectored unerringly in the installation's direction, predator towards prey.

As it reached the perimeter of Desolation Wells, the black cloud came to a halt, its hum decreasing to a whisper. Suddenly dozens of winged figures emerged from it, one after another. They poured out in a stream and clustered together. Then, at a pre-arranged signal, they scattered. With near-silent wingbeats they fanned out across the installation. A few headed for the housing blocks. The rest made for the warehouses where refined oil was stored in steel barrels, ready to be transported by truck across the Relentless Desert.

The warehouses were not locked. There were no thieves out here in this remote spot, two days' journey from anything that might be called civilisation. At least, no thieves that the owners of Westward Oil Enterprises, WOE, could have anticipated.

The winged figures only had to roll open the warehouse doors, stealthily, to gain access to the hundreds of full barrels stacked inside. They set about removing as many as they could. Each barrel weighed several hundred kilogrammes and required the strength of three of them to lift it. Struggling with their burdens, the trios of winged figures bore the barrels to the hovering black cloud and deposited them inside.

The cloud – the pirate airship *Behemoth* – slowly filled up with plundered fuel. Over the course of an hour the airship's cargo holds were loaded to capacity. Softly she purged water ballast in order to compensate for the added weight.

Meanwhile groups of the winged figures stood guard outside the entrances to the housing blocks. Their colleagues were being as careful as possible with the barrels, but it was best to be prepared, just in case. Accidents could happen.

And eventually, one did. A barrel slipped from the hands of the threesome who were carrying it. Their arms and wings were aching after an hour of transporting so many gallons of fuel up to *Behemoth*; their fingers had begun to cramp. One of them lost his grip on the rim of the barrel. The other two could not keep hold of it between them. The barrel fell for fifty metres, tumbling end over end, and hit the ground with an almighty, booming *clonnggg*. It split open on impact and thick liquid slooshed everywhere.

The noise awoke the roughnecks – oil workers – who were sleeping in a nearby housing block. They leapt from their beds, threw on some clothes, and rushed to the main entrance to see what was going on.

Waiting for them outside the door were a half-dozen of the winged figures. To the roughnecks, still shaking off the fog of sleep, these looked like something out of a nightmare.

They were lean, nervy creatures, with sores and bad skin, and each wore a motley assortment of clothing. No two of them were dressed alike, some sporting bandannas around their foreheads, others scarves around their necks, others with sashes diagonally across their torsos, others with brocaded waistcoats, or any combination of these. Most had long hair, with beaded braids and brightly coloured streaks showing here and there amid the straggly curls and spikes. Most had ornate tattoos on their arms and faces, and metal piercings glinted in ears, noses, lips, and wings. All were bearing weapons – crossbows, sabres, daggers, maces – and they brandished these as they looked sneeringly at the roughnecks, their mouths curling up at the corners in contempt.

One, however, stood out from the rest. She was tall, sinuous, voluptuous, and clad solely in black leather, from top to toe. Even her face was covered. A black leather mask encased her head and a pair of smoked-glass flight goggles hid her eyes. Her wings, similarly, were black – black as a raven's. She was like a silhouette, a shadow in the shape of a winged woman. Even the lance she carried was black. The only spot of colour on her was the patch stitched on her chest: a skull above two crossed feathers, picked out in black on red. The same motif, much larger, adorned the airship's tailfins.

'Air – Airborn?' one of the roughnecks stammered.

'Get back, emu,' barked the black-clad woman, waving the lance at him. The mask muffled her voice, making it sound distant and weird. 'Get back or I'll run you through.'

'What'm you doing? What *be* this?' another of the roughnecks asked.

The speaker was Magnus Clockweight, the 'toolpusher', or site foreman. He was a broad-shouldered, brawny, big-fisted fellow. All of the roughnecks were. You needed to be made of stern stuff if you wanted to work at Desolation Wells.

Yet, for all that, Clockweight's voice trembled as he phrased his questions. He was frightened, and so was everyone standing with him. These winged apparitions were shabby and unkempt and inhuman. They were *wrong*. The roughnecks had limited knowledge of what the Airborn looked like. Most, in fact, had never actually set eyes on a member of that race before. This was not how they expected them to be. This was almost the exact opposite of that.

'"What *be* this?"' one of the pirates echoed, with a high-pitched, demented laugh. His hair was a shock of green dread-locks and his eyes rolled in their sockets like loose marbles.

'What does it look like it is?' the sinister, leather-clad woman said to Clockweight. She spoke with the unmistakable authority and assertiveness of a leader. 'We're taking what's rightfully ours. Taking what you Groundlings should still be giving us for free. Now shut up and behave. Be obedient little ostriches. Unless you want to know how it feels to have a lance skewer your guts ...'

None of the roughnecks was keen to experience that particular sensation for himself. They shuffled warily back from the doorway.

A moment later a loud horn blare sounded from overhead. This was *Behemoth* signalling that the raid was over and she had as much booty on board as she could handle. It was time to depart.

'Thank you so much for your cooperation,' the black-clad Airborn woman said to the roughnecks. 'Till next time!' She launched herself off the ground, and the other Airborn followed suit. The green-dreadlocked one was still giggling insanely as he took to their air.

The intimidated roughnecks peered out of the doorway, watching the winged figures disappear into the darkness beyond the glow of the refinery's lights. A huge throbbing beat filled the air, and rapidly faded. Then there was just the familiar hiss of the desert winds, the tickle of sand grains against windows and walls, and the far-off, plaintive howls of a pack of hackerjackals that had been startled by the huge, unfamiliar bulk of an airship passing above them.

'Them's supposed to be our friends now, be'n't they, tool-pusher?' said one of the roughnecks finally. 'Trading partners at least.'

'Apparently not,' replied Magnus Clockweight. Grim-faced, he took charge of the situation. 'Right. Some of you go and check on the others, make sure there'm nobody been hurt. I want a full inventory of what those Ascended Ones' – he corrected himself – 'those Airborn have nicked off we. And somebody had better send a telegram to head office about all this.'

As the roughnecks rushed to obey his orders, Clockweight rubbed his brow worriedly.

'Already,' he said to himself. 'Barely a year gone and already there'm trouble. I might've known it wouldn't last.'

CHAPTER 2

A Day And A Half Later ...

... and half a world away, at the Silver Sanctum, Lady Aanfielsdaughter was saying much the same thing as Magnus Clockweight, although she was putting it somewhat less bleakly and more reassuringly.

'There were bound to be hiccups,' she said.

'Hiccups?' interjected Farris, Lord Urironson. 'If the reports we've been getting from the ground are even halfway true, then this is hardly classifiable as a *hiccup*.'

'Teething troubles, then.'

'Not that either, Serena. I honestly don't believe you can compare these incidents to – to the sort of ailments a small child might suffer.'

'Well, I do. After all, the new relationship between Airborn and Groundling is a fragile, tender thing, still taking its first baby-steps. We should treat it with the same sort of care and tolerance as we would an infant.'

Lord Urironson snorted. 'Infant. Baby-steps. Getting sentimental in our old age, are we, Serena? Maternal instincts coming to the fore? Rather late in life for that, I'd say.'

Lady Aanfielsdaughter fixed him with a frosty stare, but refused to respond directly to the taunt. Instead she said, 'Perhaps, Farris, you should give us the benefit of *your* opinion on this matter.' She indicated the other senior residents sitting in the preening parlour with them. 'We're all dying to hear it.'

Lord Urironson puffed out his wings self-importantly. The action meant that the preener who was tending to him had to dart sharply backwards so as to avoid getting smacked in the face. The preener gave a disgruntled pout, then resumed his work, using a teasing wand and a fine-tooth comb to neaten Lord Urironson's plumage.

A preening parlour might seem an unusual venue for a weighty political discussion, but that was how the Silver Sanctum operated. Government there happened casually – a lunchtime chat in the dining hall, a chance encounter in the macaw house, an impromptu get-together over a glass of wine or during a twilight flit around the turrets – although there was nothing casual about the content of these meetings. Serious topics were debated and solutions to knotty problems were thrashed out, even though to an outside observer it might look just like a few people having a bit of a chinwag while they did something else.

'I think,' Lord Urironson declared, 'that what we have here are the makings of a full-blown disaster.'

'Oh really, Farris!'

'No, no, hear me out.'

'Could you be any more melodramatic?'

'Serena, I insist on being allowed to have my say.'

'Very well.' Lady Aanfieldsdaughter gestured to the preener who was ministering to her. The feathers at the tip of her right wing needed special attention, they were getting a bit dry, perhaps a touch of scented oil there? Yes, good.

'There are plenty of people who object to what you did last year,' Lord Urironson said, pointing an accusing finger at her. In his younger days he had been a lawyer and old courtroom habits died hard. 'They resent the way you took matters into your own hands, exposing us to the Groundlings and the Groundlings to us. They feel you overstepped your authority. You flung open a door which can never be closed again, and you did so without consulting anyone at the Silver Sanctum.'

'I discussed the matter at length with Mr Mordadson.'

'Ah yes. Mordadson. I hardly think he counts. He's just your pet hawk, trained to keep his beak shut and not argue. I mean us, your colleagues and peers. Had you deigned to talk about it with us first, we might have been able to warn you of the possible consequences. Consequences such as the rise of anti-Groundling feeling throughout the Airborn realm, which, as we are seeing in one sky-city in particular, has evolved into something more than mere protest.'

'What is it that you object to, Farris?' replied Lady Aanfieldsdaughter. 'The decision I took or the fact that you weren't consulted?'

A couple of the other senior residents chortled softly. Lady Aanfieldsdaughter had struck back well.

'Because you're wrong,' she continued. 'I thought long and hard before doing what I did, and I did it, moreover, because I had very little choice. The Groundlings were making their presence felt already with the embargo on supplying materials. By the time I became personally involved in the affair, they were on the point of making their presence felt – explosively. Heliotropia was under threat, and there was no way of saving the city without interacting with the Groundlings. Without opening that uncloseable door of yours. My hand was forced. I explained this to you immediately afterwards, all of you, at a grand assembly. You didn't seem to have a problem with it then, and I certainly don't remember hearing any dire prophecies of doom from you. And yet now that we face a minority protest group and a single sky-city going rogue, all of a sudden it's I-told-you-so and woe-is-me-all-is-lost.'

'To be fair, Serena,' piped up Alimon, Lord Yurkemison, 'one or two of us at the grand assembly did query the wisdom of your actions.'

'In the mildest possible terms. The overwhelming sentiment, however, was that I had performed a good and necessary deed.'

'And I'm startled to hear you describe the Feather First! movement as a minority protest group,' offered Faith, Lady Jeduthunsdaughter-Ochson. 'They're represented in every sky-city in every quadrant and their numbers are growing fast. I happened to get caught up in one of their rallies in Pearl Town the other day. Quite a gaggle! They brought traffic to a halt all along the city's Grand Concourse, and the Alar Patrol were very slow in getting them to disperse, which made me think the Patrollers themselves might be sympathetic to their cause.'

'But it's the situation at Redspire that's the real worry,' said Lord Urironson. He was surprised, but far from displeased, to find he had allies among his fellow nobles. Usually in discussions like this, everyone went along with whatever Lady Aanfielsdaughter said and his was the lone voice of dissent. This was no longer the case, which struck him as a mark of how grave the situation had become and how much worse it could well get. 'These cases of piracy we've been hearing about, Redspirian citizens raiding the ground. What if that acts as a catalyst? What if other people start to copy their example? Ultimately we could be looking at a war.'

'Honestly, Farris, you can be such an old woman at times,' said Lady Aanfielsdaughter, rolling her eyes.

Lord Urironson huffed and went scarlet. Several of the other senior residents, and a couple of the preeners, smirked. Somehow it was doubly insulting for a man to be called an old woman by a woman who was manifestly quite old, although in no way old-womanish herself.

'It's almost as if you *want* things to turn bad,' Lady Aanfielsdaughter went on. 'As if you're *willing* this whole venture to end in tears. That's not an attitude that's going to get us anywhere. Besides, you seem to forget that I prevented one war breaking out between us and the Groundlings. What makes you think I'd let another one start?'

'I don't know,' grumbled Lord Urironson. 'Maybe you enjoyed all the excitement last time. Maybe it gave you a bit of a thrill and you'd like to do it all over again.'

'Ridiculous! What a complete pluck-wit you are!'

Even as she snapped these words, Lady Aanfielsdaughter knew she shouldn't have. Her 'old woman' jibe had been fine, but 'pluck-wit' was altogether a cruder insult. She should simply have ignored Lord Urironson's comment; risen above it. Instead, she had finally allowed her irritation to show, which meant she had lost the upper hand in the argument.

She'd been unable to stop herself, however. Lord Urironson was always an irritant. On this occasion, though, he had really managed to get under her skin. Perhaps it was because, in spite of her supreme self-confidence in all matters, Lady Aanfielsdaughter still wasn't totally sure that she had done the right thing a year ago. Had there really been no alternative but to break the long-existing barrier between Airborn and Groundlings and put the situation between the two races on an entirely new footing? Couldn't a more elegant solution have been found, one with fewer and less far-reaching ramifications?

'So what do you propose, Serena?' enquired Pendroz, Lord Luelson. He was a good friend of Lady Aanfielsdaughter's and she knew she could always count on his support. 'I take it you have some plan of action in mind.'

'Naturally,' Lady Aanfielsdaughter replied, regaining a little of her authority. 'I'll be putting my top man onto it right away.'

CHAPTER 3

The Aforementioned 'Top Man'

Mr Mordadson stood ready, legs apart, wings splayed for balance, braced for the attack. A thin, sharp wind swooped across the high-level courtyard, ruffling his feathers and his short, dark hair. Behind his crimson-lensed spectacles his eyes glinted like a pair of fine-cut rubies.

He raised a hand and flicked the fingers against the palm twice – an invitation.

'Come on then,' he said to his opponent. 'Enough pussy-footing. Let's see what you're really made of.'

Az shook sweat from his eyebrows and moved forward, fists clenched. There was determination in his reddened face – determination and a hint of something harder and fiercer. He was aware that a handful of junior Silver Sanctum residents were looking on from the cloister at one end of the courtyard. They had been there for several minutes. Partly they were interested because a fight was always worth watching; but they were also there, Az knew, because of him. He was a novelty and a celebrity, even at the Silver Sanctum. Az Gabrielson – the wingless wonder who helped change everything.

He tuned out their presence. This wasn't about putting on a show for an audience. It was about him versus Mr Mordadson. About not letting Mr Mordadson win. Again. That was all that mattered.

He closed the distance between the two of them, then abruptly lunged. He feinted left and at the last second twisted to the right, aiming an upward chopping blow at the knot of nerves in Mr Mordadson's armpit.

Had the blow struck home, Mr Mordadson's arm would have

been rendered numb and useless. But Mr Mordadson spotted the feint and parried with one wing, batting Az's fist aside. At the same time, he reached out and grabbed Az's other hand and forearm and wrenched the one backwards against the other.

The pain was excruciating. Az's wrist felt like it was about to snap. He was paralysed, his whole body locked down by the hold Mr Mordadson had on him.

He told himself to focus, take no notice of the pain, *think*. The hold was designed to hurt more if you tried to pull away. If you did the opposite, moved *into* it, it was no longer so effective.

Az thrust himself towards Mr Mordadson. Mr Mordadson, however, had anticipated the manoeuvre and released his grip at the crucial moment. He swung Az round, turning Az's own momentum against him. Next thing Az knew, he was plunging face-first onto the courtyard flagstones.

He managed to tuck and roll. Somersaulting, he came up lightly on the balls of his feet. Distant applause from the spectators told him the feat of agility had been impressive. He didn't let their clapping distract him. He wheeled round to face Mr Mordadson – *never turn your back on a foe* – only to find that Mr Mordadson was nowhere to be seen. The courtyard was empty. Where . . . ?

A fraction of a second too late, Az looked up. All he saw were the soles of Mr Mordadson's shoes descending towards him. Mr Mordadson landed on Az's shoulders with his full bodyweight, slamming him flat on his belly.

The wind was knocked out of Az. For several horrible, writhing moments he lay on the flagstones thinking he was never going to draw breath again. He heaved and gasped for air, uselessly.

Eventually his lungs began to work once more. He flopped onto his side. Panting, vision swimming, he saw Mr Mordadson's legs. They strode into view, halting just out of his reach.

'Had enough?'

'Only just started,' Az coughed out through gritted teeth.

'Then let me help you up and we can resume.'

Mr Mordadson extended a hand down to Az. Az groped for it clumsily, as if dazed. Then, quick as a flash, he kicked out at Mr Mordadson's ankles, swiping his legs from under him. Mr Mordadson toppled sideways but caught himself expertly with a beat of his outstretched wings, so that rather than hit the ground he merely brushed it with one elbow. An instant later, he was hovering five metres up, well out of harm's way.

'Sneaky,' he said to Az, with approval.

'If I hadn't tried that, you'd have done something similar to me,' said Az.

'Absolutely correct. You beat me to it, that's all. Well done. I see you've remembered the cardinal rule of combat: trust no one.'

'Least of all you.'

Mr Mordadson chuckled. 'Least of all me. Now, really – had enough? We've been at it nearly an hour.'

Wearily Az picked himself up and dusted himself down. 'Yeah, I reckon so. For today.'

'Very well.' Mr Mordadson alighted next to him. 'Then let's go and get a drink, and you can tell me what you're so angry about.'

CHAPTER 4

Angry? Who's Angry?

'You are,' said Mr Mordadson, sipping a glass of iced persimmon juice at a table in one of the Silver Sanctum's open-air cafeterias. 'You have been for several weeks. I've noticed it in our training sessions. You come at me with this mean look in your eye, like you plan on doing some serious damage.'

'Isn't that a good thing?' said Az, also drinking persimmon juice. 'You're always going on about the need for aggression.'

'*Directed* aggression. Aggression with a specific goal. Whereas what I'm seeing is a kind of unfocused, all-purpose aggression, which you're using your combat lessons as a convenient outlet for. Using me as a punchbag. Don't get me wrong, Az, your skills are improving. Even without the benefit of wings you're turning into a formidable fighter. But for all that, at present I don't think your mind is completely on the job. I beat you pretty easily today.'

'You cheated at the end. You flew.'

'Merely using the tactical advantages to hand. Any winged opponent would do the same.'

'But we had rules.'

'You don't think every opponent you come up against is going to abide by *rules*, do you? So come on. Are you going to tell me what the matter is?'

For a while Az said nothing. The sounds of the cafeteria filled the silence between him and Mr Mordadson: the chatter of Silver Sanctum residents and employees, the chink of cutlery and crystalware, now and then a flap of wings as somebody emphasised a conversational point or strongly disagreed with somebody else's opinion.

Finally Az said, 'It's complicated.'

Mr Mordadson nodded. 'It's Cassie, isn't it?'

Az failed to hide his surprise. 'How ...'

'Not hard. When a male seventeen-year-old is in a funk about something and doesn't want to talk about it, nine times out of ten the reason is girl trouble. Plus, I'm not stupid. I know how difficult it is for you and her. When was the last time you got together, the pair of you? A month ago?'

'More than that. Six weeks, nearly.'

'You went down or she came up?'

'She came up.'

'And the visit lasted how long? An hour?'

'If that.'

Mr Mordadson spread out his hands, as if to say *You see?* 'It was never going to be easy trying to conduct a meaningful, one-to-one relationship with a Groundling, Az. You must have realised that from the start. The obstacles that must be overcome. Not least, you having to acclimatise every time you go down to the ground and Cassie not being able to breathe properly every time she comes up here. In fact, all in all, it's almost inconceivable that you and she have any kind of long-term prospects as a couple.'

'Oh well, thanks for the encouragement.'

'Just telling it like it is.'

'I know, I know,' Az sighed. 'As a matter of fact, Michael said pretty much the same thing to me the other day. "Face it, Az, love's wonderful and all that, but three kilometres of altitude is a heck of a big gap to bridge."'

'Your brother has a knack for a colourful turn of phrase.'

'But ...'

'But?'

Az shifted his head and neck, as if there were an uncomfortable weight on his shoulders. 'There's more to it. Lately I've been feeling like Cassie's pulling away from me. As if she's not interested in seeing me. Little things. Like, it's awkward when we chat. We don't know what to say to each other. I try and crack a joke; she doesn't laugh. I try and touch her; she shies away. Last time I was down in Grimvale, I really got the impression she couldn't wait for me to leave. I know she's having problems with her dad, and her family's finding it difficult to make ends meet. I know life isn't a barrel of laughs for her right now. Even so ...'

Briefly Az wondered why he was sharing such personal stuff with Mr Mordadson. They were friends, yes, but hardly close ones. More than anything they were master and pupil now, thanks to their weekly combat training sessions. That lent their relationship a certain level of formality. Was it right that he should be confiding in Mr Mordadson about his love life?

But then Mr Mordadson *had* asked, and had seemed sincere in his interest. And somehow, talking about it did feel good.

'And then there's Michael's wedding.'

'Ah yes. The day after tomorrow, if I'm not mistaken,' said Mr Mordadson. 'What about it? Not written your best-man speech yet, is that the problem?'

'No, no. It's the Grubdollars. They've been asked to come and I'm hoping they'll be able to make it despite everything, you know, getting to the High Haven elevators, breathing apparatus, all the practical difficulties. Frankly I'll be amazed if they do. But I'm hoping. The thing is, I don't even know whether they're coming or not. When I invited Cassie, last time she was up here, she just shrugged and said she'd mention it to her dad and brothers and maybe they'd be there, maybe they wouldn't, it wasn't for her to say. Enthusiasm? Not much. We saw a sunbow and all she seemed to want to talk about was that.'

'Well, as you yourself said, the practical difficulties.'

'Mr Mordadson?' said a voice behind Az, a voice he knew well.

Mr Mordadson looked up. Az looked round.

It was Aurora Jukarsdaughter, Lady Aanfielsdaughter's personal assistant and Michael's fiancée.

Her expression could not have been any grimmer.

CHAPTER 5

A Summons

Aurora dipped her wings briefly to Az, an acknowledgement of his presence and also an indication that, under other circumstances, she would have greeted him more warmly.

Az, in turn, nodded to his soon-to-be sister-in-law.

'I've been sent to fetch you,' Aurora said to Mr Mordadson. 'You're to come to Lady Aanfieldsdaughter's office immediately.'

'I assumed as much. Something serious?'

Aurora did not reply, which was tantamount to a yes.

'Something to do with Redspire, I'll be bound.'

Again, no response from the ever-professional Aurora.

Mr Mordadson rose. 'Duty calls. Az? It's been a pleasure, as always, putting a few bruises on you. Same time next week.'

Aurora spread her wings and took off without a backward glance. Mr Mordadson made to follow but, before doing so, leaned back and muttered a few quick words to Az out of the side of his mouth:

'Or perhaps we shall get together sooner, if you can manage it.'

Watching Mr Mordadson soar to join Aurora in the air, Az's initial thought was: *Redspire? What's going on at Redspire?*

His next thought was: *'Or perhaps we shall get together sooner?' What did he mean by that?*

He puzzled over Mr Mordadson's parting comment. Was Mr Mordadson proposing that they have an extra training session, earlier in the week than usual? Was that it?

No, the way he'd said it, the intonation he had used, suggested more.

It implied a hint.

A challenge.

All at once Az recalled a conversation that had taken place not long after the events at Grimvale, when Mr Mordadson first said he was willing to school Az in hand-to-hand combat.

'You're asking yourself, "Why me?"' said Mr Mordadson. '"Why is a high-ranking Silver Sanctum emissary offering to find time in his remarkably hectic schedule to teach a teenage kid everything he knows about self-defence and the fine art of duffing people up?"'

'Something along those lines,' said Az.

'One reason: because you have no wings, and a person without wings is apt to get picked on.'

'I've been all right so far. A few people have made snide comments but' – Az shrugged – 'so what? Just means they're morons. That's not to say I haven't got into fights, but . . .'

'Quite,' said Mr Mordadson. 'We all know about your quick temper. But there may come a time when you'll need more than just a willingness to come out swinging. You may need some skill to back up the anger, to save yourself from real harm. Another reason: the way you handled yourself throughout this whole recent crisis, right from the start, impressed me. And I'm not, as you know, a man who's easily impressed. You have guts and integrity, which are rarer qualities than you might think. You also have a spark in you, Az, a faint glimmer of something that I believe, with the right encouragement, could be fanned into quite a flame.'

'What do you mean?'

'You'll see. Besides, be honest, what other plans do you have for your life right now?'

'Umm . . . I'm thinking of asking Captain Qadoschson if I can sign on with him as an airship pilot. You know, learn the ropes properly.'

'Very laudable. But otherwise?'

'There's school.'

'For a couple more years. And then?'

'Dunno.'

'Precisely. Az, I'm presenting you with the kind of opportunity the average man or woman in the street would pull out half their feathers for. Though I must admit to a selfish interest as well. I'd like to see if

I can adapt the combat techniques I know to suit someone who can't fly. That should be a challenge.'

'Well, as long you get something out of it,' Az said.

Mr Mordadson flashed him a half-smile. 'Promise me you'll think about it.'

Az had promised he would, and had indeed thought about it, and had come to the conclusion that he had nothing to lose by learning a few combat moves, although he doubted he would ever need to use them. What had intrigued him about the offer was that it seemed to indicate that Mr Mordadson wasn't going to stop at teaching him how to handle himself in a fight. There was more to it, as though the combat lessons were just a first step and, if they went well, lessons in other skills would follow.

What those other skills might be, Az was not sure. But his suspicion was that Mr Mordadson could be grooming him for a role as a Silver Sanctum emissary like himself. That, surely, was the opportunity he had referred to, the one that 'the average man or woman in the street would pluck out half their feathers for'.

All of which led Az to believe that Mr Mordadson had issued him with an instruction just now – 'if you can manage it'. Mr Mordadson was telling him to tag along. He was telling him to find a way to get to Lady Aanfieldsaughter's office under his own steam and then surreptitiously listen in on their conversation.

Really?

Az shook his head. No, he was being crazy.

But why else would Mr Mordadson have phrased the remark so pointedly and said it under his breath so that Aurora wouldn't hear? What other interpretation could there be?

Az stood up from the table, sat down, then stood up again, this time with finality. He squared his jaw, resolute.

Mr Mordadson wanted him to prove himself? He wanted him to show he had the nerve and the cunning to eavesdrop on a private conversation between two of the Silver Sanctum's elite members?

OK then, he would. He'd make his way to Lady Aan-fielsdaughter's office immediately.

Only one small problem.

How?

CHAPTER 6

How

To get to Lady Aanfielsdaughter's office, which lay halfway across the Silver Sanctum, Az would have to use a series of bridges and walkways, not to mention staircases. On foot, it was a lengthy, laborious journey, and by the time he reached his destination Mr Mordadson's meeting with her ladyship would almost certainly be over.

And even if he did manage to get there in good time, he couldn't eavesdrop on their conversation through the office door because the room was separated from the corridor by an antechamber, where Aurora worked. His only option was the balcony outside the office.

The office was near the summit of one of the Silver Sanctum's tallest towers. The sides of the tower were smoothly metallic. Climbing was out of the question, obviously. As, for that matter, was begging a lift off somebody. Az could just imagine the reaction when he went up to some random person and asked to be flown up to the office balcony and then had to give his reasons. *Why? Well, you see, I want to hang around outside and listen in as Lady Aanfielsdaughter briefs Mr Mordadson on some important affair of state, that's why. Perhaps you wouldn't mind hovering with me in your arms while I do it.* That was simply not going to work.

However . . .

The Silver Sanctum was adorned with countless stained-glass windows. Some of them depicted renowned leaders from the past, others showed representations of notable historical events, while a few were simply abstract designs, gorgeous sprays and swirls of kaleidoscopic colour. Keeping the windows sparklingly clean was a full-time job and required the services of a dedicated team of washers armed with cloths and buckets of soapy water.

It would have tired the washers out, hovering all day long while they scrubbed and polished the glass. So, to conserve energy, they worked sitting in slings suspended from helium-filled balloons.

Just now, a few of the window-washers were taking a tea break in the cafeteria. Their balloons were tethered nearby.

That was the answer. Both of Az's problems were eliminated at a single stroke.

Having formulated a plan, Az moved quickly, before common sense could wag its finger at him. This was an insanely risky idea, he knew. But he was still on an adrenaline buzz from the combat session, and he found his own mood of recklessness rather pleasing. At the back of his mind, thoughts of Cassie simmered. In some obscure way he felt that this was how to show her that he didn't care about things stood between them. Was he bothered by her growing coolness towards him? No. He was so little bothered by it that he was happy to attempt something as daft as stealing a window-washer's balloon and riding it through the thoroughfares of the Silver Sanctum.

The balloons were lined up in a row, tied to the balustrade at the edge of the platform on which the cafeteria stood. They bumped against one another springily in the breeze.

Az stole a glance back at the window-washers. They were huddled around a table, heads down, engrossed in an anecdote which one of them was telling. Everybody else in the cafeteria was minding their own business. Nobody was looking his way.

Az slid himself over the balustrade and into the sling of the nearest balloon. It began to sink under his weight. He reached round and undid the line securing it. Then he pushed off from the platform. The balloon bobbed outwards, still descending until it settled into buoyancy. Az waited to hear a cry from above: *Hey! My balloon! Where d'you think you're going with that?* No cry came. A current of air snagged the balloon, moving it forward with some urgency.

He was on his way.

CHAPTER 7

The Consequences Of An Idea
Not Thought Through Fully

For a minute or so Az felt only exhilaration. He didn't think about the fact that he was hanging in midair with only a two-metre-diameter balloon keeping him there. The sheer drop below him didn't trouble him. It was a hundred metres straight down to an anvil-shaped plaza, a further fifty metres to a small domed structure, then a walkway, and beneath that nothing but empty air all the way to the cloud cover. He scarcely noticed. He was too busy revelling in his own boldness, too busy congratulating himself on his success at making off with the balloon without getting caught. He grasped the ropes which joined the seat of the sling to the balloon and he floated away from the cafeteria, letting the breeze coast him thrillingly along.

It was a minute or so later when he had his first misgivings, his first inkling that he hadn't thought this idea through as fully as he should.

For it was then that a sudden, strong air current came in and swept him off at right angles. It drove the balloon towards a tower, and there would have been a collision if the air current hadn't died down as abruptly as it had arisen. Az glided past the tower with centimetres to spare. A pair of storks, nesting near the tower's pinnacle, squawked and waggled their bills at him in protest.

Tingling all over, Az let out a laugh. *That* was a close shave! Except, the laugh did not sound very convincing, even to himself. And he found he was no longer grasping the sling ropes so much as gripping them.

It dawned on him that the balloon was all very well and fine as a method of transport, as long as you had a means of steering it. The window-washers used their wings for that purpose, employing them for propulsion and as rudders. In that respect Az was at a crucial disadvantage. Which left what?

His mind raced. He had visions of himself being buffeted around, helpless, till finally he was dashed against a building and killed. Either that or the winds blew him clear out of the Silver Sanctum and sent him gusting who-knows-how-far to who-knows-where.

Another sharp, fierce current of air seized the balloon and started twirling it around and around. The sling was flung outward by centrifugal force, and Az with it. He banged into the parapet of a jutting balcony, which hurt but had the benefit of halting the balloon's dizzying spin. With his shin scraped and throbbing, Az rebounded away from the balcony, not happy at all now.

He had to end this journey. He'd been mad to embark on it in the first place. The whole thing was a mistake. He was beginning to wonder whether he had misunderstood Mr Mordadson's remark after all, and even if he hadn't, still, was it worth getting himself killed for?

The balloon was picking up speed. It was tugging him along behind it with wicked gusto, as if enjoying its passenger's mounting sense of panic. Silver Sanctum towers whisked by on either side, faster and faster.

Think, Az!

Az thought.

He was suspended from a balloon. In the most basic sense there wasn't much difference between that and being in the control gondola of Troop-Carrier *Cerulean*. Az ventured out with Captain Qadoschson and his crew regularly, once a month on average, each time discovering a little bit more about airshipcraft and aerial navigation. *Cerulean* was, all said and done, just big balloon with propellers attached. He knew how to fly her. Surely, therefore, he might be able to fly *this* balloon.

A one-person airship. That was how he should regard it.

He hurtled past the spire of another tower, coming within a whisker of impaling himself on its pointed peak. He noticed he was gaining height. The air current that had a hold on him was an updraught. Possibly he would be borne all the way up into the stratosphere if he didn't get a grip on the situation right now.

A one-person airship.

Here goes nothing, he thought.

He hauled down on the right-hand rope, hard. The balloon responded, dipping that way.

Yes!

He kept hauling down, gradually turning himself about.

Then he leaned back, straightening out his legs.

That worked too. All at once he wasn't ascending nearly as fast. He had, in airship terms, gained control of his trim.

Now: he knifed his body sideways at an angle. The balloon veered accordingly.

A human rudder.

A few more manoeuvres, a little more trial and error, and Az had mastery of his vessel. He wasn't beholden to the whim of the winds any more. He was in command.

He swooped. He sheared. He tacked into the breeze. He rose. He fell. With a yank on the balloon here, a repositioning of his body there, he was able to guide himself in whatever direction he wished.

Soon he was heading for Lady Aanfielsdaughter's office. His course took him past a pair of Silver Sanctum residents flapping sedately along. He gave them a cheery wave. They did a classic double-take, looking at him first without interest, then with startled frowns. Az steered his balloon onward, grinning.

The tower loomed. There was a broad, semicircular balcony right outside Lady Aanfielsdaughter's office. Az aimed for it. The office windows stood wide open. Gauzy curtains billowed outward. Inside, Az glimpsed the Silver Sanctum's premier resident herself, along with Mr Mordadson. The balcony was below his feet. He slipped out of the sling, letting go of the ropes. He landed on the balcony softly on all fours. The balloon shot upward, racing towards the heavens. How was he going to get down from here again? Az didn't know, and it didn't matter. What mattered was that he had made it to his destination.

He waited, breath held, to see if his arrival had been noticed.

Lady Aanfielsdaughter and Mr Mordadson kept talking, uninterrupted.

Az crept forward, closer to the windows.

The voices became clearer.

Crouching behind a huge stand of potted pampas grass, Az listened.

CHAPTER 8

Overheard

'Piracy?' said Mr Mordadson.

'Well, how else would you describe it?' said Lady Aanfieldsdaughter.

'I don't deny that technically it's the correct term, milady. But calling it piracy lends it a kind of glamour, when really it's nothing better than common thievery. So this will be their third raid, am I correct?'

'There have been three that we know of. It could be more. Accurate data from the ground is so hard to come by.'

'Three is enough. In fact it's three too many.'

'I agree.'

'And they're terrorising Groundlings, too.'

'That, to me, is the most serious aspect of the whole affair,' Lady Aanfieldsdaughter said. 'Stealing is bad enough, but threatening lives – that's beyond the pale. It's a miracle no one's been harmed yet. I imagine it's only a question of time before someone is. All the more reason, Mr Mordadson, why the matter must be dealt with, and promptly.'

'I agree, milady. I've been waiting for you to bring me in on this.'

'What these people, these pirates, are doing flies in the face of everything we Airborn hold dear,' her ladyship continued. 'It makes a mockery of our beliefs and aspirations. *And* there's the danger that it could undermine everything we've managed to achieve this past year – the Bilateral Covenant, formalising relations with the Groundlings, trading with them rather than merely receiving supplies from them. I won't have that jeopardised!' She clapped the backs of her wings together. 'I won't.'

'Of course you've communicated your concern to the officials at Redspire.'

'Of course, in a strongly-worded letter.'

'But no joy.'

'They say they're not aware of any wrongdoing.'

'They say.'

'Quite.'

'And the pirates have an airship,' Mr Mordadson said, musingly. 'That's a puzzle in itself. Where did they get hold of one? Where did they find her?'

'Who knows? Does it matter? The main thing is, I want them stopped. Permanently.'

'You want me to head down to Redspire and sort the situation out.' This wasn't a question – Mr Mordadson was confirming orders, spelling out in precise terms what was required of him.

'I do.'

'May I ask then, at what level of authorisation will I be allowed to operate?'

There was a pause while Lady Aanfieldsdaughter deliberated. 'What level do you feel you need?'

'Somewhere like Redspire – the place has long been a thorn in our side, an embarrassment to the entire Airborn community. I'm not surprised that's where these pirates hail from. If any sky-city was going to breed such criminals, it'd be Redspire.'

'Implying?'

'Implying, milady, that an example should be set. For everyone's sake, our own and the Groundlings', Redspire must be taught a lesson. A lesson it won't forget and neither will anyone else. We have to demonstrate that we have zero tolerance for this type of behaviour. Otherwise . . .'

Lady Aanfieldsdaughter's voice was sombre. 'I see where you're going with this.'

'Indeed. I'm asking to be given full discretion to act in whatever way I deem fit.'

'Yes. All right. Very well.'

'Up to and including extreme sanction.'

'I doubt there'll be any call for that.'

'With the utmost respect, I beg to differ.'

'Extreme sanction?'

'Extreme.'

Another pause from Lady Aanfielsdaughter, a long one this time. 'Well, if you feel it's absolutely necessary.'

'I do. So, whatever happens, whatever I do, you'll back me to the hilt?'

'Yes. Yes, I will.'

Mr Mordadson sounded satisfied. 'Thank you, milady. That's all I needed to hear.'

CHAPTER 9

Permission Not To Have
To Ask Permission

Moments later Mr Mordadson strode out onto the balcony, leaving Lady Aanfielsdaughter at her desk. He stood for a while with his hands behind his back, folded beneath his wings. He looked as if he was contemplating the view. Brilliant blueness stretched to the horizon where it met the creamy curve of the cloud cover. The spires of the Silver Sanctum shone.

Az remained in his hiding place behind the potted pampas. Should he come out? Or should he stay put until Mr Mordadson was gone?

Before Az could decide either way, Mr Mordadson turned his head and fixed his gaze on the very spot where he was crouching. Az gave a start. Mr Mordadson put a finger to his lips and nodded in the direction of the office. Az nodded back, understanding. Mr Mordadson walked over to the pampas grass in a nonchalant manner. Then, in a single, smooth motion, he grabbed Az by the wrists and at the same time stepped off the balcony's edge. Together they plunged in a steep dive, which Mr Mordadson converted into a glide ten metres down.

Once they were well out of Lady Aanfielsdaughter's sight and earshot, he spoke.

'So how much of that did you hear?'

'From "piracy" onwards,' Az replied.

'Excellent. You got most of it, then. Now I won't have to explain everything to you from scratch.'

'So you really did want me to listen in? That was the plan?'

'I thought I made that quite plain.'

'Well, you did, I suppose. I just wasn't sure why. Still aren't.'

'Partly, like I said, to save me the bother of having to repeat it all to you later. I'm lazy that way. Mainly, though, it was a test of initiative, to see if you could get to Lady Aanfielsdaughter's office under your own steam. And you did, so congratulations on that. A window-washer's balloon, right?'

'You saw me.'

'No. But the balloons were sitting there at the cafeteria. It seemed the obvious method. It's what I'd have done in your position. The only drawback, as you found, was having to abandon the balloon once you reached the balcony. You couldn't keep it. Something as big as that bobbing around outside would have given you away. So tell me, how were you proposing to get *off* the balcony afterwards? What would have happened if I hadn't come out to get you?'

'No idea.'

'Thought so. You left yourself without an exit strategy. That's bad. Never, ever, leave yourself without an exit strategy, Az. Always think one step beyond your immediate goal.'

Mr Mordadson canted his wings to the right. He dipped over slightly too far and adjusted with a grunt of effort. The extra weight he was carrying threw off his natural sense of balance.

Levelling out, he and Az swooped around the Hanging Garden, whose multi-tiered terraces spilled flowers like champagne frothing from goblets. There were so many blooms and they were so brightly coloured that it was almost painful to look at them. You had to squint to perceive their beauty.

'If you wanted me to know what Lady Aanfielsdaughter was going to tell you,' Az said, 'then obviously you want me to be involved in some way. Unless all you're after is my opinion on pirates.'

'Which is?'

'Pretty much the same as yours. Stealing is stealing, whatever name you give it. But pirates? Nowadays you only find them in history books and novels.'

'This Redspire lot seem to have revived the tradition, with a new twist. Instead of preying on other Airborn, they've elected Groundlings as their victims.'

'But it's more than my opinion you're after, isn't it?' Az said, as he and Mr Mordadson darted between the twin turrets of Silver Sanctum's public records office. The turrets' cupola roofs were covered with hundreds of roosting parrots, which made them look no less brilliantly gaudy than the Hanging Garden.

'Ever since a week ago, when I first got wind of what was happening at Redspire, I've had a feeling I might need your help. Now I'm certain of it.'

'And that would be because the pirates have an airship.'

'Full marks.'

'You're planning on going after them in *Cerulean*.'

'It makes sense. No other kind of vehicle has the range or fuel capacity. To find and confront one airship, we need another.'

Several more questions were jostling at the forefront of Az's mind, but one in particular begged to be asked:

'What's extreme sanction?'

Mr Mordadson flattened out his wings. They were approaching the landing apron at the city's perimeter, where a gyro-cab waited to take Az back to High Haven.

'What do you think it is?' Mr Mordadson said.

'Sounds to me like … like permission to do anything you wish. Permission not to have to ask permission.'

'Hm. Nicely put. It also means I'm entitled to act without fear of reprisals or repercussions, especially legal ones. Remember Alan Steamarm?'

Az did. How could he ever forget? He remembered, all too clearly, watching Mr Mordadson hurl the Humanist leader down into the cloud cover and seeing and hearing the detonation of the dynamite to which Steamarm had strapped himself.

'That,' said Mr Mordadson, tight-lipped, 'is a perfect example of extreme sanction.'

CHAPTER 10

A Place Of Refuge

The moment Az let himself in through the front door of his house, his mother pounced.

'Azrael, good, you're back,' she said, bustling out from the kitchen. 'Now, firstly, I've given your father instructions about picking up the buttonholes and bouquets first thing on the morning of the wedding. We both know how forgetful he is, so I want you to make sure he does it, which means you have to go with him. They're at Celestial Florists on Sunbeam Boulevard, you know the place, next door to the wing jewellery shop. Also, I've been thinking about the music. Of course Michael and Aurora are insisting on having one of those four-piece close-harmony choirs rather than the traditional harp ensemble. That's all right, they're young, it's their wedding – but isn't a song like "Hearts Held Like Hands" just a bit too, well, contemporary? Too pop? What do you think? Oh, and the seating plan. I've been considering some revisions. Mainly I'm wondering if I should put the Grubdollars all together at one table or spread them out among the other guests. That way they could meet new people and our friends could get to know some Groundlings, which would be a good thing all round. That's if the Grubdollars are coming. Are they? Have you heard anything yet?'

All of this poured out from her in one go. She scarcely paused for breath, and Az just stood there in the hallway, pinned to the spot. His mother had been like this for at least a month, fizzing-full of plans for the wedding. Now, with just two days left, her enthusiasm was shooting off in all directions like fireworks. From dawn till dusk she was making arrangements, fine-tuning the arrangements she had made, and double-checking the arrangements she had fine-tuned. There was no stopping her. She was like a force of nature. Everything had to be perfect, everything had to go right on the big day, and all anyone else could do was going along with her demands and try not to get in the way.

'Erm, yes, no, don't know,' Az said. An opportunity to speak had at last presented itself.

'What's that?'

'Those are my answers to your questions, Mum. Yes, I'll go with Dad to the florists. No, that song isn't too contemporary. And as far as the Grubdollars go – I don't know.'

'Still?'

'Still.'

His mother's face fell. 'Oh dear. I do hope they'll let us know one way or the other soon. The elevator postal service isn't very efficient yet, is it? Perhaps that's the problem. They sent a letter but it hasn't got here. Or perhaps Groundlings aren't familiar with the social niceties, such as telling people whether you're going to be at a function or not. Is that it? Their ways and ours are so different. Maybe they'll just turn up anyway. I should probably go ahead and assume they will.'

'Where's Dad?' Az asked, changing the subject.

His mother rolled her eyes. 'Where do you think?'

In the basement, which Az's father used as a workshop, calmness reigned. The rest of the house crackled with the manic energy Az's mother was giving off, but none of that energy managed to penetrate down here. The tools which lined the walls and hung from the ceiling seemed to act like insulation. On any given day Az's father was happy to secrete himself in the workshop for an hour or two. At present, however, the place had become more than a place for tinkering with gadgets and ideas for home improvements. It had become a refuge, somewhere he – and Az too, if he wanted – could go to escape the wedding-preparation storm above.

'Lucky Michael,' Az's father said, 'living all the way over on the other side of town. There's the whole of High Haven between him and your mother. Whereas you and I, lad, we're right in the thick of things. She's running us ragged, and we're not even the ones getting married! Honestly, I don't know how much more I can take. Ramona's become this mad, organising machine. I swear, if she asks me again whether I've remembered to book a barber's appointment for tomorrow ...'

'And have you?'

'No, but that's not the point. Anyway, I'm sure I can just pop in for a quick trim.' Az's father rubbed his nearly-bald scalp. 'Won't take five minutes, with a threadbare bonce like mine.'

'Look on the bright side, Dad. Only one more day. Then it's the wedding, and then everything'll be over.'

'One!' Az's father pretended to break down and sob. 'I ... just can't ... go on, son. One more ... day of this! I don't think ... I can make it. Kill me. Please ... just ... kill me now.'

Az laughed, and the laugh turned into a yawn which he was helpless to stifle.

'Ah,' said his father, 'poor chap, you must be whacked. A ten-hour round trip, plus an hour of "exercise class".' He mimed quotation marks with the tips of his wings. 'That'll certainly take it out of you.'

'I am pretty tired.'

'How was it at the Silver Sanctum today? Mr Mordadson in good form?'

'Same as ever,' said Az.

His father detected something in his voice, a hint of eva-siveness. 'What's up?'

'Nothing.'

But Az knew he wasn't going to be allowed to leave it at that. Gabriel Enochson might be pushing seventy but his mind remained as sharp as a quill tip. Az had never been able to fool his father and he was certain he never would.

'I'm going – I've *got* to go to Prismburg the day after the wedding,' he said, trying to make it sound casual.

A bushy white eyebrow rose. 'Oh?'

'Yes. For a week or so, maybe longer.'

'Silver Sanctum business?'

'No. Yes.'

'Involving *Cerulean*?'

'Yes.'

His father pondered for a moment. 'This is some kind of official assignment. Your friend Mr Mordadson has recruited you for something.'

Az gave a slow, reluctant nod.

Gabriel Enochson sighed. 'I suppose it was inevitable. Ever since you started combat training with Mr Mordadson, I've known the time was going to come when he would want more from you. It's clear he's got his eye on you and thinks you have great potential, and why shouldn't he? Wings or no wings, you're a star. We've always known that. We knew it long before you became Az the big, famous lad who went down to the ground. Without telling his parents.'

Az grinned sheepishly. It was still a sore point with his father and mother that he had agreed to go down in the elevators that first time, embarking on a journey which might well have killed him, and indeed nearly did, without their knowledge. To make matters worse, Michael had lied to them about it, sending them a message that Az was OK when he'd had no idea whether he was or wasn't. Although everything had turned out well in the end, Az's parents still hadn't quite forgiven him yet.

'But now,' his father went on, 'now, finally, old Mordy's decided to take things up a level, and I can't say I'm completely happy about it, Az. There's going to be some danger, right? Just like last time?'

'No, Dad.'

'Come on, be straight.'

The phrase *extreme sanction* ghosted through Az's mind. 'I don't think I personally am going to be in any danger.'

'But you don't know that for sure.'

'Do you not want me to go? Because I can say no. I can tell Mr Mordadson I've changed my mind and I don't feel ready. He doesn't *need* me to come along with him, I don't think. I mean, *Cerulean* is still Captain Qadoschson's vessel. I'm not even second-in-command.'

'That'd be your pal Wallimson.'

'Yes,' said Az ruefully. His father's 'your pal' had been more than a little sarcastic.

Gabriel Enochson glanced around the workshop. His gaze settled on the scale model of *Cerulean* which he and Az had not finished building. They had abandoned work on it a year ago, leaving it half done, after Az got his first taste of piloting the real airship. The model was redundant now and seemed more than ever a childish thing, a toy. Looking at it, Az's father realised his younger son was fast becoming a man, and this filled him with pride but saddened him as well.

'But still, you want to go,' he said.

'Yeah. Kind of. Yeah.'

The old man put on a brave smile. 'Then you should. You must. The only question is how to break the news to your mother.'

'I know.'

'Any ideas?'

'No.'

'Leave it to me. I'll come up with some excuse. You're taking *Cerulean* out for an extended trip, how about that? Putting her through some long-distance manoeuvres.'

Az shrugged. 'Sounds believable.'

'I'll make it believable. And I'll choose my moment. I'll mention it to her sometime tomorrow when she's right at the height of one of her planning frenzies. She won't be listening to me properly and may not even notice what I've said.'

'Thanks, Dad. You're the best.'

'Just promise me one thing.'

'Of course. What?'

With an index finger his father rubbed a lower eyelid, pushing the grey, pouchy bit of flesh back and forth. 'Promise me you won't ever forget your family.'

'How could I?'

'You say that, but for a while I've been feeling this sense of you gradually slipping away from us. There're your visits to the Silver Sanctum and down to the ground, your trips in *Cerulean*.

Don't get me wrong, I'm not saying you shouldn't go out and explore the world and learn skills and make something of yourself. You're growing up, and growing up means growing apart from your family. It's natural and proper. That's what being seventeen is all about. And you're doing important things, and that's fine. Just … just remember that we're important too. OK?'

'OK.'

'Not making you feel guilty, am I? I wouldn't want that.'

'No. No, I understand what you're getting at.'

'Do you? Good.' His father chuckled. 'Because I'm not sure *I* do. Maybe it's this wedding. One of my two lads is getting hitched and I'm starting to feel as if the nest is emptying. Even though Michael hasn't been in the nest for some time, he's still been around, he's still needed us – and now he won't need us so much, and I'm starting to get a bit soppy and sentimental about that. But still … Oh look, forget it. Ignore me. I'm being daft.' He spread out his arms and his wings. 'Fancy giving your old dad a hug? I could really do with one. Or are you too grown-up for that now?'

'Not yet.'

The arms folded around Az and then the wings, a double layer of comfort. He felt enclosed and safe and loved. He became aware of the boniness of his father's body through his clothing: the ribs pushing against the skin, the muscles that were growing stringy and scrawny with age. With care, he hugged his father more tightly still.

Pre-season Warm-up Friendly

The following day Az was too busy to think about anything except the wedding. Everything was a blur, a rush of preparation, with his mother alternately chiding and chivvying, not allowing anybody a moment's rest, least of all herself.

Az went over his best-man speech, rehearsing it out loud to his father, who laughed in all the right places. He tried on the smart suit which had been tailor-made for him (it was uncomfortable because it was new, but it fit). When Aurora dropped by in the afternoon to introduce her two bridesmaids to her fiancé's family, Az was polite and friendly, and Aurora was too. He assumed she didn't know he had been enlisted to help deal with the Redspire situation, and even if she did, he assumed she would keep quiet about it.

Then, in the evening, Michael took him out to the hoop-drome at Stratoville to watch the Shrikes take on the Azuropolis Bluejays in a pre-season warm-up friendly. The two brothers cheered as the Shrikes romped to a 37-12 victory. It was an easy win but also a good game of jetball, with some spectacular defensive work from the home side and a satisfyingly high quota of deep slams and horizontal drives. Both Az and Michael agreed that the prospects for the coming season were good, as long as the Shrikes developed their midfield play, especially at the lower levels where they weren't nearly as cohesive as they ought to be. A team like the Northernheights Goshawks, the division leaders, could rip them apart there if they weren't careful.

'You know that nothing is going to change between us,' Michael said as they flew back to High Haven in his new helicopter, an Aerodyne Aeronauticals Green Dart. It was just a few days old, hot off the production line, streamlined and shimmering. 'I mean, sure, my footloose-and-fancy-free bachelor days are over, but *we'll* still be the same, you and me. We'll still go and see the Shrikes at the 'drome every fortnight and maybe fit in some away matches as well if we can.'

'Of course,' Az said. 'Nothing's going to change. You're going to be an old married fogey, but apart from that . . .'

'Cheek!' Michael reached across the cockpit, grabbed a clump of Az's hair and shook his head from side to side. The Green Dart sank sickeningly while his hand was off the collective handle, adding to Az's discomfort. Michael maintained control by applying pressure on the right anti-torque pedal, before grasping the collective again when he had finished roughing up his brother.

'And then kids will come along,' Az went on, 'and you'll be up half the night changing nappies and you'll be so tired you won't even remember you have a brother. But *apart* from all that . . .'

Michael scanned the dashboard frowningly. 'Where's the damn ejector seat button? I know there's one here somewhere. It's fitted as standard on the Dart.'

'Oh yes, and just think, this is the last two-seater 'copter you'll ever own. Next aircraft you buy is going to be a nice, safe family-model front-prop.' Which, Az knew, was a fate worse than death as far as his brother was concerned. 'And also, you can forget about having a drink with your mates after work. You know what Aurora'll have to say about that. "Out again with those rowdy test-pilot friends of yours, Michael? I don't think so." No, from tomorrow onwards you'll be under curfew – home by six every evening or else.'

'Well, maybe not,' Michael said with a hopeful air. 'After all, Aurora's not giving up her job at the Sanctum, is she? She's going to be there four days a week, which means that for four days a week I'm going to be a free man.'

'She'll find ways of keeping tabs on you. She's not stupid, Mike.'

'That she isn't. She's incredibly smart.'

'Except,' Az added, 'she can't be that smart if she wants *you* for a husband.'

'Ejector seat, ejector seat, ejector seat.' Michael slapped the dashboard. 'Come on, work, pluck you, work!'

'I'd just hit the vanes anyway,' Az said in a smart-alecky voice.

'And they'd chop you to ribbons. Twice as effective.'

'Maybe, but they'd also break, and then you'd crash.'

'It'd be worth it.'

Az laughed. Michael laughed. It felt carefree. Their banter was the usual blithe brotherly banter. It felt like the two of them as they always had been.

And all at once Az found himself wanting to tell Michael about Redspire, about extreme sanction, about everything . . .

. . . but he couldn't do it. He couldn't bring himself to tarnish the moment. As a rule he kept nothing from Michael. If he was gloomy, he would tell Michael so. If he was sad or anxious, he would tell Michael why. Suddenly, with Michael about to get married, it seemed that that option wasn't available to him any more. Michael was embarking on a new life and, no matter what he said, Az wasn't going to be a big part of it. His brother wasn't going to have as much time for him as he used to.

Meanwhile Az felt he was embarking on a new life of his own, one in which Michael and his parents were going to play an increasingly smaller role. In spite of everything he and his father had talked about yesterday, he couldn't ignore the fact that the drift of destiny seemed to be pulling him away from his family. The difference between him and them was no longer merely a matter of wings. He was becoming involved in affairs far removed from their simple domestic existence.

So really all he could do was lark about and laugh as if everything was the same as it ever was. Because in truth, despite Michael's claim that nothing was going to change, a great deal had changed already and a great deal more was about to.

CHAPTER 12

Visit Scenic Grimvale!

Cassie huffed into the speaker tube.

'Ladies and gentlemen,' she announced. 'If you'll kindly look to your left, you will observe the Thatcherhollow sawmill. Thatcherhollow is Grimvale's largest sawmill and one of the largest in all of the Westward Territories, turning out eighteen thousand tonnes of planks per year, on average, and a similar quantity of woodpulp, the basic material for making paper.'

Fletcher was in the driver's pod with her, seated at the controls. He let out a mocking laugh. 'A simi-larr ker-wantity of woodpulp! Hark at yourself, Cass!'

'Shh!' Cassie hissed, covering the speaker tube's mouthpiece with one hand.

'You know, every day you'm getting to sound more and more poncey when you'm on that tube.'

'Just speaking to they as them'd understand.'

'Oh yes, right. Of course, your highness. Pray continue.' Fletcher changed gear, and *Cackling Bertha* let out a laugh of her own – the chugging mechanical *clank-clatter-gurgle* which earned her her name.

'Thatcherhollow were established – *was* established in the early years of the last century,' Cassie said into the tube. 'The sawmill was one of the two main factors which helped turn a remote valley village into the thriving and successful township that we know today as Grimvale. The other factor, the Consolidated Colliery Collective, we will come to shortly. Thatcherhollow's sustainable pine plantations now cover almost half a million hectares of land and the timber which is derived from its hardy trees is as highly prized on the ground as it is up above the clouds. A great deal of your furniture is constructed from it, not to mention the elegant fretwork screens and the intricately carved statuettes which your race produces and which are now finding such favour down here.'

'Honestly, girl,' muttered Fletcher. 'This'm getting bad. You keep it up and I'll be checking your back for feathers.'

'Shut *up*, Fletch,' Cassie snapped out of the side of her mouth. 'I mean it. Elsewise you'm going to be finding this speaker tube rammed up somewhere you wouldn't want it rammed. Straight up.'

'If you did, them lot down in the loading bay wouldn't notice the difference. Just be getting one kind of hot air instead of another.'

Cassie clouted her brother.

Grinning from ear to ear, Fletcher steered *Bertha* around a corner. The forest-swathed slopes which clustered behind the sawmill fell away in the rearview mirrors. Ahead, a more industrialised section of Grimvale beckoned.

Cassie resumed her tour-guide monologue, doing her best to make what she was saying sound fresh and spontaneous. She had borrowed books from the town library and toiled to memorise a huge amount of facts and figures about Grimvale and the surrounded area until she could reel them off without thinking. To make the facts and figures interesting to her audience, however, she had to pretend that they were interesting to her.

And they weren't. After just a couple of months of running these sightseeing trips, Cassie was bored. It was the same journey every time, the same circuit through Grimvale and its outskirts, the same landmarks to be passed and commented on along the way – dull, dull, dull. There was no challenge, no excitement. It wasn't like murk-combing, where there'd always been the potential thrill of discovery, the chance (and hope) of coming across a Relic; where you'd had to rely on your wits and the sharpness of your eyes; where the many hazards of the Shadow Zone kept you constantly on your toes. Trundling along metalled roads, pointing out the 'highlights' of Grimvale to a handful of Airborn visitors who sat down in the loading bay on padded benches that Fletcher had installed and looked out through the rows of portholes that Fletcher had also installed, and who doubtless found what they were being shown was glum and grey and dismal and depressing – why did she do it?

Cassie knew why. She did it because she had no choice. It was this or she and her family starved.

That, though, didn't make the job any less boring or more bearable.

Soon *Bertha* was nearing the Consolidated Colliery Collective and Cassie found herself explaining to her passengers about the mine's shared-profits policy and about the so-called Black Lake Lode, the vast, apparently inexhaustible seam of coal upon which the pithead stood. She also mentioned the CCC's annual coal-output tonnage and various other fascinating statistics.

What she didn't tell them about was the attempted revolution which had sprung up at the CCC and almost brought down a sky-city. In all likelihood the passengers knew the story already. After all, that was how it was possible for them to be here now, sightseeing. Twelve months ago they would not even have realised that there were people down here to take them on a tour such as this. Now, since the events of last year, they could visit the ground and mingle with its inhabitants any time.

Not that many of them did. Today it wasn't bad. There were eight Airborn down in the loading bay: an elderly married couple, three university students and a mother with two young children. But most days the Grubdollars were lucky if they pulled in two paying passengers and some days they didn't get any at all. Cassie had done the maths and worked out that they needed two fares per trip just to cover their fuel costs. A third fare meant they had a bit of money to pay bills and buy food. A fourth, and they were turning an actual profit.

So, on average, they were just about breaking even, and good days like today helped with that. But breaking even wasn't enough. If you took into account the fact that she and Fletcher worked from dawn to dusk and didn't draw a salary for it, then they were actually running the business at a loss.

Resentment welled up inside Cassie. She swallowed it back down. Life hadn't been perfect back when murk-combing had been the Grubdollar family trade, but it had certainly been better than this. She must not allow herself to feel hard done by, however. That didn't help anyone.

'We'll shortly be coming to the end of our journey around the Grimvale region,' she announced. 'Our route now takes us back through the Shadow Zone to the Chancel at the base of the sky-city Heliotropia. You may wish to keep an eye out for the Shadow Zone's indigenous species, verms.'

'Indigenous,' Fletcher said, to himself. 'I doesn't even know what the word means.'

'As the daylight starts to fade,' Cassie said into the speaker tube, ignoring him, 'verms emerge from their burrows to forage for food. Totally blind, they hunt by —'

Clang!

Something small and hard struck *Bertha*'s side.

'What the —?' Fletcher peered out through the windshield and a sour look came over his face. 'Damn. Should have known.'

'Who be it?' Cassie asked.

'*They*,' came the cold reply.

CHAPTER 13

The Marquee

That morning, on their way to the Chancel to collect passengers, Cassie and Fletcher had spotted a marquee pitched at the roadside. It was large and weather-stained and its entrance flaps were tied open, revealing a shadowy interior. Inside, a man had been setting out wooden chairs, arranging them in rows in front of a rostrum. Outside, parked a few metres away, was a rusty, beaten-up old van with balding tyres and a tarpaulin covering half of its flatbed. The marquee hadn't been there the evening before. It had sprung up overnight, like a mushroom.

Both Grubdollar siblings had known what it signified. A travelling preacher had come to town. To be precise: a travelling Deacon.

Fletcher's first instinct had been to steer *Bertha* off the road and flatten the marquee. And if the man inside had happened to get crushed beneath *Bertha*'s caterpillar tracks too, so be it. Fletcher's loathing for Deacons ran that deep.

But he'd resisted the temptation and settled for a few growled threats instead. The Deacon, for his part, had glanced round at *Bertha* without curiosity, then resumed laying out the chairs. Fletcher had fired a rude gesture at him from the driver's pod but the man hadn't noticed. Cassie, meanwhile, had observed that the Deacon's hair was strikingly red and flared upward from his head like flames, but he hadn't been close enough for her to get a good look at his face.

It was clear what had happened since then. The red-haired Deacon would have gone into town to drum up custom. A recently-passed Grimvale bylaw meant he wasn't allowed to preach within the town limits. Nothing, however, prevented him from gathering an audience from the town and holding a meeting with them just outside.

What had he said at that meeting?

The precise words didn't matter. But if he was anything like other Deacons who had visited the region lately, he would have delivered a long, ranting sermon against the Airborn and against anyone who was friendly with them. He would have condemned the Bilateral Covenant and denounced the Groundling governments who had so willingly, blindly signed up to it. He would have lamented the fact that Deacons like him had been thrown out of their positions of authority and out of their Chancels. He would have painted a picture of the world as it was now, emphasising the upheaval and confusion which were the result of contact with the beings formerly known as the Ascended Ones. 'So many people don't know where they stand any more,' he would have said. 'There's so much uncertainty now, and so little order.' And he would have gone on to conjure up images of a terrible future, with society breaking down, everything falling into chaos. War, disaster, death. All because the established way of doing things was gone. The division between the races was gone. The system which had been in place for centuries, and for centuries had *worked*, was gone.

And his audience would have lapped it up. They would have applauded throughout his speech. They would have grumbled their agreement with the Deacon's views on the present sorry state of the world and would have nodded dourly at his dark vision of what was to come. Gradually he would have stirred them into a froth of indignation and disgust. For his audience was made up of people who preferred the world as it used to be. They were unsettled by the drastic changes that had occurred. They pined for the not-so-distant past, a simpler time.

And then, just as the meeting was breaking up, what should these angry, seething folk see but a murk-comber growling its way towards them? A murk-comber which had been modified to carry Airborn tourists inside.

Little wonder that one of them picked up a stone off the ground and hurled it at *Cackling Bertha*. Little wonder that the rest of them started to do the same.

CHAPTER 14

The Effects Of Anti-verm Countermeasures On Humans

A second stone hit *Bertha*, striking not far from the driver's pod.

'Bastards!' yelled Fletcher. 'What'm got into they?'

'That Deacon, that be what,' Cassie said. 'Filling their bellies with his own sour grapes. Just keep driving. Ignore they.'

'But them's pelting us with stones!'

'Can't hurt we or our passengers. Damage *Bertha*'s paintwork maybe, put a couple of dents in she, but then her be'n't a perfect beauty to begin with.'

'But —'

'Keep driving, Fletch. Only thing to do. Just not too fast. Make it as if us doesn't give a fig. So as not to alarm any of they lot down below.'

More stones came sailing in from the crowd that was clustered outside the marquee. They struck like gong beats on *Bertha*'s hull. Some missed. One rebounded off the curved windshield of the driver's pod, leaving a scratch on the glass. Dimly over the sound of the engine Cassie could hear the crowd shouting. She couldn't make out what they were saying but the tone was pure wild rage, like the baying of hounds.

A voice came through the speaker tube. 'Erm,' it said nervously, 'sorry to bother you, but might I ask what's going on? Why are those people attacking us?'

Cassie recognised the voice as belonging to the male half of the elderly Airborn couple.

'Nothing to worry about, sir,' she said. 'Please stay calm. It'm just some – some rowdy locals. We'll be out of their range soon enough. You're perfectly safe.'

But even as she said this Cassie observed that the stone throwers were now running alongside *Bertha*, keeping pace with her. And rocky missiles continued to bounce noisily off *Bertha*'s exterior.

'Chaff,' she said to Fletcher.

'What?'

'Let's see they off with some chaff.'

'Against people? But that'm for verms.'

'Still. Why not?'

Fletcher smiled. 'Yeah, why not?'

He pulled a lever. At *Bertha*'s rear a small panel slid open, exposing the end of a pipe. The next instant a fist-sized paper sphere shot out from the pipe with a *choom* of compressed air. It exploded above the heads of the pursuing crowd. Several of them were hit by tiny fragments of rock salt. They fell, clutching arms and faces.

Fletcher checked the lens-projected images in the rearview mirrors. 'Got some, annoyed the rest.'

'Smoke,' said Cassie.

Her brother pulled another lever.

A cloud of white smoke spurted violently from *Bertha*'s rear, enveloping the stone throwers. Some charged through it and emerged the other side unaffected. Others staggered and col-lapsed to the ground, choking and spluttering in the billowing fumes, tears streaming from their eyes.

Cassie debated whether to deploy another anti-verm coun-termeasure.

Fletcher was thinking the same thing. 'Let's electrocute they.'

'Us only wants to hurt they, Fletch, not kill. Besides, them isn't close enough for it to work. No, I reckon us has made our point and them's made theirs. Call it a draw.'

'Ahem, excuse me.' It was the elderly Airborn man again on the speaker tube. 'Sorry to bother you again, but those "rowdy locals" of yours managed to hit one of the portholes down here.

There's a hole in the glass and, well, we're losing the pressure seal. Air's hissing in from outside.'

'Oh bugger it!' Cassie said under her breath. Into the speaker tube she said, 'Just sit tight, everyone. We'll get you back to the elevators in no time.'

She turned to Fletcher, but he didn't need telling. He thrust the control sticks forward to Full Speed.

CHAPTER 15

Under Pressure

The Grubdollars had converted *Bertha*'s loading bay into a self-contained, airtight compartment and had installed a vacuum pump so that it could be depressurised. That way they were able to replicate the thin, high-altitude atmosphere which their Airborn passengers were used to and the tourists would not suffer from ground-sickness.

With the seal breached, the air in the loading bay would return to normal ground-level pressure very rapidly. That meant the passengers were soon going to start feeling unwell. Cassie recalled Az's first time down on the ground. He had been near-comatose for twenty-four hours, on top of suffering from nausea and a splitting headache.

Then there were the two small children on board to consider. Ground-sickness might affect them even more severely than it did adults. It might even kill them.

'Faster, Fletch,' Cassie urged.

'Want we to crash? I be going as fast as I can.'

Cackling Bertha beetled along the Shadow Zone road, kicking up a plume of dust behind her. Dead ahead was the column which supported Heliotropia. Elevators shuttled up and down it, at this distance looking like aphids on a rose stem. To Cassie, the column didn't seem to be getting any closer, and she knew that with every passing second the air pressure in the loading bay was becoming denser and *Bertha*'s passengers were getting less and less comfortable.

'How'm you all bearing up?' she asked through the speaker tube, trying to sound upbeat. She wasn't aware that she had stopped imitating Airborn speech patterns.

'We're – we're OK,' said the elderly man. 'I can't say we're —'

Someone interrupted, snatching the speaker tube off him. 'Listen, Miss Grumdingle or whatever your name is. One of my friends has just been sick all over the floor. I'm starting to feel pretty dizzy. Why aren't you doing anything?'

Cassie guessed the person talking was one of the three university students. 'Us is trying to get you to the elevators quick as possible, sir, but *Bertha* be'n't exactly built for speed. Her top k.p.h. is —'

'I don't care about that! There are children here. There must be some way of keeping the air pressure down.'

'The vacuum pump be operating on full power but it'm not going to make much difference so long as that porthole be broken.'

'Then come down here and fix it somehow!' the student demanded.

'I can't,' Cassie said. 'To get into the bay I'll have to unseal the doors, which'll only make things worse for you. Maybe you could find something to stuff into the crack, like a piece of cloth or something.'

'We've already done that. It's helped, but not a lot.'

'That'm all I can think of. Sorry.'

A torrent of abuse burst from the speaker tube. Cassie hadn't known the Airborn could swear like that.

She looked at Fletcher.

All he said was, 'Well, there'm some new Airborn phrases you can use on the next tour.'

'That'm assuming there even be a next tour,' Cassie replied.

CHAPTER 16

Thanks A Lot

Fletcher steered *Bertha* into a parking space in the large, ware-house-like structure that used to be the Chancel's sorting-house. Cassie nipped out through an iris-style access point in the underside of the driver's pod, leaving Fletcher to hit the switch to open the loading bay.

There was a sigh of inrushing air as the hatch rose, although not the loud, sharp hiss that usually came. At the same time the fruity stench of vomit wafted out. Cassie had to force herself not to retch.

The Airborn passengers staggered out – the mother and children were first, then the students.

The mother said nothing. She just gave Cassie a dirty look, then hustled her children off towards the sorting-house's double-doored exit, herding them along with her wings. Council-appointed officials were waiting on the other side of the doors with a fleet of battery-powered carts to transport the Airborn visitors back to the elevator chamber.

One of the students hurried after the mother and children. He was green-faced and obviously was the one who'd been sick. He was keen to get to the elevator chamber as soon as possible.

The two remaining students rounded on Cassie angrily.

'Well, what do you call that?' the taller of them snarled. 'All part of the Groundling experience I suppose. A slice of life as it's lived down here.'

'We could have been killed!' said the other, who had flamingo feathers stitched into his plumage. These made him look very flamboyant, but their deep pink colour also matched the indignant flush that had come to his cheeks.

'I doesn't reckon you could have been killed,' Cassie replied. 'There were no real danger of —'

'Oh, you *doesn't*, does you?' snapped the taller one. 'So is it commonplace on these tours that one gets pelted with rocks? Or perhaps you arranged it. To add a little spice to the trip.'

'That'm just stupid.'

'Probably you'll start charging people extra now,' said the flamingo-feathered one. 'You know, to "guarantee security". This is a little protection racket you lot have set up.'

Cassie was finding it hard to keep an even temper in the face of such ridiculous accusations. These two were, what, nineteen? Not that much older than her, just a couple of years, and yet they were treating her like a child.

'I be truly sorry about what happened,' she said. 'It were circumstances entirely beyond our control. If there'm something I can do to make it up to you ...'

'There certainly is. A refund.'

'A full refund,' Flamingo Feathers chimed in.

'Would that make you happy?' Cassie said.

'No, but it would leave us feeling that we hadn't been ripped off.'

Reluctantly Cassie went to fetch the gifts with which the Airborn had paid for the tour. These were items of jewellery, silverware and small wooden statuettes, all of them beautifully crafted. The Airborn made artworks with a delicacy and elegance that Groundlings simply could not match.

'Which was yours?' she asked, holding out the box which contained the gifts, today's fares. It looked like a decent sum in total, although you never knew till you got to the gift-broker's shop. Cassie hated to lose any of it.

The two students plucked out a gold chain bracelet and a small mahogany figure of an eagle in flight. Flamingo Feathers also took an ivory-handled fan which the third student, the sick one, had paid with.

'I shan't be recommending you to any of my friends,' the taller student said haughtily, as he and Flamingo Feathers strutted off in the direction of the exit.

'Surprised if you's *got* any friends,' Cassie muttered under her breath.

The elderly Airborn couple had watched all of this in silence, and Cassie turned to them wearily, anticipating more of the same.

'Here,' she said, nodding to the box in her hands. 'Take what'm yours and go.'

'Young lady,' said the husband, 'I cannot apologise enough for those two.' He gestured at the departing students. 'Such ingratitude is unforgivable. Believe me, they don't represent us all. Don't judge the rest of the Airborn by their example.'

'Oh,' said Cassie, taken aback.

'None of what happened was your fault,' said the wife, 'and I honestly don't believe we were in serious danger. The young man who was ill – that was fear and panic, not ground-sickness. He just worked himself up into a state.'

'So you doesn't want your gifts back?'

The husband shook his head firmly. 'On the contrary. In fact, I think Vesta has something for you.'

He pointed to his wife, who was undoing the clasp of her necklace. Cassie had noticed the necklace earlier when the tourists were climbing aboard. It was made of opals and gorgeous. Each white precious stone was carved into a rounded, asymmetrical shape. Strung together in irregular rows, they resembled nothing quite so much as a vista of glittering white clouds.

Now, the elderly woman took the necklace off and held it out to Cassie.

'Oh no, I can't accept that.'

'You can and you will.'

'But it'm much too nice.'

'It should make up for the refunds you handed out.'

'More than make up,' Cassie said. 'But still, I can't.'

'I won't take no for an answer.' The woman laid the opal necklace in the box. 'There. It's yours. And we have to go, don't we, dear?' she said to her husband.

'We do.'

'We *will* be recommending a Grubdollar tour to our friends,' the elderly woman said, as she took her husband's arm. 'Very enthusiastically.'

'Thank you,' Cassie said again, although the phrase scarcely began to convey what she was feeling.

The elderly couple headed for the doors, leaving her gazing at the necklace in awe. Flecks of colour shone within the opals' whiteness. If she tilted the box just slightly, a multihued shimmer rippled through the entire necklace.

All at once she thought of Az and the last time she and he had met, up overhead in Heliotropia.

They had been standing at the city's edge, looking out over the cloudscape. Her visit was nearly up. There wasn't much oxygen left in her breathing apparatus. Az was asking her about Michael's wedding. Would she and her family like to come?

She made noncommittal noises. *Maybe. Perhaps. Depending.*

At that moment, the sunlight struck a gauzy peak of cloud and, out of nowhere, an arc of colours appeared. It remained there, transparent and shining, for just a few seconds, then vanished again. She asked Az what it was.

He told her: *a sunbow.* It was a trick of the light, something to do with refraction, the distortion of the sun's rays through cloud vapour.

He said it as though such a thing was commonplace, and to him, of course, it was. To Cassie, however, it was one of the most beautiful sights she had ever seen.

She knew then that there was too much separating them; too much in Az's world that he took for granted and that she never could. If this sunbow, this brief-lived miracle in the clouds, got nothing more from him than a shrug and a scientific explanation, then how could he and she ever hope to understand each other at even the most basic level? They were too unalike.

She'd recognised this as an excuse, even as she thought it. She was trying to find a reason not to be with Az any more, and the flimsiest of ones would do.

The opals reminded her of the sunbow, and that was all it took to make her happiness about the necklace vanish. The emotion popped like a balloon, punctured by a stab of guilt.

She still owed Az a reply to his invitation to Michael's wedding. It was tomorrow, and she hadn't given him a yes or a no. She had ducked the whole issue, ignored it, and it was too late now. She had left him in limbo and that was weak of her and she was ashamed.

If only things were simple! If only she didn't have all these worries, all these responsibilities!

If only, if only, if only.

'Penny for your thoughts?'

Cassie turned. Fletcher was standing beside her. She hadn't heard him walk up.

'Them be'n't even worth that,' she replied, then gave what she hoped was a breezy laugh. 'But hey, look at this!' She showed him the opal necklace. 'This be worth something all right.'

'Not bad.'

'Let's head back to town. Reckon if us makes good time, the gift-broker's might still be open.'

'You never know.' Fletcher sniffed the air, then leaned into the loading bay and recoiled with a disgusted expression. 'Phew! That'm *nasty*. Fains I doesn't have to clean it up.'

'Me either. I vote Robert.'

'Yeah. Least him can do, being as him gets to sit at home and twiddle his thumbs all day.'

'Motion carried then. Two to one. Robert it be.'

CHAPTER 17

Speaking Of Whom . . .

Robert did not actually 'sit at home and twiddle his thumbs all day'. For a start, he was still in school, so during term time he was out from eight till three each weekday being a reasonably attentive pupil at the Grimvale Central College on Loomshuttle Lane. Even during the holidays, though, he didn't get to go out in *Bertha* with his brother and sister, much as he would have liked to.

The reason was that someone had to stay home with their father, and Robert was the youngest and therefore, somehow, the job had fallen to him.

He wasn't quite sure how that had happened. Surely it was Cassie's duty, not his. As the girl in the family, she was the one you went to when there was looking-after and caring-for stuff to be done. But Robert was on the bottom rung of the Grubdollar sibling ladder, and youngest brothers and sisters tended to have to do what their elders told them to. It wasn't fair or democratic but it was the way things were. Hence, Robert was stuck with the dull and thankless daily task which he had taken to calling 'Da-watch'.

It was a necessary task too. Their father had to have someone there in the house with him. Nobody said it in so many words, but Den Grubdollar could not be left on his own.

Den was not a well man.

So unwell was he that sometimes, looking at him, Robert scarcely recognised him any more.

At this moment, Den was where he usually was: his favourite armchair in the corner of the lounge. He was just sitting there, staring into space, his hands resting in his lap, fingertip against fingertip. He wasn't talking or laughing, and at one time it had been rare to see him not doing either. Nor was he rushing around, busy with some job or other. For instance, you never saw him working on *Bertha*, which was once his favourite spare-time activity. His nails weren't permanently dirty from changing her oil; his hands weren't grease-stained from replacing gaskets and spark plugs. Nowadays, too, he barely ate, and didn't touch his beloved beer. Den used to have quite a belly on him, which he somehow managed to sustain even during the periods when the family's fortunes had taken a downturn and food (and beer) were in short supply.

He had become thin, a shadow of his former self. His eyes were sunken in his face, as if he had grown hollow inside. Sitting and staring was what he mostly did during his waking hours, though he napped as well, either dozing in the armchair or sloping off to his bedroom in the afternoon for an hour or two. Occasionally he got up to look out of a window. Sometimes you could find him down in the courtyard, peering at the clouds or the ground. Very, very rarely he might step out through the front gate and stop and gaze one way along the street then the other, perhaps sighing as he did so. But that was as active as he ever got, and he never strayed more than a few metres from the house.

He stumbled through the days of his life, mute, lost.

It had been this way ever since Martin died.

All of the Grubdollars mourned Martin. His absence was a constant pang in their hearts. They missed him horribly. They remembered him as temperamental, hot-headed, opinionated – and ultimately brave and true, a hero. He could not be replaced and the pain of his death would not go away. The family was not the same without him. It functioned but only just. There was a vital component missing.

Their father, though, was taking it harder than any of them. He had lost his wife thirteen years ago, and now he had lost his oldest son. It had knocked the stuffing out of him. Robust, good-natured, cantankerous Den Grubdollar was gone, and in his place was an empty shell of a man, a shrunken effigy.

His children were worried that he might do something drastic and foolish one day, like kill himself. Even if he didn't go that far, they feared he might continue to neglect himself to the point where he would waste away to nothing. Perhaps rattle-lung or some other disease would invade him while his defences were down and destroy him from within; perhaps misery alone would be enough to do the trick.

So Robert was tasked with keeping an eye on him while Cassie and Fletcher were off conducting their tours, and when Robert was obliged to be at school, Colin Amblescrut filled in.

Colin had elected himself Den's faithful friend and was only too happy to keep him company when required. He probably – Robert thought ruefully – did a better job of it than he, Robert, did. Colin chattered all day long to Den, regaling him with story after story about the extensive Amblescrut clan and their unusual and frequently illegal exploits. The run-ins they had with the police were the stuff of legend. So were their skills at brewing moonshine and their artful methods of making money without doing any actual work. Colin's fund of Amblescrut tales was apparently endless. Whether Den enjoyed listening to them or not was unclear, but Colin certainly relished telling them. It entertained *him*, even if his audience seemed indifferent.

Robert, by contrast, just left his father to his morose staring while he himself got on with other things. He felt his dad couldn't be helped unless he decided he wanted to be. Until then, he checked on him at regular intervals, made him lunch and cups of tea, but otherwise stayed out of his way. It was odd how boring and irritating someone else's depression could be. Without question Robert still loved his father but he detested the surly, silent presence the old man had become. In Robert's view, if Den truly cared about his family he would make the effort to break out of the slump he had fallen into. Obviously he just didn't care enough.

The long trial of another day of Da-watch was coming to an end. As nightfall deepened the grey of the clouds to black, Robert heard a far-off clank-and-trundle which announced that *Bertha* was nearly home. He wondered what sort of a trip it had been, how many paying punters there'd been aboard, and how much cash Cassie and Fletcher had got at the gift-broker's in exchange for the Airborn's artefacts. He felt a keen edge of envy. At least his brother and sister got to tootle around in *Bertha*, even if it was along the exact same route every time. At least they got to see something other than the four walls of the family homestead, which were prison walls to Robert while he was on Da-watch. At least they *did* something with their days. Did they have any idea how frustrating his existence was right now?

It appeared to have been a good outing. Cassie emerged from *Bertha* clutching a sheaf of banknotes, which she eagerly showed off to Robert.

'Hundred and fifty!' she exclaimed. 'We had five tourists and one of they gave us a necklace that was real opal. Gift-broker were well impressed.'

'Strictly speaking it were eight, not five,' said Fletcher, coming up the spiral staircase behind her.

'What, you lose three of they halfway round?' said Robert. 'Pretty careless.'

The story came out: the Deacon's marquee, the enraged townsfolk, the hail of stones, the pressure-seal breach.

'Mind you,' said Fletcher, 'us may have made some decent money today but it'm going to cost us to get *Bertha* mended and shipshape again. New porthole, plus a lick of paint and some panel-beating to get the dents out of her.'

'Us can do that ourselves,' Cassie said. 'And maybe us can get the porthole glass at the reclamation yard, cheap and second-hand.'

'You'm certainly looking on the bright side today, sis,' said Robert.

'Someone has to,' Cassie replied, sounding determined and also ever so slightly desperate.

Robert was about to comment on this when a distant, deep voice spoke up from the lounge. Robert had heard the voice so seldom these past few months that he almost didn't know whose it was.

'Hurt *Bertha*?' it rumbled.

Den was up out his armchair. He was hunched and swaying, and in his sunken eyes there was a look which none of his offspring could remember seeing there before and none of them much liked. For once, his eyes were lively again, but the light that animated them was yellow and baleful. It spoke of curdled emotions and a despair that needed an outlet and had found one.

'Who,' Den intoned, growling out the words, 'hurt she?'

CHAPTER 18

Deacon Gerald Hardscree

Deacon Gerald Hardscree was reading to himself in his marquee by the light of a kerosene lantern. It was too early to get out his bedroll and turn in for the night, and anyway he wasn't much of a sleeper. His brain was always so busy that he had a hard time shutting it down. Thought after thought raced through it like the trucks of a freight train, keeping him awake with their rattle and clang.

The book in his hands was a slim pamphlet entitled *The Death of Faith, The End of Days*, written by one Archdeacon Corbelgilt. It was smudgily printed on cheap paper and not the sort of thing that could be found in an ordinary bookshop. Copies cost nothing and were distributed privately through a network of Deacons. One had come into Hardscree's possession a week ago when he was preaching thirty miles away at a town called Breaker's Harrow. There had been a Deacon in his audience, sitting there in plain clothes. He had come up to Hardscree after the meeting and pressed the book on him.

'You should read this, brother,' he had said.

Hardscree had known who Corbelgilt was. He had also known that he was planning to pass through Grimvale on the next leg of his travels. Grimvale, whose Chancel the selfsame Corbelgilt used to be in charge of. Hardscree had thought this an omen.

He studied the book, taking occasional sips from the hip flask of whisky by his side. Moths and other winged insects swirled in the lantern's orbit. Every so often one of them would hurl itself at the hot glass with a loud *plink* and sometimes a sizzle.

Corbelgilt wrote that the forced eviction of Deacons from

their Chancels had been an act of gross heresy. Not only that but it was foolish and short-sighted and had damaged civilisation, perhaps beyond repair. For, if there was no promise of an Ascended life after this earthbound, cloud-shrouded one, then what did anyone have to look forward to beyond death? Nothing. All across the land, Corbelgilt said, people were slowly waking up to this dire fact. They had had hope ripped away from them. It surely wouldn't be long before they wanted it back, and the best way for that to happen would be to reinstate the Deacons.

Hardscree found himself nodding in agreement with Corbelgilt's book in some places. In others, he found himself shaking his head in strong disagreement. For instance, Corbelgilt insisted that the only way to normalise the world again was to tear up the Bilateral Covenant, break off relations with the Airborn, and put the Deacons back in the Chancels.

Hardscree didn't believe that that could be done. You couldn't have things exactly as they were before, not after such a fundamental shift in the way the world worked. A broken china cup could be glued back together but it would never be as good as it had been previously. A brand new cup was called for.

It so happened that Hardscree had an idea what that new cup should look like and how it might be fashioned. In the months that he had been roaming the Westward Territories, his thundering freight-train brain had been pondering the matter. Lately, an answer had become clear to him.

Footfalls outside the marquee caught his attention. Hardscree laid Corbelgilt's book down and looked out, shading his eyes against the lantern light.

A man appeared, panting. He was dishevelled and furious-looking. His eyes glared, his hair was scrubby, and he didn't have many teeth.

Hardscree sensed trouble but remained calm. He knew he and his kind weren't popular. That was why they were banned from preaching within town limits. For now, the public mood was against them and all that they stood for. Many wandering preachers didn't wear their Deacon robes any more for that very reason. A minority of people wanted to hear what they had to say, but the majority did not and could get quite aggressive about it. So it was wise to travel incognito whenever possible.

Hardscree himself was not ashamed of who he was and wore his robe openly and with pride. He had things to say, truths to spread, and didn't care if people were upset by that.

However, as a precaution, he wore something else too, beneath his robe: a sheath knife with a twenty-centimetre blade, strapped to his shin.

He didn't carry the knife idly, either. It wasn't for him to take out just for show, to try and scare people off with. He knew how to handle it and could do so with great skill. Before becoming a Deacon, Hardscree had been a huntsman. He had been born and raised in the Pale Uplands, that mountainous region where tracking and killing wild game wasn't a sport, it was a way of life. Hardscree was lethally accurate with a bow and arrow. He could hit a bullseye at a hundred paces. And he was no less deft with a knife. Once, he had skewered a rock hare from over sixty metres away, hurling the knife so that the blade impaled the fleeing creature in the back of the head, ending its life instantly.

Many times in his recent travels Hardscree had been under-estimated by irate, indignant citizens. They thought that because he had spent much of his life in a Chancel, he was soft and pampered – an easy target.

They'd been wrong.

And this man was about to learn the same lesson, if he wasn't careful.

'Hello,' said Hardscree evenly. 'I'm afraid I've finished pre-aching for the day. I plan on holding another meeting tomorrow if you're interested. Perhaps you should come back then.'

'I be'n't after listening to your Deaconish jabber,' said the man, striding up the aisle between the rows of chairs. 'I want to know one thing, and that'm why you be stirring up all this trouble and getting folk to attack my *Bertha*.'

'Your . . .' Hardscree deduced what he was referring to. 'Ah. The murk-comber.'

'Yes, the murk-comber,' growled the man. 'Where d'you get

off, rabble-rousing like that? Us has had enough trouble from your sort in the past, and here you come along raking up bad feeling again and preying on people's fears, and I won't have it!'

The man halted just a few metres from Hardscree. His fists were clenched and his body was quiveringly rigid. Hardscree assessed him carefully, thinking that the man had once been larger and sturdier than he was now. His clothes hung loosely off his frame. There was an unhealthy sallowness to his complexion. Once upon a time, Hardscree might have been wary of getting into a ruckus with this fellow, knife or no knife. As it was, he knew he'd have no difficulty subduing him, if it came to that.

But Hardscree didn't want it to come to that. The man seemed to deserve his pity rather than his hostility.

'Your name?' he enquired. 'At least let's introduce ourselves before this goes any further.'

The man blinked. 'Grubdollar. Den Grubdollar.'

'Pleased to meet you, Den. I'm Gerald Hardscree.'

He held out his hip flask.

'Fancy a nip?' he asked.

CHAPTER 19

Waking Up From A Long Dream

Den hesitated, then reached for the small, brushed steel container. It was almost a reflex. Someone politely offered you a drink, you accepted. At the same time he was confused by his own response. He'd come here to harangue the Deacon and maybe knock him around a little bit. Not give him a serious beating, just vent some frustration and indignation on him, a bruise here, a scuff there. Perhaps smash up a few of his chairs.

But now he wasn't even sure why he wanted to do that. It had struck him as a good idea when he learned about *Bertha* getting bombarded with stones, and he had felt a wonderful clear-headedness as he stormed out of the house and out of town. For the first time in ages he had something to aim at, something to do, a purpose. He'd felt as though he was waking up from a long dream.

And then, this.

He was abruptly deflated, empty. His fingers closed around the hip flask. He unscrewed the cap and took a swig. It was good whisky. Single malt, if he didn't miss his guess. Quality stuff.

A Deacon who drank whisky? Wine, maybe. That was a typical Deacon's sort of tipple. Port too, and brandy. But whisky?

'I'm from the Pale Uplands,' said Hardscree, as if reading his thoughts. 'Whisky's like water there. As babies we have a drop of it in our milk every night, or so it's said. I'm not convinced that's healthy but I imagine it ensures a good night's sleep for everyone, baby *and* parents.' He chuckled, then went serious. 'Now listen, about your murk-comber – I'd like to say sorry

68

and ask your forgiveness. It was an unfortunate episode and I didn't mean for it to happen.'

'Yes? Really?' said Den. Half-consciously he took another swig from the hip flask.

'It all took place after I'd finished preaching. Everyone had left the tent and by the time I realised what was going on, it was too late. I shouted at them to stop but no one heard. For what it's worth, your murk-comber retaliated. Gave as good as she got. Chaff, smoke – it was pretty funny to watch, as a matter of fact. There were some sore feelings afterwards, I can tell you, but I managed to soothe egos and convince everyone that they had had it coming. You needn't fear any reprisals.'

'Still, none of it would have happened in the first place if you hadn't got those folk all so fired up with your speechifying and pontificating,' Den said.

'I agree. Guilty as charged. That's why I'm apologising.'

Den was more confused than ever. The Deacon seemed entirely sincere. That alone set him apart from every other Deacon he had encountered before. As a rule, a Deacon wouldn't know sincerity if it came up and bit him on the well-fleshed backside.

The other thing that distinguished this one was that hair of his. Like fire, it was. Den found himself mesmerised by it. He'd never seen hair quite so red, although he had heard it was a common feature of folk from the Uplands.

He cleared his throat. 'Well. Hmph. Apology accepted, I suppose. No real harm done. Not to *Bertha* at any rate. Them Airborn who was on board, them was all right too, apparently. Bit shaken, bit peeved, but no bruises, no bones broken. It'm just . . .'

'Yes?'

'Us has had some bad experiences with mobs and rabble-rousers here in Grimvale. Not so long ago . . . but you probably know the tale. Most folk does.'

Hardscree gave a nod. 'The Grimvale Humanist uprising. It was the catalyst, the reason why everything's the way it is now.'

'So you see, I fancied you was another Alan Steamarm. But

you be'n't. You'm just another wandering Deacon.'

'From the way you said that,' said Hardscree, 'I take it you're no fan of Deacons.'

Den seesawed a hand in the air. 'Fair to middling about they. My son, see, my eldest boy ... him were ... him died. Died in a fight with a Deacon. A bad man, that Deacon were. Rotten and corrupt and, it turned out, insane. Martin, my son, died stopping he from doing something that'd've killed a whole load of people. No question, that were a reason worth dying for. But if it hadn't been for that Deacon, Martin'd still be ... be alive.'

Deacon Hardscree gestured to a chair. Den accepted the invitation and sat. For a while he couldn't speak. He was lost in a swirl of memories, painful ones, guilt-ridden ones. Everything he had been brooding on and tormenting himself with this past year boiled up inside him. He tipped some more whisky down his throat without even thinking about it. What if he had got to the Chancel sooner on that dreadful day? What if he had been able to locate Martin in the furnace chamber? Would he have been able to save him? Couldn't he have sacrificed *himself* in the struggle with Deacon Shatterlonger? Wouldn't that have been infinitely better, him dying instead of Martin? Sons should bury their fathers, not the other way round.

And all at once Den was crying – crying so hard he could barely draw breath. Sobs coughed out of him. Tears coursed down his cheeks, burning like acid.

He felt helpless and hopeless. The impulse that had brought him to the Deacon's marquee had vanished utterly. It had been like a struck match, flaring briefly then gone.

He didn't know anything any more except his own grief and remorse.

He felt a hand on his shoulder.

'Tell me more, Den,' said Hardscree. 'Tell me everything.'

CHAPTER 20

'People Need Mystery'

The kerosene lantern guttered and hissed. More insects perished, drawn to its incandescence, flying too near, dying on singed wings. Outside the marquee, the clouded night was dark and still.

Much of what Den had to say was stuff Hardscree was already familiar with. The events at Grimvale had already entered into history, and into folklore as well. All across the world, people told one another about the Humanist siege of the Chancel and the arrival of the Airborn which quelled it, and with each telling they added their own invented details, their own embroiderings, and so the story mutated and got more complicated and grew.

Archdeacon Corbelgilt's book contained its own version of what had happened, although the account Corbelgilt gave was one-sided and concentrated less on description and more on criticism. Treachery! Outrage! Desecration! Those were the sort of terms Corbelgilt used, exclamation marks included.

Like Corbelgilt, Den had first-hand experience. He'd been an eyewitness to the events. He'd participated. And like Corbelgilt he had paid for his involvement, although far more dearly than the Archdeacon. In the end Corbelgilt had been deprived of luxury and prestige, whereas for Den the price of being caught up in the Grimvale Humanist uprising was nothing less than the loss of his eldest child.

Hardscree listened to him recount the whole tragic tale. Every so often he would stumble over some particularly difficult recollection, such as his arguments with Martin over Martin's Humanist beliefs. Hardscree would then coax the next portion of the story out of him with a soft query or two:

How did you feel about that? Do you think you can explain yourself a little better?

Finally there was no more to tell. Den was left hoarse, drained, and somewhat bewildered.

'Never said it all like that before,' he said. 'Never been over the whole lot in one go, from start to finish. And telling it to a complete stranger, what'm more.'

'Sometimes it's easier talking to a stranger than to friends or kin,' said Hardscree. 'There's less at stake emotionally. You can open up without fear of hurting someone's feelings or irritating them or boring them or whatever.'

'But you'm a Deacon and all.'

'And I can see you'd have every reason to resent what I am. However, from what you said earlier I'm guessing that you feel, in a way, that Deacons aren't altogether a bad thing.'

'It'm odd, but I's always had the impression that us needed you lot. Personally speaking, I needed you, my family needed you, because us used to make a living off of you. But more'n that, us *all* needed you, all of us "Groundlings", as us is supposed to call ourselves these days. Us all needed you to be there between we and them lot above the clouds. A kind of . . . curtain, I suppose. A human curtain. Someone to keep the mystery a mystery.'

'People need mystery in their lives.'

'Exactly! Bless my bum, that'm just the phrase for it. People need mystery. And that be'n't there any more. Us meets the Ascended Ones all the time now. Us knows they on a personal basis. Us sees they, and them's much like we, apart from the, you know.' He mimed having wings on his back. 'Them may be a bit more highfaluting than most of we, and I won't deny that as a rule them's better-looking too. Not more handsome but just more . . .' He groped for a word to describe the Airborn's general appearance.

'Groomed?' Hardscree suggested.

'That'll do. Groomed, yes. Clipped fingernails, nicer clothing, suntans, all that. But still, them's just people. My daughter be pretty good pals with one, him's a good kid.'

'That's Az, right? The one you mentioned. The wingless Airborn boy.'

'That'm he. And the simple fact that her and him can be friends – it makes things all a bit too normal, you know what I mean?'

'You preferred it when you believed we could Ascend after death and become reincarnated as winged people and live a glorious second life in the sky-cities.'

'Yes. No. I were never too sure about it either way. It seemed kind of unlikely. A bit too far-fetched. But I felt it were important that us did believe it anyway, because then this life in this grey world where the sun never quite shines – it were bearable. It were like the savoury course of a meal, the part you have to get through so's you can then have the sweet. Do that make sense?'

'It makes an admirable amount of sense.'

'Don't get me wrong. The world weren't perfect the way it used to be. For starters, it were clear you Deacons were taking advantage of everyone else. You exploited we and you looked after what you had very carefully.'

Hardscree gave a shrug that said he agreed.

'You admit it?'

'Freely, Den. I was never comfortable with that aspect of our lifestyle. In my own Chancel I often clashed with the Archdeacon about all the creature comforts we surrounded ourselves with. I argued that we should be more restrained and self-denying. It would set a better example to everyone on the outside. But my Archdeacon never saw it that way, and I spent many a week in the Contrition Cells to atone for the sin of openly challenging him.'

'Know what?' said Den, looking Hardscree in the eye. 'I reckon you did and all.'

'Let me tell you, Den,' Hardscree went on, earnestly. 'You're not alone. I've travelled far and wide since I and all the other Deacons were thrown out of our Chancels, and everywhere I've been I've come across people who think the same as you, although few have expressed themselves anywhere near as

73

concisely and even-handedly as you have. I've spoken with fishermen on the Granite Coast and farmworkers up on the Plains of Silence. I've met mayors and miners, manufacturers and musicians. I've pitched my tent outside countless cities, towns and villages, and preached to audiences as small as one and as large as a hundred and had their feedback afterwards. And what I've heard from them is what I'm hearing from you. "OK, the world wasn't perfect beforehand, but it's even further from being perfect now."'

Hardscree paused there, to make sure he had Den's full attention.

'But you know what?' he carried on. 'I think it could be perfect after all.'

High Spirits

Later, Den traipsed homeward. The road was dark but he had the distant, glimmering lights of the township to guide him. He reached his house without difficulty, and once indoors he let his anxious children make a fuss of him.

'You's been gone for hours, Da.'

'You'm all right?'

'Us was worried. You said not to follow and us didn't, but the way you rushed off, it were hard to know what to make of it.'

'You didn't get into any trouble, did you?'

'Kids,' Den said.

The firmness in his voice, and the serenity, surprised them. But it was a pleasant surprise. Fletcher, Cassie and Robert looked at their father and realised that somehow, by some miracle, their old dad was back. He had gone off to remonstrate with the Deacon and had returned fuller-faced and brighter-eyed. He even looked a little taller than before. They hardly dared believe that he was himself again, but they could not deny the evidence of their own eyes.

'Kids,' he said again. 'I been a useless old lump lately. Don't say no. You know I has. No good to you nor anybody. That'm all done with. Never going to happen again.'

'What did you do with the Deacon, Da?' Robert asked. 'You give he a thrashing?'

'What went on between I and that remarkably red-headed fellow be my business. All I want you to know be that I love you, always has, always will, and thanks for putting up with I being such a miserable mope for so damn long. Like I said, never going to happen again. Straight up.'

'Oh, Da!' said Cassie, and leapt on him and planted a fierce kiss on his stubbly cheek.

'Now, how about us takes some of that hard-earned of yours and buys ourselves dinner at the Hole and Shovel? I know about saving money for our overheads and debts and that, but when were the last time us ate out? When were the last time us actually went out for a nice meal like an ordinary family? Let's *live* a little.'

It was late but food was still being served at the Hole and Shovel, Grimvale's largest pub-cum-restaurant. The Grubdollars clustered around a table in the snug, and ordered pies, cake and beer. A band was playing jigs and reels in the next room, and the music spilled out through the doorway, jaunty and bright, a sound like a ray of hope. The food and drink arrived, and the Grubdollars pounced on it and devoured. Then, with gorged bellies, they sat back and chatted and bantered. For a time, they were once again a close-knit family unit.

'Cass and Fletch made I mop up Airborn puke!' Robert complained at one point. 'Why should I have to clean up Airborn puke? Be'n't fair. Tell they, Da. Tell they it be'n't fair.'

His father just laughed.

Back home, the three Grubdollar siblings went to bed in high spirits. Cassie in particular hadn't felt so optimistic in ages. Was it possible – just possible – that everything was going to be OK after all?

The next morning, she, Fletcher and Robert woke up to discover that their father wasn't there.

His bed had not been slept in. Clothes were missing from his wardrobe. His boots weren't where they should have been, at the top of the spiral staircase.

There was no note, or at least none that anybody could find in the house. He had left behind no indication of where he was off to or for how long or why.

He had simply slipped out of the house sometime during the night.

He had left.

Disappeared.

Gone.

CHAPTER 22

The Big Day

The wedding of Michael Gabrielson and Aurora Jukarsdaughter went smoothly, much to the relief of the bridegroom's mother. Ramona Gabrielson spent almost the entire day in the state of agitation, fretting over every single stage of the proceedings from the moment the High Haven Assembly Hall opened its doors to guests to the moment the newlyweds departed in Michael's helicopter (with ribbons and tin cans dangling from the undercarriage and a JUST MARRIED banner strung across the fuselage, courtesy of Az).

Mrs Gabrielson's nerves were not helped by the fact that Lady Aanfieldsdaughter was an invitee to the occasion, along with a number of other Silver Sanctum dignitaries and several members of management from Aerodyne. She feared that with such illustrious guests present, something was bound to go wrong and embarrass her. But Lady Aanfieldsdaughter, as if realising this, made a point of coming up to her just before the start of the ceremony and saying that the decorations looked marvellous and it was clear that every last detail had been taken care of. This did much to put Mrs Gabrielson's mind at rest.

And nothing did go wrong.

The ceremony itself was simple and beautiful. A local official intoned the rites. Rings were exchanged, and Michael and Aurora screened themselves behind their wings for their first, tender kiss as husband and wife. Meanwhile the close-harmony choir soared, and their voices soared too, filling the hall with song.

Then there was the traditional feather-blessing as the newlyweds wafted down the aisle. Each guest plucked a single feather from his or her wings and tossed it towards the happy couple. Az's father gave Az one of his own to use. Michael and Aurora passed hand in hand through a blizzard of slow-tumbling white down.

The reception was held at one of High Haven's fanciest restaurants, the Panorama. Encircled by views of nothing but sky, the guests tucked into sparrow pâté, honeyed duck breast, eggs Elysian and cloudberry ice cream. To wash it down there was wine from the Silver Sanctum vineyards, generously donated by Aurora's employers.

The speeches were good, and also short, which meant the guests paid attention and the less polite ones didn't start to yawn or heckle. Gabriel Enochson found himself too choked up with emotion to do much more than welcome his new daughter-in-law into the family and drop a broad hint about grandchildren. 'Look at me. How many more years do you think I've got? I can't hang on for ever.' To which Aurora, in her speech, replied that she and Michael would strive their utmost to see that he wasn't disappointed. She added that, having lost her own mother and father while she was young, she couldn't think of two people better suited to be her new parents than Gabriel and Ramona.

When Az's turn came, he had the room in stitches. He'd been nervous but as soon as he stood up and began speaking, the butterflies in his stomach vanished. If the purpose of a best man's speech was to keep everybody laughing, then unquestionably Az succeeded.

'I'm not here to make Michael look stupid,' he said. 'He's perfectly capable of doing that himself.'

And: 'I doubt Michael could love Aurora more – unless she was an AtmoCorp double-prop Bladecopter with radial fins, walnut dash, silver-chase detailing and flush-mounted teardrop undercarriage.'

And also: 'I can't possibly reveal what my brother's nickname at school was. He'd hate you to know that he was called Mike the Mirror because he used to spend all of break time in the boys' toilets getting his hair right.'

Not to mention: 'It's been said that marriage is a meeting of opposites. In which case, no wonder Aurora is beautiful, brainy, talented and thoughtful.'

'You are so dead,' Michael said mock-menacingly to Az during the applause afterwards. 'When I come back from our honeymoon, you'd better have found a good place to hide because I am going to hunt you down and kill you!'

'Az, I feel you and I need to have a chat sometime about my husband,' said Aurora. 'I'm already starting to think I may have made a mistake.'

'See, little brother? That's why I'm going to kill you.'

Then came the cutting of the cake, and following that the guests rose from their tables and mingled.

Lady Aanfieldsdaughter sought out Az.

'Excellent speech,' she said. 'Very droll.'

'Thanks.'

'I was expecting to see Cassie here today.'

'She couldn't make it.'

'Ah. Any reason why not?'

'Just ... you know. Hard for Groundlings, being up here for any length of time.'

'Quite. A pity, though. I was looking forward to catching up with her. Seeing how things are for her. I think fondly of Cassie and I'd like to believe she feels the same way about me.'

'Um, yeah. Yeah, she does.'

'She helped us so much, didn't she?'

'That she did.'

Lady Aanfieldsdaughter's bright blue eyes narrowed. 'I'm getting the impression this isn't a thread of conversation you particularly want to follow.'

'No, no, it's not that.'

'What, then?'

Az racked his brains to figure out why he found it so uncomfortable talking to Lady Aanfieldsdaughter. It wasn't anything to do with Cassie. He realised it was because he had crouched on the balcony outside Lady Aanfieldsdaughter's office the day before yesterday, snooping like a spy. Guilt gnawed at him. He regretted what he'd done now and he wanted to confess to her about it but couldn't. She would be shocked and disappointed.

Lady Aanfieldsdaughter decided not the press the matter. Instead, she peered across the roomful of guests and said, 'Oh look. There's an old acquaintance of mine. I must go over and say hello. Nice to see you, Az. Again, a fine speech. And well done on gaining such a worthy sister-in-law. Aurora will adorn your family.'

It was a neat, diplomatic way out of an awkward impasse. With relief, Az watched her ladyship flit off.

He spent the rest of the day avoiding Lady Aanfieldsdaughter, and she managed not to bump into him either. Meanwhile, he continued to play his part as best man and bridegroom's brother. He chortled at a distant cousin's rude joke and let a blowsy great-aunt smother him with affection and the reek of too much perfume. He also dealt with the relatives from the further branches of his extended family who never quite knew how to feel about his lack of wings. Some pitied him and couldn't help letting it show; others strenuously tried to stick to topics of conversation that had nothing to do with wings and usually ended up talking about exactly that and stumbling horribly. Az faced them all with a tactful, patient smile.

There were plenty of guests who demanded he give them an account of his adventures down on the ground. He was used to telling the story now and could rattle it off in his sleep. The novelty of being famous had worn off long ago but he understood that other people were interested in what he had done, so he didn't treat them with disdain or an air of boredom. He answered their questions and modestly brushed aside their praise and their awe.

Throughout, he kept an eye out for Cassie, although he knew she wasn't going to come. He hoped she'd been delayed by some unexpected hitch. He hoped she would put in a last-minute appearance. But at the same time he was reconciled to the fact that neither she nor her family were going to show up.

It told him what he needed to know and yet didn't want to know.

The next day, he was up at dawn and waiting out on the house's landing platform with a packed bag. The gyro-cab which was booked to take him to Prismburg could not have arrived too soon.

A Fruitless Search

The Grubdollar siblings turned Grimvale upside down looking for their father.

On foot, Fletcher and Robert checked all of Den's known haunts – pubs, friends' houses, the skittles alley, even the bluff in the hills above town where he and their mother had courted. It was one of his favourite spots, somewhere he used to go when his mood turned melancholy and he wanted to recall happy times with his wife, when they were both young and nothing mattered more to them than each other. He wasn't there now.

Cassie, meanwhile, gave herself the job of searching further afield. She clambered into *Bertha* and started her up.

Or rather, tried to start her up.

With every press of the ignition button *Bertha* remained stubbornly silent. Not a cough, not a whine, not so much as a titter came from her, and certainly no cackle.

A quick rummage under the engine cowling identified the problem. *Bertha*'s distributor cap had been neatly removed and placed to one side. Without the distributor cap to direct the charge from the battery to the sparkplugs, *Bertha* wasn't going anywhere.

'Sabotaged she,' Cassie said to herself, her brow knitting in perplexed annoyance. 'How could you, Da? And why didn't you do a proper job of it, if you didn't want us to follow you?'

She picked up the dome-shaped cap in order to reconnect the wires. As she did so, something fell out of the cap: a small piece of paper, folded into a tight wad.

Cassie opened up the piece of paper. It was a note, and straight away she recognised the handwriting as her father's.

The note said:

Kids,
So sorry about this. I won't be gone long. You just carry on
without I. I be off looking for a needle in a haystack. Which'm
another way of saying I be looking for hope.
All my love,
Da

Cassie read the note several times and still couldn't understand what it meant, particularly that reference to a 'needle in
a haystack'. What she did understand was that that her father
had placed the note inside the distributor cap for a purpose. He
was making a point. By removing the cap to disable *Bertha* (if
only fleetingly), he was warning his family not to go searching
for him.

That made Cassie all the more determined to do so.

She reattached the distributor cap wires, started *Bertha* up
and trundled off through the outskirts of Grimvale, pausing
to ask anyone she passed if they had seen her father. No one
had. Eventually she made her way out to the Chancel. She
couldn't imagine what reason the old man would have to
go in that direction, but this was how desperate she was
becoming.

No sign of him there. No sign of him anywhere.

Meeting up back at the house with Fletcher and Robert, she
showed them the note. Together they racked their brains to
fathom what it meant, and couldn't come up with an answer.

'Let's go over everything us knows,' Fletcher suggested.
'Might help. Last night Da went off to see that Deacon, then
him came home and him were back to normal. His old self
again.'

'In hindsight,' Robert said, 'anyone else reckon that were
kind of odd? One moment Da's all doom and gloom, next him's
all sweetness and light. Like somebody threw a big switch inside
he.'

''Cause him took it out on the Deacon, that'm my theory,'

Fletcher said. 'All the stuff inside that was bothering he. Sort of like squeezing a zit.'

'Squeezing a zit?' said Cassie.

'Yeah. All the pus and gunk spurted out.'

'Who'm the zit?' Robert wanted to know. 'Da? The Deacon?'

'No, the zit's the feelings inside Da.'

'So who were squeezing it? The Deacon?'

'No, it were — Oh, never mind. I were just drawing a parallel.'

'Bad one,' Robert muttered.

'Yeah?' said Fletcher, bristling. 'Well, pardon I for making an effort. Pardon I for trying to understand what might be going through Da's mind so's us can figure out where him's got to and why him doesn't want we knowing. Just trying to help, that'm all. But maybe you has some better idea, Bobby-boy. Being as you's clearly so much smarter'n I.'

'Never said I were smarter,' his brother replied. He was becoming annoyed too. One of Robert's pet hates was being called Bobby-boy, which, of course, was why Fletcher had called him that. 'But at least I be'n't talking gibberish about zits and pus and that.'

'No, you'm talking about big switches instead. That makes *so* much more sense.'

'Boys,' Cassie snapped. 'Enough. Bickering won't get we anywhere. For what it'm worth, I reckon there be truth in what both of you's saying. Obviously this comes down to the Deacon. But maybe it weren't something Da did to he, maybe it were something *him* did to Da.'

'Such as?'

'Not sure, Fletch. But I can tell you that his marquee be'n't there any more. I passed the spot in *Bertha* on my way to the Chancel. It'm gone, every last guy-rope and pole of it, and his van too.'

'You think Da and the Deacon has gone off *together*?'

'I be beginning to think it'm the only logical explanation.'

'But Da hates Deacons!' Robert said.

'But remember what him said last night when him came back? You asked if him'd given the man a thrashing, and Da

84

replied, "That'm my business", or something more or less like that. Which weren't a no but neither were it a yes.'

'Da trotting off with one of them black-robed bilge-spouters,' Fletcher said wonderingly. 'Don't seem real. What if, instead, the Deacon kidnapped he?'

'Our da? Kidnapped? Never. Him'd never let it happen. Besides, the facts don't fit. Him left the house of his own accord. There weren't no struggle. And the note makes it clear him went off because him wanted to.'

'All right, not kidnapped then. Bad choice of word. *Persuaded*.'

'Yes,' Cassie said, slowly nodding. 'Those be my thoughts. Not liking to think they, but thinking they all the same. This Deacon somehow talked Da into heading off somewhere with he, to find this so-called needle in a haystack, whatever that actually be.'

'So if him doesn't want we coming after he,' said Robert, 'shouldn't us respect his wishes?'

'Nope,' said his sister firmly. 'Not if him's fallen under the Deacon's sway. That'd be —'

She was interrupted by a shout from the storage area at the bottom of the spiral staircase.

'Yoo-hoo! Grubdollars!'

It was Colin Amblescrut. They heard his heavy tread on the stairs, and then his melon-like head appeared above floor-level, followed by the rest of him.

'I banged on the front gate,' he said. 'No answer, so I let myself in. Thought perhaps you was still out and about and I'd wait for you to come home.'

'You know us has been out and about?' Cassie said.

''Course!' said Colin, beaming proudly. 'Be'n't much that goes on in this town that my family don't know about. The Amblescrut web's been tingling and quivering all day. You'm searching for your da, right?'

'Right.'

'Well, it just so happens I may know where him's at.'

CHAPTER 24

Loaded For Battle

No sooner did Az get a glimpse of *Cerulean* than he knew that she had been modified. The airship had gained a number of add-ons which would have been almost undetectable to the untrained eye but which Az spotted immediately.

She bobbed at her moorings, a great oval of pale blue, with Prismburg's sun-shot glass towers and apartment blocks forming a gleaming, iridescent backdrop behind her. In her size and ponderous majesty she was unchanged.

However, set beneath the tip of her control gondola there was now a fan of small, forward-pointing steel tubes, which Az had a pretty good idea were grappling hook launchers; and just above her nose-cone a kind of gun had been mounted, one which – if Az knew anything about aerial warfare, and he did – fired bolas shells, weighted knots of steel cable that would snarl up an enemy airship's propellers and rudders.

'You've been busy,' he said as Mr Mordadson picked him up from the landing apron and carried him aboard.

'Haven't slept a wink in forty-eight hours,' came the reply. 'I've been charging around like a blue-bottomed bluebottle and I'm absolutely exhausted.'

'Where did it all come from? The weaponry?'

'Museums mostly. I had to call in a lot of favours and wave my Silver Sanctum seal under a lot of noses, but it got results.'

'And does it really all work? If those weapons have been mouldering in museums for decades, surely they'll have seized up and rusted.'

'We've overhauled them and greased them and replaced the parts that needed replacing. They've tested fine.'

'Well, maybe we won't have to use them anyway. Maybe we can get the pirates to back down simply by turning up in *Cerulean*. A show of strength.'

'Maybe, Az, and I admire your optimism, even if I don't share it. For which reason, I'm not relying on weaponry alone. I have a back-up plan.'

'Which is?'

'You'll see.'

Az did as soon as they entered by the aft hatch. A squadron of Alar Patrollers were billeted in the airship's cabins. For the first time since she was decommissioned all those years ago, Troop-Carrier *Cerulean* was carrying troops again.

One Patroller had quadruple-grooved gold wing hoops, indicating that he was a wing commander. He snapped a brisk salute at Mr Mordadson. Mr Mordadson returned the military gesture with a civilian one, a touch of finger to forehead. The wing commander went back to polishing his lance.

'That's Iaxson,' Mr Mordadson said. 'Good man. We were at Alar cadet academy together. He's in charge of the Patrollers and he answers to me. You should get to know him. You'll like him.'

Az wasn't so sure. Iaxson had a pinched, wary look about him, like that of a man who always saw the worst in people and refused to try to see anything else.

Down in the control gondola, a far kinder face was waiting to greet him. Captain Qadoschson clasped Az's hand in both of his and shook it warmly.

'A bit out of the ordinary, this, eh?' he said. 'Not the usual four-hour there-and-back with a load of daytrippers. Quite something else altogether.'

The crew were at their stations. Az returned their welcoming glances, pleased to see them. It had been nearly two months since his last visit to Primsburg. In the run-up to the wedding he hadn't been free to pop over and join *Cerulean* on one of her regular tourist outings. He'd missed being aboard the airship and he'd missed her crew, whom he counted as friends.

With one exception. A man whose absence in the gondola Az

87

quickly noted, as he would have noted a rotten tooth that had at last been pulled.

'Is Flight Lieutenant Wallimson not here?' he asked the captain.

He was hoping the answer to his casual-sounding enquiry would be something like: *Oh no, Wallimson won't be coming with us today. In fact, we had to get rid of him.*

Instead, disappointingly, the answer was: 'He should be. I've no idea where he's got to. Notoriously unreliable fellow, as you know.' Qadoschson consulted his watch. 'Still, there's half an hour before cast off. I'm sure he'll make it.'

Az made a noncommittal sound, halfway between *ah* and *hmph*. It had been a nice thought that he wouldn't have to put up with Wallimson on the trip to Redspire, but that hope was now dashed. Oh well. You had to take the rough with the smooth, as the saying went, and in this case that meant Az had to accept that the pleasure of flying in *Cerulean* also brought with it the surly attitude of Captain Qadoschson's second-in-command. Unfortunately, he couldn't have one without the other.

He took the opportunity to quiz Qadoschson about various technical matters such as payload size and pressure height. This was so that he would have all the relevant data for this particular flight at his fingertips. If he was well-informed on *Cerulean*'s operational status, then Flight Lieutenant Wallimson, when he turned up, would have fewer excuses to criticise him or catch him out.

'I take it we'll be doing shifts,' he said once he had gleaned what he needed from the captain. 'Rotating command between you and Wallimson, with me pitching in between the two of you. I could oversee a skeleton crew at night, perhaps, if we're night-running.'

Captain Qadoschson turned to Mr Mordadson with a frown. 'You mean you didn't tell him?'

'Tell me what?' Az asked.

Mr Mordadson just smiled.

'Az,' said Qadoschson, 'all I'm here to do is supervise the

arming and loading. Make sure everything's put together properly.'

'You're not coming with us?'

'I'm no spring chicken,' the captain said. 'I've a few too many grey hairs on my head and not all the feathers I should have on my wings. Time was, I'd have happily taken *Cerulean* out for a week or so. It would have been a treat. An adventure. But these days, at my age, I'm more of an early-to-bed-with-a-cup-of-cocoa kind of chap. Then there's the fact that we have weapons and Patrollers on board, with everything that that implies. We all know what could be waiting for us down at Redspire and, well, frankly I can't see myself taking part in that sort of malarkey. I'm too old and too tired and too keen on enjoying the life I have left. I made all this clear to Mr Mordadson the moment he got in contact with me. I told him I'd help outfit the old girl. I'd help him source weaponry for her. I'd see she had what she required. But as for actually captaining her ...' He shook his head.

Az's heart sank. 'So Lieutenant Wallimson's in charge?'

It was too awful to contemplate. *Captain* Wallimson?

Az could just see what was going to happen. Wallimson had taken a dislike to him almost from the outset, and it was obvious why. He felt Az was a threat. Qadoschson made no secret of favouring Az over him. Wallimson regarded Az as a usurper, someone who was after his job.

Without Qadoschson there, Wallimson would no longer have to confine himself to harsh stares and snide, just-audible comments. As captain, he could say and do whatever he wanted. He could give his spite for Az free rein. Az would be lucky if Wallimson let him take charge of *Cerulean* for even a minute. More likely, he would have him priming ballast tanks or unblocking latrines the whole way.

Az wanted to get off the airship right now. Forget the mission. Wallimson, captain? Having to answer to *him*? Follow *his* orders? No way.

'No,' said Qadoschson. 'Not Wallimson.'

'Who, then?' said Az, perplexed. 'Who's got the job? One of the crew?'

Mr Mordadson's smile broadened and sharpened.

'Isn't it obvious, lad?' said Captain Qadoschson. 'You have.'

CHAPTER 25

Feather First!

Prismburg received a higher than average number of Groundling visitors. There were three reasons for this. One: it was close to one of the largest and populous cities on the ground, Craterhome. Two: its architecture was a visual marvel. And three: *Cerulean* was berthed there, and Groundlings were keen for a glimpse of the famous and, until now, one and only Airborn airship.

Equipped with breathing-apparatus kits, Groundlings ascended by elevator, toured the sky-city via its walkways and bridges, and returned to the ground full of tales to tell their friends and families. The way the refractive-panelled walls of the buildings shone in every colour. The brightness of the sun and sky, so dazzling it hurt the eyes. The birdsong that in certain places was deafeningly raucous. The graciousness of the Airborn guides who ushered you around.

However, not every Groundling could manage the long journey up and back down in the elevators. Only the fit and healthy could endure the slow reduction in air pressure, which sometimes hurt the ears, and use the breathing apparatus, which could tax even the strongest of lungs. If Groundlings wished for a glimpse of how the other half lived, they had to be in good shape, not too old, not too young, with no history of respiratory problems. They had to be resilient and hardy.

Nevertheless those who could come came. They saw. They admired. And mostly they went home again happy, convinced it had been worth the effort.

Mostly.

Unless they happened to run foul of a group of Feather

First!ers. That could soon sour the experience for them.

The majority of Feather First! demonstrations took place on six-way street corners or on public plazas and were relatively restrained affairs. Slogans were chanted. Placards were waved. GROUNDLINGS DOWN! AIR FOR THE AIRBORN! IF YOU CAN'T FLY, DON'T DROP BY! Traffic flow might be interrupted; ordinary sky-citizens might be inconvenienced; that was all.

Groundlings seldom got to witness these demos. They didn't occur often and they didn't last too long.

The Feather First! guerrilla protests, though, were a different matter.

On this day in Prismburg, for instance, a six-strong Groundling tour party was making its way along the prearranged route, heading towards Vitreous Park. Escorting the six were a pair of Airborn guides. The Groundlings were gazing around in wonderment and awe. They had the latest design of breathing-apparatus kits on. These were more comfortable than the old ones, with lightweight oxygen tanks and masks that covered just the nose and mouth rather than the entire face. In addition they were wearing tinted goggles, to protect their eyes from a degree of sunlight they simply weren't used to.

They were enjoying themselves. Everything was going fine.

Then, out of nowhere, a dozen Feather First!ers homed in. They encircled the Groundlings and began yelling insults.

'Emus!'

'Ostriches!'

'Go home! Go back down to your shabby hovels and stay there!'

Not content with that, the Feather First!ers began chucking handfuls of soil at the Groundlings. Dirt granules showered down on their heads. The Groundlings ducked and swore.

The guides rose to remonstrate with the Feather First!ers. They told them to stop. This was not the way to treat guests.

But the Feather First!ers just carried on. The guides tried to drive them away, but they were only two and the protestors were many. Each could tackle only one protestor at a time, which left the others free to continue hurling insults and soil at the Groundlings.

They kept it up till the bags of soil they were carrying were empty. Then, their malicious stunt complete, they zoomed off. Afterwards the guides could only express regret and the Groundlings could only shake the dirt from their hair and try not to feel offended and degraded.

Among the group of Feather First!ers was a man in his mid-thirties who flew a little more slowly than the others and struggled to keep pace with them. This was due to one his wings, the left, being malformed. It was crooked at the arch and did not flap as efficiently as the right.

As a boy he had been hit by an airbus when crossing a street and had broken the wing. Doctors had set it but, despite their best efforts, the bones had not knitted properly. Intensive physiotherapy had also not helped. The wing had healed badly, and the doctors had shrugged and told him it was 'just one of those things' and he would have to live with it.

Possessing a lame wing had done little for this man's self-esteem and character. He did not like being different from everyone else, being *less*. He held a grudge against the world for it. Permanently bitter, he purged his resentment by taking it out on others. In recent months he had developed a particular loathing for Groundlings. Such ungainly creatures. Coarse and crude. Cluttering up Primsburg's bridges and walkways. Stomping along.

The soil protest had been his idea. There was a pleasing symmetry to it, he felt. Sprinkling Groundlings with stuff from the ground.

Now, he called out to the other Feather First!ers. 'Good work, everyone,' he said. 'Well done. We'll meet up again soon. In the meantime, I'm running late. Must fly!'

With that, he parted company from them, banking left down a narrow alleyway which was a shortcut to the city's perimeter.

He knew he was cutting things fine, punctuality-wise. He would get into trouble for not being where he should be at the time he was supposed to be there. He didn't care, though. The guerrilla protest was worth any reprimand he would receive.

Besides, he wasn't looking forward to what lay ahead.

A lengthy trip in *Cerulean*.

With that little wingless plucker as captain!

Flight Lieutenant Wallimson's face hardened into a sneer as he wended his somewhat wonky way towards the docked airship.

CHAPTER 26

Leave-taking

As Wallimson entered the control gondola, Qadoschson gave him a withering look.

'Nice of you to show your face, lieutenant,' he said. 'Hope we weren't keeping you from anything important.'

'I was held up, sir. You know how hard it is for me to get around.' Wallimson flapped his bad wing feebly.

'Yet Az here hasn't got any wings at all, and he always manages to be on time. Funny, that.'

'Gabrielson is a better man than I am, captain. Clearly. After all, there's me with nine years of service on *Cerulean*, and yet *he* gets to take charge of the ship on this outing. A kid with less than a hundred hours of flying time under his belt, as opposed to a grown man with nearly a thousand.'

'Stop sulking, lieutenant. My decision is final, and I have the crew's full agreement. Don't I, men?'

The crew members assented.

'Aye-aye.'

'True enough, captain.'

They were as fond of Flight Lieutenant Wallimson as Az was.

'So let's not hear any more about this,' Qadoschson said to Wallimson. 'An order is an order. You are to regard Az as your commanding officer from now on and obey his every instruction and demand. Is that understood?'

Wallimson's reply came through clenched teeth. 'Perfectly, sir.'

Without so much as a glance at Az he stalked off to the forward viewing windows and stood there, grasping the brass handrail, his back hunched. You didn't have to be able to see his face to know he was scowling.

Az felt that, all in all, Qadoschson had let Wallimson off pretty lightly. The lieutenant had deserved a much more severe dressing-down than he had just received. Qadoschson probably hadn't wanted to antagonise him and deepen his resentment of Az. Still, Az sensed his and Wallimson's relationship wasn't going to get any sweeter in the foreseeable future.

'Az?' said Qadoschson.

'Sir?'

'*Cerulean*'s all yours. Look after her. Be as kind as you can with her. And, if possible, do try and bring her back in one piece.'

'I will.'

Qadoschson took a last look around the control gondola, his lips pursed, his eyes wistful and tender. Then, with something like a sigh, he flapped up to the ceiling hatch and climbed through. Moments later Az caught sight of him out on the landing apron, gazing at his ship, hand to forehead in a salute.

'Right, men,' Az said, taking charge. 'Let's get cracking, shall we? Mooring lines detached and reeled in?'

'Aye-aye, sir. We're floating free.'

'Then give her quarter reverse thrust on the fore props.'

'Quarter reverse, aye-aye.'

Cerulean's engines started to hum. Gradually she began to pull back from Primsburg, although to Az it seemed more as if the sky-city was the one withdrawing, somehow shifting itself away from the airship. In the gut-knotting exhilaration of the moment, he felt that he was standing still and everything else was moving.

'Helmsman? Half a degree to starboard. Gently, gently. Easy does it.'

He uttered the commands with a calmness and confidence that surprised him. The launch procedures weren't new to him, but until today he had never had to execute them unaided, without Qadoschson at his shoulder, a reassuring presence. He realised that there was nothing to be afraid of. The crewmen were skilled, too, which helped. If he put a foot wrong, they would correct him.

'Bring thrust up to half. Disengage port fore prop. Engage starboard rear prop. Trim-master? Picking up some downward drift there. Fix it.'

'Aye-aye.'

Cerulean slowly came about. Presently the sky-city was behind them and there was nothing ahead but open sky.

Az glanced over at Mr Mordadson to see what he was making of the new captain's performance so far. But Mr Mordadson was sitting with his head canted against a bulkhead and his mouth agape, snoring softly.

'Take her up a hundred metres,' Az said. 'Let's sniff the jet stream currents, see which way they're running.'

The airship began to climb.

'And then,' he said, 'we plot a course for Redspire.'

CHAPTER 27

Desolation Wells Again

That night, the Airborn pirates returned for a second bite of the cherry.

This time, however, the cherry bit back.

Westward Oil Enterprises did not take kindly to having one of its assets raided and robbed. Magnus Clockweight's telegram to company headquarters had been received with astonishment and indignation in the boardroom, and also with consternation. WOE's executives were in a tricky position. Product had been stolen from them, and that was bad. But the people doing the stealing were Airborn and the executives found it hard to contemplate retaliation. The Airborn were everyone's new friends. More than that, they were officially WOE clients now. The company made money from them, as opposed to before, when half of its output had gone up the elevators for free. WOE's profit margins had swelled significantly since the Bilateral Covenant came into play. To fight back against the raiders would be to risk antagonising all the Airborn, and thus risk losing them as customers. The Airborn might decide to boycott Westward Oil Enterprises and take their business to another oil corporation.

All the same, the attack on Desolation Wells could not just be ignored and forgotten about.

So the executives did two things. First, they complained to the Airborn leadership through the proper channels. A message of protest was sent to the nearest Chancel, was relayed in letter format up via the elevators, and from there was transported by carrier dove to the Silver Sanctum. The reply followed the same route in reverse. It stated that the matter was being taken in hand and the culprits would be brought to justice. There were several signatures on the reply, including those of Lady Aanfielsdaughter and Lord Urironson.

The WOE executives felt that this was satisfactory as far as it went. Their complaint had been noted and they had an assurance that it was being acted upon. Good.

But not good enough. Steps must be taken to show that a Westward Oil Enterprises extraction and refining installation was not a soft target. Nobody should be allowed to feel that they could swoop in and make off with a couple of hundred barrels of fuel any time they liked. It was just not on.

So the second thing the executives did was send a telegram to Desolation Wells, which read as follows:

```
INCIDENT OF ONE WEEK AGO MUST NOT BE REPEATED
+ STOP + REASONABLE PRECAUTIONS ADVISED +
STOP +
```

The message was very carefully worded, although it might not appear so. Nobody was saying that Magnus Clockweight and his team should do anything drastic or violent if provoked. Equally, nobody was saying they shouldn't.

The term for this was deniability. It was a corporate stratagem to provide a cover story for everyone involved. If something went wrong, the executives could blame the workforce for misinterpreting their instructions, the workforce could blame the executives for not making their intentions crystal clear, and that way no one had to take any actual responsibility.

Clockweight, at any rate, understood precisely what the suits in the boardroom were after. He knew he had been given carte blanche to defend Desolation Wells against the raiders if they came back, and defend it by whatever means he could manage.

So he and his men built a flamethrower.

A massive great flamethrower.

They took one of the installation's fire extinguisher trucks, drained the water from its tank, and filled it up with petrol instead. Thus a machine for stopping fires was transformed into a machine for starting them.

They tested the flamethrower out in the Relentless Desert. A pleasingly huge jet of burning liquid shot from the nozzle of the truck's hose. It arced fifty metres into the air, dripping small fiery gobbets onto the ground.

When *Behemoth* loomed once more from the night-dark clouds, the roughnecks were waiting and ready. This time Clockweight noticed the skull and crossed feathers on the airship's tailfins, visible even in the dark. He felt a surge of resentment, recalling that the pirates' leader bore the same motif on her chest. There was something aggravatingly brazen about it – the sheer shameless arrogance of it.

He tightened his grip on the control valve of the flamethrower.

Behemoth herself was too high to hit.

The pirates who emerged from her, however, were not.

As they came flying in towards the installation, Clockweight took aim and opened fire.

Literally opened fire.

He got three of the pirates with the first burst. They plummeted to the ground, spiralling down, wings burning.

The next few minutes were a frantic blur of driving and shooting. A colleague steered the truck crazily around, chasing after the scattering pirates. Meanwhile Clockweight, on the back, directed blast after blast of flame at them. At the same time, other roughnecks used portable, battery-powered searchlights to pinpoint the pirates in the sky and dazzle them. All of this took place some distance from the installation, of course, since it would have been madness to deploy the flamethrower on-site, near all that combustible material.

The flamethrower truck charged this way and that across the bumpy desert terrain, and the pirates darted this way and that overhead. Some attempted to attack the truck but Clockweight swung right and left, repelling them with devastatingly accurate shots.

In all, he brought down eleven of the pirates before *Behemoth*'s horn sounded, signalling retreat.

As the airship withdrew, the roughnecks whooped and cheered. Victory was theirs.

But only for now, Clockweight thought. The raiders would be back, and next time they'd be out for revenge. There was no real way of stopping them.

Unless, somehow, that airship could be destroyed.

CHAPTER 28

Coincidence And Bad Timing

'Explain to I once again, Colin, why you'm coming with we,' said Cassie. 'Just so's I be totally clear on it.'

Colin Amblescrut paused, about to load another carton of tinned food into *Bertha*.

'Den be my friend,' he said simply, then swung the carton effortlessly up to Fletcher, who was standing inside the murkcomber. Fletcher in turn passed the carton to Robert, who stacked it with others in a corner of *Bertha*'s loading bay. Both of them found the carton far heavier than the hulking, bulky Colin did.

'Also,' Colin added, 'I be the one who discovered where him's off to.'

'No, you didn't. You were told. It be'n't quite the same.'

Colin shrugged. 'Still and all. If I hadn't come and told you, you wouldn't have had a clue.'

'And,' Cassie went on, 'you doesn't know *exactly* where him and the Deacon is. All you said was them's headed out of town on the Craterhome road.'

'Yup.'

'And if it hadn't been for your relative – what'm his name?'

'John-John. My ma's aunt's brother-in-law's stepson.'

'If it hadn't been for he, you wouldn't have known at all. Now, you'm absolutely sure it were them him saw?'

'Absolutely. John-John were coming home from, er, from doing something near the Ridgerider farm, and an old half-tarp van passed he by. It were early in the morning and misty, but him got a good look at they inside, and it were definitely your da, and a Deacon alongside. John-John were with we during the attack on the Chancel. Him wouldn't mistake Den for anybody else. And as for the Deacon, him had the reddest hair John-John had ever seen, and as us all knows, that Deacon who were preaching outside town the other day were a ginger-nut.'

'It'm true,' said Fletcher. 'I saw that for myself. But what I want to know be what this John-John were doing out near the Ridgeriders' place at that sort of hour, Colin. Nothing illegal, I hope.'

'No,' Colin replied quickly. 'Not at all.'

'Nothing like poaching, perhaps?'

A firm shake of the head from Colin was followed by a reluctant, acknowledging nod. An Amblescrut's first instinct was always to deny accusations of wrongdoing, but with the Grubdollars it wasn't necessary. They knew as well as he did the sort of things his family got up to.

'What *I* want to know,' said Robert, 'is how come you actually know the name of your ma's aunt's – what were it again?'

'Ma's aunt's brother-in-law's stepson,' Colin said. 'And it'm easy. You see, him's John-John from the lower-township side of the family.'

'And?'

'Well, that means him be'n't upper-township John-John. Or John-John from the bunch who live out by Whitewater Rapids.'

Fletcher looked at Robert, Robert at Fletcher.

'Nope, still none the wiser,' Robert said.

'Suppose you has to be an Amblescrut for it to make sense,' Colin said.

'Suppose you does.'

'But Colin,' said Cassie, 'it be'n't that us doesn't appreciate you informing we about Da. Honestly, us is very grateful. It'm just that ... well, this be family stuff. Family deals with its own family things. You of all people should understand that.'

'And friends deal with friend things, Cassie. Your da, him once showed me kindness I didn't deserve. Robert'll tell you; him were there. I owe your da for that, and I's been trying to repay he ever since. This'm just a part of that.'

'I isn't going to be able to talk you out of this, is I?'

'Nope,' said Colin, hoisting another carton of tins onto his shoulder and carrying it over to *Bertha*. 'I be coming with you and there'm an end of it.'

You just can't argue with an Amblescrut! Cassie thought.

She tried to look on the positive side. Colin's muscle-power was coming in very handy right now. That was a point in his favour. And an extra person on board when they were out on the road meant the driving workload would be shared between four rather than three. Their father had a head start on them and was in a faster vehicle, and they had lost further time kitting *Bertha* out for a long journey. In order to have a hope of finding their da, wherever he was, they had to be prepared to drive round the clock, taking it in turns at the controls. Shorter driving shifts for everyone could only be a good thing. Cassie wasn't sure her brothers would like the idea of Colin taking *Bertha*'s controls, but maybe if they started him off an hour at a time, supervised, they could see if he could be trusted with the murk-comber on his own.

She turned her attention to the canisters of diesel fuel which had yet to be stowed aboard *Bertha*. These were for emergency purposes, in case *Bertha*, greedy old gas-guzzler that she was, started to run dry somewhere out in the middle of nowhere, with no filling station within range. For *Bertha*, the fuel canisters were the equivalent of the tinned food. They meant that, like the humans inside her, she could travel with the minimum number of stops for replenishment.

Cassie had bargained hard and got a good deal on the food and fuel. Even so, she only had a little of the tourist-gift money from two days ago left in her pocket. The cash they'd got for the elderly woman's opal necklace was all gone. In effect, the necklace was funding the whole trip. So if it hadn't been for the attack on *Bertha* by the Deacon's audience, Cassie and her brothers would not have been able to afford to go after Den. There was a kind of balance to that. It almost made her think that some things were meant to happen; that there was such a phenomenon as destiny.

Then again, destiny and coincidence could often be confused for each other.

Flap-flap.

Cassie looked up. What was that? Had she just heard —?

Flap-flap.

There it was again. The beat of wings. Airborn wings. Cassie had no difficulty recognising the sound. She was more familiar with it than most Groundlings.

'Hello down there?' called a voice from above. 'Hello?'

Cassie recognised the voice as well.

Two Airborn, a man and a woman, hovered into view above the courtyard. Their wings shone a shimmering white against the murky grey sky.

'Michael?' said Cassie. 'Aurora?'

'In the flesh,' said Michael.

'What'm you two doing here?'

'First, would you seal up that murk-comber and depressurise her?' Michael said, coming in to land. 'My head feels like it's about to burst.'

'Mine too,' said Aurora.

'Boys,' Cassie said to her brothers. 'Do as him says.'

At the same time, she restrained a sigh. This was all they needed, another delay. Talk about bad timing.

CHAPTER 29

Aurora's Offer

'We told everyone we were going to Heliotropia,' Michael said through the speaker tube. 'Only the most clichéd place in the world for a honeymoon. But it wasn't exactly a lie. We spent last night there. A very nice night it was too. Then today we came down in the elevators, because we actually want to spend our honeymoon in a less clichéd place.'

'You mean Grimvale?' said Cassie.

'The ground. We want to tour the ground for a week. And we'd like to hire you and your murk-comber to take us around.'

'*Bertha* be'n't for hire at present.' Cassie couldn't be bothered to put it less bluntly. 'Her'm already engaged. Us has business with she ourselves.'

'Oh. You sure about that?'

'Maybe if you'd given advance warning, Michael, us could have sorted something out. As it be, you'm out of luck. Try Roving Sightseer Enterprises, them that used to be Relic Seeker Enterprises. Them does tours too.'

'But we really fancied the idea of travelling with the Grub-dollars. Seeing as you're Az's friends and all that. We'll pay well.'

'I told you,' Cassie said adamantly. 'You'm out of luck.'

'Well, that's nice, isn't it?' Michael's voice turned harsh. Even tinnily distorted by the speaker tube, Cassie could hear the sourness in it. 'You're not even prepared to think about it. A flat-out refusal. What is it with you, Cassie? What have you got against us?'

'What do you mean?'

'You know what I mean. Treating Az the way you have. Then

106

simply not turning up to our wedding. Now this. Have we done something to offend you? Is that it?'

'No, that be'n't it,' Cassie replied, hotly, 'and you's no right making accusations like that. You know nothing about I or my life down here. Nothing. You may think you do but you don't. Anyways, don't bring Az into this. This be'n't about him, or you, or the Airborn, or anything of that kind.'

'Then what is it about?'

'None of your concern.'

Faintly she heard Aurora say, 'Give me that.' Next moment, Aurora was talking through the speaker tube, and her tone was measured and far mellower than Michael's.

'Cassie,' she said, 'look, Michael didn't mean any of that.'

In the background Michael grumbled, 'Oh yeah?'

'Ground-sickness, that's all,' Aurora went on. 'The air pressure in here is down, thank you very much, but our heads haven't quite cleared yet. That's why he's a bit grouchy. I just want to say, I appreciate the fact that you're unable to take us touring. We're disappointed, but you obviously have your reasons and I respect that. We're just grateful you've allowed us to use *Cackling Bertha* to catch our breath and straighten ourselves out. Once we're fully recovered we'll head over to the other tour company you mentioned. I'm sorry if we've inconvenienced you in any way.'

'You haven't, not as such,' Cassie said.

'I feel we have. I can see you're preparing to go somewhere. All this food you have here. Quite a long trip, I'd say. I can also see that . . . may I be frank a second?'

'Suppose.'

'Something's the matter. You're very tense. So are your brothers. And – well, I don't see your father anywhere. Now, I know your father's been a bit down in the clouds lately.'

A bit under the weather did she mean? That was putting it mildly!

'Him has,' Cassie admitted.

'And you're such a close family. Where is he? If he isn't here, where has he gone?'

Cassie was stuck to know what to say. It was uncanny. Aurora had diagnosed the Grubdollars' situation perfectly, from just one glance.

'My da,' Cassie replied slowly, 'has scarpered off somewhere and us is planning to find he.'

'Oh. How dreadful. You've no idea where he's gone?'

'South. Vaguely south. That'm all.'

'How do you intend to follow him?'

'Us'll ask around in towns and villages. Him's in a half-tarp van. That'm quite a recognisable vehicle. And him's with a Deacon. Also quite recognisable. People who see they two, them'll remember they.'

Even as she said this, Cassie was unconvinced. Yes, a half-tarp van and a red-headed Deacon were things that stood out. But they weren't *that* remarkable. Besides, if her father really didn't want to be followed, he would have the sense to keep a low profile. He'd make the Deacon stay out of sight as much as possible, and the two of them would stick to back roads and avoid highways and large towns. They wouldn't leave an easy trail of clues behind them.

The enormity of the task facing her, and the remote likelihood of success, suddenly weighed heavy inside Cassie. She was filled with a feeling that was close to despair. Her own phrase – *vaguely south* – resounded with a bleak hollowness. There was a vast amount of country *vaguely south*. A million roads to choose from. Endless land to get lost in.

'Let us help,' said Aurora.

'Huh?'

'We'd like to help you, Cassie. Let us. Let us come with you.'

CHAPTER 30

Cassie's Choice

Her first instinct was to reject the offer. What good would it do having passengers on board? Airborn passengers, what was more. All it meant was the food rations wouldn't go as far and *Bertha* would have a little more weight to carry and therefore use up that much more fuel.

She consulted with her brothers and Colin outside. She told them she could see no significant advantage to Michael and Aurora coming along for the ride, and several disadvantages.

Robert agreed. 'T's nothing against they. I just can't imagine them'll be much use to we.'

Fletcher, however, held a different view. 'For one thing, don't you reckon folk'll be more kindly disposed if us has Airborn with we? Whereas them mightn't tell the truth to *we* if them's seen Da, them might well to a couple of winged types.'

'And them has money,' Colin chipped in. 'You said them said them'd pay for a tour in *Bertha*, Cassie. With that cash us could travel further and for longer if needs be.'

'And I don't think us need really worry about extra fuel consumption,' Fletcher added. 'The Airborn doesn't weigh hardly anything, what with them porous bones of theirs. Remember, Robert, when you picked up Az and carried he? Barely had to bend your back to do so, and you'm such a weedy little tyke.'

'Oi!'

'So you both be saying you reckon us should bring them along?' Cassie said to Colin and Fletcher.

'I can't see it'll do any harm,' Fletcher replied.

'Me either,' said Colin.

'Myself, I doesn't exactly mind either way,' said Robert. 'There be room enough for all of we in *Bertha*. A tighter squeeze than before with them two aboard, but only slightly.'

'But in the end it'm your call, Cass,' said Fletcher.

'Be it?' Cassie frowned. It wasn't like Fletcher to defer a decision to her. Being older, he usually felt he outranked her and Robert, and whatever he said went.

'You know they better than us does, girl. You's met them up there in High Haven a few times. You know their minds and characters. In practical terms, it can't hurt for they to come along with we. But if you reckon there might be problems personality-wise or whatever, then that'm a reason to say thanks but no.'

Cassie climbed back into *Bertha*, shinned up the ladder into the driver's pod, and unhooked the speaker tube.

'Mr and Mrs Gabrielson?' she said.

'Ooh, that's us,' said Aurora with a chuckle. 'It's weird to be called that.'

Aurora's remark made up Cassie's mind for her. She realised she would enjoy this woman's company on the trip – even if she wasn't so sure about Michael.

'Us has talked over your offer,' she said, 'and it'm a yes. Us would like your help.'

CHAPTER 31

Southward

An hour later, *Cackling Bertha* gave her signature mechanical laugh, spouted fumes from her exhaust, and pulled out of the Grubdollars' courtyard. Cassie was at the controls; Fletcher, Robert and Colin were ensconced in the observation nacelles; Michael and Aurora were sealed in the loading bay. It was late afternoon. The sky was shading from ash-grey to slate-grey, a change that was occurring earlier each day as autumn settled in. The darker half of the year brought more rain and also a spiritual dampness and gloom. Autumn and winter were the time when people were apt to contract rattle-lung and other fatal diseases; the time when life on the ground became least bearable. The sun was a pallid wraith, showing itself for just a few hours and shedding little light and no warmth at all through its veil of cloud. Shadows hung everywhere. The world was cobwebby and dim.

Cassie switched on *Bertha*'s headlamps, casting a yellow glow on the road ahead. She was grappling with wintry thoughts herself, with feelings of hopelessness and foreboding. She steered through the town's outskirts and joined the Craterhome road, which ran arrow-straight for four kilometres before unravelling into a series of twists and turns as it climbed over the southern hills out of the Grimvale region.

A hundred kilometres to the east, and a couple of thousand metres above, *Cerulean* was also wending its way southward.

Had Cassie known this, would it have made any difference to her mood? Had she known Az was guiding the airship in a similar direction, on a journey with no more certain an outcome than hers, would it have helped comfort or console her in any way?

Who could say?
Night was falling.
Bertha's cackle grew subdued in the thickening twilight.
Cassie drove on.

CHAPTER 32

The Rudiments Of Falconry

Lord Urironson knocked and entered.

'Farris,' said Lady Aanfieldsdaughter. Her voice carried a hint of quizzicality, just enough to leave him in no doubt that she found it odd he was visiting her in her office. One-to-one conversations, unless they were of a non-official or friendly nature, were frowned on at the Silver Sanctum, and she couldn't imagine Lord Urironson had anything to say to her that was non-official or friendly. Their mutual animosity ran too deep for that.

'I'll get straight to the point,' Lord Urironson said, with a businesslike flourish of wings.

Lady Aanfieldsdaughter slid the paperwork she was perusing to one side. It was a pile of written applications from people wishing to join the Silver Sanctum. Dozens of these arrived every day and each had to be assessed impartially and carefully before an invitation to come for an interview was sent out.

'Please do,' she said.

'You're aware there's been a second attack on that Westward Oil Enterprises installation?'

'I have heard about it.'

'And the workers there retaliated?'

'So I understand.'

'I'm very concerned by this development.'

'As am I.'

'The Redspire pirates won't take it lying down, you know. Up till now they've raided with impunity. They hit that small Groundling village first, didn't they? Took some timber, some coal. No casualties on either side. Then they went for a steelyard. Again, no casualties. Now, if what we're hearing from the ground is true, ten or so of them are dead. Burned to a crisp, by all accounts. They'll want to get their own back, you can bet your pinfeathers on that.'

'I won't deny, it is a regrettable escalation of the problem,' Lady Aanfielsdaughter said. 'But one can see the Groundlings' point of view. The pirates stole from them. Little wonder they decided to strike back.'

'You're siding with them? Condoning what they did?'

'I never said that, Farris.' Lady Aanfielsdaughter's eyes flashed like chips of ice. 'And I feel this discussion is at an end. If you have anything further to say to me on the subject, say it in a public place with other people around.'

'I would, Serena, if only I weren't trying to help you.'

Lady Aanfielsdaughter blinked. 'I'm sorry, I didn't quite catch that. Did you just say "help"?'

Lord Urironson moved closer to her, his wings furling behind his back to indicate submissiveness and a lack of threat.

'Listen to me,' he said. 'You may not realise it but the atmosphere around this place is getting pretty anxious, and what the Silver Sanctum feels is a pretty fair reflection of what the Airborn in general are feeling. We're the barometer of the race's mood, or at least we should be. People here are talking in frightened tones. I hear them. Maybe you don't because they don't dare do it around you. They put on a brave face because you're the mighty Lady Aanfielsdaughter and they don't want you to think them weak or alarmist. But I hear what they're saying, and what they're saying is that Airborn are dead, killed by Groundlings. Never mind the circumstances, never mind the provocation – Airborn are dead, and that cannot simply be ignored.'

'What would you have me do about it?'

'What *are* you doing?'

'You know full well. *Cerulean* should be arriving at Redspire within a few days.'

'And your Mr Mordadson will solve the pirate problem?'

'Indeed. I have every faith in him.'

'Well, good. Let's hope he does. But even so, it still won't address the issue of Groundlings murdering Airborn. That's what's critical here. The pirates stole but they didn't kill. The Groundlings killed. Granted, they were defending themselves and their livelihoods, but instead of a proportionate response they overreacted. Which leaves us with a stupendous mess.'

'What would have been a proportionate response? Stealing something of the same value off us?'

'I don't know. But not murder.'

'And how is it helping me, telling me this?'

'Isn't it obvious?' said Lord Urironson. 'The whisper running round the Sanctum is that you've gone soft, Serena.'

'Soft. Really.' Lady Aanfieldsdaughter arched an eyebrow. 'I despatch *Cerulean* south with Patrollers on board and with extreme sanction authorised, and apparently I've gone soft. How interesting.'

'The feeling is that more affirmative action is required.'

'Such as?'

'At the very least, a proclamation to the Groundlings. A strongly worded statement to all their governments letting them know that attacks on our kind will not be tolerated.'

'I can't see the benefit of that. It would smack of self-right-eousness and hypocrisy.'

'We need to be firm with the Groundlings. We need them to respect us. It's like training a hunting falcon. The bird is a wild creature, a law unto itself, and in order to tame it you have to bend it to your will. You must teach it to obey your commands first and its own instincts second. Otherwise it will never do as it's told.'

'Ah, an aviary analogy,' said Lady Aanfieldsdaughter with a sardonic twist to her lips. 'You do realise you're talking to a fowl-farmer's daughter? Someone who knows more about the rearing and taming of birds than you ever will?'

'I don't know anyone at the Sanctum who *isn't* aware of your humble origins, Serena. You never tire of telling us about them.'

'Then you'll bow before my expertise on the subject. You've clearly had no experience of falconry, whereas my father was a skilled falconer and I learned the rudiments of the art from him. One doesn't bend the bird to one's will, as you claim. One works in harmony with the bird. A falcon is naturally aggressive and the whole point is to harness that aggression and make use of it. In the process, one should be prepared to receive the odd scratch or peck. It's only to be expected. But the injuries would be that much worse if one were actually trying to break the falcon's spirit using punishment and scare tactics. It wouldn't respond well to those at all, and in the end there'd be a disgruntled, petulant bird that won't hunt and a falconer covered in cuts and blood. One must woo the bird and gain its trust. Then it will be a loyal partner for life. Do you see what I'm saying?'

'With great clarity,' said Lord Urironson. 'But I believe you're wrong. I believe that showing the Groundlings any kind of weakness, any level of tolerance, will simply encourage them to behave worse. Give them a centimetre and they'll take a kilometre, to coin a phrase.'

'Not everyone perceives tolerance as weakness, Farris.'

'Many do. Not least in this very city.'

Lord Urironson thought this a nice line to exit on, and so about-turned and did. Outside Lady Aanfielsdaughter's office he paused long enough to grin to himself, then leapt into the tower's central shaft and plunged twenty floors, braking at the last moment before he hit the bottom, his wings catching him with a *whoomph*.

As for Lady Aanfielsdaughter, she sat for a long time staring into the middle distance. Try though she might, she couldn't dispel Lord Urironson's comments from her thoughts. He had touched a nerve. Were people talking behind her back and lying to her face? Did they really think she wasn't doing enough to contain the situation? Or was Lord Urironson merely stirring up trouble? Muck-raking? Seeding doubts in her mind? If so, why? What did he hope to gain?

For the first time in her long and distinguished career, Lady Aanfielsdaughter wondered if she wasn't getting too old for this job.

CHAPTER 33

City Of Number-crunchers

A brilliant sunrise shot the surface of the cloud cover with streaks of pink and blue. The dawn light was so pristine that almost every fold and billow seemed perfectly delineated, as though the clouds were etched on glass. To starboard, *Cerulean*'s shadow moved ripplingly, broad and elongated, like a bizarre follower, a warped second airship faithfully dogging her tail.

Gazing out from the viewing windows with bleary eyes, Az fought the urge to yawn. He had managed four hours' sleep last night and not much more the night before. It was all he could allow himself. *Cerulean* was running constantly, twenty-four hours a day, and her crew were on overlapping double-shifts and taking naps when and where they could. Az could do no less himself.

They were all exhausted – all except Flight Lieutenant Wallimson, who had no qualms about leaving the control gondola whenever he felt like it and retiring to his cabin for a nice long snooze. 'Someone has to be fresh and alert', was his excuse, but that cut no ice with the crew. 'Just plain lazy', was their view, which they expressed in several different ways, although never within Wallimson's hearing.

Several kilometres ahead, rising from the pink-blue clouds, lay the city of Gyre. *Cerulean* was already scheduled to make a refuelling stop there. Az had decided a rest stop would be a good idea as well. There was no way the crew could maintain this pace indefinitely. Better that everyone got a period of uninterrupted downtime before carrying on. Otherwise they would be beyond exhausted by the time they reached Redspire and unable to perform effectively.

Gyre was helical in shape, a single cone-like spiral three kilometres in diameter at its base, mounting to a sharp apex. All its buildings faced outward in rising, terraced tiers. It was home to mathematicians and accountants, statisticians and actuaries – a city of number-crunchers. The arithmetically-minded gravitated to Gyre and lived there in almost total isolation. They had little contact with the outside world except to take in bookwork. Otherwise, they spent their days lost in the realms of abstract calculation. By and large, it was a city of weirdoes, or so its reputation went. Az would have chosen anywhere else to halt, except that would have meant a significant and time-consuming detour. Gyre was directly on the route to Redspire.

One further unusual feature of Gyre was that it still had a mooring mast at its summit. Most other sky-cities had dismantled theirs long ago. With officially only one airship in existence, the masts had become a skyline-cluttering waste of space. Gyre lacked either the will or the manpower to take its one down.

Docking at a mooring mast was a tricky procedure and Az had never practised it. Now was not the time to try. *Cerulean* would use the landing apron at the sky-city's base.

He pressed the button which rang an alarm in the crewmembers' cabins. Within minutes he had a full complement of crew on deck, rather than just the night-time skeleton crew of three. They manned their stations, rubbing their eyes. A few of them had buttoned up their uniform tunics the wrong way.

When Az announced that they would be taking some time off at Gyre, a low cheer went around the gondola.

'Nice one, skipper,' said the navigator, Ra'asielson. *Skipper* was what the crew had taken to calling Az. It was deferential but not quite *captain*.

'Time off?' Mr Mordadson had arrived. 'Are you sure?'

Az explained his reasons. 'Unless you want them men nodding off at their stations while we're hunting the pirates' airship, I'd say a rest period was utterly necessary.'

'Fair enough. We've made good progress so far. I think we can spare a few hours. And it's hard to imagine a more soporific place than Gyre. Ideal spot for a bit of shut-eye.'

As *Cerulean* drew nearer the city, Flight Lieutenant Wallimson put in a belated appearance in the control gondola.

'Mooring mast,' he observed, peering out. 'There's something you don't see every day. I don't suppose you've ever docked at a mooring mast, Gabrielson.'

Az was irritable with tiredness. It was an effort to keep his cool and not snipe back at Wallimson.

'I haven't and I don't plan to today.'

'Really? Why not? It's far from difficult.'

'That's not what I've heard.'

'All it takes is nerve and a good command of your vessel. But perhaps you don't have either.'

Az threw a look at Mr Mordadson, as if to say, *Can't you do something about this pain-in-the-backside?*

Mr Mordadson's response was a slow, neutral blink. It told Az that Wallimson was *his* concern, no one else's. Mr Mordadson couldn't fight his fights for him. It was up to Az to sort Wallimson out.

'If you're so keen on using the mast, flight lieutenant,' Az said, 'why not take over and manage it for me?'

'Oh, I couldn't. Captain Qadoschson made you boss, not me. I couldn't go against his wishes.'

'Well, I'm not going to do it.'

'A pity. The crew would think more of you if you did.'

Az knew he was being goaded. Wallimson was trying to shame him into attempting the manoeuvre.

Unfortunately, the tactic was working.

'All right,' he said, as coolly as he could. He thought he could see a way of turning Wallimson's act of provocation to his own advantage. 'Men? We're going to aim for the mast. Start unspooling the mooring line and take her up a hundred metres.'

To Wallimson he said, 'You, flight lieutenant, are going to help. I want you to be my co-pilot. You'll be my eyes at the front. You keep us on track.'

Wallimson made a show of considering this, as if it was an offer rather than an order. Finally he gave a nod.

Cerulean lifted her nose, her propellers canting downwards. Decelerating, she zeroed in on the mast. Az dished out commands, listening to what the crew were telling him. He was careful to consult Wallimson on each phase of the manoeuvre. The flight lieutenant curtly corrected him once or twice, otherwise saying nothing.

If this worked as Az hoped, Wallimson would perhaps feel more involved in the running of the ship. He might even come to respect Az more.

There was a catcher at the top of the mast, a V-shaped metal armature mounted on a swivel. It swung in the prevailing wind like a weathervane and was fitted with a spring-loaded pressure switch which snapped the catcher shut as soon as a mooring line touched it and triggered it. *Cerulean*'s course of approach had to be directly into the wind and at the correct height so that the line, trailing below her, slotted into the catcher.

Steering headlong into the wind meant she began to jump and lurch about. The mast, her target, seemed to dance this way and that.

'Hold her steady,' Az said. 'Steady.'

He was starting to wonder if he hadn't bitten off more than he could chew. But he couldn't back out now. He was committed. If he called off the manoeuvre and went down to dock at the landing apron instead, he feared it would do irreparable damage to his standing with the crew.

He glanced over at Mr Mordadson. The Silver Sanctum emissary's expression was unreadable.

'Two degrees to port,' he said.

A hush had settled over the control gondola. Everyone was concentrating hard. Wings were tensely folded.

'Another two. That's it. Bring the engine power right down. Let the wind brake us.'

'Gabrielson, we're a little too high,' said Wallimson.

'Are we? Doesn't look it to me.'

'Trust me. The line will miss if we don't come down slightly.'

Az hesitated, then said, 'Down ten metres.'

'Aye-aye, ten metres.'

'More,' said Wallimson.

'More?'

'You asked me to co-pilot. I'm co-piloting. We need to go down more. The wind's strong and it's blowing the line beneath us at an acute angle. It won't reach the catcher.'

'Rigz? Can't we pay out more of it?'

'It's at its fullest extent, skipper,' said Chief Engineer Rigzielson. It was Rigz's duty to operate the mooring line winch during launches and dockings.

'Then, another ten metres,' said Az.

The top of the mast seemed alarmingly close to the airship. The catcher loomed like a pair of metal pincers.

'All engines, full stop.'

Cerulean drifted forward under her own momentum, still juddering in the headwind. The mast was now twenty metres away.

Fifteen.

Ten.

The wind dropped.

Cerulean lost lift. Her nose dipped.

'Up!' Az yelled. 'Bring her up! Bring her up!'

The crew reacted, but just too late.

Time slowed to a crawl. Everything that happened next, happened with a kind of appalling leisureliness – a snail's pace disaster.

One side of *Cerulean*'s balloon rubbed against the top of the mast.

The catcher dug into the balloon canvas.

The canvas split and the catcher dug deeper. It scored a gash that lengthened and widened. The tearing sound was horrible, like a deep groan of pain.

The catcher continued to rip through the canvas until it hit one of the main frame sections, the giant circular braces which gave the balloon its cylindrical roundness. Steel screeched on steel. Then the catcher snapped shut, and *Cerulean* rocked to a halt. Everyone in the control gondola who wasn't seated staggered forwards a step.

For several seconds there was silence. The crew waited to see if that was the end of it; if the crash was over or there was more to come.

It was over. *Cerulean* was stuck fast, her balloon impaled on the mast.

'Oh well done,' said Flight Lieutenant Wallimson, and he started a slow handclap. 'Bravo, "skipper". Nice going.'

Az, mortified, did not know where to look.

CHAPTER 34

Damage Assessment

It was bad but it could have been a great deal worse.

The catcher had failed to penetrate any of *Cerulean*'s gas cells. They were all intact, no helium leaking.

Which still left a gash in her canvas 20 metres long, but that could be mended relatively easily. The result would be unsightly, like a newly stitched scar, but would not affect *Cerulean*'s flight performance.

What was a problem was the structural damage to the balloon's frame. Where the catcher had collided with the circular brace, the brace had bent and twisted. Rivets had popped out and several of the support wires strung within the brace had snapped. A large section of the thing was deformed and needed to be straightened out before *Cerulean* could continue on her way.

'At least two days' work,' said Rigz, lugubriously eyeing the broken, dangling cables. He was standing with Az and Mr Mordadson in the airship's axial corridor, a skeletal steel tube which ran the length of the balloon from stem to stern. A chilly wind was hissing in through the tear in the canvas. 'We'll have to cut out the bent bit, hammer it straight and weld it back into place, then reattach all those cables. I suppose we could manage it in a day and a half, if we bodge.'

'We can't just fly with it as it is?' Mr Mordadson asked.

'Not unless we want *Cerulean* to keep corkscrewing. The distension in the balloon would drag on that side, creating a torque effect. We'd have a struggle to keep her from turning upside down.'

'Tell me, Rigz,' said Az, although he didn't want to hear the answer, 'was it my fault?'

The chief engineer scratched the back of his head and let out a whistle through his teeth. 'Yes and no, skipper. Yes, because maybe you shouldn't have attempted docking at the mast. No, because nobody could have foreseen that sudden wind drop. That's what knackered us. That and . . .'

'And what?'

'And the fact that we were coming in too low.'

'But Wallimson said —'

'Wallimson misjudged,' said Rigz. 'Not wishing to cast aspersions or anything, but the flight lieutenant obviously didn't gauge our height right. He should have given us more leeway, in case of exactly what occurred, the wind letting up. He had us in too tight, no margin for error.'

'Then I'm not to blame.'

'Afraid so. See, it's your responsibility as captain, or whatever you are, to double-check all the information you're given by the crew. You can trust us but you can't *rely* on us. Because we're fallible. We're only human. We make mistakes. You have to know better than us and not accept everything we tell you at face value. Tough, I know, but there it is. Someone has to be the big fellow who makes the decisions and lives with them. Someone has to carry the can. That, for better or worse, is you.'

Az swallowed hard, the chief engineer's words a bitter pill. 'Let's get started on the repairs immediately. I'll go and tell the Alar Patrollers what's going on. And then Mr Mordadson and I will head down into Gyre and explain things to people there. Is that a good —?'

He had turned to address Mr Mordadson, only to find him gone. At some point while he and Rigz were talking just now, the Silver Sanctum emissary had flitted off without a sound. He was nowhere to be seen.

Az hoped there was an innocent reason for his abrupt departure, but, knowing Mr Mordadson, there probably wasn't.

CHAPTER 35

The Sound Made By Someone With A Thumb Digging Into His Throat

'Ghnnk!' said Wallimson.

Mr Mordadson ground his thumb harder into the flight lieu-tenant's windpipe.

'What was that?' he said. 'Didn't quite catch it.'

'Ghnnk!' said Wallimson again. His eyes were bulging and his face had gone purple.

'Nope. Still not making yourself clear. You want me to pull my thumb out of you neck? Is that it?'

Frantically Wallimson nodded.

'I don't know. I'm having such fun watching you squirm. I think I might leave my thumb where it is till you stop squirming altogether. How about that? Good idea?'

Wallimson gave a pitiful shake of his head. He was terrified. All he could see in Mr Mordadson's crimson-shaded eyes was implacable determination. The man was going to kill him, he was quite sure of that. Already he could feel his lungs bursting for breath. His vision was growing hazy. It would be a miserable death, here in *Cerulean*'s latrines, where Mr Mordadson had lured him with a request for 'a quick word'. What a sordid and unseemly way to go, being throttled in a toilet cubicle with your head pressed up against the lavatory cistern.

He pleaded with his eyes, begging the Silver Sanctum emis-sary to let him live.

Mr Mordadson cocked his head, seemed to ponder for a moment, then withdrew his thumb.

With a gasp, Wallimson collapsed onto the toilet seat. He

took several raspy gulps of air, sitting limp, overjoyed to be alive.

'Right,' said Mr Mordadson, 'here's the deal. I know you deliberately sabotaged Az's attempt to moor at the mast.'

'I didn't —' croaked Wallimson.

Mr Mordadson poised his thumb over Wallimson's throat. 'Shut up. I'm talking.'

The flight lieutenant clamped his lips tight together.

'I don't believe you meant for us to crash,' Mr Mordadson went on. 'I do believe, though, that you were hoping we would miss the mast or perhaps scrape it. Then you'd put a dent not only in *Cerulean* but in Az's credibility. You'd make him look incompetent, you'd undermine his authority, and in the process you'd make yourself look like a better candidate for captain. Well, congratulations. You succeeded. Trouble is, you've delayed us now. In messing with Az you've messed with *my* mission, and as you can see I'm not best pleased by that. I'm taking what you did very personally.

'I want to make one thing clear,' he continued. 'I don't care what your beef is with Az. I know you don't like him and he was promoted over you. That's got to hurt. But maybe what you really hate about him is that he has no wings and manages fine, while you have two wings – OK, one and a half – and still find life a struggle. Maybe it's jealousy, the worst kind of jealousy, the kind that has a little bit of admiration mixed into it.

'Thing is, I *just don't care*. All I care about is fulfilling my mission, and anyone or anything that gets in the way of that, I will deal with harshly. You've been given a warning, Wallimson. Buck up your ideas, or the next time this thumb gets planted in your epiglottis, it stays there. Understood? You may speak now.'

'Understood,' said Wallimson, coughing out the word.

'Bear in mind, I'm not doing this to protect Az. He has to learn to stand on his own two feet where you're concerned. He has to work out his own strategy for dealing with you. All this is about is you and me. And I think we've straightened things out between us, haven't we?'

'We have.'

'If I had my way, I'd bung you off this airship right now, but we need a back-up captain, someone who can take over if Az is indisposed. So I'm stuck with you. And you're stuck with me. But that shouldn't be a problem for either of us any more, should it?'

'No.'

'Good man.'

Mr Mordadson patted Wallimson on the cheek, as though they were close chums. The flight lieutenant flinched.

'Now, clean yourself up and get back to work,' Mr Mordadson said, and he stepped out of the cubicle.

Seconds later, Wallimson heard the door to the latrines swing shut. Only then was he able to relax.

He was puzzled by Mr Mordadson's remark about cleaning himself up, till he noticed that his trousers were soggy at the crotch.

In his terror, Wallimson had wet himself.

He staggered to his cabin and changed clothes. While he was doing so he thought of the moment he had stared into Mr Mordadson's eyes and seen his death in them. He felt he would carry the memory of those eyes for the rest of his life – the memory of his own helplessness and dread.

There was a small vanity mirror mounted on the cabin wall. Wallimson looked into it. He saw his face, pale in the aftermath of his near-murder. He saw his crooked, lame wing.

The last of his fear sank away and his old, ingrained resentment resurfaced.

Mr Mordadson was right in one respect, Wallimson thought. Wallimson hadn't intended to harm *Cerulean* as badly as he had. He'd been hoping for a collision with the mast but a glancing one, nothing quite as drastic as what did happen. He loved *Cerulean*, in his way, and he regretted the damage he had helped cause.

But Mr Mordadson was wrong if he thought their encounter in the latrines was going to persuade him to mend his ways.

All it had done was sharpen his hatred of Az. What was that kid? Nothing more than a jumped-up Groundling lookalike, that was what. Everyone thought of him as a somebody, a hero, because he had played a part in saving Heliotropia and bringing the Airborn and the Groundlings into contact with each other.

Well, big deal. Wallimson had played a part too. He'd been on *Cerulean* when they flew down through the cloud cover. He'd been there when they carried a bunch of Groundling passengers up to Heliotropia and given them their first glimpse of a sky-city. Yet no one was calling Wallimson a hero and giving him plum jobs on Silver Sanctum missions! No, all the honour and glory went to Az Gabrielson, a snotty wingless teenager who just got lucky.

If it hadn't been for Az, there might not be Groundlings roaming the sky-cities now.

If it hadn't been for Az, the Airborn might not have to share their space and their wealth with those ostriches.

Yes, when you got down to it, Az Gabrielson had a lot to answer for.

'And you won't always have mean old Mr Mordadson to look out for you,' Wallimson said to his reflection in the mirror, as though he were addressing Az. 'He can't be there the whole time, hovering at your shoulder. A moment will come when you're on your own and at my mercy. You can count on it. For the time being I'll play nice. I'll simper along all meek and mild. I'll be the finest flight lieutenant you could wish for. But when the moment comes ...'

Wallimson didn't need to complete the threat. His reflection's grin said it all.

CHAPTER 36

Harried By A Potter

The Grubdollars picked up their father's trail in Timberwolf Knoll, thirty-five kilometres southeast of Grimvale. Then, promptly, they lost it again.

The half-tarp van had been spotted near Timberwolf Knoll heading for the Fishkill River, but once they crossed that by the bridge at Ladenford they couldn't find anyone who had seen the van coming that way. For lack of an alternative, Cassie decided they should follow the river east, but a day of driving along bumpy roads and halting at every steamboat landing and mill town along the way yielded no results. They doubled back and went west, travelling as far as Glass Lake and the Heartberry Dam. No sign of the half-tarp that way either.

Then a ferocious rainstorm broke. They had to halt because the downpour was too torrential for *Bertha*'s wipers to cope with and there was a risk she might pitch sideways into a drainage ditch.

Down near Hillcrest they had what they thought was a stroke of luck, although it proved to be a false alarm. Robert was at the controls, when Colin, in one of the front observation nacelles, started yelling over the speaker-tube system: 'There! There! A half-tarp! There'm a half-tarp parked by the roadside!' Robert slammed on the brakes and all four of *Bertha*'s Groundling occupants piled out and hurried over to the van.

It certainly was a half-tarp and in shabby condition, just like the Deacon's. Unfortunately it didn't belong to him but to a potter who used it to transport his earthenware urns and flowerpots to the weekly market at Croaker Gulch. His house was up a small path in the woods and he was busy ferrying his produce between it and the van. He was not happy to come down the path and find a quartet of youngsters clustered around the vehicle, peering into it. He thought they were about to steal his merchandise, so he set down all but one of the flowerpots in his arms and charged at them.

Sensibly he elected to tackle the largest of the four kids first, and swung the pot at Colin's head. He couldn't have known that Amblescruts were born with notoriously thick skulls. The pot shattered, and Colin turned round to look at his attacker with a puzzled frown, as though he'd just been tapped on the shoulder. The potter peered at the fragment of clay remaining in his hand, then got very afraid.

But Cassie stopped Colin before he could give the potter too severe a beating. The man got away with just a few lumps and bruises, and knew he had been fortunate.

They carried on their quest through the Diamondcrop region and further south into Harkaway, not far from Craterhome itself, capital of the Westward Territories.

Meanwhile, inside *Bertha*'s loading bay, Michael was growing increasingly bored, and then frustrated, and then annoyed.

'Some honeymoon,' he said. 'Cooped up inside this blasted lumbering hunk of junk. Nothing to do but stare out of the windows all day. Whose idea was this again, Aurora?'

'Yours.'

'You sure?'

'Quite sure. You said, and I quote, "Let's do something no one else has done. Let's have an adventure."'

'Yeah. And I meant it and all. I just didn't imagine an adventure could be quite so – well, so unadventurous. Not to mention so claustrophobic. I'm going nuts in here. I need to be out for more than a few minutes at a time. I want to really spread my wings. I'm sick of this.'

'You think I'm not?' said Aurora. 'Apart from anything else I'd be glad of some time alone, so that I don't have to keep on listening to you whinge.'

'I don't whinge.'

'What do you call this, if it isn't whingeing?'

'Just stating how I feel.'

'Also, if I recall rightly, you had an ulterior motive for hiring the Grubdollars to take us on a tour. You were going to use the time to work on Cassie and find out why she's been making Az so miserable. I haven't seen you doing much of that.'

'Haven't had the chance, have I?' Michael said. 'She's been so wrapped up in looking for her dad, I've barely managed to talk to her for more than a couple of minutes. And that damn tube isn't the ideal medium for in-depth heart-to-hearts.'

'Do you want to give up? Call this off as a bad idea? We could ask to be dropped off at the nearest Chancel and then go up and find ourselves a nice hotel and spend the rest of our honeymoon honeymooning properly.'

'Do *you* want to do that?'

'I'm sorely tempted. We're not being much use to the Grubdollars, except maybe financially, and we're taking up all this room while they're stuck in those cramped observation-bubble things.'

The decision was more or less made. Michael and Aurora agreed to speak to Cassie about being offloaded at a Chancel. The Grubdollars would still get paid in full, but would be able to go on without the inconvenience of Airborn passengers on board.

Then Fletcher had a brainwave.

CHAPTER 37

Fletcher's Brainwave

'Pressure,' he said to Michael and Aurora. 'I's been thinking about it and what to do about it. Be'n't kind or fair that you two's hunkering inside *Bertha*'s belly all the time so as you won't be ground-sick. Us could simply open up the loading bay and you could be ill for a day till you acclimatise, like Az do on his visits. Or ...'

'Go on,' said Aurora into the speaker-tube mouthpiece.

'Or us could equalise the pressure between you and the outside little by little. Lower the pump speed a notch at a time. Make the adjustment a gradual thing. Then you mightn't feel too unwell. Mightn't feel unwell at all, in fact.'

'Do you think that'll work?'

'Us can only try. Question be, you'm up for trying?'

Aurora turned to Michael, who nodded. For the first time in several days he looked almost enthusiastic.

'Why not?' she said to Fletcher. 'Let's give it a bash.'

They gave it a bash, and it was successful. While the search went on, Fletcher decreased the power on the air pump at half-hourly intervals. To begin with Michael and Aurora found this uncomfortable. Their ears popped painfully and they complained of a buzzing, headachey sort of dizziness. However, Fletcher found that if he increased the pressure slightly for a quarter of an hour, the next half-hourly decrease was easier to bear. And so it went, in a kind of two steps forward, one step back pattern. Gradually the air pressure in the loading bay became denser and more closely equalised with the air pressure outside, and the Airborn newlyweds experienced no further ill-effects.

In all, the procedure took seven hours. At the end of that period the pump was turned off and the loading bay hatch opened. Michael and Aurora stepped out and waited to feel ground-sick, and waited, until eventually it became clear they weren't going to. Then Michael launched himself into the sky and turned cartwheels and spun around and around in loop-the-loops and figure-of-eights, whooping and cheering.

'You're a genius,' Aurora said to a blushing Fletcher. 'I was beginning to think our marriage was over almost as soon as it had started. We weren't even going to make it through the honeymoon without coming to blows.'

'Divorce avoidance – all part of the service, ma'am,' Fletcher replied.

In truth, he was pretty pleased with himself. He had hit on a way of making the transition between sky and ground much easier and more comfortable. It was so simple and obvious he was surprised nobody had thought of it before. Already he could see the technique being applied at every Chancel, and at the top of every elevator column as well. After all, if it worked for the Airborn coming down, might it not also work in reverse for the Groundlings going up? People could acclimatise before they made their journeys, or else just after they arrived, reasonably quickly. He needed to put his mind to it a bit more. Special tanks could be built. They could be called Fletcher Tanks . . .

'Shall us be on our way?' said Cassie, intruding on Fletcher's thoughts. She was watching Michael's aerial antics in an impatient stance, hands on hips. 'Time be wasting.'

'It'm all go-go-go with you, be'n't it?' her brother said. 'Give he a little longer to frolic. Him's been going stir-crazy.'

'Well, 'scuse I for my sense of urgency,' Cassie shot back. 'There'm I thinking us is trying to find Da and every second counts as him gets further and further away. *Obviously* us should let Michael doodle about up there for as long as him likes. Matter of fact, why doesn't us jack in looking for Da altogether and just do whatever them ruddy Airborn feel like doing.'

'*Cass*,' Fletcher hissed. Aurora was within earshot. 'Clip it down, girl. A few minutes won't make any difference. Besides which, the trail's gone cold. You's no more idea where Da be now than any of we.'

'All the more reason to keep searching.'

'Where? How? Do you even have a plan? Or is us just going to carry on thrashing around the country hoping to get lucky again?'

'Yes!' said Cassie hotly. Then: 'No.' Her eyes brimmed with tears. 'Oh Fletch, it'm useless, be'n't it? Da's really pulled a vanishing act. Us is chasing after shadows.'

'No, lass.' Fletcher reached for her and enfolded her in an embrace. 'No, that be'n't so. Us is going to find he, I swear. Don't know how, but us is.'

'I hope you's right, really I do.' She buried her face in her brother's chest, sniffing. 'If only Martin was here. Him always knew what to do. I miss he, Fletch.'

'I miss he too,' Fletcher said, thick-voiced. 'Every day. It'm odd but I keep thinking him's still around. You know, at home I walk past his room and I think, *Oh, Martin must be in there, that'm why the door's shut*. Then I remember him be'n't in there and it just hits me, hard, this twisting feeling in my guts, like someone be digging a knife there.'

'Yeah, same with I. It'm like him died only yesterday, not a whole year ago. Even remembering what an old bossy-boots him could be – I don't mind. I'd give anything to hear him boss I around again.

'Martin mayn't have been right all the time but more often than not him was,' Fletcher said, with a rueful nod.

'So what do you think him would have suggested us do?'

'Now?'

'Yeah. With Da.'

'No idea. Let I think. Maybe – maybe him'd've said something like go to Craterhome.'

Cassie stepped back, wiping her face with a hand. 'Craterhome? Why would Da be there?'

'Why not? Great big city. Lots going on. Whatever him and the Deacon be after, Craterhome be as likely a place as any for they to find it. And also, Da's note said a needle in a haystack.

Well, haystacks don't come much bigger than Craterhome. Metaphorical haystacks, I mean.'

'Reckon?'

Fletcher was starting to like his own idea more and more. 'Crowds of people, too, in a city. That'd help we. Loads of pairs of eyes that might've seen they if them's there.'

'That'm not bad thinking at all,' Cassie said, brightening. 'You know, Fletch, you'm not nearly as dumb as everyone says.'

'All depends on how dumb them says I be, doesn't it?' Fletcher retorted with a grin. 'And being as I's actually the smart one in the family, however dumb I be, that'd make you even dumber.'

'The smart one? Oh yeah?'

'Oh yeah!'

'Says who?'

'Says me,' declared the inventor of the Fletcher Tank, a device he was confident would revolutionise the way the two races of the world travelled to and fro and interacted.

But that was for later.

For now, Fletcher and his companions' immediate goal was Craterhome. And as soon as Michael had had his fill of aerobatics, Craterhome was where they set off to.

CHAPTER 38

The Outlier

The Count of Gyre was old and as thin as it was humanly possible to be without actually being a skeleton. His cheeks were sunken and cadaverous, his shaven head skull-like. The white toga he wore, with its purple hem and gold braid, revealed knobbly shoulders, stick-thin legs and in general more of his scrawny, mole-riddled, lived-spotted physique than you might care to see. It swished around him as he ushered Az and Mr Mordadson through a series of adjoining chambers to his private office.

In each chamber, Az saw scores of men and women working in large cubbyholes stacked a dozen high. Every one of them had an adding machine or an abacus in front of him or her, along with reams of graph paper and a plethora of pens, and every one was tapping away and jotting down intently. The adding machines' keys clacked, the counters on the abacuses clicked, and these noises built up into a insistent background clatter-chorus which was counterpointed by the wingbeats of clerks who flitted from cubbyhole to cubbyhole, delivering or gathering documents.

Like the Count, all these people had shaven heads, male and female alike, and were clad in white togas, albeit without the trimmings. Az noted a peculiar serenity about them. They were industrious but at the same time tranquil. It was as if they found the act of compiling figures and making calculations hypnotically soothing. Many had blissful smiles on their faces as they toiled away.

Maths was not one of Az's strong subjects at school. That made it all the more extraordinary to him how the citizens of

Gyre could derive such happiness from their jobs and why they loved providing accounts and statistical analysis for the whole of the Airborn realm. Basic algebra alone was enough to give him a headache.

Definitely a city of weirdoes.

And the Count of Gyre, governor of this place, the arch-calculator, was the biggest weirdo of them all.

'Now,' the Count said, after he had despatched a minion out of his office to fetch herbal tea for his guests. 'What can I do for you again?'

'This is a courtesy call,' said Mr Mordadson. 'We need to berth for a couple of days here at your city while we carry out repairs on *Cerulean*.'

'Of course. You are welcome. A couple of days? Can you be more precise with that estimate?'

'I'm afraid not.'

'Oh dear, oh dear,' said the Count, fluttering his wings. Somehow even his wings looked bony and skeletal. 'Too vague. I find vagueness distressing. But I shall try to accommodate.'

'We'd also like to buy fuel.'

As he said this, Mr Mordadson produced his Silver Sanctum seal. Normally the sight of the seal was enough to prompt people into doing their civic duty and willingly providing whatever goods or services the bearer asked for.

In this case, however, it seemed not to have the desired effect.

'That thing,' the Count said with a dismissive sniff.

'You have a problem with the Silver Sanctum?' said Mr Mordadson, his eyes narrowing.

'Not as such. We do your book-keeping. You're a major client. There is no lack of respect here for the Sanctum. No, my problem is with the seal itself.'

'What about it?'

'Its influence is out of all proportion to its intrinsic value,' the Count said. 'Even if we factor in its net worth as so many grammes of precious metal, it still represents far more than it is, to an absurd degree. Can we assess, in real terms, how much it can obtain? No. Can we provide a clearly itemised bill for all the services that have been rendered gratis over the years, every time one of those seals is shown? No. Can we know if its usage obtains us taxpayers a fair outlay-to-reward ratio? No. The seal is problematic because it cannot be quantified with any accuracy. It is of no establishable cost-effectiveness.'

'It's an emblem,' Mr Mordadson replied. 'You can't quantify emblems. By definition they have to be more than they actually are. A flag, for example, can't just be thought of a rectangle of printed cloth. It has to embody everything that the people who it stands for feel. Otherwise, what's the point?'

'What indeed? Hence Gyre has no flag, no insignia, unlike every other sky-city. Because we cannot see the point. We cannot assign a direct value to it. However, let us not argue about this. You will get your fuel. We shall provide it. Grudgingly, but we shall. It so happens there's something I am more interested in.'

'And that would be?'

The Count swivelled round and pointed at Az. 'You.'

Az mirrored the gesture, pointing at himself. 'Me?'

'Yes, you. The great Az Gabrielson. The wingless wonder. Don't look so surprised. Of course we've heard of you, even in Gyre. You're well-known throughout the Airborn realm, and on the ground too, I should imagine. But we have taken a particular interest in you, ever since your exploits first came to our attention. And now lo and behold, at the extremity of all the laws of probability, here you are, arriving right on our doorstep.'

'We had to stop here. It was expedient.' The Count was fond of long words so Az thought he would match him with a little verbosity of his own. 'It so happened that our flight path —'

The Count bared his teeth, an arresting sight. His teeth were yellow and unusually long, poking out from their gums like clothes pegs.

In fact, he was grinning.

'Expediency, coincidence, accident, happenstance,' he said. 'Let me tell you, young man, none of these things exists. They are merely names people give to varying contingencies of measurable probability. There is no turn of luck, no chance meeting, no confluence of events, which cannot be rationalised and accounted for by means of figures and statistics. There is no outcome that cannot be predicted with the proper calculation, and thus no set of circumstances that is not preordained.'

'I don't understand.'

'I didn't think you would. Let me put it more straight-forwardly. You stopped here because you were meant to stop here. You crashed your airship on our mast because you and I were meant to have this conversation.'

'Meant by who?'

'By *whom*,' said the Count, correcting his grammar. 'And it's the wrong question. You should be asking, by *what*?'

'All right then. By *what*?'

'By the underlying order of numbers. By the tendency of mathematics to work out. By the arithmetical structure which underpins the world's apparent randomness. Hence the *what* rather than the *whom*. That which I'm talking about is not an entity, not a guiding sentience, although some have mistaken it for that and called it God. It's at once simpler and more intricate. It's the dimension of pure mathematics, that whole beautiful para-realm where one and one always equals two, two and two four, and so on ad infinitum. Where every fraction can be reduced to its lowest common denominator and every equation can be balanced and every theorem can be proved. Where the —'

'Sorry to butt in.' Az was feeling a mixture of bafflement (*para-realm?*) and boredom. He suddenly seemed to have become stuck in the worst maths lesson ever. 'You said you've taken a "particular interest" in me.'

'Indeed.'

'Well, why? Because I was the pioneering sky-ground go-between?'

'Partly that,' said the Count, 'and also because you are what's known as an outlier.'

'Beg pardon? Did you just call me a liar?'

'Outlier,' the Count reiterated patiently. 'Something which

lies outside the norm. In the strictly statistical sense it means a value that is extraordinarily large or small and does not fit into the data set as a whole. It cannot even be accounted for by standard deviation. In the broader sense, I'm talking about an anomaly. One of a kind. Unique, even.'

'Ah. The no-wings thing. As a matter of fact, I'm not unique there. Apparently there's this woman in the Cumula Collective. Mr Mordadson here told me about her. No wings, eighty years old, half-blind. They had to decide which of us to send down to the ground, her or me. Funnily enough they plumped for me.'

Either flippancy was lost on the Count or he would not deign to acknowledge it.

'We know of her too,' he said. 'She does not matter, except in so far as her lack of importance points up *your* importance the more greatly. In contrast with the relative uneventfulness of her long life, your short life has already been packed with incident. As an outlier, that makes you statistically significant and impossible to ignore. It points to a qualitative purpose to your existence.'

'Oh?'

'Yes, Az. May I call you Az? You see, we at Gyre have an inkling that you are pivotal to the future of the Airborn race, and the future of the Groundling race too.'

Az groped for something further to say but couldn't find it. No more facetious comments sprang to mind. The Count's words, and the utter solemnity with which he spoke them, had set the skin on the back of his neck crawling. He felt he had strayed into uncertain territory. This wasn't a situation ripe for poking fun at any more. Things had taken a turn for the strange.

'And I can prove it to you,' the Count went on. 'Would you care to come with me? You too, Mr Mordadson. It's not far but some flying is required.'

CHAPTER 39

The Ultimate Reckoner

As the Count led them along a series of winding, cross-connecting corridors and shafts, deeper into Gyre, Mr Mordadson bent his head close to Az's and whispered: 'I wonder if he's taking us to see what I think he is.'

'Which is ...'

'Something I've heard only rumours about. Something I didn't believe really existed.'

'Tell me.'

'No. Let's just wait till we get there.'

At last they arrived at a spacious hallway which was, Az guessed, close to the centre of Gyre, if not right at the city's core. As Mr Mordadson set him down, he became aware of a low, churning, clanking background clamour. He could feel the sound as well as hear it. It made the polished marble floor tiles beneath his feet vibrate.

At one end of the hallway were a gigantic pair of doors, each so big it could let an army through. This was a portal designed to dwarf you and make you feel awestruck and insignificant. All over the doors there were mathematical symbols, inlaid in gold. Az recognised many of the symbols: $+$, $\div$, $=$, $>$, $<$, $\neq$, and so on. Some, though, were not so familiar, for instance $\approx$, and ∞, and Δ, and $\cap$. And a few were so ornate and exotic-looking he wasn't certain they were genuine mathematical symbols at all.

The Count threw a large lever, and the doors started to grind ponderously apart, sliding sideways into recesses.

Az knew that what lay on the other side was a vast chamber full of machinery. Judging by the racket coming from there, it had to be. He imagined it to be similar to the supply-arrival depot at Heliotropia or the elevator chamber in the Chancel below, an immense space filled with moving, whirring, thundering technology.

He was surprised, therefore, when the doors opened to reveal . . .

. . . a room not much larger than the living room at home.

The walls, floor and ceiling were bare and white, and there were just two items of machinery visible, right at the centre. One of them was a kind of pedestal, on top of which was a sloping panel with buttons on it, which reminded Az very much of the adding machines he had seen earlier. Larger, slightly more complicated-looking, but essentially the same.

The other was a freestanding printing device, which was busy turning out a ribbon of tickertape that gathered in loose, unruly coils on the floor. The tickertape was four centimetres wide and covered in rows of numbers.

With a flick of his hand, the Count invited Az and Mr Mordadson to follow him into the room.

The thrum of machinery came from all around them but was barely any louder here than in the hallway. The Count had to raise his voice in order to be heard, but only a little.

'This,' he said to his two guests, 'is the Ultimate Reckoner.'

'Doesn't look like much,' Az remarked. *Ultimate Reckoner* seemed a grandiose name for just those two pieces of apparatus.

'What you're looking at is simply the Reckoner's input and output portions,' the Count explained. 'They represent a small fraction of its full bulk. All around us, if you'd care to imagine it, is a system of brass rods, linked by sprocketed flywheels. Each rod is thirty centimetres long and contains ten dials numbered with the digits nought to nine. In all, there are fifty thousand rods. The machine as a whole extends a hundred metres in every direction, give or take a metre or two. As such, the Ultimate Reckoner represents forty years' worth of construction by a total of more than three hundred residents of Gyre. Forty-three years, to be exact, and three hundred and twenty-nine residents in all. A million-plus man-hours of labour. To be exact, one million, one hundred and seven thousand —'

'Yes, yes, we get the picture,' said Mr Mordadson. 'Tell us what it *does*.'

'Why, it's nothing less than the most sophisticated calculating tool ever built. It is to the ordinary adding machine as a human brain is to the brain of a common-or-garden sparrow.'

'And what's all this?' Az said, indicating the growing pile of tickertape on the floor.

'That is the task the Reckoner is currently engaged on. At present, we have the machine working out π to a trillion decimal places. That's its default setting, a calculation we use to keep it ticking over, so that the sprockets and rods don't seize up with disuse. We're collating and analysing the results, looking to see if there are cycles of repetition within the number string. It's something of an outlier in itself, is π. A mathematical operation which refuses to conform to any rules. Circles and spheres occur spontaneously in nature. That means π is a biological construct and therefore, to our way of thinking, ought to demonstrate a pattern and be finite. In the end, seven *must* go into twenty-two. The division *must* be achievable. And if anything can prove that, the Ultimate Reckoner can.'

'A *trillion* decimal places?' said Az.

'We're not there yet but we're well on the way. And if, after a trillion, we haven't shown that π has repetitions and is finite, we'll try a trillion more. It's a long-term project, you might say. However, the Ultimate Reckoner has another, more significant use.'

'Which is?'

The Count fixed Az with a steely gaze.

'It can tell the future.'

CHAPTER 40

The Sealed Envelope

Az assumed he must have misheard.

'Seriously? Tell the future?'

'Destiny, for want of a better word, is simply a product of interdependent chains of event,' the Count of Gyre said. 'One thing leads to another. If we translate that in terms of sequences of probability, it means the likely thing leads to the next likely thing, and so on and so forth. I could explain about continuous and discrete random variables and probability density function, but I'd doubt I'd leave you any the wiser. What it boils down to is that the Ultimate Reckoner has the computational power to determine the course of a plan of action, a city's fortunes, or even a person's life.'

'I don't believe it.'

'It doesn't matter whether you do or not. The Ultimate Reckoner works. It is a divination tool. It can prophesy. It predicted your coming here.'

Az was sceptical and didn't hide it.

'Oh yes,' said the Count. 'We perform regular data surveys with the Reckoner. It helps us map out our upcoming workload so that we can deploy our personnel resources with the greatest efficiency. We feed in information – in the form of graphs, tabulation, Venn diagrams, flowcharts – via the control panel on that pedestal. The Reckoner then returns its outcome-prediction, which we call an evaluation, through the tickertape printer. Twelve days and nine hours ago, we ran one of our usual surveys and received an evaluation strongly indicating that you, Az Gabrielson, the Airborn outlier, would be paying us a visit.' He folded his hands together. 'And here you are.'

'And now you're asking me if I'd like my fortune told by this – this big whizz-bang bunch of cogs and dials?'

Az was starting to think the Count of Gyre wasn't just weird. The man was downright mad. Being fanatical about figures and calculations, amid a city full of people who were similarly obsessed, had messed up his brain.

'No, not in the slightest,' the Count said.

'Well, that's a relief.'

'No, because we knew you were coming, Az, and because you fascinate us, we took the liberty of setting the Reckoner to construct an evaluation for you in advance.'

'Riiight.'

'Believe me, it spent a long time coming up with a result. What with you being an outlier, it had to reach far beyond the normal parameters and the standard quartiles and percentiles to plot your evaluation.'

The Count reached into a fold of his toga and produced a somewhat crumpled envelope.

'And here it is,' he said.

He held the envelope out.

Az deliberated for several moments before finally taking it from the Count.

'It's sealed,' the Count said.

'Have you looked at it?'

'I have.'

'And?'

'I found it striking and intriguing, although hard to fathom fully. But you should not have a problem interpreting it. It is specific to you, after all. You know more about yourself than I do, therefore you will perceive nuances and levels of meaning in it that I cannot.'

'Can't you even give me a hint about it?'

'No. It is your evaluation. It's up to you whether or not you look at it, and it's up to you whether or not you act on what it tells you.' Gravely, the Count added, 'I would rather, though, for the sake of all of us, that you did.'

CHAPTER 41

Tickertape Prognostication

Az returned to *Cerulean* with the envelope still unopened. The meeting with the Count and the trip to the Ultimate Reckoner had left him with a queasy feeling in his stomach. He didn't know what to think. On the one hand, he simply couldn't see how a piece of machinery, however cunning and intricate it was, could foretell the future. But on the other hand, what if it could? Did he really want to find out what lay in store for him?

'What would you do?' he asked Mr Mordadson as they arrived at the airship.

'Me? With a "prophecy" like the one you have there? Read it, laugh, and chuck it in the bin.'

Az didn't do that. Instead, he left the envelope in his cabin and went to see how the repairs were coming along.

Under Rigz's supervision the crew were slicing away the bent section of brace using blowtorches. While one crewman did the cutting, another three hovered around him with fireproof blankets to catch and smother any stray sparks. The helium gas which gave *Cerulean* her buoyancy was not itself flammable – in fact, it was a natural fire retardant. However, if her canvas caught alight, the whole ship could burn, so the sparks from the blowtorches had to be carefully contained.

By afternoon the section of brace was ready to come away, and all hands were put to work levering it free and then lowering it to Gyre's landing apron, where a space had been cleared in readiness. Some of the Alar Patrollers helped with this. Then Rigz and the rest of the crew set about pounding the brace back into shape with mallets.

Flight Lieutenant Wallimson joined in, which was unlike

146

him. He usually regarded any form of manual labour as beneath him, and yet there he was, down on the apron, hammering away and meekly doing whatever the chief engineer told him to. How had this remarkable change of attitude come about? Az didn't like to think that Mr Mordadson had had something to do with it, but that seemed the most plausible explanation.

At dinner in the crew's mess, Rigz pronounced himself pleased with the day's efforts. They were making good progress. Az commended everyone on their hard work, but otherwise he was quiet and subdued at the meal. The crew assumed he was still feeling guilty about the crash (which he was), and they teased him in the hope of cheering him up.

'Don't worry, skipper. There'll be other masts.'

'Don't say that! You'll put him off ever trying to moor again.'

'Yeah. No more mooring for Az.'

'Never*moor* will he moor!'

'*Moor*'s the pity!'

'The *moor* the merrier!'

Az smiled gamely. If they were ribbing him, at least it meant they were halfway to forgiving him.

Guilt, however, wasn't the reason he was subdued.

The envelope still waited for him in his cabin.

And eventually, when everybody went to bed for the night, he was confronted by it. It sat on top of the tiny, tubular-steel desk in the corner of the cabin. Just an oblong of gummed paper, but it seemed to taunt him. It seemed to say, *Don't you want to know? Aren't you even a little bit curious about what's inside me?*

Az remembered the Count of Gyre telling him he would be pivotal to the future of both races. He also remembered Mr Mordadson's recommendation: *Read it, laugh, and chuck it in the bin.*

With a sudden burst of recklessness, he snatched up the envelope and tore the flap open. He fished out the short length of tickertape inside and spread it out on the desktop.

He didn't laugh.

Neither did he chuck the tickertape in the bin.

He scowled.

A prophecy?

If so, it was one he couldn't make head or tail of.

What the Ultimate Reckoner had produced for Az was a symbol that looked like this:

It was meaningless as far as he could see. A two-way arrow? Up and down? With a question mark? What did that represent? What sort of a prophecy was *that*?

After a while he slid the piece of tickertape back into the envelope and stashed the envelope away in the desk drawer, out of sight. He resolved not to think about it any more. It was a joke. A hoax. The Count was either a charlatan or deluded, or both, and the so-called evaluation was pointless, nothing more than machine-generated nonsense.

Az lay down to sleep, and sleep came, though not till after he had lain awake for over an hour, wondering, pondering.

CHAPTER 42

Craterhome Sweet Craterhome

The seven boroughs of Craterhome were named, imaginatively, First to Seventh. They occupied a septet of immense cauldron-like depressions in the ground, clustered close together and linked by a series of tunnels through which road traffic and trams passed to and fro constantly. The smallest borough was three kilometres in diameter and 200 metres below sea level at its base. The largest, the Third Borough, had a span of nearly eight kilometres and plunged to a depth of one and a half kilometres below sea level.

Six of the boroughs were mainly residential, and one in particular, the Fifth, considered itself Craterhome's most gentrified area, with grand apartment blocks decked around the inside of its rim and beautiful mansions nestling in its interior, each set in its own grounds, encircled by lavish, mossy gardens.

The Third Borough, by contrast, was the city's commercial and industrial hub, and was a warren of shops, factories, foundaries and tenements. Day and night it teemed with activity. It never rested, never slept. Its streets and alleyways were perpetually packed with people and threaded by vehicles and clanging trams. A tide of workers flooded in at dawn and flooded out again at dusk, and after dark the borough played host to rowdy throngs of drinkers and fun-seekers who filled the pubs, clubs, restaurants and music venues to bursting. With them came an attendant swarm of thieves and muggers who preyed on the merry revellers like parasites. Crime flourished at night in the Third Borough, under a sickly gas-lamp glare, and prospered only slightly less during the dimness of day.

There were mazy covered marketplaces in the Third

Borough. There were teetering-tall curiosity shops and basement-based antique stores. Cobblers and shoeshine men operated out of kiosks that were effectively alcoves in walls. Dodgy doctors hawked potions and nostrums on street corners. Purveyors of 'quality second-hand goods' peddled their wares from the backs of pushcarts, vanishing at the faintest whiff of a police constable. Newsboys roved, yelling out headlines as they brandished copies of the latest edition of the *Craterhome Messenger* and the *Westward Territories Gazette*. One-man bands shuffled from place to place, strumming, bass-drumming, tooting, hooting, cymbal-crashing. Hand-wound barrel organs churned out tunes. Beggars sat slumped, caps ready for coins, showing off the mangled limb or blinded eye or missing hand which prevented them from holding down gainful employment.

It was —

'Mad,' said Robert

'Like an Amblescrut get-together, times a hundred,' said Colin

'Damn hard to drive through,' said Fletcher.

'Scary,' said Michael.

'Bewildering,' said Aurora.

Cassie herself said nothing. She was too busy scanning the crowds to comment. A river of bodies flowed around *Bertha* as the murk-comber crawled along. Cassie, in one of the front nacelles, flicked her gaze from one face to another, hoping, hoping, that suddenly she would spy her father. But stranger after stranger passed by, and several of them glared back up at her and shouted snarky comments which she couldn't hear through the glass. Residents of Craterhome's Third Borough did not, it seemed, take kindly to being peered at.

'Seen a place to park yet?' she asked Fletcher.

'Not a chance round here. There'm barely a scrap of roadway without somebody on it.'

Eventually Fletcher found a spot for *Bertha* in a broad alley, next to some overflowing dustbins and an open drain which carried a trickle of sludgy, lump-filled water towards a sewer grating.

As Cassie clambered out, the stink of putrid garbage and human waste hit her. These smells mingled with a darker odour, an acrid background miasma of coal smoke and other burnt fuels. She coughed and spluttered. Parts of Grimvale were bad, but never *this* bad.

Fletcher emerged after her. He coughed too, and spat out a wad of phlegm. 'Filthy place. How does them stand the stench?'

'Live here long enough, suppose you must get used to it.'

'Well' – Fletcher glanced around the alley – 'I be'n't leaving *Bertha* here unguarded, straight up. Reckon just you and me should go out and everyone else stay behind.'

The proposal was put to the other four and met with no objections. Robert was entrusted with responsibility for keeping *Bertha* and her Airborn passengers safe and secure. Colin was assigned patrol and lookout duties. He would wander around and keep an eye out for potential trouble. He was not, though, to stray far. He should remain within sight of *Bertha* at all times.

'Within sight, right you be,' he said.

'Can I use anti-verm countermeasures if I has to?' Robert asked.

'Yes,' Cassie said. 'But only if you absolutely have to.'

'Ace!'

'Michael? Aurora?'

The Airborn honeymooners stood just inside the loading bay hatchway. Michael had a handkerchief pressed over his mouth and nose. Aurora was gripping the doorframe with one hand, as if to anchor herself.

'I doesn't know how long us'll be,' Cassie said. 'I'd suggest you don't go off exploring, in case you get into difficulties.'

'Don't worry,' Aurora replied. 'I think Michael and I will be very happy staying right here.'

'Good.' Cassie turned to Fletcher. 'OK then, big brother. It'm you and me. Let's see what us can turn up.'

CHAPTER 43

Hundred Ways

No member of the Grubdollar family had visited Craterhome before except Den, who had come here once, long ago, in a fit of youthful curiosity. He'd stayed for a very short time, and all he would ever say about the city was that it was a squirrelly kind of place and he never wanted to go back.

By 'squirrelly' Cassie took her father to mean frantic and devious, and Craterhome was. If she hadn't realised that from her first exposure to it while inside *Bertha*, she certainly did now. She and Fletcher hadn't walked more than a couple of hundred paces before someone tried to sell them a man's wallet, complete with a small lithograph of a woman and two children inside, and someone else invited them to come and watch a 'bed show' (Cassie wasn't sure what this was, but she had a pretty good idea it didn't involve sleeping). A few paces further on, and a basket of laundry tumbled from a fourth-storey balcony and crashed at their feet, scattering clothes everywhere. Fletcher had come within a whisker of being hit, but when he and Cassie looked up they didn't receive an apology. Instead, they were subjected to a torrent of abuse from a waspish-faced woman leaning over the balcony rail. She yelled at them for failing to catch the basket and preventing her laundry from being strewn all over the pavement. Look at it! It was getting trampled! And whose fault was that? Theirs, not hers!

They hurried on. They were heading for a place called Hundred Ways, the nucleus of the Third Borough, a large open square where a number of streets converged, although not actually a hundred; more like twenty. It was renowned as somewhere you could go and spout an opinion on any topic you liked. People would gather and listen, and if they approved of what you were saying they might throw money at you. If they didn't approve, then they would throw other things – rotten vegetables, bad eggs, stones, and worse. Plenty of wandering Deacons came to Hundred Ways. Perhaps *their* wandering Deacon was there now, or had preached there recently.

Having obtained directions from a passably civil passer-by, Cassie and Fletcher soon reached Hundred Ways. A tumult of shouting and jeering echoed around the square. Individuals stood perched on chairs and crates, holding forth on a variety of subjects. Some spoke softly and with a measure of restraint, while others hectored and harangued till they were red in the face. Some pleaded intelligently on political issues such as greater electoral transparency and the reform of prison conditions, while others were clearly madmen and argued, for instance, that fish should be treated as honorary humans or that everyone should build themselves wings made out of wood and feathers and flap up through the clouds to join the Airborn. Each had drawn an audience of anything up to three dozen, and the audience members seemed not to care too much whether what they were being told made any sense or not. They abused the speakers and attempted to drown out their voices with booing and catcalls. Occasionally a decaying-food missile flew through the air, lobbed more for comic effect than with accuracy.

There were several Deacons to be seen, and the two Grub-dollars made a slow circuit of the square, stopping to look at each one. On the way they passed a Humanist, who was busy proclaiming his particular creed. Humanism had become widely discredited since the Grimvale uprising. Most people considered the movement and its followers to be irrelevant and out-of-date, in much the same way that Deacons were. The world had moved on.

But if so, no one had told *this* Humanist, who was delivering a scathing attack on the Deacons as if they were still lording it over everyone in their Chancels and the upsets of the past year had never happened. The Deacons who were close enough to hear him would pause from their preaching every so often to tell him to shut up. The Humanist, in return, would advise them to 'shove it up your robes'. The crowds loved it and egged the two sides on, hoping the verbal clash would turn into something more physical.

Cassie sensed Fletcher stiffening as they came near the Humanist. His hands became fists.

'Let it go,' she said, placing a hand on his arm. 'It'm in the past. Him's just a clapped-out windbag with nothing to say.'

Fletcher's fists unclenched. His face was rueful.

'Can't believe I ever thought him and his kind was the way forward,' he said. 'How wrong can a bloke be?'

They completed their circuit of Hundred Ways without seeing a Deacon who matched the description of the one they were looking for. Cassie felt her heart begin to sink.

She also felt a hand delving into the back pocket of her trousers.

Without thinking, she spun round and thumped the owner of the hand.

He, a nine-year-old boy, fell to the ground with a yelp. He was clutching a wad of banknotes which just a second earlier had been in Cassie's pocket. As he scrambled back up onto his feet, Cassie grabbed hold of him by the shirt collar. He struggled to get away, but she shook him roughly till he stopped squirming. Then she plucked the money out of his hand.

'Cass? What'm you doing?' said Fletcher. He had seen nothing except his sister hitting the boy and taking the banknotes off him.

'Him were trying to steal from I,' she said. 'Wasn't you?' she snarled at the youngster.

The boy shook his head vigorously.

'Want I to hit you again?'

The boy shook his head even more vigorously.

'Then 'fess up.'

Slowly, hesitantly, the boy nodded. 'I *were* trying to steal from you. Only, it weren't supposed to go like that.'

'What d'you mean?'

'You wasn't supposed to catch me. And you wouldn't've, either, if I'd been using my proper hand.'

He held up his right hand. The index finger was wrapped in a thick, grubby bandage.

'It'm hard for a pickpocket to make a decent living,' the boy said, 'with his finger busted and his pinching hand out of action.'

CHAPTER 44

Pickpocket With A Broken Finger

Cassie couldn't believe it. 'So you admit you'm a pickpocket.'

Neither could Fletcher. 'Brazen little tyke, be'n't he?'

'Look around,' the boy said with a shrug. 'See all those folk? See how none of they is looking at we? Not even curious, despite all the hollering and frothing you's made? That'm because at least one in ten of they be in the same trade as I or something similar, and the rest'm so used to it them doesn't care when one of we gets caught. It'm only people like you who makes such a big song-and-dance about being thieved from.'

'People like we?'

'Out-of-towners. Country bumpkins.'

Cassie gaped at him. Not only was this boy unashamed about being a professional thief, but he had the nerve to insult her, his intended victim.

'Don't mean it harshly,' he went on. 'But it comes off of you like a reek. The way you was staring around all bug-eyed and baffled. The fact that you had that money making a big fat bulge in your pocket. Nobody in Craterhome carries cash in their *pockets*. Nobody be that stupid. This'm your first time in town, eh?'

Dumbly, Cassie nodded.

'Well, it could be you's been very fortunate, then. Think of I as your wake-up call. From now on you'll be a whole lot more city-savvy, unless you want the same thing to happen again in an hour or so, or less.'

Fletcher burst out laughing. Cassie looked daggers at him, but then she too saw the funny side.

'Got to admit, sis, him's a live wire.'

'I know. I be'n't sure whether to drag his sorry bones to the nearest police station or just give he a pat on the head and let he go.'

'Oh, I wouldn't bother taking I to the cops,' the boy said, tugging himself free of Cassie's grasp and straightening out his shirt. It was a cheap woollen shirt but he smoothed it down like it was a tailored garment woven from the finest silk. 'Them's no better than anyone else in this town. All I has to do is offer they a small, ahem, contribution and I'll be on my way in no time, free as a bird.'

Cassie couldn't help but think that this must be true. In Grimvale the police were reasonably honest, but then that was down to there not being much wealth around. No one could afford to bribe them, so the constables had no choice but to do their job properly. Here in Craterhome, where money abounded and thievery was commonplace, all sorts of opportunities for police corruption were available.

'Tell me then,' she said, 'how come you got your finger broken? Were it an unhappy accident or did someone else catch you trying to nick from they?'

'The second one,' the boy replied, with a hangdog look. He eyed his bandaged finger as if the unfortunate digit had somehow let him down.

'Really?' said Fletcher. 'So maybe you'm not as skilled at the old pocket-picking as you thought.'

'No, I be pretty damn good at it,' the boy said with some force. 'Had plenty of practice. Been doing it since I were four. It were just that this Deacon I were snatching from – him were something out of the ordinary.'

'You tried to steal from a Deacon?' said Cassie.

'I be liking this little pipsqueak more and more,' said Fletcher.

'Yeah, well, I had to, really. The man had this lovely-looking knife strapped to his ankle. A hunter's knife. I saw it when him were going up some steps into a shop. His robe flapped up in a breeze, and there it were. I only caught a glimpse but I knew that knife were worth something and I knew I had to have it. So I waited for him to come out, and him was carrying all this stuff him'd bought, whole big bunch of it in brown paper bags, so I saw this were my chance and I snuck forward, got in his way, bent down like I were tying my shoelace, and made the grab as him stepped around me. Only . . .'

'What?'

'It were uncanny. That'm the only word for it. Uncanny. It were like him *knew* what I were going to do. I mean, Deacons, right? Not exactly worldly-wise, is them? Fresh out of the Chancels and all naïve and clumsy. So I thought him'd be an easy mark. Why not? But him weren't at all. Kicked me here.' The boy pointed to his chest. 'Didn't even see his foot move, I didn't, and next thing I know I's flat on my arse and the wind's knocked out of me and the Deacon's put down his shopping and him's got hold of my finger and hand and . . . *snap.*'

Cassie and Fletcher winced in empathy. Whatever else he was, the kid was still just a nine-year-old.

'"There," him says to I,' the boy went on. '"You won't be trying that again in a while." And here I be, just three days later, back in the game, sort of. But even so, him were so cool and calm about it. Just yanked back my finger quick as you please, like pulling a wishbone. Then him stood up and smoothed out that red hair of his and picked up his bags and waltzed off, and I be left there with a finger pointing up in a direction it had no right to and with enough pain coming from my hand to make me dizzy and feel like throwing up, and —'

'Hold on,' said Cassie, interrupting. 'Back up a moment. Did you say *red* hair?'

'Bright orangey red, it were, and all sticking up like flames.'

She glanced at Fletcher and could tell that he was thinking what she was thinking. Neither could quite believe it. Their Deacon? It couldn't be. Could it?

'Were there another fellow with he?' she asked the boy. 'Tallish, stubbly chin, not too many teeth?'

'Not that I saw.'

'Then did the Deacon by any chance have a van?'

'Yup, that him did.'

'What type?'

'It were a cruddy old half-tarp. I saw it from behind. Barely roadworthy, by the looks of it. And a pile of stuff bundled up in the back, like canvas or something, ropes, poles.'

Cassie stared the boy in the eye. 'Where precisely did you see he? What shop were him buying stuff from?'

The boy stared back. 'I'll show you – for a tenner.'

They held each others gazes for a long while. Then, reluctantly, Cassie peeled off one of her banknotes and waved it front of him. He snatched it from her and tucked it inside the waistband of his trousers.

'Take we there,' she said. 'And if there'm even a hint of any funny business, you'll have another broken finger to go with the one you's already got.'

CHAPTER 45

The Ignorance-Is-Bliss Imperative

Colin Amblescrut was taking his sentry duty very seriously indeed. He marched up and down the alley, performing a smart about-turn at each end. He bore in mind the instruction not to let *Bertha* out of his sight, so that even when he was walking away from her he kept his head swivelled at an angle to make sure she was always within the scope of his vision. Once or twice he collided with a wall because he wasn't properly looking where he was going, but this was a small price to pay. The main thing was that he was following his orders to the letter. He wouldn't let anyone down.

Up in *Bertha*'s javelin turret, Robert sat and lovingly fingered the auxiliary set of anti-verm countermeasure controls. He was envious of Fletcher and Cassie, who had had the opportunity to use the countermeasures against people. It wasn't that Robert had a burning urge to hurt anyone, just that he was tickled by the idea of exploding a chaff bomb, say, in the face of some deserving human victim. That would be much more satisfying to watch, he thought, than doing the same thing to a dumb old verm.

As for Michael and Aurora, she was giving him a lecture on the origin of the craters in which Craterhome was built and he was nodding and seemed to be very interested in what she said, although in fact he was already developing the ability common to many husbands, namely the knack of appearing to listen to a wife's comments while not actually listening at all.

'They were formed during the Great Cataclysm,' Aurora was saying. 'The whole of the ground is pocked with them, although it's rare to get so many all in one spot like this. As best we can tell, they're the result of gigantic rocks which hit the planet from space. The impacts left these immense dents and also threw up a thick pall of dust and debris, which collected vapour around it and formed the cloud cover. No one is a hundred per cent certain this is what happened but it's the fairest guess, based on the evidence. People remember the Cataclysm as a time when fire fell from the sky, but the fire was those rocks burning up as they entered the atmosphere.'

'Atmosphere, yes,' said Michael.

'It's fascinating, isn't it? The thought of rocks out there among the stars, big as city blocks, hurtling through space. What were the chances of them hitting us? What did they come from originally? Why were they out there in the first place? Nobody knows. But whatever life was like beforehand, the Cataclysm changed it in a flash. Literally.'

'Literally.'

'Lady Aanfieldsdaughter says there's a huge amount of history that was eradicated by the Cataclysm. There's also a huge amount of Airborn history that has been forgotten or else lies buried so deeply in libraries and archives that it might as well have been forgotten. A lot of it's kept at the Sanctum and there are scholars whose job is to excavate and study it – but what they find out always remains in the Sanctum. The rest of the race doesn't need to know about these things and probably doesn't want to. Lady Aanfieldsdaughter calls this the ignorance-is-bliss imperative. The Sanctum harbours secrets which the general population is better off not having revealed to them.'

'Them.'

'It's like the way we used not to know about the Groundlings. I'm not saying we're worse off now. It was a phase that had run its course. It had to end. But while it lasted, it made the Airborn's lives that bit easier. And the same with all those other secrets. I'm told that the higher up in the Sanctum you are, the more of them you learn. Someone in Lady Aanfieldsdaughter's position is privy to a whole host of facts about our race that would weigh heavily on a lesser person's shoulders. It's almost like the Sanctum elders know about these things so that no one else has to. Which makes me wonder about my own ambitions. Do I want to get to the top, if getting to the top means finding out all sorts of dark, hidden truths? What do you think, Mike?'

'Oh yeah. Definitely.'

Aurora frowned at him. Then her expression turned sly. 'Yes. And I suppose when we have children you'll be happy to look after them full time. You wouldn't mind that?'

'Hmm? No, wouldn't mind.'

'So that I can be free to pursue my career. That's excellent. You promise? Even though I want to have at least ten kids. That won't be too much for you?'

'No way. Too much? No.' Michael glanced up, suddenly worried. 'Wait a second. What are we talking about?'

'Oh, nothing, dear.'

'No, tell me.'

'You just made a promise, that's all.'

'To do what?'

'You don't remember?'

'No.'

'Well, a promise is still a promise. It's not my fault if you weren't listening.'

'You can't hold me to something I said if I didn't know what I was saying.'

'I can and I will.'

Michael rose up, wings outstretched. From tip to tip they spanned half the width of the loading bay.

'You better tell me what I just agreed to,' he said, moving towards Aurora mock-menacingly. 'Or else.'

'Or else what?'

'I may be forced to feather-smother you.'

'For one thing, don't you dare,' said Aurora, grinning. 'For another thing – feather-smother? How old are you? That's straight out of the playground!'

Michael bent his wings towards her, as if intending to cocoon her in them. 'Tell me.'

'Never!' Aurora leapt backwards, propelling herself out through the loading bay hatch.

Michael followed, and together they spiralled upward, batting each other with their wingtips as they went. Peals of laughter spilled from them. It was the sort of blithe, young-couple horseplay which wouldn't have garnered much attention in a sky-city.

But of course, they weren't in a sky-city.

CHAPTER 46

Barnswallow's Practical Goods Emporium

'Hoo. Hum. Yes,' said Cyrus Barnswallow, proprietor and sole sales representative of Barnswallow's Practical Goods Emporium. 'The Deacon. I've had a few Deacons come through my door lately, but how could one forget *him*? Such hair! Like a burning brazier atop his head. A northerner, if I'm not mistaken. There was a hint of the Uplands in his accent, a whisper of the snows and frost.'

'There, can I go now?' said the pickpocket. 'I's done my bit.'

Cassie shushed him. 'Him were on his own?' she asked Barnswallow. 'There weren't anybody with he?'

'I told you —' the boy began, but Fletcher poked him and he fell silent.

'On his own?' said Barnswallow. 'Hoo. As far as I recall, yes.'

'And what did him buy, if I might ask?'

'What did he buy? Huhhh. Hmm. Let me think.' Barnswallow looked around at the tall, tightly packed shelves of his shop, blinking through his brass-rimmed pince-nez spectacles. The room bulged with apparatus and paraphernalia of all kinds. There were fire irons and fishing rods, umbrellas and thermal underwear, gumboots and galoshes, towels and trowels, mousetraps and catflaps, baking trays and camping stoves, fly swatters and ink blotters, binoculars and bin bags, doormats and hardhats, paintbrushes and painkillers ... In fact, rather than list what the Practical Goods Emporium sold, it would be easier to list what it didn't.

'I remember he bought a compass,' said its owner. 'A Magnet

Opus, what's more. Top of the range. He bought a quantity of beef jerky. He bought some hardtack biscuits. Bags of raisins. What else? Hoo. My memory – it's not what it was, you know. Ah yes, a shovel and a mattock.' Barnswallow pointed to a rack of tools which looked like pickaxes with flattened blades. 'In fact I think he bought two of each. And flashlights. It was quite a shopping list he had, let me tell you. Insect repellent. A first-aid kit. Did he buy a first-aid kit? Yes, he did. One that included antivenin for snakebites. He was very specific about that. Huhhh. There was more, I'm sure.' Barnswallow levelled his gaze sternly at Cassie. 'But what I'm wondering, young lady, is why you're so keen to know. What business is it of yours, the purchases a certain Deacon made?'

Before Cassie could answer, the pickpocket piped up. 'Them's chasing he. I heard they chatting about it on the way here. The Deacon's taken their da hostage or something like that. Them's been looking for he all over, and I be the first real lucky break them's had.' He beamed with pride, as if the small matter of his attempted larceny meant nothing now that he was being so useful.

'Well, there's a thing I never heard of before,' said Barnswallow, stroking his chin. 'These Deacons are a funny lot, eh? Hoo. It's almost as though they're beginning to go crazy, now they don't have a clearly defined role any more. You listen to them preaching at Hundred Ways and their words seem to smack of desperation. So, somehow, it doesn't surprise me to learn that one of them has resorted to kidnapping, or whatever it is he's done with your father. I am surprised, though, that he would be taking him where he appears to be taking him.'

'Him said?' Cassie asked, excited. 'Him told you where them was going?'

'Not as such. I'm merely inferring from his selection of purchases. Hoo. I could be completely wide of the mark, of course. But ...'

Barnswallow paused for a long time, uttering a stream of those peculiar throat-clearing noises. Cassie was afraid he had become stuck and would simply *hoo* and *huhhh* and *hum* from now till he died. She fought the urge to snap him out of it with a kick in the shins.

Finally he said, 'A map of the south. Did I mention that earlier? He bought one of those. A map covering the area from Craterhome all the way down to the shores of the Centric Ocean. That and the snakebite antivenin . . . Yes. Do you see?'

Cassie thought she did.

'Him's going into the desert,' she said.

'Must be,' said Barnswallow.

'The Relentless Desert,' the pickpocket said wonderingly. 'Be him some kind of nutter? Has him got a death wish or what!'

CHAPTER 47

The Power Of The Press

Yesterday, the *Craterhome Messenger* had carried the following headline on its front page:

CRATERHOMERS
ASSAULTED
BY AIRBORN!

The article below began:

A grotesque prank was played on a group of Craterhome residents visiting the sky-city of Prismburg last week.

The incident, which has only just come to light, involved a tour party whose number included several prominent Craterhomers. Among them were two prosperous local industrialists and the undersecretary to the mayor.

In a wholly unprovoked attack, at least a dozen Airborn descended on the tour party and showered them with dirt. The Airborn also hurled racist abuse. They were heard to use such terms as *ostrich* and *emu*, a reference to the legendary flightless birds of those names.

The victims of the attack were unhurt but were left shaken and distressed.

Inside the paper, an editorial piece tried to strike a note of conciliation but could not quite manage it:

This newspaper abhors conflict of any kind and has been a keen promoter of harmonious relations with the Airborn. We praised the Bilateral Covenant and we have openly welcomed the new economic circumstances that exist between the inhabitants of ground and sky.

We even changed our title from *Examiner* to *Messenger* and redesigned our masthead to feature a winged figure, all in the name of fostering closer ties between us so-called Groundlings and those formerly known to us as the Ascended Ones.

However, the recent unpleasant incident at Prismburg (reported on today's front page) has left us fearing that we might be forced to reconsider our views. Although no one was physically harmed, nonetheless this malicious violation of the newly formed trust between the two races leaves a nasty taste in the mouth.

Are we to accept the Airborn leadership's assurances that it was an isolated event, unlikely to be repeated?

Not if stories the *Messenger*'s newsdesk has been receiving from other regions are true. We are aware of at least three separate accounts of similar outrages being perpetrated on innocent visitors to the sky-cities – tourists whose 'crimes' were nothing more than inquisitiveness, and an absence of wings.

Craterhomers are well known for their tolerance and generosity of spirit. This paper would urge the people of our great city not to do anything in retaliation for the indignity committed upon their own kind. Acts of petty vengeance will help nobody.

At the same time, we must not allow the Airborn to feel that further such attacks will be graciously endured. The insult should be forgiven, but not forgotten.

As a point of interest, one of the 'prominent Craterhomers' who was bombarded with soil by the Feather First!ers in Prismburg was a close friend of the owner of the *Messenger*. He, in fact, brought the incident to the newspaper's attention and had a hand in writing the editorial. He sincerely did not want to stir up trouble but he also could not help letting his chagrin show through.

Consequently, the *Messenger*'s readers – the paper had a circulation of some 200,000 – were infected with a similar sense of hurt and indignation. Contrary to the editorial, Craterhomers were *not* well known for their tolerance and generosity of spirit. They seethed at the thought of Airborn treating their fellow citizens with such contempt. The seething had spread through the city, until it became a pulsing undercurrent of anger that ran everywhere, from borough to borough, mansion to tenement, factory to pub.

So when several people spotted a pair of Airborn sporting around above the rooftops, it didn't take long for news of the sighting to travel the length and breadth of the Third Borough. Nor did it take long for an irate mob to form.

Airborn? Right here in the city? Flying about, free as you please?

Time for a little payback.

CHAPTER 48

The Mob

Outside Barnswallow's, the pint-sized pickpocket raced off without so much as a goodbye. Cassie watched him go with a mixture of amusement and pity. She was dismayed that a kid his age was forced to steal to survive. However, he was a sparky little tyke and seemed to relish his precarious criminal lifestyle, and for that she almost admired him.

A moment after the pickpocket vanished around a corner, Barnswallow came puffing out of his shop.

'Which way did he go?' he demanded, looking right and left.

Cassie pointed.

'Little monster! Hoo! Nabbed a handful of cigarette lighters while I was distracted talking to you. I just noticed.' He lumbered off in pursuit of the boy, shouting over his shoulder: 'If I don't catch him, I'm holding you two liable!'

'Then it'm best if us be'n't here when him comes back,' Fletcher said to Cassie with a chuckle.

'Him's a cold-hearted bastard, though, that copper-topped Deacon,' he added as they set off back in the direction of Hundred Ways. 'Even by Deacon standards. Snapping the kid's finger...'

'Da wouldn't stand for that,' said Cassie, firmly. 'Which makes me wonder if him's still with the Deacon.'

'I think him is. I think Da were in the van and didn't see what happened. Also, Barnswallow said him bought *two* shovels and mattocks, remember? Why'd him want two if it were just he travelling alone?'

'Good point. Still, more and more I be thinking them makes

a strange pair, him and Da. What does them have in common? What be them after together?'

'Dunno,' said Fletcher, 'but I reckon us'll see soon enough.'

Locating Hundred Ways again was not as simple as they thought. Streets seemed familiar but weren't. Distinctive urban landmarks were few and far between. One factory or tenement block looked much like another. The two Grubdollars soon became disorientated, and finally found their destination more by accident than on purpose. Once there, it took them a while to identify which of its converging thoroughfares was the one they had originally entered by earlier.

They both observed that the square was half as full of people as before. There were the same number of speakers but they were addressing significantly smaller audiences.

Cassie then became aware of a rumble of noise. It was coming from some distance away, roughly the direction in which she thought *Bertha* lay. This made her apprehensive.

Fletcher had noticed the noise too. 'What'm that?' he wondered, cocking an ear.

'Not sure. Sounds like voices. Shouting. I reckon us should go and see.'

Other people were heading towards the rumble, and Cassie's apprehension deepened as she joined them. No one was running but equally no one was walking. They were all moving at an eager jog, as if summoned towards something exciting.

She quickened her pace to match theirs. Fletcher did so too. Cassie was picking up murmurs around her. One word she kept hearing was 'Airborn', and it was being said in a fierce, sneering way. She knew now beyond any doubt that *Bertha* was at the centre of the source of the noise. This wasn't premonition; it was a horrible logical deduction.

Finally she and Fletcher arrived at the alley where *Bertha* was parked. They had to fight their way through a milling, baying throng to get within sight of her. All around them fists were being shaken and mouths were yelling with spittle-flecked fury: 'Birdbrains out!' 'Back up where you belong, you wingnuts!' 'Fly away home!'

Bertha was totally surrounded. Hands were hammering on her. Some of the mob tried rocking her from side to side but she was too heavy for that, so they swarmed over her instead and began pounding on her windscreen, portholes and nacelle bubbles.

Cassie caught a glimpse of Robert in the javelin turret, peering out with panic in his eyes.

'Come on!' she urged Fletcher.

The alley was packed tight with people. It was hard to make headway through the crush of jostling bodies. Cassie trod on toes, clambered over shoulders, jabbed with her elbows, but even so she struggled to get any closer to *Bertha*. It was like some nightmare where she needed to move but was stuck fast and no amount of effort could help. She knew – *knew* – that the situation, which was already dire, was about to get a whole lot worse. She might just be able to prevent that, if she could make it to *Bertha* in time.

She couldn't, and the dire situation did indeed get worse.

CHAPTER 49

Bertha Besieged

It had happened appallingly fast. Colin was striding the length
of the alley for the umpteenth time, with no less enthusiasm
than when he had started out. Michael and Aurora had returned
to the loading bay, their brief, japesome jaunt over. Everything
seemed calm and normal.

Then Colin saw a half-dozen people appear at the end of the
alley. Then a dozen.

'Oi!' he called out. 'What'm you wanting?' He didn't like the
way they were looking at *Bertha*.

'Be there Airborn in that murk-comber?' one of the people
asked.

'What if there be? What of it?'

The people exchanged looks and muttered to one another,
too low for Colin to catch what they said.

Colin puffed out his barrel chest and flexed his arm muscles.

The people melted away.

Job done, thought Colin.

But a few minutes later they returned, and there were more
of them this time. Many more. They started to stalk towards
Bertha purposefully.

Colin gulped. Not good.

He set off towards *Bertha* at a sprint. He was nearer to her
than the small crowd of Craterhomers were. They broke into a
sprint too, but Colin got to the murk-comber several seconds
ahead of them. He leapt aboard, startling Michael and Aurora,
who were having a nice, cosy cuddle in the loading bay.

'Us has got trouble,' was all he said, and he hit the button to
close the hatch.

The hatch came down painfully slowly. There was still a metre-wide gap left when the frontrunners of the crowd reached *Bertha*. Two of them hurled themselves through into the loading bay, and a split-second later the hatch shut tight with a *clang*.

Colin knocked the first of the intruders cold with a single punch to the head. The other one made for Michael and Aurora with a growl, but Colin grabbed him by the belt and yanked him back, sending him crashing against a bulkhead. The man staggered upright.

He was similarly proportioned to Colin, slightly shorter but no less stocky. He punched Colin twice in the face. Colin shrugged and punched him back twice as hard. Blood spurted from a broken nose. A dislodged tooth went flying. But the Craterhomer didn't seem fazed. With a roar, he launched himself at Colin, arms outstretched.

Michael and Aurora looked on as a brutal fight ensued. Colin and the Craterhomer slammed each other around the loading bay, trading blows. A knee to the groin. An elbow in the stomach. A head butt. Both of them seemed to relish the carnage, baring grins at each other and grunting deliriously as they grappled.

Then an uppercut from the Craterhomer caught Colin under the chin. The legendary thickness of the Amblescrut cranium couldn't protect him there. Colin reeled dizzily, stumbled against a seat, and fell to the floor. The Craterhomer loomed over him. Colin was trying to get up. His opponent raised a leg, ready to stomp his face.

A carton of tinned food came thudding down on the Craterhomer's head. He staggered, his eyes rolled up, and he crumpled like a marionette with cut strings. He landed beside Colin on the floor, unconscious.

Michael dropped the carton, bent down, and helped Colin to his feet.

'I had he,' Colin insisted, between gasps for breath. 'I were just ... lulling he into a ... false sense of security.'

'I know,' said Michael, with a smile.

That was when the hammering outside started, dozens of

fists beating against *Bertha*'s bodywork. Within the loading bay the sound resounded deafeningly. It was like being inside a vast kettledrum.

Robert shouted down through the speaker tube: 'There'm hundreds of they! All over the place! And more coming!'

Furious faces glared in through the portholes. The hammering intensified. Aurora ran to Michael and they clung to each other. Colin, still dazed, bellowed abuse at the mob through the porthole glass. There wasn't much else he could do.

Robert's voice came over the speaker tube system again, now scarcely audible above the thunderous racket.

'OK, it'm OK,' he said. 'I's got a plan. Hang on. Watch this.'

Next moment, there was a colossal

ZZZZZAP!!!

followed by a massed shriek from the mob, then a quieter aftermath of groans and moans and pitiful sobs.

'Oh bugger,' said Robert. 'I didn't mean to press *that* one.'

CHAPTER 50

Trail Of Carnage

Nobody was killed, a small miracle for which Robert would be forever thankful. So many Craterhomers were clustered around *Bertha* that, when he accidentally hit the button to electrify her hull, the charge was shared among all of them. Nobody received a dose of voltage large enough to die from. The people closest to *Bertha* got the biggest shocks, and several of them were knocked senseless and suffered superficial burns. The people touching those people were stunned but unharmed. The worst that happened was that their hair shot straight upwards and stayed that way for hours. Further outwards, members of the mob leapt and yelped, but more in surprise than pain.

To Cassie, it was like watching a small earthquake sweep out from the murk-comber, losing strength as it spread. People fell, jumped or twitched according to how far they were from the quake's epicentre. By the time the electricity touched her and Fletcher there was scarcely any power left in it at all. Cassie felt nothing more than a nipping sensation in her palms, which were pressed between the shoulderblades of the person in front of her. Bee stings hurt worse.

She saw her chance.

'Now!' she said, grabbing Fletcher by the wrist.

While the mob was still reeling from the electric jolt, Cassie lunged towards *Bertha*, dragging her brother behind her. They shoved some of the Craterhomers aside and stepped on others, and within seconds they were standing below the driver's pod, which stuck out from *Bertha* like a head on a neck.

A short metal ladder hung from the pod's underside, leading to the access point. Fletcher gave Cassie a boost. She climbed the three rungs and grasped the recessed handle above her. A half-turn clockwise and three half-turns anticlockwise unlocked the access point. It dilated, triangular steel plates retracting with a scraping screech. Cassie hauled herself inside. Fletcher leapt for the ladder and followed her in.

The mob was beginning to stir. People were recovering their wits and stoking up their anger afresh.

Cassie slipped into the driving seat and fired up the ignition. *Bertha* cackled into life. Cassie honked the horn long and loud to warn everyone to get out of the way. She gave them five seconds to do so, then engaged gear.

The mob scramble-tumble-dived clear of *Bertha* as she moved forwards. The murk-comber sliced through the crowd like a plough through soil. The mob shoved themselves up against the walls of the alley and clambered on top of each other to avoid her, or else scattered ahead of her, spilling out into the street at the end.

Soon *Bertha* was in the street too and trundling along at speed, slewing this way and that as her tracks slithered and freewheeled on the cobblestone roads. Cassie didn't much care what *Bertha* hit, as long as it wasn't a person. Her sole concern was leaving Craterhome as fast as possible. Thus a greengrocer's stall was overturned, strewing fruit and vegetables everywhere; a barrel organ got flattened; a stack of baskets containing live chickens received a glancing blow and freed birds fluttered briefly into the air, clucking and squawking; and there was a glancing, sidelong collision with a tram which dislodged that vehicle from its tracks and sent it skidding into a piece of municipal statuary, a stone effigy of one of the city's foremost sons, a long-dead field-marshal who had commanded his army to victory a century ago in the War of Intervention between the Westward Territories and the Axis of Eastern States. The tram shunted against the statue's plinth, and the field-marshal and the horse he was riding slid forwards and landed nose-down on the cobbles. Both broke into chunks.

Cassie winced and drove on. What else could she do? Stop and say sorry?

Shortly afterwards she arrived at a stretch of dual carriageway. Signs pointed a way out of the Third Borough and out of Craterhome. Cassie joined the road, entering the flow of traffic which was heading for one of the tunnels between boroughs. Just before she reached the tunnel, a light on the dashboard came on. It indicated that the loading bay hatch was opening.

'What'm you doing down there?' she asked through the speaker tube, as she applied the brakes.

'Just getting rid of some excess cargo,' Colin replied.

In a rearview mirror Cassie saw him dump the limp form of a man onto the roadside. Seconds later, a second man was dropped out the same way.

'There,' said Colin. 'Much lighter load now. On you go.'

Cassie shoved the control sticks forward and *Bertha* rolled on into the tunnel. In roaring darkness she switched on the floodlights.

The tunnel was two kilometres long. Now at last there was time to think.

And all she could think was: *the Relentless Desert.*

A vastness of rocks and sand, howling winds and lethal wildlife.

A huge, hostile emptiness at the heart of the Westward Territories.

And somewhere in it – who knew where? – was her father, and with him the finger-breaking, knife-carrying Deacon.

Fletcher, crouching beside her, picked up on his sister's mood. 'Things be looking up,' he said.

'How d'you reckon that?'

'Out in the desert there'm only a limited number of roads them can travel on. So our job be that much easier now.'

'What if them doesn't stick to roads, though?'

Fletcher gave the dashboard a pat. 'Where can them go in a half-tarp that a murk-comber can't go better and faster?'

It was a tiny crumb of comfort but Cassie took it and fed on it as though it were a feast.

Desolation Wells, A Final Time

Night after night Magnus Clockweight watched the skies, waiting for the airship to return.

Night after night it failed to appear.

Had he and the other roughnecks won? Had they really driven the pirates off?

His men certainly thought so. They were swaggering around, crowing about their victory over the Airborn. They'd shown those winged raiders a thing or two. You didn't mess with Groundlings and get away with it.

Clockweight himself wasn't so confident. He insisted that the flamethrower truck remained at the ready and he posted night-time lookouts around the perimeter of the installation. The men called him over-cautious, but he wasn't taking any chances.

The desert had taken care of the burned Airborn bodies. Scavenging animals, hackerjackals most likely, had picked the remains clean. All that was left was a few chewed bones.

Clockweight didn't believe the pirates would let these deaths go unpunished. The leather-clad woman, their leader, had struck him as forceful and ruthless. Even though he had had only the briefest contact with her, he knew she was someone not to be taken lightly.

That was why, although the pirates had not yet got around to taking their revenge on Desolation Wells, he was sure it was only a matter of time until they did. And that was why he was formulating a back-up plan to defend the installation.

The day before yesterday he had sent out a couple of men in a company dune-buggy, with a map and precise instructions.

Clockweight knew of a rumour, one that had circulated in this region for decades. He had no idea if the rumour had any basis in truth or not. The mission of the two men was to find out either way.

Strange stories abounded in the Relentless Desert. An area like this – largely uncharted, mostly uninhabited – was rife with tales that stretched credibility, tall stories of the sort that travellers loved to tell. There were unexplained disappearances, isolated tribal communities surviving through cannibalism, valleys haunted by ghosts and ghouls, holes in the ground which were the lairs of giant fire-breathing termites, lakes of quicksand which shifted from place to place as though alive, that sort of thing.

This particular rumour could just be one of those.

But if it wasn't, it might hold the key to combating the pirate airship, and so it was worth investigating.

Another night had fallen, and the two-man search party had not yet returned. Clockweight was expecting them back soon. They'd be here by tomorrow at the latest. Unless, that was, they had fallen foul of a giant fire-breathing worm or a roving quicksand lake!

Clockweight prayed that the black airship would not make its reappearance tonight. If the pirates were to hold off for just a couple more days, he and his men might have a better chance of fighting back.

But his prayer, alas, was not answered.

Around midnight, *Behemoth* descended from the clouds.

Directly above Desolation Wells.

One of the lookouts spotted her. Scarcely had he raised the alarm, when an object fell from the airship's rear hatch.

It tumbled lazily, like it had all the time in the world. It was an oil barrel, and there was a bright white flame at one end of it, sparking and sputtering – a fuse.

The barrel hit one of the storage tanks and exploded.

A split-second later the storage tank itself exploded. A million litres of crude oil ignited at once. The fireball was the size of a city block and illuminated the desert landscape for kilometres around. The thunderclap of detonation was loud enough to burst eardrums.

Then the adjacent storage tank went up. Another city-block-sized eruption of fire tore the night air apart. The shockwave shattered every pane of glass on the site that hadn't been shattered by the first explosion. It also blew the installation gates clean off their hinges.

Men ran out of the housing blocks. They scurried this way and that like ants whose nest had been stamped on. Deafened, dazzled, dazed, they didn't know where to go. Clockweight tried to marshal them, directing them towards the fleet of tanker trucks. He knew Desolation Wells was doomed. Fire was everywhere. The inferno at the storage tanks was spreading to the refinery and the drilling towers. Lesser explosions thumped all around, one after another. The only sensible course of action was to abandon the installation.

But the pirates had anticipated this. *Behemoth* turned towards the area where the trucks were parked. Another of those home-made oil-barrel bombs was jettisoned from her rear hatch. It landed in the midst of the trucks. The ground rocked as it blew up. Most of trucks were destroyed instantly; the rest caught light and burned to charred wrecks.

Clockweight ordered the men to head for the desert. He could barely make himself heard above the roar of flames. The air was searing-hot and filled with black, choking smoke. Clockweight grabbed workers by the scruff of the neck or gave them a kick up the backside. Get moving! Get out! Go!

To venture into the Relentless Desert after dark, on foot, was the next best thing to suicide, which was why many of the men hesitated even though the installation was coming down around their ears. They had an ingrained fear of what lay out there beyond the perimeter fence. Nevertheless, it was certain death to stay put. They hurried towards the gates, with Clockweight urging them along every step of the way.

Behemoth hadn't finished with them, however.

Gliding serenely above the blazing chaos on the ground, she dropped three further barrel bombs. Each was aimed at the fleeing WOE employees. Each found its mark.

Men died screaming. Some were incinerated on the spot. Some ran with their clothes and hair afire, like human torches. They rolled on the ground and beat at themselves to put out the flames, but with little success. The lucky ones got away with patches of scorched flesh and blistered skin. No one was left unscathed.

Behemoth performed a circuit of the installation, as if gloating over the devastation she had wrought. Here and there, fresh fires were breaking out. Gouts of flame shot upwards. A derrick keeled over with a huge crash, like a dying dinosaur. A drilling tower collapsed in on itself. Smoke billowed. Flame-light cast everything in an eerie, pulsing yellow.

Finally the airship lofted her nose and slipped up into the clouds.

Down on the ground, a safe distance from the immense, twisting funeral pyre that had been installation number 137, Clockweight gathered the survivors together and counted heads. Barely fifty remained alive, out of a workforce of almost two hundred.

Before dawn, twenty of those fifty succumbed to their injuries. They shuddered and gasped on the sand, and there was nothing their toolpusher or anyone else could do except watch them expire, slowly, in agony.

Clockweight himself had lost most of the skin off his left arm and cheek. One eyebrow had been singed off. He was dizzy with pain and shock.

But even as Desolation Wells was reduced to an expanse of smoking rubble, a fire of a different kind was kindled in his belly.

CHAPTER 52

Two Pieces Of Very Bad News

She couldn't get it out of her thoughts. She tried to dismiss everything Lord Urironson had said to her, and couldn't. His words had bored into her brain and were gnawing at her like a worm.

Every corridor Lady Aanfielsdaughter walked down, every shaft she flew through, every room and chamber she entered, she felt that she was being surreptitiously watched. People she passed glanced at her then glanced away again, furtive. Anyone who greeted her seemed to mean more than he or she actually said. Every *hello* and *how are you?* seemed pregnant with implication. Even friends and close confidants were wary around her, or so she felt. Their talk was guarded, as though there was a lot they had to say but they were holding their tongues for fear of upsetting her.

She thought she heard whispering behind her back. At times she thought she heard giggling.

No matter how often she told herself she was being silly and paranoid, she just could not shake the notion that Lord Urironson was right. The mood around the Sanctum was uneasy, jittery. People were worried, and they blamed her for it. No one accused her directly of anything. No one came out and said what they were feeling. But she could see it in their eyes.

Not everyone perceives tolerance as weakness, Farris, she had said.

Many do, Lord Urironson had replied. *Not least in this very city*.

The situation wasn't helped by the arrival of two pieces of very bad news from the ground.

In the city of Craterhome there had been an incident involving two Airborn. Reports were sketchy but it appeared that a rabble of locals ganged up on the Airborn and some kind of retaliation occurred, resulting in a number of minor injuries among the Groundlings. Something to do with a murk-comber.

Lady Aanfieldsdaughter wasn't sure what to make of this story but some instinct, some intuition, told her she knew the people concerned. There were plenty of murk-combers around. This one didn't *have* to be the Grubdollars'. Yet somehow she was convinced that Cassie's family were mixed up in the affair.

The other piece of news was that Westward Oil Enterprises had lost all contact with installation number 137. Telegram messages weren't reaching it. Truck shipments of refined oil had stopped coming from it.

There was cause to be alarmed, the WOE executives said.

Lady Aanfieldsdaughter concurred.

Every hope she now had was pinned on *Cerulean*. If Az and Mr Mordadson failed in their mission, her position at the Sanctum was in jeopardy but, more importantly, so was the entire fledgling relationship between Airborn and Groundlings.

She waited for some good news to come from Redspire.

And waited.

CHAPTER 53

Dangers Of The Relentless Desert:
A Field Guide

It was a hard journey.

Once civilisation petered out and there was only desert, the roads dwindled to dirt tracks (and frequently were not even that). There were gravelled patches where the bigger potholes had been filled in; otherwise it was just a bumpy, rock-strewn surface all the way. Now and then the edges of the road blurred into the surrounding terrain so that it was almost impossible to tell where one ended and the other began. Now and then, too, the rusted hulks of trucks loomed at the roadside, half buried in sand, testament to the desert's power to conquer even the sturdiest means of transport.

The half-tarp kept trying to join the ranks of those abandoned trucks, breaking down an average of three times a day. Dust would clog up the engine air intakes, or the radiator would overheat, or sand would get into the brake cylinders and jam a wheel. The van was not at all suited for this kind of environment. But Den kept it going. His skills as a mechanic were repeatedly put to the test but each time he rose to the challenge and triumphed.

On one occasion he was lying on his back beneath the van, plugging a crack in the oil sump, when he felt something touch his ankle. It was a brushing, tickling sensation.

Immediately he froze. 'Gerald?' he said softly. 'You there?'

Deacon Hardscree was standing at the rear of the van, taking sightings with his compass while also keeping an eye out for predators. 'Yes.'

'There'm something on my foot.'

Hardscree went round to where Den's legs were sticking out from under the van.

'Well? What be it?'

Hardscree's answer was barely a whisper. 'Don't move, Den.'

'I be'n't moving.'

'Stay like that.'

'All right, but what be it?'

No reply.

The tickling sensation grew worse. Something was exploring the skin around his ankle – something small with sharp little claws or feelers.

Den was very frightened. All at once he was sweating from every pore and his mouth had gone bone-dry.

For what seemed like ages, nothing happened. He couldn't see Hardscree and he began to wonder if the Deacon was actually doing anything.

Then there was a scrabble of activity, a thud, a wet squelchy sound, and finally the words he had been longing to hear: 'It's OK now. You're safe.'

He slithered out, to find Hardscree holding up a hunting knife. Impaled on the blade was the ugliest creature Den Grub-dollar had ever clapped eyes on. It was so loathsome it made a verm look like a cute fluffy kitten.

'Scorpipede,' said Hardscree.

The thing was still alive, thrashing and writhing around on the knife. It was a handspan in length from end to end and had four sets of pincers, a dozen little blue-black eyes like elderberries, and a segmented body with a pair of legs on each section. Its abdomen tapered then forked into three tails. Each tail had a barbed, semi-transparent bulb at the tip and each bulb contained a venom of a different colour: one yellow, one red, one black. The venoms were dripping out through the barbs and splattering uselessly on the ground. Thick dark goo was oozing down the knife blade from where it pierced the scorpipede's thorax.

'It uses a particular venom according to its prey,' said Hard-scree, gesturing at the tails. 'Yellow for other insects, red for reptiles and black for mammals. Each is designed to kill that particular species in an instant. You, for instance, would have been injected with the black stuff, and it'd've stopped your heart in a few seconds. Ingenious creature, really.'

'Maybe so,' said the scorpipede's intended victim, 'but I'd be happier if that "ingenious creature" were a lot more dead than it be now.'

'Of course.'

Hardscree flicked the scorpipede onto the ground and crushed it underfoot.

'Nice knife, by the way,' said Den, mopping his damp forehead with his sleeve.

'Isn't it? I was given it by my father when I turned twenty-one.'

'You Uplanders. It'm all weapons and hunting with you lot. Surprised you still carry it, though, being as you'm a Deacon and all.'

Hardscree grinned. 'You can take the boy out of the mountains but you can't take the mountains out of the boy. Now, how are the repairs coming along?'

'Should be done soon.' Den crouched down to crawl back under the van. He paused to check there weren't any more scorpipedes lurking in the vicinity, then nodded at the knife. 'Best keep that handy, eh? Just in case.'

Hardscree wiped the blade clean on his robe. 'Don't you worry, Den. You're far too valuable for me to lose you.'

There were plantlife hazards as well as wildlife hazards in the Relentless Desert. Early the next morning, after breakfast, Den went off in search of a place to relieve himself. A large clump of bushes seemed the ideal spot, providing shelter and a little bit of privacy – until he heard the Deacon call out, 'I wouldn't go there if I were you.'

'Why not?'

'Weltwort. Releases a puff of caustic mist when disturbed. We have a similar species in the Uplands. It burns like the blazes and the blisters last for days. All you have to do is brush against it and you'll get a squirting.'

'Ah. Understood.'

Den tiptoed delicately around the weltwort bushes and found somewhere else to do his business, far away from any vegetation.

Not all the difficulties they encountered were living ones, either. Late one afternoon a sandstorm of staggering ferocity rose up, engulfing the half-tarp and shaking it so viciously that driving became impossible. There was no alternative but to pull over and wait for the storm to pass.

It raged for an hour, buffeting the stationary van and its occupants. Den watched particles of sand etch tiny scratches in the windscreen glass. Every so often the van felt as though it was about to be plucked off the ground and sent rolling over and over. Somehow it stayed put.

While the sandstorm was at its height, a grim-faced Hardscree said, 'You must be wondering right now whether any of this is worth it.'

The thought had crossed his companion's mind. 'I don't known which'm tougher,' Den replied ruefully. 'Getting to where us is going or the fact that I had to leave my kids behind and keep they in the dark about it all. I's never deceived they before in any way.'

'It was necessary. We both agreed on that. You wouldn't want them to face these risks you're facing.'

'But if I dies out here and them never knows what became of I ...'

'We aren't going to die, Den.'

'You sound pretty certain.'

'Trust me,' said Hardscree, with a skewed smile. 'I'm a Deacon.'

'But what if, after everything, this place us is looking for – what if it don't exist?'

'It does.'

'But you's never seen it. You's never been there.'

'Deacon after Deacon has told me about it over the years. It's an open secret among our fraternity.'

'And you really believe the stuff that'm kept there be what us needs?'

'I do. I believe it's "stuff" that will pave the way to a better tomorrow. It will put us on a fairer footing with the Airborn. It will enable us and them to interact as equals – true equals. It's our race's best chance of safeguarding our future. You see, Den, as long as the Airborn look down on us, literally look down on us as well as figuratively, we're never going to be more to them than something unpleasant beneath their feet. Rather like that scorpipede of yours. Something they'd much rather squash than embrace. But we, you and I, can change that, and will.'

Den thought of Az, the one Airborn he knew at all well. The lad wasn't the type to look down on anybody. But then Az wasn't representative of his kind, was he? He was himself looked down on by other Airborn. So there was no reason to think the rest of Az's race weren't just as Hardscree described. After all, they'd spent centuries not even acknowledging that Groundlings existed. They had lived off the sweat of Groundling backs, conveniently forgetting who it was that was making their lives so easy for them. Now, everyone on the ground was meant to be thankful for no longer being taken for granted – but the fact was, Groundlings were giving away as much of their material wealth as ever, and receiving just trinkets and knickknacks in return. It wasn't right.

All the way from Grimvale through Craterhome to here, Hardscree had quietly but insistently reiterated these arguments. He'd claimed his proposed solution would work. It would be the first step towards evening up the scales, which were at present heavily weighted in the Airborn's favour.

Den was once more convinced. Even with the sandstorm still battering away at the half-tarp, he felt a renewed firmness of purpose. He had already decided he liked this Deacon. Now, more than that, he was starting to admire the man.

The sandstorm ebbed and subsided.

With the shovels and mattocks purchased from Barnswallow's Practical Goods Emporium, the two men dug the van's wheels out from the drifts of sand that had banked up around them. Den cleaned out the air intake filters, yet again.

The journey across the Relentless Desert continued.

CHAPTER 54

Absence Of Evidence

Redspire, unsurprisingly, was red and consisted of lots of spires.

Legend had it that you couldn't accurately count the spires. Anybody who tried to ended up with a total that was either one more or one less than the previous total somebody had arrived at.

Legend also had it that Redspire was the first of the sky-cities to be built. Or the last. One or the other.

What was certain about Redspire was that it lay at the extreme southern tip of the Western Quadrant. It was the remotest sky-city. It stood at the very edge of the Airborn realm.

An outlier, Az thought. *Like me*.

Then he told himself to shut up. He was determined not to think about Gyre, outliers, or anything connected with the Ultimate Reckoner's so-called prophecy. He shunted all such thoughts to the back of his brain and left them in the darkness there to wither and die.

So: Redspire.

Like a huge scarlet pincushion.

No, like an upturned hairbrush with hundreds of bright red bristles.

Whatever it resembled, there it lay, dead ahead. Destination. Journey's end.

And *Cerulean* was approaching it at low speed, with an escort of Alar Patrollers around her. This was a necessary precaution as well as a show of strength. No one knew what to expect from Redspire. No one had any idea what sort of reception *Cerulean* would receive.

'I don't see any airship,' observed Rigz, scanning the city.

'She could be berthed on the far side,' Az said. 'That's why we're going to do a circuit.'

Cerulean was also going to fly once around Redspire to let all the inhabitants know she was there.

It took half an hour to complete the orbit of the sky-city. The Alar Patrollers maintained perfect formation the whole way. They flew in V-shaped units, seven men per grouping. Wing Commander Iaxson used shouts and a whistle to keep them tightly together. He didn't allow any Patroller to deviate more than a metre from position. It was configuration flying at its finest and most precise.

No airship could be found. Redspire's civic landing apron had the usual complement of single-seater planes, airbuses, cargo transporters, helicopters, autogyros and private passenger craft, but nothing that even remotely resembled a lighter-than-air troop carrier.

'You don't suppose this was all a false alarm?' Az asked Mr Mordadson.

'No, I do not,' came the thin-lipped reply. 'Absence of evidence is not evidence of absence. Let's move in and dock. The airship may not be here but someone in the city will know where she is.'

CHAPTER 55

A Huge Collective Hangover

The silence was eerie. The whole of Redspire appeared to be asleep. Or worse.

Az, Mr Mordadson, Wing Commander Iaxson and a trio of Patrollers padded across the landing apron, waiting for someone to hail them and ask what their business was.

No one did. The landing apron was populated only by parked aircraft. There wasn't a living soul in sight. The Patrollers gripped their lances, looking around, wary and uncomfortable.

'Eleven-thirty a.m.,' said Mr Mordadson. 'You'd have thought there'd be *somebody* up and about.'

They ventured further into the city. Everywhere, there were indications that Redspire was usually an inhabited, bustling place. Shops, though shut, had merchandise on display in their windows. Municipal fountains gurgled. The greenery in public parks had been tended to, more or less.

Yet, for all these signs of normality, no people. Where were they?

Finally, on a triangular plaza suspended between three spires, people were sighted.

Three men and two women lay sprawled together in a heap. Their heads touched and their arms and wings were thrown around one another.

Dry-mouthed, Az asked, 'Are they . . .'

'Dead?' Mr Mordadson stepped closer to the jumble of bodies, sniffed, then straightened up again. 'No. Dead drunk. Look.' He pointed to a litter of empty wine bottles strewn around the slumbering figures. 'They've been having quite a party.'

'Want us to wake them up?' asked Iaxson.

'Why not?'

The Alar Patrollers took great delight in prodding the sleepers with their lances.

'Come on, you lazy lot!'

'Wakey-wakey, rise and shine!'

Soon all five were blearily on their feet and standing in a dishevelled line. Mr Mordadson flashed his Silver Sanctum seal and started interrogating.

It turned out that not just these five but the whole of Redspire had been carousing the night before. Apparently, this wasn't uncommon. Roughly once a month Redspire went on a massive bender. The city's population danced and drank from dusk till dawn, then spent all of the next day in a state of disarray, nursing a huge collective hangover.

'How nice,' said Mr Mordadson. 'Do these celebrations commemorate anything in particular?'

'No,' said one of the bloodshot-eyed citizens with a shrug. 'We just like to do it.'

'Tradition,' said another.

'What about your kids?' Az asked. 'What happens to them while the grown-ups are boozing themselves into a stupor?'

'Where are your wings? Are you a Groundling?'

'No, I'm not. Now answer me.'

'Our kids? We keep them up. They're usually so exhausted by morning that they sleep late, so their parents get a lie-in too, much needed. Now, is that everything? Only, my head's killing me and I'd really like to close my eyes and get a bit more kip, if you don't mind.'

'Oh, that's definitely not it,' said Mr Mordadson. 'I have plenty more questions to ask. However, out of respect for your delicate condition, I'll confine myself to one. Where's the airship?'

All five of the Redspirians shuffled their feet and fluffed their wings. None was keen to answer.

'Come along,' said Mr Mordadson. 'You all know what I'm talking about. But it appears I'm not speaking clearly enough. Perhaps it would help if I RAISED MY VOICE SLIGHTLY.'

In fact, he shouted these words, and the five Redspirians flinched and grimaced. Loud sounds were unpleasant when you were suffering the after-effects of too much alcohol.

'SO?' Mr Mordadson went on. 'WHICH OF YOU IS GOING TO TELL ME ABOUT THE AIRSHIP? EH?' He was yelling right in their faces. 'OR WOULD YOU LIKE ME TO **REALLY TURN UP THE VOLUME?**'

'All right, all right,' said one of the women, clutching her brow as though trying to prevent her brains from spilling out. 'Please. We'll tell you anything. Just ... please keep it down.'

'It's all Naoutha's doing,' said another of the five. 'Naoutha Nisrocsdaughter.'

'Her and her gang,' said another. 'They're the ones to blame.'

'Interesting,' said Mr Mordadson. 'Explain.'

Between them, haltingly, the five did.

CHAPTER 56

Prodigal Daughter

Redspire had long harboured a grudge. Because it was so far from anywhere else, it always felt neglected and overlooked. It felt that the rest of the Airborn race didn't care about it and preferred to pretend it didn't exist.

The city was fine with that, mostly. It took a perverse pleasure in being on the fringes, isolated and ignored. That was why it would do things like hold mammoth monthly parties – to show how little concern it had for conventional behaviour and the niceties of polite society. It regarded the other sky-cities as a snooty club to which it had no desire to belong. They rejected it, it thought, so it rejected them in return.

All the same, deep down, Redspire resented the way it was sidelined and disregarded. It had a long list of complaints, many of them legitimate grievances. For instance, every time one of its citizens applied to join the Silver Sanctum, he or she was turned down (the reason usually given was 'irreverent attitude'). And then there was the fact that Redspire alone, of all the sky-cities, did not receive supplies from the ground and therefore had to rely on imports from its neighbours. For this it was charged a steep mark-up, which was justified on the grounds that everything had to travel a long distance and there were transport costs. However, goods exported out of Redspire fetched the same prices as those from anywhere else. Was that fair? No, it was not.

Redspire, then, was in a dilemma. It yearned for respect and proper treatment, but at the same time couldn't bring itself to act in a responsible manner which would guarantee those things.

The city's sense of injustice was sharpened when the presence of Groundlings was acknowledged officially and the Bilateral Covenant was signed. Suddenly Redspire was having to pay a further premium on incoming supplies of daily necessities, to compensate for the amount the other sky-cities were now having to pay.

That was when Naoutha Nisrocsdaughter decided to take matters into her own hands.

Naoutha was a rebel even by Redspire standards. One of that rare minority born with black wings, she had been insolent as a child and a hopeless tearaway as a teen. By the time she reached adulthood she was completely out of control, and had gathered a gang of like-minded types around her, a good forty or fifty of them. While the city was content to enjoy a major shindig once a month, Naoutha and friends made it their goal to drink and be merry every single night. They were troublemakers and vandals, and the city had tried its hardest to tame them but without success. You just couldn't control Naoutha. All her life she had stood out thanks to those black wings. She had been bullied at school because of them and had learned to fight back. She had embraced Redspire's outcast ethic and taken it to the next level. She was a source of eye-rolling despair to most people, but those who admired her, admired her ardently. Her young band of followers worshipped the air she flew through. They were disciples as much as partying pals. She ruled them, and they loved her and would do anything for her.

Not only that but they were into pterine.

Pterine was a recreational drug, a stimulant derived from a hormonal secretion contained in the gall bladders of eagles. Powerful stuff, it sharpened the reflexes and increased the body's strength and endurance. While its effects lasted it was like having an extra set of wings. You felt wonderful. Invincible. Indestructible.

It was terribly addictive, of course. It was also terribly expensive. Naoutha and her gang got into pterine in a big way and, since none of them was any good at holding down a job, they needed to find some other method of funding their habit.

That was when they started making trips to the ground.

Having learned there were people down there after all, Naoutha spied a commercial opportunity. She started to go exploring, and more often than not her gang went with her. They descended in aircraft and overcame ground-sickness through sheer willpower, or so they claimed, although it was reckoned that they medicated themselves with pterine beforehand to armour themselves against the worst symptoms of the condition. Either that or their hard-partying ways had increased their tolerance to dizziness, nausea and fatigue.

They returned with extraordinary tales of what they found down there in the vicinity of Redspire. Largely they found wilderness – vast tracts of uncultivated land, rugged, barren, intimidating. There were pockets of Groundling habitation, but these were few and far between. The rest was just emptiness.

Then one day they came back with an airship.

She was old and decrepit. That she could fly at all was nothing short of a miracle. Naoutha and co. managed to get her up to Redspire, just. They refused to say where they had found her. Instead, they set to work fixing her up. They toiled zealously, patching the holes in her balloon canvas, reconditioning her ailing engines, and replacing her broken propeller arms with new ones they forged themselves. They scavenged and borrowed the materials they needed. They spent weeks making the airship as good as she had ever been, and then, doubtless as a tribute to Naoutha's wing colour and peculiar dress sense, they painted her matt black all over, adding the black-on-red skull and crossed feathers motif to her tailfins.

It was safe to assume that the airship must be a troop carrier from the wartime era, although nobody knew which one she was or how she had survived when all the rest had been decommissioned. The only clue to her origins was the sky-city insignia on her tailfins. Before being covered with Naoutha's own emblem, the fins had sported the colours of Brightspans.

Whatever the airship had been called formerly, Naoutha had dubbed her *Behemoth*, and that seemed as good a name as any.

In *Behemoth*, Naoutha and her gang took off one evening and weren't seen again for several days. When they sailed home, they brought with them a substantial cargo of timber and coal. They offered this to the city for a reasonable sum, less than the usual asking price for such items, and the city, reasonably, bought it. No questions were asked. Among Redspire's officialdom the opinion was that Naoutha had struck a deal with some Groundlings somewhere. That was what they told themselves, at any rate. They were getting a bargain, so they didn't want to dwell too hard on the matter of where the stuff was coming from or how Naoutha had obtained it.

They felt the same way when *Behemoth* came back with a consignment of steel.

And, even more so, when she came back with barrels of fuel.

Above all else, Redspire was pleased that Naoutha appeared to have mended her ways. She and her gang were still into pterine, but that aside, they had transformed themselves into enterprising individuals who wanted to help out their hometown. Naoutha was coming good after all. The prodigal daughter had become a proper Redspirian.

That said, she had not been seen for nearly a week now. It was assumed *Behemoth* was off scouting for further supplies; Naoutha was trying to locate more Groundlings to do deals with.

And that was everything the five hung-over citizens knew about the airship and its crew.

Or almost everything.

CHAPTER 57

The Aircraft Mausoleum

'What if I told you this Naoutha of yours wasn't buying these supplies but *stealing* them?' said Mr Mordadson. 'What would you say to that?'

The five Redspirians exchanged looks. Then one of them said, 'Well, it would explain why you're here with Patrollers.'

'Stealing?' said another. 'For real?'

'But you knew all along,' Mr Mordadson said. 'There's no point trying to act surprised. You didn't want to think it, you certainly didn't want to say it aloud, but you knew. Your city had got a nice little black-market thing going, so nobody was willing to ponder too deeply on the whys and hows.'

'Didn't the local Alar Patrol get even a tiny bit suspicious?' Iaxson asked. 'I'd have thought they would have questions even if no one else did.'

'This is Redspire,' came the reply. 'We barely have an Alar Patrol.'

'The bats,' said another of the five, with a sheepish grin. 'That's what we call them, bats. As in blind as. Because they never quite manage to see any crimes happening.'

'They're bribed to be that way,' said a third. 'No one really wants the Patrollers sticking their beaks into other people's affairs. A little extra cash in their wage packets every month makes sure of it.'

'It's our system,' said a fourth. 'It's always worked OK.'

Iaxson scowled and spat. 'Yes, that makes sense. A place like this gets the policing it deserves.'

The five nodded in agreement, as if the wing commander had spoken approvingly.

Mr Mordadson turned to Az. 'What do you reckon? Do you think we've been given enough information to find this *Behemoth*?'

'Not really, but I don't feel we're going to get anything else useful from this bunch.'

'You may be right. I fear even shouting at them again won't help.'

One of the men said, 'For what it's worth, I bumped into one of Naoutha's gang recently and we had a brief chat. It was in a bar, as a matter of fact.'

'In a bar,' said Mr Mordadson, deadpan. 'Why am I not shocked?'

'This was shortly before *Behemoth* last went off,' said the Redspirian, unfazed. 'This guy was there in the bar along with a few of his mates. They stand out because they dress pretty outlandishly. Silks, scarves, brocade waistcoats, beads in their hair, plenty of leather. That's on top of all the tattoos and piercings they already had.'

'Playing at being pirates,' said Mr Mordadson, with a sneer. 'And still no one stopped to think, "Hang on, where are they getting this stuff they're selling to us so they can buy their next pterine fix? Can their source really be legit?"'

'Do you want me to tell you this story?'

'Oh, yes please. Do proceed.'

'So anyway, it so happened that we were ordering drinks at the same time,' said the Redspirian, 'and I told the guy what a good job he and the rest had done with that airship, fixing it up the way they did. It's not as if there are airship maintenance manuals you can just buy in any bookshop, are there? And he scratched at the scabs on his face – pterine scabs, they all get them if they use it too much – and then said, "Labour of love. Plus, we improvised a lot."'

'Is that it? What a charming anecdote.'

'No, that's not it. I'm trying to remember how the conversation went after that. He started going on about how he used to be a professional aircraft mechanic but got the sack because his boss said he was unreliable. And he said he did most of the repair work himself, with the others helping. They didn't want to but Naoutha bullied them into it, telling them she'd withhold their pterine if they didn't make themselves useful. You can work extra hard if you're on pterine. You can also work extra hard if your pterine supply is under threat.'

'I almost admire the woman,' Mr Mordadson commented drily.

'So then I think I said something like, "So why's it such a big secret where you got the airship from?" And the gang guy said – now I remember, his name's Abuzaha Biletson – he said, "It's only a big secret because we don't want anyone else finding the place." I said, "Why not?" and Biletson said that there were other items there which he and his friends might like to use in future so they wanted to keep the place's whereabouts to themselves.'

'Go on.'

'So I said, sort of making a joke, "Come on, you can tell me." I thought maybe I'd pushed it too far and he would just clam up, but he was pretty far gone and he did reveal something about the place. He used the phrase ... oh, what was it?'

The Redspirian racked his aching brains. Mr Mordadson struggled to contain his impatience.

Finally the man said, 'An aircraft mausoleum. That was it. I'm sure that was how he described it.'

'An aircraft mausoleum.'

'Right, and he said it was this weird mix of junkyard, museum and, you know, tomb. Then his drinks arrived and that was the end of the chat.'

'Biletson didn't give any clue where this place was? Direction? Distance? Anything?'

'Somewhere south, that's all I know. Quite a way south, I think.'

Mr Mordadson sighed. 'Fair enough. It's a lead, although not much of one. I'd like to thank all of you for being such fine upstanding citizens. You're a credit to your race. You can collapse now.'

With grateful groans the five Redspirians sank to the floor.

CHAPTER 58

The Fate Of The Brightspans Empress

'Brightspans,' said Az as he, Mr Mordadson and the Patrollers made their way back to *Cerulean*. 'Then the airship would have to be the *Brightspans Empress*.'

'You think?' said Mr Mordadson.

'Stands to reason.'

'The *Brightspans Empress*,' said Iaxson. 'Rings a faint bell. How come she wasn't decommissioned like the rest?'

'She was meant to be,' Az explained. 'She was on the list. But her captain was a sentimental old sort, couldn't bear the thought of her being torn apart and sold for scrap, so shortly before the decommissioning was due to begin he hijacked her. That's if you *can* hijack your own airship. At any rate, he and a few other crewmen sneaked into the breakers' yard and made off with her. Then they abandoned her somewhere far out from the airlanes, letting her fly off unmanned into the sunset while they went home in another aircraft. She was never seen again, so presumably she must have gradually lost height, sunk through the cloud cover and floated to the ground more or less intact. Of course nobody knew back then that there were people down there. The captain just thought he'd rather see her go all in one piece, with some dignity. I can see his point. I'd feel the same way about *Cerulean*.'

'Did he get into trouble?'

'He certainly did. He was stripped of his rank and pension and had his pilot's licence torn up. Same with his accomplices. They ended their careers in disgrace. But even so, I bet they thought it was worth it.'

'And now the *Brightspans Empress* is back,' said Mr Mordadson, 'and under the control of a bunch of pterine-heads.'

'Yup,' said Az. 'So what's our next move?'

'Fancy a trip below the cloud cover?'

'Not much,' Az replied, 'but I reckon we don't have a choice.'

CHAPTER 59

The Maze

Bertha loved the desert. This was her kind of terrain. This was what a murk-comber was built for.

The cruder and more uneven the roads became, the deeper and throatier *Bertha*'s cackle grew. She hadn't been particularly happy on ordinary roads, asphalt too smooth and slippery for her liking, and she hadn't relished the cobbles of Craterhome at all. Here, though, with grit and sand and sprigs of scrubby vegetation beneath her tracks, she thrummed along, kicking up a joyous cat's tail of dust in her wake.

Her good mood wasn't shared by most of her passengers.

Robert was in the doghouse with Cassie after the incident at Craterhome. No matter that it had been an accident, his sister still couldn't get over the fact that he had electrocuted all those people, including her and Fletcher. She suspected that there had been no serious casualties and thought Robert had been very fortunate in that respect. She appreciated, too, that he had been frightened and flustered. Nonetheless it had been a grave mistake, and she was sure there would be unwelcome consequences for the Grubdollars further down the line.

Meanwhile, as a result of the same incident, Colin had become insufferable. It didn't take much to give an Amblescrut a swollen head. The clan had an inbuilt streak of pride which emerged at the least excuse. In Colin's case, he couldn't stop bragging about protecting Michael and Aurora, his 'Airborn pals', from the two Craterhomers who'd got into the loading bay. Each time he told the story, the fight became longer and more violent. In addition, he could not forget that Michael had saved him at the last moment, so some of the slavish devotion which he felt for Den Grubdollar was now transferred to Michael. He kept badgering Michael to reminisce about the fight. He felt that the pair of them had been bonded by battle.

'Be'n't it amazing?' he said. 'You and me, Mike, us comes from different worlds, and yet us is so close now. Like brothers. Brothers in arms.'

Michael found it highly irritating. Aurora found it highly amusing, at least to begin with, although she, too, grew weary of Colin's incessant chatter. It didn't help that she appeared to be suffering from a slight touch of ground-sickness again. She complained of feeling faintly nauseated but told Michael not to make a fuss or bother Fletcher about it. She was sure it would pass and she would re-acclimatise soon.

With Cassie annoyed at Robert and with tension in the loading bay, Fletcher took on the role of cheerleader, trying to keep everyone's spirits up. From the driver's pod or his observation nacelle he would deliver droll, sarcastic comments about what he saw outside. 'Oh look, there'm another rock,' he would say, or 'Interestingly, us is passing another large patch of sand.' Sometimes he managed to raise a weary laugh or two.

All of them could feel it, however, as they voyaged further and further into the desert – a mounting sense of futility, of despair.

The Relentless Desert was huge, its vistas impossibly distant. The emptiness was relieved by an occasional outcrop of boulders or a towering mesa, here and there a scrubby shrub or some kind of twisting cactus, and perhaps the hollowed wreck of a vehicle. But otherwise it was a flat expanse of brown nothing beneath a similarly flat expanse of sullen grey sky. Being in the middle of it was like being sandwiched between two immense voids.

This landscape stared in through *Bertha*'s portholes and windscreen. It stared into her passengers' hearts and oppressed them.

The roads were straight and monotonous, long scratches in the sand that extended from horizon to horizon. Sometimes a junction would appear without warning, a two-way fork marked by a metre-high cairn of stones. There was never a signpost.

There was just a choice: right or left. It was up to whoever was at *Bertha*'s controls at the time to make the decision. Then, soon, the junction would be far behind and the road had become another straight stretch virtually indistinguishable from the last.

At each turning, *Bertha*'s passengers knew they weren't getting anywhere, even though the junctions gave the illusion that they were. Simply, they were driving around in a vast maze whose layout they had no conception of. Somewhere else in the maze was Den Grubdollar. In trying to find him, they were becoming lost.

They kept going regardless. They had to. They had come too far to give up.

With *Bertha*'s cackle as encouragement – their only encouragement – they travelled on.

CHAPTER 60

The Smoke Pillar

It was Robert who spotted the smoke, and in doing so he managed to redeem himself in Cassie's eyes.

'Hey! What'm that over there?'

Cassie peered. All she could see was a tiny, curving black line like an apostrophe on the eastern horizon.

'Don't know,' she said. 'Looks like smoke. Some kind of bonfire or cooking fire, maybe.'

'Worth investigating?'

'Definitely. Those'm some sharp eyes you's got there, little bro.'

Robert felt a warm glow. It was the first nice thing anyone had said to him in four days.

Cassie steered off-road, making a beeline towards the smoke. *Bertha* growled with glee as she tackled terrain that was even bumpier and rougher than before.

Soon it became clear that the source of the smoke wasn't some minor conflagration. Distance had made the size of the smoke pillar hard to judge. In fact it was massive, bridging the gap between earth and sky. Its dimensions were those of the column of a sky-city, although of course it lacked the smoothness, straightness and solidity, and its head flattened and fanned out as it hit the clouds, dispersing into them like ink into water.

On board *Bertha* there was speculation as to what was generating the smoke. Whatever it was, Den and the Deacon might have seen it too and gone in for a closer look. The smoke was visible from a long way away in all directions. Anyone who caught sight of it would be drawn in, out of curiosity if nothing else.

Shortly another road appeared ahead. It arrowed straight towards the smoke, with a line of telegraph poles running alongside which from a distance looked like a stitch sewn across the desert. Cassie drove onto it.

A large metal sign by the roadside read:

WESTWARD OIL ENTERPRISES
EXTRACTION AND REFINING
INSTALLATION
137

At the bottom someone had added, in slapdash paint:

DESOLATION WELLS

Half a kilometre further on, the road ended at a tall chainlink fence, the perimeter of an enclosure covering several hectares of land.

Much of the fence lay flat on the ground. Beyond was a scene of devastation.

Ruined buildings.

The shattered, charred remnants of cranes and steel-girder towers.

Storage tanks like huge, cracked-open eggs.

And everywhere, fires. Small ones, large ones. Some were low and pulsing like furnaces, others jetted into the air like geysers. Each sent up a plume of smoke which merged together overhead with the others to form the single billowing pillar.

Cassie halted outside the entrance to the installation. For a while no one aboard *Bertha* dared speak. They all looked out at the carnage in awestruck silence.

Finally Fletcher said, 'What be this? How did it happen? Were it an accident or what?'

'Dunno,' Cassie replied, 'but I vote us should get out and look for survivors.'

CHAPTER 61

Bodies

The three Grubdollar siblings put on the retrieval suits which were still stowed aboard *Bertha* even though they hadn't been needed in over a year. The last time any of them had worn one of the suits was when they discovered Az out in the Shadow Zone, being pursued by verms. Since then there hadn't been any Relic-hunting for the Grubdollar family and the suits had lain in their lockers getting musty and creased. Cassie felt a pang of nostalgia as she wriggled into hers. The stiffness of the padding and the coldness of the chain-mail gloves evoked a purer, happier time in her life. Even the helmet, with its narrow slit of a visor, felt somehow cosy.

Michael insisted on coming out to help. Aurora did, too. Her mild dose of ground-sickness had eased and she was feeling more like herself again. They took off and flew in criss-crossing patterns to reconnoitre the area. Meanwhile Cassie, Fletcher and Robert trudged on foot through the entrance to Desolation Wells. The installation's gates were lying several metres from where they should have been, tangled and twisted like crumpled paper. Colin, in the driver's pod, tooted *Bertha*'s horn to let everyone know he was there if they needed him.

Even through the retrieval suit's padding Cassie could feel the heat of the fires. The acrid stench of the smoke was thick in her nostrils, despite the helmet. She and her brothers roamed the site, keeping clear of the largest and fiercest of the various infernos. They didn't come across any survivors but they did see dead bodies – twisted, half-cremated forms which only just resembled human beings. Cassie flashed back to Martin's burned remains. The memory made her horror that much greater but also filled her with compassion for the dead people, whoever they were. She felt as though she knew them. They weren't just strangers.

Every so often she checked the sky to see if Michael and Aurora had found anyone alive. Finally she spotted Aurora waving to Michael. He flew to his wife's side, looked down to where she was pointing, then soared over to the Grubdollars.

'Over that way,' he said. His eyes were red and streaming from the smoke. His mouth was hard and sombre. 'I've got to warn you, though. It's not pleasant.'

'Be'n't all that nice here either,' Cassie replied.

With Michael leading them, the three Grubdollars trooped back out of the installation and headed for the spot above which Aurora was hovering.

On the ground, in a neat row, lay twenty or more bodies. These were not as severely burned as the ones inside the installation. They had, however, been left there for at least a day and were starting to bloat and putrefy. Their limbs were contorted with rigor mortis, their eyes were pale and bulging, and their skin bore a hideous purple-black mottling. Even worse than the sight of them was the smell. Cassie got no closer than ten metres from them, and still the stench was atrocious. Her helmet did nothing to keep it out. Bile rose in her throat. It was an effort not to retch.

'Someone laid they out,' Fletcher said. 'Them didn't die in the fire, them died out here afterwards.'

'So there *be* survivors,' Cassie said. 'Just not here. Them's gone on somewhere else.'

'Stands to reason. And, hey, look over there.' Fletcher indicated a patch of ground not far away. A large quantity of pebbles had been set out, carefully arranged to form words. It was a message, accompanied by an arrow pointing off towards the south-west.

Before Cassie had a chance to go over and read it, however, she was distracted by a shout from above.

'Down there!' Michael yelled. He was gesticulating wildly at something he could see, and the Grubdollars couldn't, on the other side of a nearby ridge.

'What be it?' Cassie called up.

'I don't know. I don't have a name for it. I've never seen anything like it. But there are lots of them and they're coming fast.'

A sudden coldness filled Cassie's gut.

'Run,' she said to her brothers. 'Run like you's never run before.'

Moments later, a pack of dog-like animals came bounding into view.

Hackerjackals.

CHAPTER 62

Attack Of The Hackerjackals

The hackerjackals would have smelled the roughnecks' corpses sooner and come to eat them, but the smoke and fire had confused their senses and scared them away from the area. Only now had they plucked up the courage to return.

The alpha male, the pack leader, was the first of them to catch a whiff of rotting meat in the air, and with a soft yelp he conveyed this information to his wives, offspring, cousins and the couple of young pretenders who had attached themselves to the pack and would one day fight with the alpha male in the hope of usurping him and becoming the new dominant member. As one, the pack moved off, following the scent trail. With the alpha male at the fore, they homed in unerringly on the gorgeous, delicious odour of death-decay. Bellies rumbling, mouths slavering, they gouged furrows in the desert sand with their sickle-like claws. The black hackles along their spines bristled with eagerness.

Eagerness turned to joy as the hackerjackals crested the ridge of rocks and spied not just dead creatures but living ones too. There was only thing hackerjackals liked more than the taste of carrion, and that was the taste of freshly killed prey. To wrench flesh from bone while it was still springy and moist, to lap up blood as it poured hotly from torn veins – this was truly heaven.

With bloodlust lighting up their pus-yellow eyes, the pack hurtled past the row of dead humans, making straight for the three who were alive.

The three Grubdollars, naturally enough, had no desire to be chomped on, and turned and fled from the hackerjackals as fast as their legs could carry them. The bulkiness of the retrieval suits hampered their progress. Nonetheless they ran, skidding, slithering, arms pistoning, thinking only of getting to *Bertha* and safety.

Above, an alarmed Michael and Aurora knew they had to help. They might never have laid eyes on a hackerjackal before but they recognised a carnivorous predator when they saw one. They'd watched kestrels dive on sparrows, hawks sink their talons into pigeons. These large, fanged mammals were the same, just without feathers.

Michael folded his wings and plunged towards the hackerjackal at the front of the pack. His feet collided with its back, slamming it flat on the ground. The hackerjackal shrieked, rolled over, and leapt up snapping. Michael just managed to hoist himself out of range in time. The hackerjackal's teeth clacked on empty air.

Aurora came down too and kicked one of the hackerjackals in the side of the head. It responded by pouncing at her with its claws outstretched. It slashed a hole in her shirt, missing her skin by mere millimetres.

The hackerjackals were quicker and tougher than the Airborn newlyweds had anticipated.

They were also a whole lot smarter.

The alpha male yipped, giving orders. Two of the larger bitches broke away from the pack. One went after Michael, the other Aurora. Snarling, fangs bared, they sprang at the winged humans, driving them backwards and higher and higher into the air.

The rest of the pack bounded on after the non-winged humans.

Cassie's frantic, panting breaths echoed inside her helmet. She didn't know if the retrieval suits would protect her from the hackerjackals' wicked claws and finger-length fangs, and she didn't want to find out. The suits were designed for dealing with verms, whose teeth were comparatively small and whose claws were blunted from burrowing. The beasts pursuing her and her brothers looked like they'd have no difficulty tearing the padding apart. Even the helmets and the chain-mail gloves might not deter them.

Bertha still seemed far away. Cassie was sprinting with all her might and the murk-comber somehow didn't get any closer. She prayed that Colin would see what was going on and would start *Bertha* up and drive to meet them. It was perhaps their only chance. A swift glance over her shoulder told her that the nearest of the hackerjackals was now less than twenty metres away. It was the biggest of the pack and it moved with a sinewy grace and purposefulness. Its eyes met Cassie's, and she saw a horrible intelligence in them. In that moment it seemed to lock onto her, making her its sole target. Cassie had the impression that this hackerjackal, obviously the leader of the pack, had singled her out as the leader of *her* small pack. Therefore, out of a sense of symmetry, it had resolved that it ought to be the one to eat her.

She dug deep inside herself, finding an extra level of speed. Robert was just behind her, Fletcher just behind him.

She was aware of a scream building in her throat.

Colin! she begged mentally. *Colin! See we and start the bloody engine!*

CHAPTER 63

Banjo Musings

Colin was sitting with his feet up on the dashboard. He was picking at a scab on his knuckle, a legacy of the punch-up in the loading bay. He was humming the tune of a folksong one of his quarter-brothers liked to play on the banjo ('My Heart's Been In The Coal Pit Since My Girlfriend Got Her Wings' was its title). He was thinking that he would like to learn the banjo himself one of these days. He was thinking that he would like to do a lot of the things which he never actually got around to doing.

Colin was supposed to be monitoring the situation outside, in case the Grubdollars got into difficulties. But then Amblescruts were not famous for the length of their attention span.

Then something – a flicker of motion at the periphery of his vision – prompted him to glance up.

Next second, he was scrambling to hit the ignition.

Unfortunately Colin didn't know *Bertha* like the Grubdollars did. She didn't always fire at the first attempt, unless you leaned on the ignition switch for just the right amount of time. Panicked, he gave her too little juice. Then, when he tried again, he gave her too much. Both times *Bertha* spluttered but didn't start.

Third time, he got it right. *Bertha* roared. Colin shoved the control sticks fully forwards. *Bertha* ground dirt and accelerated skiddingly.

'Idiot!' Colin berated himself as he made for the Grubdollars and the ferocious canids that were pursuing them. 'Numbskull! Moron! Poop-for-brains! Mule-head! Useless, woolgathering, all-the-sense-of-a-cheese, dribble-mouthed dingbat!'

No amount of self-recrimination, though, was going to make up for lost time or get *Bertha* to go any faster. Judging by the Grubdollars' speed compared with that of the animals, Colin estimated they had less than five seconds before the animals caught up with them. And he was at least half a minute from reaching them.

CHAPTER 64

Joining The Airborn

Robert felt himself being grabbed from behind and knew he'd had it. The hackerjackals had caught up with him. He had a strange sensation of being lifted, his feet parting company with the ground. Everything was syrupy-slow and surreal, as in a dream. He waited for the pain, the crunch of hackerjackal teeth sinking into his neck, the agonies of death. Maybe it had already happened. Maybe he'd already been attacked and killed, and this feeling of lightness was his soul slipping free from his body and Ascending. People said that often when you died violently, you didn't feel a thing. Shock numbed you. You drifted away.

So this was it. He was going up into the next life. He was going to join the Airborn, if that was what really happened.

Then, at the corner of his restricted field of vision, Robert glimpsed Fletcher. His brother was beside him, rising into the air too. But that was because Michael had his hands locked under Fletcher's armpits and was carrying him.

Belatedly Robert realised that he himself was being carried in the same fashion, by Aurora.

He looked down and saw Cassie was on her own, still running, with the entire hackerjackal pack at her heels, bounding after her.

Then he was borne over his sister's head, in the direction of *Bertha*. He could feel Aurora was struggling with the extra weight. The two of them kept dipping downwards, and then Aurora would grunt as she strained to haul them aloft again. Michael seemed to be having similar difficulties with Fletcher, and Fletcher wasn't helping matters by thrashing around in Michael's clutches. Faintly Robert heard his brother yelling at

Michael: 'Put I down! Get Cass! Don't worry about I! Cass!'

They flew over a rift in the ground, a jagged scar that had been carved in the earth by a river, long since dried up. It looked to be about seven or eight metres deep. *Bertha* lay on the other side. Aurora was almost sobbing with effort as she covered the last stretch to the murk-comber. She deposited Robert on *Bertha*'s roof, then collapsed beside him in a heap, heaving for breath, wings limp.

Michael dropped Fletcher beside them, and instantly flipped around in midair and made his way back towards Cassie.

She was just a couple of strides from the rift. The hackerjackal pack was almost on top of her.

Michael was exhausted from carrying Fletcher. He flapped as hard as he could, but everyone, including him, could see that he wasn't going to reach Cassie in time.

CHAPTER 65

Try Or Die

The rift had to be at least five metres across. Cassie didn't know if she could leap such a distance, even with a run-up. She didn't think it mattered. There was no choice. It was try or die. If she turned left or right along the edge of the rift, the hackerjackals would catch her. Straight over was the only way.

The thumping lollops of the hackerjackals' paws rumbled behind her. Ahead, on the other side of the rift, Cassie could see *Bertha*, with Aurora and her brothers safely on the roof. Michael was flying towards her.

Reaching the rift, she didn't hesitate. She kicked off with her right foot and launched herself into space.

She made it.

She didn't make it.

One moment, her left foot landed squarely on the far edge. The next moment, the ground gave way, her leg shot from under her, and she was slithering helplessly downwards.

She caught herself with her arms. Her chain-mailed fingers clawed for purchase in the crumbly soil. Her toecaps dug frantic grooves in the sheer wall of the rift. There was an immense thump as one of the hackerjackals hit the edge of the rift right next to her. It had jumped after her but its leap fell short. It tumbled down into the riverbed, rolling end over end and hitting the bottom with a yelp. When it tried to get up, it stumbled and whined. One of its hindlegs was broken.

All the other hackerjackals stopped at the rift. All but one. The alpha male swiftly assessed the situation, turned and took a short run-up. Its leap was more successful than that of its over-eager packmate. It touched down gracefully on the other side, next to Cassie, and spun round.

Cassie was still trying to fight her way out of the rift, but the bulkiness of her retrieval suit hampered her movements. In fact, it was all she could do just to stop herself sliding further down.

The alpha male seemed to feel it could take its time. It padded over in an almost leisurely fashion and lowered its muzzle to Cassie's face. The slit of her helmet visor was filled entirely with the sight of two rows of fangs. The creature's teeth slotted together almost perfectly, a solid mesh of lethal sharp ivory, glistening with saliva. The hackerjackal's breath was like a gust of wind from hell.

'Hold on, Cassie!' Michael yelled. But he sounded like he was a million kilometres away.

Cassie closed her eyes. There was only one thing for it.

She let go of the rift's edge and fell.

CHAPTER 66

Out Of The Blue ...

On top of *Bertha*, Fletcher was kneeling beside the javelin turret with his arm thrust into the slot through which the javelin launcher protruded. He was trying to grab one of the spare javelins that were racked at the back of the turret. It was futile, he knew, but he had to try and do *something* to help Cassie. Reaching in as far as he could, he managed to brush the shaft of the topmost javelin with his groping, gloved fingers. He almost had it – then he dislodged the javelin from its mounting and it rattled onto the turret floor.

He howled with frustration.

'Fletch ...' said Robert softly.

'I can do this,' Fletcher said. 'Shut up. Let I do this.'

'No, Fletch,' said Robert, tapping him on the shoulder. 'Look. Just look.'

Something in the tone of his brother's voice made Fletcher turn. Robert's gaze was directed straight upwards. Aurora's was too, and there was a hint of a smile on her face.

Smile? thought Fletcher. *How can her smile at a time like this?*

Then he became aware of a sound – a sound he recognised. A steady, reverberating drone.

Overhead, casting a huge shadow before it, was the very last thing Fletcher would have expected to see and perhaps the very best thing he could have hoped to see.

Huge, stately, graceful, descending ...

Cerulean!

And out from the airship, uniformed men were pouring in a stream. Alar Patrollers.

Lances poised, the Patrollers descended on the hackerjackals at the rift's edge. One after another they hit the pack. One after another the hackerjackals were impaled with lance-thrusts. They squealed and yelped as they died. Some of them retaliated, leaping at their attackers, but the Patrollers quickly learned to stay out of range. Their lances were long enough for them to be able to inflict fatal wounds with minimal risk to themselves.

It was brisk, efficient, methodical slaughter, and Fletcher was overjoyed to see the hackerjackals getting their comeuppance.

Finally the hackerjackals' collective spirit was broken. Pack unity gave way to panic. The few surviving beasts scattered in all directions, and the Patrollers gave chase, picking them off individually.

Fletcher surveyed the scene of carnage that was left behind. Dead and dying hackerjackals lay strewn alongside the rift. One of them snapped angrily at the blood-gushing hole in its own flank. Another struggled to walk, but with each trembling step more of its entrails spilled out from its ripped-open belly and dragged behind it in a clump.

He searched for Cassie, but could see no sign of her.

Where was she?

And where, for that matter, was Michael?

CHAPTER 67

Down In The Rift

The alpha male hackerjackal escaped the cull.

It did this simply by plunging after Cassie. Digging its talons into the side of the rift, it slid and skidded downward in a reckless headlong rush. It ended up at the bottom in one piece, with a landslide of loosened earth and stones spilling behind it.

Its packmate with the broken hindleg crouched nearby, whimpering. The alpha male strode past, pausing only to tear out the other hackerjackal's throat with a single, almost casual snap of its jaws. An instinctive habit. A wounded hackerjackal was no use to the pack. Better off dead.

The alpha male homed in on Cassie, its eyes glowing like lamps in fog.

Cassie lay stunned on the floor of the rift. Her retrieval suit had protected her from serious harm, but her slithering, precipitous descent down the wall of the rift had left her bruised and shaken. She wanted to get up but neither her arms nor her legs seemed to have any strength in them.

The alpha male knew it had been overconfident before, when the human pack leader had been clinging onto the edge of the rift for dear life. Then, it had let its prey get away. It was not going to make the same mistake twice.

With a low, hungry snarl the hackerjackal bent its head over Cassie's neck and opened its maw wide.

'No!'

Michael came crashing down feet-first on the beast's back.

Last time, this had worked for Michael, knocking his victim flat. But that hackerjackal had been one of the smaller members of the pack. The alpha male was much larger and stockier, a

hefty brute, and scarcely seemed to feel the impact. With startling speed, it turned and lashed out with a forepaw.

Michael cried out as the talons raked his calf. The pain was
blinding, red-hot. He flew up several metres, blood pattering
down from his leg onto the hackerjackal's spine bristles. The
alpha male, with a kind of rolling shoulder shrug, lowered its
head again over Cassie and gave a growl. This was unmistakably
a sound of gloating satisfaction. *No more interruptions*, it said.
Now you're mine.

Michael's intervention, however, had alerted Cassie to the
danger she was in. A rush of fear lent her the co-ordination she
needed. Her hand found a rock the size of her fist. She swung
it round with all her might, slamming it into the hackerjackal's
snout.

Blood spurted. Fangs splintered. The alpha male yowled and
recoiled.

Cassie drew the rock back for a second strike.

Then there was a *whump* of wings and the hackerjackal shot
into the air.

The beast gave an almost comical yelp of surprise as it
hurtled vertically upwards, suspended by its hindlegs.
Cassie had a glimpse of the person who was carrying the
hackerjackal aloft, and was surprised to see that it wasn't
Michael. She saw dark clothing, close-cropped hair and ...
crimson spectacles?

Up they went, Mr Mordadson and the upside-down dangling
hackerjackal, zooming up out of the rift, shooting skyward,
heading for the clouds. Now they were 100 metres high, now
150, now 200. By the time the startled animal had gathered its
wits enough to bend round on itself and start snapping at Mr
Mordadson's hands, the two of them were at least 250 metres
above the ground.

The alpha male didn't seem to realise that it was putting its
own life at risk by attacking the human who was holding it. All
it wanted was to make him let go.

For reasons of self-preservation as much as anything, Mr
Mordadson did just that.

The hackerjackal plummeted to the desert, howling and flailing the whole way.

The impact was loud and wet and messy, a great blood-spattering *thud* which cut short the hackerjackal's cries, and also its life.

Mr Mordadson floated down into the rift and landed beside Cassie, brushing his palms together.

'Cassie,' he said. 'It is Cassie inside that outfit, isn't it?'

Cassie nodded.

'Are you all right?'

She nodded again.

'Then come with me. There's someone who'd like to say hello to you.'

CHAPTER 68

Reunion #1

Az folded his arms, unfolded them, put his hands in his pockets, took them out again, leaned against a bulkhead nonchalantly, decided this didn't work, and was still trying to figure out what sort of stance he should adopt as Mr Mordadson ushered Cassie into the control gondola.

In the end, instead of looking in any way cool or casual, Az stood there, arms hanging by his sides, and said, simply, 'Hi.'

Cassie, with her retrieval suit helmet tucked under one arm, said 'Hi' back.

'So,' Az said. He was conscious of the presence of the crew. They weren't looking at him but he knew they were listening. If only this meeting could have taken place somewhere else, somewhere private. But Az had thought that it might impress Cassie, seeing him in the control gondola, in an obvious position of authority. He realised he should have known better. She was never the type to be easily impressed.

'It's funny,' he said, after an awkward silence.

'What'm funny?'

'Me saving you from a pack of wild animals. It's like the first time we ever met, only with the roles reversed.'

'Except,' Cassie pointed out, 'it were Mr Mordadson and those Patroller fellows who saved we. Not you.'

'Let's not split hairs. If I hadn't spotted *Bertha* when I did, and then you, you'd be those creatures' lunch by now.'

That came out sounding more brutal than he intended.

'What were those things anyway?' he asked in a placatory tone of voice.

'Them's called hackerjackals.'

'Nice name. Sounds like the way they look.'

'You wouldn't think it so nice if them was chasing you.'

'I wasn't saying *they* were nice. I just meant the name is — Oh, never mind.'

Az told himself he wasn't going to get spiteful or peevish. He had every reason to be annoyed, he felt. Cassie had treated him unfairly and now, against all odds, here they were, the two of them, reunited. They had run into each other in the middle of nowhere, he had saved her life (or at any rate *helped* save her life) and she was repaying that by continuing to be as difficult and defensive as she had been during their last few get-togethers. She could at least have said thank you. Was that too much to ask?

But then he looked at her, at her tousled, chunkily-cut hair, her large brown eyes, the soft contours of her face, and he remembered everything that he liked about her – her courage, her humour, the kindness that lay just beneath that couldn't-care-less exterior, the way she used to touch him, how it felt to kiss her and be kissed by her . . .

He remembered all of that, and knew he couldn't bear a grudge.

'We don't have much time, I'm afraid,' he said. 'We have to get back above the clouds soon before everyone on board starts feeling unwell.'

'Yeah,' Cassie said, and in that single syllable Az heard, or thought he heard, a profound sorrow for all the things that divided him and her. It was more a sigh than a word.

It gave him hope.

'Yeah,' he said, echoing her tone. 'We're hopping up and down, you see, spending a few minutes below the clouds every hour. We're searching for someone. Or rather, some*thing*. Another airship.'

'I thought *Cerulean* were the only airship in service.'

'So did I. So did we all. But apparently not. Somehow, some Airborn have got hold of another one. They're a bad lot and they're using the airship to raid the ground. We suspect this may be their handiwork.' He indicated the smouldering ruins below. 'That's why, as soon as we saw the smoke, we came in for a look.

We thought they might still be here. And instead we found you.'

'Quite a coincidence,' Cassie said.

There's no such thing as coincidence, Az thought, then cursed himself. The Count of Gyre had really got inside his head, hadn't he?

'Maybe,' he said. 'The smoke was pretty hard to miss, though, and we couldn't ignore it. I assume it's what brought you and your family here too.'

'To this spot, yes.'

'Why *are* you here, by the way? I mean all the way out here in this wasteland. We're a long way from Grimvale.'

'Us has . . . reasons.'

Az waited for her to elaborate. 'But you're not going to tell me them,' he said, when she didn't.

'It'm a private matter,' Cassie said.

'Right. I see.'

Mr Mordadson coughed. 'Sorry to butt in, but I'm curious. Just wondering, Cassie – do you know anything about the raids this airship's been doing? Have you heard about them?'

'Honestly, no. Until now I hadn't heard a thing. But that'm not saying much. I's been kind of busy with other stuff lately.'

Az hated it that Cassie seemed much more comfortable speaking to Mr Mordadson than to him.

'So your reasons for being out here would have no connection with our mission?' Mr Mordadson said.

'Not as far as I be aware.'

'Fine,' said Mr Mordadson. 'Only, if you told us what you were after, perhaps we could help.'

'Doubt it. Besides, you's got this big, important mission you be on, whereas us has just a little personal business to take care of, that'm all. No need to waste your time on we.'

'We'd like to help, Cassie,' Az said, taking his cue from Mr Mordadson.

'I'm sure you'd like to,' she replied curtly, 'but you can't.'

Az lost patience. He'd had enough of Cassie's surliness. He was about to give her a piece of his mind – but then someone else entered the control gondola.

'Little brother!'

CHAPTER 69

Reunion #2

Michael? Michael as well?

'I don't believe it,' said Az.

'Me either,' said Michael. He came limping across the control gondola to brace his brother by the shoulders and give him a loving shake. 'But here I am. And here you are. How you doing?'

'Not bad. What's up with your leg?'

'This? A scratch. One of those beasties got me. Aurora bandaged it up. She did a good job.'

'Aurora's here too?'

'Why shouldn't she be? We are on honeymoon after all.'

Michael filled Az in on his and Aurora's decision to stay for only one night at Heliotropia, then spend the rest of the time travelling on the ground.

'You lied to us,' Az said, amazed but also admiring.

'We didn't want anyone worrying, specially not Mum and Dad. And as honeymoons go, this one's certainly had its worrying moments. Hasn't it, Cassie?'

She nodded.

'So you're the reason *Bertha*'s here,' Az said. 'You're exploring the desert. You're the "personal business" Cassie's taking care of.' He glanced at her, looking smug.

'Huh?' said Michael. 'No. That's not it. Actually, we're searching for her father.'

'Her . . .'

Now it was Cassie's turn to look smug. 'Don't know everything, do you, Az?'

'But . . .' Az floundered. 'Why didn't you just say so, Cassie? Why be so secretive?'

'Maybe it be'n't the same for you Airborn, but for we, family deals with family stuff. No one else gets involved.'

'Michael's involved. Aurora's involved.'

'Yes, well, them made we an offer us couldn't refuse.'

'*I'd* have got involved, if you'd asked me. What's happened to Den? Where is he?'

Cassie explained as briefly as she could. Az could see that it hurt her to admit to the breakdown within her family. Her pride was strong, he thought. So strong that she found it hard to allow herself any failure. So strong that she automatically spurned offers of assistance from anyone but her immediate kin.

'Ahem.'

This came from Flight Lieutenant Wallimson.

'Yes?' Az said. He had been trying to figure out if there was anything he could do for Cassie. Given that *Cerulean*'s goal was stopping the pirates, he doubted he could be sidetracked from that. The mission came first. He couldn't see any possible overlap with the hunt for Den Grubdollar.

'The last of the Patrollers are back on board,' Wallimson said. 'I hate to break up the happy meeting, but if we don't get up above the clouds again soon, we're going to have a ship full of very ground-sick people.'

'Of course. You'd better head back down, Cassie. Mike? What about you? Do you want to come with us or stay with the Grubdollars?'

'Haven't asked the missus,' Michael said, 'but I imagine we'll carry on with the Grubdollars for the time being. If I know Aurora, she'll want to see this through to the end. I know I do.'

The parting was over with quickly, a few goodbyes, then Michael and Cassie were gone. Az watched his brother descend with Cassie in his arms. Michael strained against gravity with laborious downbeats of his wings. He looked exhausted by the time he alighted close to *Bertha* with his dense-boned cargo of Groundling.

'Set a course for the clouds,' Az told his crew.

He kept his gaze fixed on the tiny figures below until *Cerulean* nudged up into the cloud cover and the ground disappeared in a white haze.

CHAPTER 70

The Shape

During *Cerulean*'s turbulent ascent through the clouds, Flight Lieutenant Wallimson had his second glimpse of a large, dark *something* out there in the whiteness.

His first glimpse had come during *Cerulean*'s last but one trip through the layer of vapour. Since Wallimson was not assigned to any particular station in the control gondola, his duties as flight lieutenant consisted of keeping lookout at the viewing windows. Two hours ago, as the airship was bumping downward for yet another recce of the ground, he had spied a vague shape, a distant dim blot, roughly elliptical in outline, a few degrees off starboard.

He had been about to say something but held his tongue. The other crew members were concentrating on their controls and instruments, and the 'skipper' was busy doling out commands. Wallimson had felt he was better off not mentioning the shape. He had probably imagined it anyway. It had appeared fleetingly, there one second, gone the next.

The second time, he was certain he was not imagining it. Although the shape flitted into view for just an instant, Wallimson knew now that his eyes were not playing tricks on him. This wasn't some optical illusion brought on by the juddering of the airship or the roiling of the clouds or even mild ground-sickness. There was definitely a murky, elliptical silhouette out there, and Wallimson had absolutely no doubt what it was.

Report it?

Again, he nearly did. He was minded to. For everyone else's sake, he knew he ought to have.

But then he had, just a few minutes earlier, witnessed a

nauseating display of friendliness towards a Groundling. He'd watched Az, Mr Mordadson and Az's brother all speak to that Groundling female as though she were their equal and in some way worthy of respect. They'd grovelled to her, in fact. That ... that *ostrich* had had them behaving in a manner that was wholly unbecoming of their race.

Traitors, that was what they were. And Az Gabrielson, he was the worst of the lot.

Whereas the pirates ...

Flight Lieutenant Wallimson was forming the view that the Redspire pirates, far from being renegades or criminals, were a credit to the Airborn. They knew exactly how to treat the Groundlings. None of this pussyfooting around, no 'please', no 'thank you', no squandering money on supplies, no pretending the two races were the best of chums now. They went down, took what was rightfully theirs, and that was that. And if the pirates *were* the ones who'd destroyed that oil refining place, they had clearly had good reason to.

All in all, he was thinking he had more in common with them than he did with the bleeding-heart, Groundling-loving do-gooders aboard *Cerulean*. If the opportunity arose, he would gladly defect to the other airship and join the pirates' cause.

So, although he was sure *Behemoth* was stalking *Cerulean* through the clouds (and he was the only one aboard *Cerulean* who realised it), Wallimson kept the information to himself.

Life, he thought, was about to get rather interesting.

CHAPTER 71

But What Of The Roughnecks?

With Desolation Wells destroyed, Magnus Clockweight and his men were left facing a stark choice: stay put and wait for help, or find some means of transportation and get the hell out of there.

Staying put was not really an option, not in the Relentless Desert. A rescue mission would surely be mounted, once the WOE executives realised that contact with the installation had been lost. But who knew how long it would take for the rescuers to arrive? The desert might finish off the roughnecks long before help came.

So a brave team of volunteers, led by Clockweight himself, ventured into the still-burning installation. They foraged for food and found some, but their main task was to see if any motor vehicles had escaped the catastrophe.

Somehow, a few had.

Desolation Wells possessed a fleet of eight dune-buggies. These were short-range vehicles intended for use in and around the installation. For instance, visiting geologists would go prospecting in them, looking for fresh oil deposits in the vicinity, and the workers themselves employed them to get from one corner of the site to another quickly.

One of the dune-buggies was already spoken for, of course. Clockweight had no idea what had become of the two men he had sent out in it on a search expedition. He hoped they were OK but was beginning to fear the worst.

Three of the remaining seven dune-buggies were damaged beyond repair.

That left four workable, serviceable vehicles. Clockweight

and team drove them through the installation, avoiding piles of rubble and the gouts of flame flaring from decapitated wellheads. Avoiding, too, the corpses of friends and co-workers.

The roughnecks outside the installation were delighted to see their toolpusher emerge through the gateway in a dune-buggy, accompanied by volunteers driving three others. They did have a chance of getting back to civilisation after all.

But then Clockweight confronted them with an offer.

'Us can run home, tails between our legs,' he said, 'or us can get our own back on the buggers who did all this to we.' And he explained how.

While the workers deliberated, who should turn up at that moment, as if on cue, but the two men whom Clockweight had begun to despair of ever seeing again?

They were breathless, wind-burned and dust-caked. Once they had got over the shock of seeing what had happened to Desolation Wells, they were only too happy to announce that their expedition had been a success.

'Us found it!' one exclaimed.

'Can't believe it'm there, but it be!' said the other.

'Us looked but didn't go in, toolpusher, as per orders.'

'But if outward appearances be anything to go by, it'm huge. Huge!'

Clockweight turned to the thirty-odd survivors. 'Up to you, lads,' he said. 'No shame, whichever way you decide. Home, or vengeance? Let's put it to a vote.'

The vote was passed without objection or abstention.

Vengeance.

Immediately Clockweight told his men to gather up pebbles. They would leave a message for the rescuers, telling them where they had gone. Using the stones, Clockweight laid out five words on the ground not far from the bodies of his fallen comrades:

GONE SOUTHWEST
LOOK FOR NEEDLE

He added an arrow pointing in the right direction, just to leave no room for error.

Then the roughnecks piled into the dune-buggies. It was a tight squeeze. Each car was designed to carry no more than four people and had only the smallest of back seats. Several of the men had to perch on the rear spoilers and cling to the roll bars for support.

The crammed dune-buggies set off in a convoy, the one with the two explorers leading the way. Thick tyres churned sand. High, fat exhaust pipes spewed smoke.

A thirty-six-hour trek that began at Desolation Wells ended at a distinctive, teetering mesa which lay due southwest.

The mesa was shaped like a gigantic sewing needle. Eons of desert wind had worn a hole through the summit and eroded its base to a remarkable thinness. It was a unique and striking geographical feature and a very handy landmark, one that was visible from several kilometres away, one that could not possibly be mistaken for anything else.

The convoy of dune-buggies drew up in front of it. Clockweight climbed out and addressed his two explorers.

'Out of curiosity,' he said, pointing towards the mesa's base, 'were *that* here last time?'

'No, boss.'

'You'm sure about that?'

'Quite sure.'

Clockweight frowned.

Between the time his explorers had left the spot and now, someone else had arrived.

Sitting parked at the foot of the mesa was a half-tarp van.

CHAPTER 72

Cavern

'Echo,' said Den.

Echo ... echo ... echo ...

'Knock it off, Den.'

'Sorry. Just trying to keep my spirits up. I doesn't much like this, being underground. I could never have been a miner.'

'Keep walking. Watch your footing. I don't think it's far.'

Den grimaced and shone his flashlight upwards, hoping to see the ceiling of the cavern. But it was too high for the beam to reach, so he had no alternative but to imagine what lay overhead: sheer rock, with wickedly sharp stalactites suspended here and there.

Not a comforting thought – all that tonnage of rock, all those jagged stalactite points, seemingly ready to fall onto him and Hardscree. He knew the cavern was vast. The size of its entrance had told him so, as did the way his and the Deacon's voices and footfalls echoed once they were inside it. Nevertheless he was beginning to feel cooped up and claustrophobic.

Nope, he could definitely have never been a miner. Lucky for him that murk-combing was the trade he'd been born into.

He and Hardscree were following the course of a broad-gauge railway track which ran from the cavern's mouth deep down into the ground. They had put daylight (and that extra-ordinary needle-like mesa) behind them half an hour ago. They were walking through pure darkness, with just their flashlight beams to guide them – and the illumination from those beams seemed pitifully wan, barely adequate to the task. There was so much darkness for the flashlights to hold back. Thick darkness, which seemed to get thicker with every step.

The track itself gleamed dully whenever the flashlights played across it, two parallel lines of iron that hugged the shallow downward gradient of the cavern floor. It originated beside a broad, sloping concrete platform just outside the cavern entrance.

Den wondered how long the track had been in place. The aridity of the desert air meant that rust formed slowly, if at all. He reckoned it could have been at least a couple of centuries since those rails were laid down, maybe even three.

Something must ride up and down the track, but he had no idea what.

He and Hardscree continued to descend further and deeper. Den was just starting to think that the cavern went on for ever, right into the bowels of the planet, right to its very core, when abruptly Hardscree halted.

'There,' he said.

The glowing yellow cone from his flashlight picked out a large diesel-driven generator. Seventy, eighty horsepower output, Den estimated. A lot of energy.

After a few false starts and quite a bit of un-Deacon-like cursing, Hardscree got the generator running. As it chugged into action, lights came on. Here, and now here, and now here, one after another, dozens of bulbs began to brighten. Soon a whole section of the cavern was lit up brilliantly by the electric constellation overhead.

And, blinking, dazzled, Den and Hardscree saw things – wonderful things.

The two of them were standing at the edge of a big dome-like area, a natural subterranean hollow which had been enlarged and improved by human hands. Steel joists helped support and brace the roof, while all of the rocky surfaces had been sanded and smoothed to a near-gemlike sheen.

The floor of this area was filled with flying machines.

Most consisted of just parts and portions. Here a random wing, there a rudder, the odd propeller, a segment of fuselage.

A few, however, were complete.

There were helicopters and autogyros, some with solid,

umbrella-like rotors, and there was a range of fixed-wing air-craft, including a few elderly-looking biplanes made of wooden frames covered with a skin of canvas. There were a couple of larger planes – airbuses, Den thought they were called – multi-passenger public transport vehicles. And there were a number of strange things that were scarcely recognisable as flying machines. Early models, he guessed, from far back in Airborn history.

He let his gaze roam over them all, wide-eyed like a treasure hunter who'd just discovered the ultimate trove.

Hardscree's face bore a similar expression.

'You told I,' Den said at last. 'You described it. But you didn't do it justice.'

'How could I? I didn't know. I was only going by what others had said. It's a whole different thing to see it for oneself.'

'Relics. Them's all Relics.'

'Decades' worth.'

'And some of they is intact, all but,' Den said, scratching his head. 'Bless my bum. How come that happened? Given how far they has to fall, you'd have thought them'd end up as nothing but flinders.'

'It's amazing but some of these planes practically glide to earth. Especially the earlier models, the ones made of wood and canvas – their lightness saves them from harm. Although not so the people in them. When it comes to crashes, even the canvas aircraft turn out to be a lot more robust than their porous-boned pilots.'

'Us picked up bits of aircraft ourselves, me and my kids, in the Shadow Zone, once or twice. Just fragments. I presumed them got stowed in the Chancel Reliquary.'

'Maybe temporarily, but in the end they'd have been brought here. Every piece of Airborn aircraft that ever came down anywhere in the Westward Territories wound up here. We were running out of room for them in the Reliquaries so we started shipping them out from the Chancels on articulated lorries under cover of darkness, driving them to this cavern, and depositing them out of sight.'

'So's us Groundlings couldn't have they.'

'Precisely. So that Groundlings would not be able to fly. It was in our own interest, as Deacons, to ensure that nobody else got their hands on any of this.'

'But the Deacons doesn't rule the roost any longer.'

'Which means these planes are up for grabs.'

'What used to be *there*, I wonder.' Den indicated a large gap near the middle of the aircraft collection. It was approximately 300 metres long and shaped like a stretched-out oval, with stanchions at both ends from which ran thick lengths of hawser. Now lying limp on the floor, the hawsers had clearly been used to secure something once.

'No idea,' said Hardscree, with a shrug.

Den was reminded of *Cerulean*. An airship would have fitted neatly into a space like that.

'But our job,' the Deacon went on, 'is to see how many of these craft are fit for purpose and figure out how to make them fly.'

'How's us supposed to get they up to the surface?'

'Easy. They can go out the way they came in.' Hardscree directed Den's gaze to where the railway track terminated. Resting against a set of buffers was a large flatbed rail trolley. 'It uses a pulley and counterweight system, much like one of the sky-city elevators. There's a release mechanism at the top so that it always returns down here after use. That way it won't ever be left sitting out exposed to the elements for months on end.'

'What about actually loading the planes onto the trolley?'

Hardscree gestured to the cavern roof. Up there was a hoist which operated on a grid pattern of metal runners. Hook-tipped chains dangled from it. The hoist could reach any part of the cavern.

'There's a control console for it somewhere,' Hardscree said.

'It's all pretty much sorted then, be'n't it?' said Den. 'So when does us get started?'

Deacon Hardscree started rolling up the sleeves of his robe. 'No time like the present.'

CHAPTER 73

Hamstrung

'Skipper?'

'Yes, helmsman?'

'I'm ... I'm having a spot of bother here.'

'What sort of a spot of bother?'

'The rudder's behaving oddly. I'm not getting much response from it.'

'Problem with a cable?'

'Could be.'

Cerulean had just emerged above the cloud cover and was at cruising speed. Az had been looking forward to a brief respite from turbulence, a stretch of plain sailing.

No such luck.

'Keep trying. Rigz? Could you go aft and check the rudder cables? Maybe one of them snapped or came loose while we were being shaken around just now.'

The chief engineer was on the point of carrying out the order when he hesitated. He'd spotted something peculiar outside.

'Skipper? You ought to take a look at this.'

Az joined Rigz at the viewing windows. He saw a patch of darkness down on the clouds to starboard.

'That? That's just *Cerulean*'s shadow, Rigz. Been with us all the way!'

'With all due respect, skipper, it isn't. The sun's high and we're heading east. Our shadow should be portside, and is.'

A prickle of fear ran up Az's spine.

Before his very eyes, the patch of darkness began to rise. It wasn't *on* the clouds, it was *in* them. And it was gradually surfacing, breaking through the topmost layer, starting to open up a V-shaped furrow in the white.

Behemoth.

Up she came. The cloud cover parted around her nose-cone, flowing back along her balloon in gauzy ribbons. Up she came, trailing skeins of vapour from her tailfins. Up, with her black-painted canvas shining dully in the sunlight.

'We didn't find them,' Az breathed. 'They've found *us*.'

'Skipper?' said the helmsman. 'I have no control at all any more.' He spun the conn wheel to prove it.

'They've severed the cables,' said Rigz.

'But how?' said Az. 'They're nowhere near us.'

The answer came a moment later. A garishly dressed man winged up to the viewing windows and waved to everyone inside the gondola. He had wild eyes and shaggy, lime-green dreadlocks, and in his hands were a large pair of bolt cutters. He mimed using the bolt cutters, gave a gleeful giggle, then darted down towards the still-rising *Behemoth*.

Rigz swore.

Mr Mordadson smiled mirthlessly.

Unseen and unheard by anyone, Flight Lieutenant Wallimson snickered.

'In midair,' Az said, disgusted and incredulous. 'He flew across while we were in the clouds, latched on and started snipping.'

'He's crippled us,' said Rigz. 'We're hamstrung.'

'Perhaps so,' said Az, 'but we still have Patrollers on board. Let's sound the alarm and send them out. The pirates won't be expecting that.'

No sooner had the words left Az's lips than the viewing windows shattered inwards.

Three pirates had darted up in front of the control gondola from below. Using short-handled maces, they knocked out all the windows in swift succession. The crew ducked as shards of glass sprayed in all directions. Freezing-cold air whistled into the gondola.

The pirates clambered through the empty window frames.

Each tucked his mace into his belt and drew out a long-bladed dagger. Their eyes were crazy and bloodshot, their cheeks were sallow and acne-pocked, and their movements were jerky and agitated. These were the familiar indicators of sustained, long-term pterine abuse.

Mr Mordadson stepped forward to intercept them, but Az grabbed his arm.

'Let go, Az.'

'No. There's three of them and they're armed.'

'So? I've faced worse odds before.'

'And they're off their faces on pterine. I can't risk you getting injured.'

Mr Mordadson sneered, as if to say he thought the chances of *that* happening were pretty slim.

Then two more pirates entered the gondola.

Glass crunched as the new arrivals strode past the other three pirates, heading straight for Az and Mr Mordadson.

One of them was the grinning, dreadlocked creature they had seen earlier, the one who'd appeared outside with bolt cutters. He tittering softly to himself, as if at some priceless private joke.

As for the other . . .

Leather trousers creaked.

Black wings unfurled.

'Gentlemen,' said Naoutha Nisrocsdaughter. 'Let's parley.'

CHAPTER 74

Ultimatum

She was tall, brawny-shouldered, statuesque. The all-over leather she wore hugged the contours of her body, showing off a curvaceous figure. Her wings were as glossy as a raven's and shimmered with highlights of midnight blue.

The crew stared at her, awestruck. Az found it impossible not to do likewise. Even Mr Mordadson seemed startled and a little bit tongue-tied at the sight of her.

What was her face like behind that mask and those goggles? One could only assume that it matched the rest of her and was stunning.

'Your ship is useless now,' Naoutha said. 'We have you at a complete disadvantage. I am giving you one chance. If you agree to turn home and cease all efforts to interfere with what we're doing, we shall leave you alone.'

'And if we don't agree?' said Mr Mordadson.

'So far we've done nothing that can't be fixed. Keep pursuing us, however, and we'll do something ... unfixable.'

Her green-haired sidekick tittered loudly at this.

'Not much of a choice, is it?' said Az.

'No, Azrael Gabrielson, it isn't.'

'You know my name?'

'Don't be flattered, boy. How many wingless teenage air-shipmen are there? Though, in truth, I suppose I should say thank you to you.'

'What for?'

'You visited the ground and opened up all these possibilities for us. In a way, you're responsible for me and my friends becoming what we are. Without you we'd still be frittering away our lives at Redspire. We'd be just another bunch of dead-end layabouts, doing dull, stupid jobs so we can enjoy ourselves a little in the evenings. Whereas now, look at us. Pirates! Actual, living, breathing pirates! We used to be so bored and lazy, and now we've found a dramatic new purpose in life, and it's all down to you.'

'I'm honoured.'

'You should be.'

'But if you're so pleased with yourself,' Az said, 'why wear that mask? Do you have something to hide? Are you secretly ashamed of what you do, maybe?'

Naoutha lowered her head so that there was less than a hand's breadth between her face and his. Az saw a mirror-image Az reflected dimly, twice, in the goggles' black lenses.

'I wear it to intimidate,' she said. 'Is it working? Are you intimidated?'

Az shook his head, but in truth he was. The mask and goggles, in combination with the leather outfit, made Naoutha look less human and more like an insect – a large beetle, perhaps, or an oversized flying ant. She was sexy but at the same time very creepy.

'Your eyes say you are,' she said. 'And if *you* are, imagine how Groundlings must feel when they see me.'

'We've a ton of Alar Patrollers on board,' Az said, hoping to intimidate Naoutha in return if he could. 'Some of them are probably coming for'ard right now to see why we've stopped.'

'So what?' Naoutha replied. 'We aren't planning on staying long. We're just here to —'

Mr Mordadson had been waiting for an opening, a moment when Naoutha was distracted. That moment had come, and he sprang at her, fists clenched.

But Naoutha was not caught unawares. Her pterine-enhanced reflexes worked at lightning speed. Blocking Mr Mordadson's fists with her forearms, she lashed out with her left wing. Its upper arch smacked him across the nose. His spectacles flew off. Blood spurted. Mr Mordadson grabbed his face in pain. Without pausing Naoutha brought her right wing around, low, and swept his legs out from under him, toppling him onto his back.

The other pirates were on him in a flash. Kneeling, they pinned down his limbs and wings. The green-haired, giggling one straddled his chest and placed a dagger against his neck.

'I only have to give the word,' Naoutha said, 'and Twitchy Ziz there will carve you a new smile. Won't you, Twitchy Ziz?'

Twitchy Ziz tittered and mimed throat-cutting with the index finger of his free hand. His bulging eyes dared Mr Mordadson to resist. He clearly yearned to do some bloodletting.

'He's never been right in the head, has our Zizulph,' Naoutha added. 'Born an addled egg, as the saying goes. As a boy he used to torture birds.'

'Pull their legs off,' said Twitchy Ziz with relish. 'Twist their heads round. Squawk! Crunch! Robins especially. Friendly little fellows. So trusting. Redbreast, deadbreast.'

'And he's no better now,' Naoutha added, almost fondly.

Mr Mordadson glared up at the madman leaning over him, but he did not struggle. He knew it was useless.

Naoutha swivelled her head, looking around the control gondola in an imperious manner. 'Any more have-a-go heroes here?'

The crew looked at their hands or inspected the floor.

'Didn't think so,' Naoutha said.

Az was tempted, but thought better of it. Not while Mr Mordadson had a dagger to his neck. Then there was the fact that Naoutha had bested his friend in hand-to-hand combat so easily. If Mr Mordadson couldn't win against her, what chance did Az have?

'You know we can't let you and your pirates just carry on raiding,' he said defiantly. 'We have clear instructions from the Silver Sanctum. You're to be stopped at any cost.'

'And how are you going to do that with your rudders out of action?' Naoutha retorted. 'You can't even steer now.'

'We'll find a way.'

'Is that so?' She cocked her head, as if studying him. 'Well, we shall see. You've had your ultimatum, at any rate. How you choose to proceed from here on is up to you.' She snapped her leather-gloved fingers. 'Guys? Time to go.'

Twitchy Ziz kept his dagger against Mr Mordadson's throat

while the other three pirates let go of his limbs and wings and stood up. Then, carefully, Twitchy Ziz himself stood and backed away, leaving his blade in contact with Mr Mordadson's skin till the last possible moment.

He joined Naoutha and the other pirates at the shattered windows. Then, together, all five back-flipped out into the open air. They kept pace with *Cerulean* for several wingbeats, then peeled off in a line towards *Behemoth*.

Mr Mordadson staggered to his feet. He was bleeding profusely from the nose. He drew out a handkerchief, wadded it up and pressed it to his nostrils to stem the flow

Az picked up his spectacles and handed them to him. Mr Mordadson tried to put them on but winced and hissed.

'Broken,' he said thickly.

'They look fine to me.'

'No. My nose. She broke it.'

'Oh. Ouch.'

'Ouch is the word.'

Outside, *Behemoth* gathered speed, drawing ahead of *Cerulean*. The latter airship was starting to veer to starboard, and there was nothing anyone could do to correct her heading.

'So,' Mr Mordadson said through the handkerchief, 'are we just going to let them sail away?'

'Of course not,' said Az. 'Rigz? Can you fix the rudder?'

'Sure. It'll take a while, though. If they had any sense, they'd have cut out a whole section of each cable – as much as is exposed between the balloon and the tailfins. I'll have to find some extra from somewhere and patch it in.'

'How long?'

'Three or four hours.'

'Get on it,' said Az.

Rigz flew up through the ceiling hatchway.

'In three or four hours' time they'll be long gone,' said Mr Mordadson. 'In fact, less than that.'

'Maybe,' Az said. 'But not necessarily.'

'You have an idea?'

'I think I do.'

CHAPTER 75

Common Ground

The trolley trundled up the final section of track towards the light at the cavern mouth. The brightness ahead was blinding. Den and Deacon Hardscree squinted as their eyes adjusted.

The cavern mouth formed an almost perfect semicircle. Just outside, where the desert began, Den thought he saw figures moving. Rapidly they swam into focus. He counted ten men. No, twenty. No, more.

'Gerald?' he said in a low voice.

'I see them,' said Hardscree.

'Who be them?'

'Wish I knew,' said the Deacon, and reached down to his ankle.

As the trolley drew out into the light, the strangers swarmed around it. The trolley rolled along the last few metres of rail, coasting to a halt next to a short section of raised platform with a ramp at the end. The plane which Den and Hardscree had loaded onto it was one of the newer and more airworthy-looking models, a single-seater craft with swept-back wings and a raised cockpit. The strangers were fascinated by it – and warily curious about the two men who had brought it up from the cavern depths.

'Who'm you?' one of the strangers demanded. The skin on his face and arm was red raw with burns.

'I could ask you the same question,' replied Hardscree.

'The name's Clockweight,' the other man said. 'Toolpusher of Desolation Wells. That's foreman, in common parlance. Or at least, I was toolpusher of Desolation Wells, till just recently. And you, it goes without saying, be a Deacon.'

'Obviously.'

'And you'm stealing from your own stash of aircraft, I see.'

'Not exactly. It can't be stealing if it's *my* stash, now can it?' Den guffawed.

Clockweight's expression hardened. He leapt nimbly onto the trolley and walked towards Hardscree with an air of unmistakable menace. 'You'm a smart-mouthed one, eh, Deacon? Snooty, too. Think you'm better than the rest of we, just like all your kind does.'

Hardscree whipped out his knife.

'One step closer and I'll gut you,' he said, levelling the knife at Clockweight's stomach.

Clockweight froze, then laughed. 'Reckon you'm bluffing. Reckon you doesn't have the first clue how to use that.'

'Try he,' said Den. 'Just try he and you'll find out. Him's a Pale Uplander, see. Up there in the north, folk gets knives as birthday presents.'

Clockweight frowned at him, then at Hardscree. 'Really. Well, it doesn't make much difference. Us is here for the aircraft, and there'm thirty of we and only two of you. You could kill I but I doubt you could kill all of we. So drop the knife and surrender. That way nobody gets hurt.'

Hardscree did not drop the knife but he did raise it to vertical, an indication that he didn't necessarily wish to see anyone hurt either.

'Might I ask what you want the aircraft for?'

'Don't see as it'm any of your business,' was Clockweight's reply.

'You never know, it may be very much my business. It may even be that you and I, Mr Clockweight, have some common ground.'

'How d'you suppose that?'

'Logic. Intuition. An understanding of character. Evidently you want these aircraft for a specific purpose, and from your body language I'm guessing it isn't, for instance, to take them and sell them to someone else. There's a determination about you, an aggression, which suggests a less mercenary motive. Am I right so far?'

'Go on.'

'You said you were foreman of Desolation Wells "until just recently". Judging by your burns, and the similar injuries I see among your colleagues, I'd say something regrettable happened at your oil refinery.'

'That'd be an understatement.'

'A tragedy of some kind.'

Clockweight blinked and said, softly, 'Yes.'

Den looked from Hardscree to Clockweight and back again. The Deacon was working his wiles and Clockweight was being swayed. Den recalled how Hardscree had won *him* over when he'd gone to the tent to remonstrate about the attack on *Bertha*. Whatever charisma was, Hardscree had it in bucketloads.

Den began to feel uncomfortable, however. He knew the Deacon a lot better now. He knew him as a person. Watching someone else get charmed by him was like watching a conjuring trick when you were in on the secret behind the illusion. The magic was still there but you were aware of the deceit as well.

He saw himself in Clockweight's place. He saw himself being disarmed just as Clockweight was being. Somehow it seemed patently obvious what Hardscree was up to. He was using words to defuse a sticky situation. He was manipulating Clockweight, saying whatever he had to in order to get Clockweight on his side.

Was it that easy? Could Hardscree make anyone fall for him like that, at the proverbial drop of a hat?

'Care to tell me about it?' said the Deacon to Clockweight, oozing empathy.

Clockweight scratched his singed forearm, then nodded. 'Yeah. All right.'

CHAPTER 76

Disenchanted, Disenfranchised And Discarded

Soon, the roughnecks were busy fetching aircraft up from the cavern and wheeling them off the trolley, onto the platform, down the ramp, out onto the sand. Hardscree looked on with a satisfied air. When Den came up to him, the Deacon offered a quick arch of the eyebrows as a greeting.

'So what do you think of our hard-working new friends, Den?' he asked.

'I be thinking them seems a decent enough bunch as far as it goes. But I also be thinking us has rather strayed from the point, Gerald.'

'Meaning?'

Den hesitated. How to put this?

'When us set out on this exploit of ours, I were under the impression the plan were to liberate the Airborn's flying technology. Our ultimate goal were going to share it with everybody, make it accessible to everybody. Balancing the scales and all that. People could take the planes and back-engineer they and build planes of their own.'

'And?'

'And now us is giving it to these roughneck chaps so's them can get their own back on the airship that blew up their refinery and killed their mates.'

'So?'

Den tried to honey his words with a laugh. 'Well, don't that strike you as a misuse of it? Be'n't that precisely the wrong way to go about making the world a better place? Us is encouraging violence against the Airborn.'

'Airborn who've murdered people.'

'Yes, but from what Clockweight said, them's the one that started it. Those roughnecks. *Them* murdered first.'

'Under provocation.'

'Even so.' Den gritted his teeth. 'Look, Gerald, I be'n't saying this'm a mistake, just saying this be'n't what I signed up for.'

'No, Den, you *are* saying this is a mistake,' said Hardscree coolly. 'You're too polite to tell me flat out but that's the gist of it. You want me to stop what's been started here. But I'm not going to. Would you like to know why?'

'Sure.'

'Because, for one thing, I couldn't even if I wanted to. Clockweight said it himself. Thirty of them, two of us. Overwhelming odds. We've no choice but to let him have his way. But you know what else? I believe they have a good case. The people in that black airship cannot be allowed to get away with theft and mass killing and destruction. Someone has to bring them down, and if these planes' – he waved an arm at the fleet of aircraft which was steadily being amassed outside the cavern – 'if these planes are the means of achieving that goal, then so be it. To my mind, that *is* balancing the scales.'

Bitterly Den replied, 'I thought you was a moral man. Even for a Deacon. I thought you had a fair grasp of right and wrong. I had you pegged as somebody who looked a bit further, saw the bigger picture.'

'I am. I do.'

'Then how come you can't see that there'm a cycle of violence spiralling out of control here? And d'you know where it'll end? *I* do. It'll end in just more people dead. Like my son. It'll end in pointless, futile, stupid bloody slaughter. It'll make a whole lot of corpses, like my Martin's, and nothing will be gained. And maybe worse'll happen. Maybe it'll anger the Airborn and them'll retaliate somewhere else, and our governments'll feel the need to fight back, and then where will us be? I's seen this sort of thing before, and I tell you, Gerald, us has to prevent it, not aid and abet it. And you *can* prevent it. I's sure of that. With your speechifying and your talent for persuasion, you can talk these men round, knock some sense into they. If you try to. If you want to.'

Hardscree looked him up and down, as if seeing him in a whole new light. He was silent for a while. Then, one hand smoothing back his brush of flame-orange hair, he said, 'The aircraft will need a thorough overhaul before they can be flown. Clockweight and his men have the knowhow, but I'm certain your additional expertise would be welcome.'

Den knew in that moment that he had been downgraded from close companion to mere motor mechanic. Perhaps that was all he had been all along.

And guess what? He didn't care.

'No, Gerald,' he said evenly. 'Them'll just have to muddle through without I. As of now, I be officially out. I want nothing to do with this any more. Nothing. I quit. Hear I?'

'Loud and clear, Den. Loud and clear.' Hardscree smiled without warmth. 'You've made your position known. I'd recommend, though, that you don't try anything rash.'

'Such as?'

'I shouldn't have to spell it out. Just don't get in the way. Let things run their course. I'd take a dim view of any opposition from you, and so, I feel, would our newfound allies.'

Den said nothing, merely snorted.

'Stick around,' Hardscree went on. 'Like it or not, we're in this together, all the way. Stay and see the Groundling race take its first steps to becoming airborne like the Airborn. I think it's going to be quite a show, Den!'

Hardscree gave another warmth-free smile.

Den, in return, spun on his heel and stomped off.

CHAPTER 77

Ruminations Of A
No-longer-useful Tool

Den walked as far away from the activity at the cavern mouth as he dared – which was not far. The yells and banter of the roughnecks, as they unloaded the planes, afforded a kind of protection. While he remained within sight and sound of other people, the dangers of the Relentless Desert were held at bay, or so it seemed.

He halted in the shadow of the needlelike mesa and gazed out into the surrounding emptiness.

What a fool he'd been!

He had learned just how little Hardscree actually thought of him. If the Deacon could switch allegiance away from him so quickly and readily, that told him he had meant nothing much to the man in the first place. He'd been a useful tool, that was all, a way of ensuring Hardscree and his half-tarp got to where they were supposed to. His usefulness was now at an end. Hardscree had altered his plans, and the new plans did not include him.

'Kids,' Den said to the desert, his voice a lonely croak. 'Fletch, Cass, Robert, I be so sorry. What must you think of I? Your da's been a sad, deluded old prune. Him ran off and left you in the lurch, and what for? For a dream that'm gone and turned into a nightmare. If only I could see you all now! If I did, I'd chuck myself down at your feet and beg you to forgive I, straight up.'

But his children were hundreds of kilometres away. There

was half a desert, and a lot more besides, between him and them.

It seemed scarcely plausible to Den that he was going to see his family again any time soon.

CHAPTER 78

Riding The Jet Streams

Cerulean continued to climb, her propellers vertically down-turned for maximum lift. She was still skewing to starboard, however, and *Behemoth* was a shrinking black speck on the horizon.

'There's a crosscurrent up here,' said Az, tight-lipped. It was more a prayer than a statement of fact. 'There's got to be.'

The jet streams varied at different heights. At any given altitude you might find one running northerly, southerly, south-easterly, or from any other direction. They interleaved in layers, invisible sheets of wind sliding silkily across one another.

Captain Qadoschson had explained this to Az, saying that clever use of the jet streams could lessen journey time con-siderably. He'd added that, in the event of rudder failure, you could also use the jet streams to steer. The principle was simple: find one that was going the way you wanted to and stick with it, letting it blow you along. If it changed heading or petered out, then all you need do was rise or fall until you found another.

'It isn't an exact science,' Qadoschson had said, 'but in case of emergency it'll do.'

And if this wasn't an emergency, Az didn't know what was.

But *Cerulean* couldn't seem to locate a jet stream that was travelling the same way as *Behemoth*. So far she'd gone up nearly 1,000 metres, and the prevailing wind was still driving her on a course perpendicular to the other airship's. If she didn't hit a useable crosscurrent soon, *Behemoth* would be lost from sight.

'Come on, come on,' Az intoned. His voice trembled in time to his shivers. Everyone in the control gondola was shivering. Somebody had fetched blankets for people to drape around their shoulders, but even so warmth was hard to come by. With the windows gone, there was nothing to keep the sub-zero air outside from entering. Ice crystals were forming on dials and metal surfaces. Breath was visible.

Az reckoned if they didn't get lucky soon, he would have to abort the manoeuvre. *Cerulean* couldn't go much higher without risk of someone in the crew succumbing to frostbite or even hypothermia.

Just a few more metres. Surely, surely, the wind would change.

Az became aware of a rocking motion. *Cerulean* was being gently nudged from behind.

Could it be . . . ?

It was!

The airship was turning round towards *Behemoth*. She had penetrated into a new jet stream and it was pushing her on almost exactly the right heading. It was strong, too. Seventy knots, according to the navigator's wind-speed gauge. *Behemoth* appeared to be managing less than sixty.

'Brilliant,' said Mr Mordadson, with an approving nod. His nose had begun to swell and was turning an ugly shade of mauve. Without his spectacles on, his eyes had a diffused, lost look to them. For the first time in Az's experience, the mighty Mr Mordadson seemed vulnerable. Az knew, though, that in his heart he was scheming away. Naoutha Nisrocsdaughter had got the better of him once. It wasn't going to happen again.

'We should be able to make up lost ground,' Az said. 'As long as this jet stream keeps up, we'll be within striking distance of *Behemoth* in about four hours.'

'And then there'll be a reckoning,' said Mr Mordadson.

He didn't have to say any more.

It wouldn't be long before extreme sanction was due.

CHAPTER 79

Preparation For Assault

Slowly but steadily the gap between *Cerulean* and *Behemoth* narrowed. The black airship grew from a speck to a dot to a blob, and was soon close enough that Az could make out details such as her propellers and her tailfin assembly with the skull and crossed feathers on it. *Cerulean* was still a thousand metres above her, more or less. She was also coming towards her out of the sun. In other words, it was unlikely anyone aboard *Behemoth* would spot *Cerulean* approaching until it was too late.

This time, *Cerulean* had the advantage, not the pirates.

She also had steering again, to a certain extent. Rigz had cannibalised support wires from the balloon frame in order to replace the missing sections of rudder cable. He had plaited the wires together for strength before welding them into place. The helmsman reported that he had approximately 75 per cent of full control. Not bad, under the circumstances. Enough to do the job.

The crew were now swaddled in several layers of blankets, but were still blue-lipped and shuddering.

Az assured them they would be descending to warmer climes shortly. 'We can't afford to lose the boost we're getting from the jet stream just yet,' he said.

Then, looking around the control gondola, he added, 'I need a volunteer to go out and man the grappling hook.'

Really there was only one logical candidate, only one crewman who could be spared. Az's gaze zeroed in on him.

'Me?' said Flight Lieutenant Wallimson, pointing at his own chest.

'You,' said Az. 'Are you up for it?'

Wallimson considered, then gave a grin. 'I'd like to make myself useful,' he said. 'Count me in.'

He headed for the ceiling hatch.

Az was a little taken aback by how eager Wallimson was to help. He'd expected some grumbling at the very least. Then again, the flight lieutenant had been nothing but reliable and conscientious since Gyre. Once such a thorn in Az's side, he had metamorphosed into a trustworthy crew member. Whatever Mr Mordadson had done or said to get him to change his attitude, it had, in spite of Az's initial misgivings, done the trick.

Behemoth loomed closer, and closer still.

'We're nearly within range,' Az said. 'Descend.'

Cerulean sank.

'Sound an alarm.'

A klaxon hooted back near the cabins.

'Action stations.'

At the aft of the ship Patrollers formed a line to the rear hatch, clutching their lances. Mr Mordadson was with them. They dived out in pairs, somersaulting then righting themselves and peeling off to the left and right.

In the control gondola the crew tensed. Az himself found he no longer felt cold. Adrenaline was rushing through his body, making his pulse race and his blood pump faster, warming him.

'Here we go.'

CHAPTER 80

Treachery, Sabotage, Betrayal, Undermining, Double-cross, Deceit, Etc.

Cerulean slotted in at *Behemoth*'s rear, bumping in her wake. Wallimson was gliding outside the control gondola, holding on with one hand, priming the spring-loaded grappling hook launcher with the other. The Patrollers and Mr Mordadson, meanwhile, flanked the airship in attack formation. Mr Mordadson had borrowed a spare lance. He wasn't going to miss out on the chance to strike back at Naoutha.

The pirates still didn't appear to have spotted *Cerulean*. Obviously they believed they had sorted her out and left her far behind. Their overconfidence, Az felt, would be their undoing.

'We still have the element of surprise,' said Rigz, tentatively, as if he didn't want to jinx things.

'Let's hope so,' Az said. Raising his voice, he called out, 'Wallimson? I want you to —'

That was when everything started to go wrong.

From outside the gondola came a hollow, metallic *choomph* sound, and Az saw a grappling hook shoot towards *Behemoth*, trailing a wriggly line of rope. *Cerulean* was still slightly higher than the other airship, too high for the hook to find anything to latch on to. Az had been about to tell Wallimson to hold off from firing for at least another minute. Now, he watched in dismay as the grappling hook reached its limit. The rope snapped taut and the hook fell, landed flat on *Behemoth*'s balloon, slithered down the canvas, bounced outward, plummeted past the propellers, and continued in an arc down past *Behemoth*'s control gondola. From there it flopped back towards its point of origin, *Cerulean*.

'Wallimson!' Az shouted, running to the viewing windows. 'You moron! I never said fire.'

But the flight lieutenant wasn't beside the launcher any more. He was making for the grappling hook, which dangled below the gondola, swaying around like a useless pendulum. He grabbed the hook and flew with it strenuously, lopsidedly, towards one of the forward propellers.

Az's jaw dropped.

No.

No!

No, he wouldn't!

But he would. With an almost casual flick of the arm, Wallimson tossed the grappling hook at the propeller, then darted to safety.

The hook itself overshot the propeller but its line got snagged in the whirling blur of the blades. It wrapped around them, yanking the hook back. Metal screeched against metal as the blades chewed into the hook's prongs. Next instant, the whole propeller disintegrated in a burst of twisted fragments.

Some of the fragments tore holes in *Cerulean*'s canvas. Others bombarded the control gondola like lethal hail. Ra'asielson the navigator cried out in pain, as did Rigz. Az saw the chief engineer slump to the floor, steel shards sticking out of his arms and chest.

The propeller mounting was bent out of true, and the drive chain broke. It flailed around its cogs before unravelling and spinning off into space.

Az yelled out an order to stop the other forward propeller so that *Cerulean* would not veer off-course.

Then he saw that the pirates were emerging from *Behemoth*.

The misfired grappling hook had warned them of *Cerulean*'s approach. Naoutha and her gang were coming out to meet their enemy.

Clash At Sunset

The pitched battle between the pirates and the Patrollers took place in late afternoon, as the sun was sinking. Its reddish rays formed a fitting backdrop to the proceedings, staining sky and clouds the colour of blood.

The initial wave of pirates from *Behemoth* unleashed a volley of crossbow fire. Steel-tipped hickorywood bolts whisked through the air towards the Patrollers, forcing Wing Commander Iaxson to give the order for evasive manoeuvres. His men broke formation, scattering in all directions.

The pirates kept up the barrage. Their crossbows were short-range weapons, ineffective at more than fifty metres. None of the Patrollers was hit or hurt. But that wasn't the pirates' goal anyway. They were buying time, keeping the Patrollers busy while reinforcements appeared from inside *Behemoth*.

Soon there were equal numbers of pirates and Patrollers in the sky. The pirates put away their crossbows, and Iaxson blew the whistle command for his men to re-form. The Patrollers rapidly arranged themselves in neat ranks and files, lances at the ready. The pirates, meanwhile, gathered in clusters and brandished their own weapons – a daunting array of close-quarter implements, some sharp such as swords, daggers and axes, some blunt such as maces and clubs, and some, such as spiked iron balls on chains, that were both.

The motley throng of pirates jeered at their uniformed opponents, calling across to them, making coarse gestures of invitation, telling them to come and get it. Some of them howled with derisive laughter, others chanted rude rhymes. Leading the insults was the pirate called Twitchy Ziz. He danced a war dance in midair, jerking his limbs up and down and shrieking like a macaw, his dreadlocks flopping around his face.

'Kind of reminds me of the Sinking Cities Panic,' said Iaxson to Mr Mordadson. 'Remember, just after we graduated?'

'Yes, except those people weren't armed and they weren't hopped up on pterine. It was a wave of mass hysteria. They hardly knew what they were doing. This lot not only know what they're up against but think the drug will give them the edge. And they could be right.'

'But we have discipline and training on our side. Given a choice between that and drugs, I'll go with discipline and training any day.'

'Me too,' said Mr Mordadson, then narrowed his eyes. He had just located Naoutha Nisrocsdaughter in the pirates' midst, distinctive with her black wings. She was his primary target. He and she had unfinished business.

Iaxson readied himself to order an attack, but Naoutha got there first. She let out a high-pitched, ululating scream, and the pirates took it up and flew towards the Patrollers, coming at them in a swarm. All at once the Patrollers were on the defensive. Each found himself on the receiving end of a flurry of sword slashes or axe blows and was so busy using his lance to parry that he couldn't deploy it in attack.

Several of them perished under the onslaught. The pirates hacked wings and stabbed bellies and clouted heads. Dead or dying, their victims fell towards the clouds.

Finally Iaxson was able to establish control again. He ordered the Patrollers to withdraw and regroup, and then gave the signal for a counterattack. The Patrollers hurtled at the pirates in a Flying Spearhead, a configuration shaped like a pyramid on its side and famously effective in dispersing crowds of rioters. The pirates scattered but some were not fast enough and ended up with lances through their torsos. They too fell, figures who became doll-sized then dot-sized as they descended, like the recent Patroller casualties, who still had not reached the cloud cover yet.

The pirates' response was to fight dirty. They assembled in

pairs and trios and then picked on single Patrollers. One pirate would come at the Patroller from above, another from below, and, if there was a third involved, he would attack from behind. Pincered in this way, beleaguered on at least two fronts, the Patroller was hard pressed to protect himself.

The skies around *Cerulean* and *Behemoth* became a torment of shrieks, grunts, growls and clanging metal. Loose feathers swirled. Blood rained. Chaos reigned.

In the thick of it, Mr Mordadson battled as fiercely as anyone. He ripped the jaw off one pirate with a sideways swipe of his lance. He despatched another pirate by grabbing the man's hair braids and swinging him round and round till a section of his scalp tore away. Blinded by the blood streaming down his face, the pirate blundered through the air until, accidentally, he flew into the arc of a sword being wielded by one of his friends. An artery was severed, and the pirate spiralled downward, leaving a dotted spray of crimson in his wake. Mr Mordadson threw the handful of scalp and hair after him.

All the while, Mr Mordadson was keeping an eye out for the pirates' leader. He had lost track of her in all the confusion.

Finally he spied her, not far from *Behemoth*. Naoutha was clinging to a Patroller's back, her legs scissored around his waist. The Patroller was struggling to break free from her grip but could not. As Mr Mordadson looked on, she seized the man's head with both hands and wrenched it round. The sound of neck vertebrae snapping was audible even about the tumult of battle and the drone of the airships' engines – a sharp, sickening *crack*. She let the dead man go, and his limp form began its long, inexorable plunge to the ground.

With a cry of fury, Mr Mordadson flattened his wings and dived at her.

Naoutha saw him coming and went into a steep dive herself, chasing after the Patroller she had just killed. She snatched the lance out of the dead man's clutches and rose again to meet Mr Mordadson. She had a sword as well, and launched herself at him with both weapons to the fore.

The impact of lance against lance shivered up Mr

Mordadson's arms. An instant later, Naoutha's sword slammed down, hitting the spot on his lance where his right hand had been holding it. Had he not snatched the hand back just in time, Naoutha would have chopped it off at the wrist. In return, he lashed out with his foot, catching her a glancing blow on the thigh. At the same time he tried to strike one of her wings with one of his. He was aiming to numb the wing and paralyse it, if lucky break a bone, but Naoutha's pterine-fired reflexes enabled her to anticipate and deflect the shot. His wing tangled with hers. Feathers meshed, white and black. Then Naoutha planted her feet in Mr Mordadson's chest and kicked, separating them.

The two adversaries circled one another warily. Mr Mordadson feinted with his lance. Naoutha feinted with hers.

'I'll grant you this,' Naoutha said. 'You're a worthy opponent – for an old geezer.'

'Middle-aged geezer, if you don't mind,' Mr Mordadson replied.

'Whatever. How's the nose, by the way? Hurting?'

'The pain is a useful reminder why I have to kill you.'

Behind her mask Naoutha laughed, raucously and contemptuously. 'You can try, middle-aged geezer.'

She lunged at him abruptly. If her face had been visible Mr Mordadson might have had an inkling that the attack was coming. The face gave subtle cues – a narrowing of the eyes, a tightening of the mouth – which foreshadowed an opponent's intention.

As it was, Mr Mordadson managed to twist sideways as her lance jabbed at him ... but he was a fraction of a second too slow. The tip of the lance skewered his left arm at the biceps and gouged out a chunk of flesh.

He bit back a scream. Agony flared up from his arm, but he forced himself to ignore it. Bringing his own lance round, he thrust it at Naoutha. He was aiming for her chest emblem or thereabouts.

The thrust found its mark, but Naoutha's leather, and the fact that one of his arms wasn't fully-functioning, saved her from serious harm. He managed to embed the lance tip a couple of centimetres deep into the top of her pectoral muscle. She shrugged off the wound, knowing that the injury she had inflicted on Mr Mordadson was far more severe.

She sliced at him with her sword. Mr Mordadson parried with the lance handle. By dint of good fortune more than anything, he knocked the sword from her grasp.

Now, armed equally, the two of them went for it, using their lances like quarterstaffs. They collided and collided again in midair, the lances thudding together in an X-shape each time. Mr Mordadson drove Naoutha backwards; then it was Naoutha's turn to drive Mr Mordadson backwards. Locked in this ferocious private struggle, they hammered at each other. They pounded at each other. They matched blows like for like. Mr Mordadson's features were set in a contorted, spittle-flecked snarl. Naoutha's, presumably, looked similar.

It could perhaps have gone on for ever. Neither one seemed able to gain the upper hand; neither one was willing to weaken.

Then, suddenly, Mr Mordadson felt someone grab his wings from behind and pin them against his back. He stretched his wings out, shaking the person off. It was just a brief distraction.

Naoutha didn't hesitate.

She whipped the butt of her lance across Mr Mordadson's skull.

Mr Mordadson, knocked cold, began to fall.

CHAPTER 82

The Bolas Gun

Az sprinted along the axial corridor towards the nose-cone. He couldn't tell how well the battle outside was going but he knew he had to do something other than simply keep *Cerulean* on a steady course. He had to help in a more proactive way.

By doing some harm to *Behemoth*, for instance.

Reaching the nose-cone, he pulled out a box knife which he had taken from Rigz's storeroom.

Rigz. Was the chief engineer all right? He had looked badly hurt, as had Ra'asielson.

Az told himself he could worry about that later. Crew members were administering first aid to the two stricken men. There was nothing he personally could do for them right now.

He began cutting the canvas. It was tougher than it looked and he had to saw at it holding the knife with both hands. Eventually he succeeded in hacking a jagged sideways tear in the canvas, large enough for him to push through. He forced his head into the tear, then wriggled his shoulders and torso through after it.

He emerged just below the bolas gun which had been screwed onto the nose-cone. While still half inside the balloon, he grabbed the framework of the gun and hauled the rest of his body out. His legs swung free and for a terrifying moment he was supporting the whole of his bodyweight with just his hands. His grip started slipping. Scrambling frantically, he gained a foothold on the gun. Then he pulled himself up and over, and collapsed, panting, into the gun's seat.

No time to rest.

The gun's mechanism was straightforward enough and it was

already loaded. He pumped the air compressor arm till the gauge read green. Then he grasped the guide-handles and swivelled the gun barrel round, taking aim at *Behemoth*'s rear starboard propeller. He peered down the sights and curled his finger around the trigger.

A pirate soared into view directly in front of him.

The pirate raised his weapon, a mace, and heaved it down towards Az's head.

Instinctively Az pulled the trigger.

The bolas slammed into the pirate, hurling him back. The five steel strands coiled around his body and wings, wrapping him tight. One of them encircled his neck, strangling him. The pirate plummeted, choking, clawing madly at his throat.

Az never found out if the pirate managed to unpick the bolas strands and save himself. He fell rapidly out of sight and Az did not see him again.

He guessed, though, that he had just killed someone.

Extreme sanction, he thought.

But it was him or me, was his next thought. *He'd have smashed my skull open if I hadn't done what I did.*

That eased his conscience a little. But only a little.

He reached for another bolas round. Each bolas was kept in a compact cylinder which slotted into the gun breech.

Load.

Pump.

Aim . . .

Shoot!

The bolas whirled towards *Behemoth*, its strands unfurling till it was like a five-pointed star with a spherical weight at each tip.

Az's aim was good. The bolas struck the propeller and snarled it, bringing it to a halt. The result wasn't as explosive as Flight Lieutenant Wallimson's act of sabotage, but it would do. *Behemoth* was hobbled, like *Cerulean*. One prop down, three to go.

Just as he was about to load another cylinder, Az spotted two figures fighting not far from *Behemoth*.

Both were clad in black. One of them had white wings, while the other's wings matched her outfit.

Mr Mordadson and Naoutha Nisrocsdaughter.

They were going at each other mercilessly and unrelentingly with their lances. The skirmishes that Az could see elsewhere were vicious enough. The Patrollers and the pirates were not holding back. But these were nothing compared with the tussle between Mr Mordadson and Naoutha. Every blow, every lunge, every strike spoke of a deep and abiding enmity, and also of the combatants' evenly matched skills. As much as each of them wished the other's death, neither could find a way of bringing it about.

Then a third figure entered the fray.

Even if this third party had not been wearing a *Cerulean* crew uniform, Az would have identified him by his unique flying style. He approached Mr Mordadson from behind in an awkward, effortful fashion, twisting himself sideways with each wingbeat to compensate for the reduced thrust he was getting on his left-hand side.

Az yelled out a warning which he knew wouldn't carry as far as Mr Mordadson's ears, but what else could he do? Apart from that he could only watch in helpless horror as Flight Lieutenant Wallimson seized Mr Mordadson's wings. Mr Mordadson shrugged Wallimson off but was momentarily unbalanced, and Naoutha was quick to make the most of it.

Next thing Az knew, he was watching an unconscious Mr Mordadson fall, helpless, towards the clouds.

CHAPTER 83

Defection

'Who the hell are you?' Naoutha demanded, turning her lance on Wallimson.

'A friend,' he replied. 'Someone who just saved you and who wants to join your group.'

'You didn't save me. I'd have beaten him anyway, in the end. All you did was take away the satisfaction of a proper victory. For that I ought to run you through.'

'Didn't you hear what I said?' Wallimson pushed the lance aside. 'I want to join you. I want to be one of you.'

'But you're one of *them*,' Naoutha said, gesturing at his uniform.

'Which would make me a valuable asset to you. I know their methods. I know how they think. I know their weaknesses. I can help you defeat them.'

'We are defeating them.'

'No, Naoutha, with the greatest respect, you're not. Look around.'

Naoutha quickly scanned the battle scene.

Wallimson was telling the truth. While she had been focused on her fight with Mr Mordadson, the tide had turned against her and her gang. There were more Alar Patrollers left in the air than pirates. In the end, discipline and training had paid off, even against pterine users. They were hounding the pirates, gradually herding them back towards *Behemoth*.

'Here's what you need to do,' said Wallimson. 'Retreat and take me with you. Pull back to fight another day. *And* – take Mordadson hostage.'

'Who?'

'That's the name of the man you've just been having your little set-to with.' Wallimson pointed down at the dwindling form of Naoutha's adversary. 'Catch him, get him onto your ship. He's more use to you alive than dead, believe me. Think about it. A Silver Sanctum emissary in your clutches. Think of the power that'll give you. Think of the demands you can make then. He's a valuable bargaining chip.'

'Don't presume to give me orders.'

'I'm not. I'm pointing out a golden opportunity, that's all. But be quick about it. If you're going to catch him, you'd better get after him right away.'

'You go.'

Wallimson extended his lame wing as far as it could go. 'Can't. Sorry.'

Naoutha debated the sense of his words. Finally, with a *tsk*, she jack-knifed forward and went into a sheer vertical dive. Within seconds she caught up with Mr Mordadson, whose wings, loosely extended, were acting as a brake on his descent. She veered beneath him, scooped him up in her arms, and soared back towards *Behemoth*.

Wallimson followed her into the black airship. She hadn't invited him to, but she had taken up his suggestion about Mr Mordadson, and from that he inferred that he was now on her team.

How things could change.

A Feather First!er and former airship flight lieutenant had just become a pirate, a renegade, an outlaw.

Wallimson was thrilled.

CHAPTER 84

Who'd Have Thought A Hostage Would Come In Handy Quite So Soon?

The Patrollers continued to chase the pirates towards *Behemoth*, trying to pick off as many as possible before they gained the safety of the airship.

Wing Commander Iaxson led the pursuit on board. He wasn't happy about taking the battle into a confined space but he wanted to carry out a thorough mop-up operation. Not one of the pirates was to be left alive.

Entering *Behemoth* via the rear hatch, he was prepared to have to claw through the opposition, fighting hard for every centimetre of ground gained. He anticipated that the pirates would close ranks and come at him and his men in a rush.

What he wasn't expecting was to find *Behemoth*'s keel catwalk all but deserted. The pirates had dispersed into other sections of the airship, leaving a lone representative on the catwalk.

It was Naoutha Nisrocsdaughter, and she was crouching over a man's body with a knife poised at his heart.

Iaxson saw that the man was his friend Mordadson and that he was alive but unconscious.

Calmly Naoutha said, 'You have three seconds to get off my ship. Otherwise he dies.'

'You wouldn't —' Iaxson began, but Naoutha dug the knife-point into Mr Mordadson's lapel.

'One,' she said. 'Two.'

Iaxson had a moment to decide, and decided.

'Fall back!' he called out to the Patrollers behind him. 'Off the ship. Return to *Cerulean*.'

'A wise move,' said Naoutha.

'This isn't over,' Iaxson told her, retreating. 'Not by a long shot.'

'Of course it isn't over,' she replied. 'But for the moment I think it is.'

CHAPTER 85

Back In The Control Gondola

Quarter of an hour later, Az was finding it hard to believe that Iaxson had simply left Mr Mordadson there.

'He wouldn't want that,' he said. 'He'd want you to finish the job.'

'She was going to stab him through the heart,' said Iaxson.

'It was a bluff.'

'No, kid, it wasn't. I've more experience with this sort of thing than you. She'd have gone through with it, no question.'

'So we just let them waltz away?' Az flapped a hand towards the viewing windows. *Behemoth* was putting air between her and *Cerulean*, creeping off into the twilight. 'With Mr Mordadson as their captive?'

'I can't see an alternative,' said Iaxson.

'But we had them on the run. When I saw you and the Patrollers board *Behemoth*, I thought that was it. You'd rescue Mr Mordadson, deal with the remaining pirates, commandeer the ship, hurrah, end of story, let's go home. That's why I didn't fire another bolas. I assumed we'd won. But then you all came out again, looking downcast and slack-winged ...'

'You think I'm not frustrated too? Not as disappointed as you are?' There was steel in Iaxson's eyes. 'I lost good men out there. I'd gladly see every last one of those pirates exterminated.'

'And don't you think Mr Mordadson would agree?' said Az. 'I reckon he'd rather you let him die than have the pirates get the better of you.'

'Then lucky for him it wasn't your call to make. How long have you known Mordadson? A year or so? I've known him for twenty. We bunked together at cadet academy. I wouldn't sacrifice him. I couldn't. It was a life-or-death situation, and I chose life. You, kid, are probably not familiar with life-or-death situations.'

'Oh, I know about them all right,' Az retorted, thinking of the pirate he had shot with the bolas gun. 'I also know that we're not leaving Mr Mordadson. We're getting him back.'

'No.'

'Yes, wing commander, we are.'

'No. There's another way. There must be.'

'There isn't. I'm in charge of this airship. I say where she goes, and right now, where she's going is wherever *Behemoth* is going.'

'Mordadson will die!'

'Not necessarily. Think about it. Naoutha saved him. Wallimson must've convinced her she needs him alive. As long as we chase them, then, he has his uses to her. He's her trump card. I'm betting that while we're on the pirates' tail, she'd kill him only as a last resort.'

'That's a twisted sort of logic.'

'Maybe, but Naoutha's a twisted sort of person. Wing commander, us staying with *Behemoth* is Mr Mordadson's best chance of survival. I'm sure of it.'

'Perhaps we should ask your crew for their views,' Iaxson said, looking around the gondola. 'After all, we're in a pretty sorry state here.'

There was no disputing that. Wind was now hissing in not only through the empty windows but also through the debris-impact holes in the gondola's starboard wall. Broken glass littered the floor, and with it were spatters of blood from Rigz and Ra'asielson. Those two had been taken to the cabins, so the crew was down to just four, not including Az. Plus, a propeller was missing and the steering had been compromised.

It would have been the easiest thing in the world just to admit defeat and give up. Enough was enough. The ship couldn't – shouldn't – have to take any more punishment.

'Guys,' Az said, addressing the remaining crewmen. 'It's up to you. I have no idea what Captain Qadoschson would say or do under these circumstances. To me, it's simple. The pirates have caused us no end of grief, and it doesn't seem right that they should get away with it. Flight Lieutenant Wallimson nobbled us, and he's now on their side. Naoutha Nisrocsdaughter has Mr Mordadson captive, and there's no telling what she'll do to him. Those are the facts.

'Then there's *Behemoth* herself. She was once the *Brightspans Empress*, a troop carrier like *Cerulean*, a sister ship. I know transporting soldiers is hardly a peaceful occupation, but that was a long time ago. *Cerulean* may not have had a spotless past but she's made up for it since, whereas the *Brightspans Empress*, as *Behemoth*, is being used solely to plunder and kill. I don't know about you but it pains me to see her the way she is. She's a mockery, a black-painted perversion of an airship. Like a sick cage-bird, I think she ought to be put out of her misery.

'What it comes down to is whether you have the heart to carry on and see this to its conclusion. Whether you, like me, want to put right all the wrongs that have been done. Whether you feel, after the battering we've taken, that you've enough left in you for a last, determined push.

'This wasn't meant to be a big motivational speech,' he concluded. 'I just wanted to say what I'm feeling. The choice, really, truly, is yours. Whatever you lot decide, we do. But you have to decide quickly, before *Behemoth* sails out of sight.'

The crew were silent.

Then the trim-master said, 'We'll go on.'

The helmsman said, 'Let's get 'em.'

The other two agreed.

Az turned to Iaxson. 'Well?'

Reluctantly, sombrely, the wing commander nodded. 'All right.'

'Full speed,' Az announced. 'All engines.'

'Aye-aye, captain,' said the helmsman.

Only Az noticed. Nobody else even batted an eyelid.

Not *skipper*.

Captain.

CHAPTER 86

A Groundling Gains His Wings (Though Not In The Metaphorical, 'Ascending' Sense)

The roughnecks worked hard all afternoon, using toolkits from the dune-buggies, and by early evening their efforts bore fruit when the engine of a biplane let out a spurt of fumes and started to roar. Other planes swiftly followed suit. Choked carburettors coughed, clearing the sediment from their barrels. Seized-up propellers turned, slowly and stutteringly at first but soon with a smooth, pearly whir. Once-awkward ailerons articulated and angled on demand.

The first attempt at flying took place at dusk. Magnus Clockweight settled himself in the cockpit of a single-seater, pulled the glass bubble-canopy shut over his head, and hit the ignition. The plane rolled towards open desert, gathering speed.

Clockweight and Hardscree had pooled their knowledge of aeronautics, such as it was. Neither was in any way an expert but between them they were able to establish a solid theoretical base to work from. It was all about lift. A plane's wings were shaped so that the air flowing over the top of them was faster than the air flowing underneath. The rounded upper surface of the wings meant the air travelled slightly further than it did below the flat underside, but at the same speed. The difference between the two rates of flow created a partial vacuum above the wing and thus provided lift. It raised the plane off the ground.

In order to achieve lift, though, you had to be going

quickly. Clockweight leaned on the throttle and the single-seater juddered forward, faster, and faster still. The tail end kept skidding and he had to maintain a firm grip on the joystick to stay on a straight course. All the while, his heart was in his mouth and his belly ached with fear. This was madness, utter madness!

Suddenly, unexpectedly, and all too briefly, the single-seater took off. Clockweight had a delicious, tingling sense of weight-lessness. Flying. He was *flying*.

Then the undercarriage touched down and he was rumbling along the ground again.

He gunned the engine. He'd had a taste of being aloft. He liked it. He wanted to get back up there.

The single-seater gave a lurch and a leap, and all at once become airborne and this time stayed that way. Clockweight let out a whoop of joy. The watching roughnecks did the same. Hardscree smiled.

Clockweight flew for less than a minute, remaining at a height of ten metres or so. He experimented tentatively with steering, but for the most part he concentrated on keeping the single-seater up and going. At last he pushed down on the joystick and descended. He realised, almost too late, that he also needed to decrease his speed. The ground was rushing up to him at an alarming rate. He pulled back on the throttle, hit the desert with an almighty bang, and lurched frighteningly upwards again. His stomach did a weird kind of flip-flop. For several seconds he feared he had lost control and the plane was going to roll over and land on its top. But the single-seater then seemed to take command, levelling out, as if it wanted to touch down safely as much as its pilot did. Its wings stopped seesawing, and Clockweight was able to bring it down to the ground bumpily but in one piece.

The roughnecks were clapping one another on the back and cheering as their toolpusher taxied to a halt in front of the cavern. Clockweight stepped out of the cockpit a bona fide hero. All of his men wanted to be next to have a turn, to follow the boss's example and shake off the bonds of gravity. Only a couple got the chance before the last of the daylight leaked from the sky and it was too dark to see.

With the onset of night, the roughnecks retreated to the shelter of the cavern, lit a fire, and cooked their supper on it. Hardscree had gone out and caught over a dozen patchrabbits, little burrowing mammals with piebald fur that were native to the desert and considered, by some, to be a delicacy. Though their meat was stringy, it was also tangily tasty, and while the roughnecks gnawed, they talked eagerly about tomorrow. Come tomorrow, they would all be pilots. They had plans for weapons, too, cunning improvised devices which they could use to attack the black airship with. They would find the pirates and give them what-for. Those Airborn scumbags would have no idea what hit them.

While the roughnecks schemed and predicted, Den Grub-dollar kept himself to himself, chewing quietly on a patchrabbit leg. He had plans of his own.

CHAPTER 87

Dishonourable Men

It was midnight, or later. Den had lost track of time. Finally, finally, the last of the roughnecks had stopped chatting and dropped off to sleep. Now was his chance.

He stole out from the cavern and moved towards the needle mesa. The moon was fingernail-thin and the little light it shed was further dimmed by the clouds. He walked like a blind man, arms feeling in front of him, every footstep careful and considered. Now and then he tripped on a patch of uneven ground. Each time, he stood stock still, listened out, and heard nothing but snores from the cavern. Bit by bit the snores got further away. The needle mesa loomed closer, a giant, shadowy obelisk rising against the field of faint silver that was the sky.

Would it be the half-tarp van? Or one of the dune-buggies?

Den still hadn't made up his mind which type of vehicle to take. He would surely get further in the half-tarp, but then a dune-buggy was better suited to the rough terrain and therefore faster in the short term.

Before he set off in either, though, he had to disable all the other vehicles so that nobody could go after him. Removing the distributor caps would do the trick (with regret, Den remembered how he had immobilised *Bertha* that way).

Only problem was, taking out a distributor cap was a labour-intensive procedure and difficult to accomplish quietly, especially in the dark. A simpler, better solution was to let down the tyres on each vehicle. There was a foot-pump in the half-tarp. He would leave that behind so that the tyres could be reinflated. He doubted whether anyone would even think it worthwhile to pursue him, but if they did, he wanted a decent head start.

He located the first of the dune-buggies by blundering straight into it and barking his shin on its front bumper. Cursing under his breath, he rubbed the shin till the pain faded. Then, crouching down, he groped for the valve on the nearest tyre.

He didn't understand why his neck suddenly felt odd. There was a line of coldness running along the side of it, across his jugular vein, as though someone had placed an icicle there.

'Den, Den, Den ...' said a voice right next to his ear.

Deacon Hardscree's voice.

And then Den knew that the line of coldness was the blade of Hardscree's hunting knife.

He hadn't heard a thing! The man had crept up on him in the dark without making a sound.

'I knew you'd do something like this,' Hardscree carried on, with soft menace. 'I just knew it. Even though I told you you'd have to stay, you couldn't, could you? But where did you think you could go? There's a huge amount of desert to cross. Did you think you could just drive out of here, putter along for a couple of days and then, hey presto, you'd be back in civilisation? You must know how unlikely it is that you'd have made it.'

'That'm no reason not to try,' Den growled. 'Somebody in authority needs to know what you's doing. Somebody needs to be told so as you can be put a stop to, straight up.'

'And you'd be the one to do the telling? How brave, Den. How noble. I'd admire you, if I didn't think you were so misguided. Can't you see that this, what we're doing, *this* is how to realise our dream of equality with the Airborn? Not merely by using their aircraft but by using their aircraft against them. It's completely logical, completely appropriate. It's —'

'Oh, bless my bum, just kill I,' Den snapped. 'Do it. Get it over with. Anything rather than have to listen to your long-winded, pontificating guff for one more moment.'

Hardscree chuckled cruelly. 'I think I may kill you at that. You're proving to be a nuisance and frankly we'd all be better off without you. Hmmm. Yes. I'd have to make it look like an accident, like some wild beast got you – but I'm sure I can manage that. The right sort of slashes here and there. Clockweight and his men would be none the wiser. I could even make myself look good by saying I heard your screams and rushed out to help. I wasn't able to save you, alas. I didn't get to you in time.'

'My screams,' Den said in soft, chilled tones.

'Oh yes. Being savaged by a wild beast – of course you'd scream.'

Den's right hand began to move, picking its way sidelong across the ground like a crab. There must be something around here, something he could use to defend himself.

'You'd murder I in cold blood,' he said, stalling for time. 'And here I were, having you pegged as an honourable man.'

'Mostly I am,' said Hardscree. 'But sometimes there comes a point where honour meets practicality head-on and one of them has to give way to the other. This is one of those times and I've reached that point with you. I'm indebted to you for all you've done to help, Den, but as of now you've become unhelpful and you're in the way.'

'Be that so? 'Cause I reckon' – Den's exploring hand came across a narrow, sharp-edged stone – 'I reckon all that'm happening here is you's taken a fancy to the notion of killing a person.' His fingers closed around the stone. 'As opposed to an animal, I mean. You'm a Pale Uplander, you's used to killing animals. But here be a human being, and you's got an opportunity to do away with he and not face any consequences, and you'm going to go ahead with it. And you know why?'

Hardscree heaved a sigh. 'I'm sure you're about to enlighten me.'

'Because I were wrong about you. You doesn't have a scrap of honour after all. Turns out you'm just a psycho-nutter fanatic like all them other Deacons. But that'm OK.'

'OK?' echoed Hardscree, quizzically.

'Yep.' Den picked the stone off the ground. 'When it comes down to it, you see, I doesn't have a scrap of honour either.'

So saying, he lashed backwards with the stone, ramming it with all his strength into Hardscree's knee. It wasn't a knife but it was almost as good as. He felt it pierce the Deacon's robe and cut through into his kneecap. He heard Hardscree give a sharp cry. Thrusting the knife away from his neck, he sprang upright and started running.

There was no direction to his running, no specific objective he was heading towards. He ran through the dark, stumbling across sand and scrub, simply in order to get away and be somewhere, anywhere, that Deacon Hardscree wasn't.

He continued to run long after he would normally have collapsed from exhaustion. Panic and fear carried him far, far into the night-shrouded wastes of the Relentless Desert.

CHAPTER 88

Point Of No Return

Cerulean dogged *Behemoth* through the night. Az kept the running lights off so that everyone's eyes would remain dark-adapted. It was just possible to make out the shape of *Behemoth* ahead. She was visible despite her coloration because she stood out against the stars. Where there was an oval hole in the starfield, that was where *Behemoth* was.

Both airships were operating at half capacity, so their mean speeds were the same. Thanks to Az's handiwork with the bolas gun, the pirates would not be able to outrun *Cerulean*.

Or so he hoped.

Cerulean, however, had started to make some very unhappy noises. Creaks and groans shuddered through her frame, and every so often the usually steady rhythm of her propellers skipped a beat. For all her size, she was a delicate thing. She had taken a battering, she had wounds, and now she was being pushed to her limits. She couldn't carry on like this indefinitely, and Az knew there was a real risk of her suffering a breakdown, potentially a catastrophic one.

The issue of fuel consumption was also raising its head. The gauges showed that the tanks were running dry, and although *Cerulean* had reserves, it was debatable how far they would get her. With a favourable tailwind, back to Redspire, possibly. But not necessarily. Ra'asielson would have been able to give Az a precise estimate of the distance involved and a formula for optimal speed and altitude ... but the navigator was lying coma-tose in one of the cabins, close to death.

Az was aware that the outcome of the entire mission now rested squarely on his shoulders. But more than that, lives were depending on him, and he knew that in this respect he would shortly be facing a stark and awful dilemma. At some stage he was going to have to weigh up the safety of one person, Mr Mordadson, against the safety of many, the crew and the remaining Patrollers. He was going to have to choose whether to keep pursuing the pirates for as long as it took or cut his losses and turn for Redspire. If he did the former, there was a good chance *Cerulean* might run out of fuel and fail to make it back to civilisation. But if he did the latter, Naoutha would doubtless see that her hostage was surplus to requirements and get rid of him.

Soon the point of no return would come, the moment when the fuel gauges said it was Az's last chance to make a bid to reach Redspire, now or never.

Twelve hours, he reckoned. That was how much longer he could afford to stay on *Behemoth*'s tail. That was how much longer this pursuit could continue. After that, he would have to break it off and abandon Mr Mordadson to his fate.

CHAPTER 89

'A Lovely Chat'

Mr Mordadson came to with a start.

His skull ached. His brain was a fog.

He breathed evenly and carefully, long slow ins and outs, restoring his equilibrium.

The ache lessened. His thoughts became clearer.

He assessed his predicament.

He was tied to a chair. Ropes bound his arms and wings tightly to the chair's back. His ankles were fastened by more ropes to its legs. He twisted and writhed, but the knots were good and there was no slack to work with. He was held fast, for the duration. The lance wound in his biceps blazed excruciatingly.

He was in a cabin, and by the starlight glow coming in through the porthole he was able to confirm that it wasn't one of *Cerulean*'s cabins. The place was a mess, particularly the floor, which was littered with empty booze bottles and also with drug paraphernalia – discarded hypodermic syringes and little glass ampoules with their caps snapped off. These various glass containers rattled around, tinkling musically with the vibration of *Behemoth*'s engines.

The engines themselves, Mr Mordadson could tell, were going flat out. That might mean the airship had somewhere she urgently had to get to or it might mean she had someone she urgently had to get away from.

Before he could ponder more deeply on this matter, the cabin door was flung open and in came Naoutha Nisrocsdaughter, along with Twitchy Ziz and Flight Lieutenant Wallimson.

Mr Mordadson was startled to see Wallimson in Naoutha's

company, but immediately worked out what must have happened. The flight lieutenant had swapped sides. And it was a fair bet that Wallimson was the one who had grabbed him from behind during the fight, giving Naoutha the window of opportunity she needed to knock him out.

'Ah, awake!' said Naoutha. 'Shame. I was looking forward to rousing you with a couple of slaps. Oh, what the hell. I will anyway.'

She cuffed Mr Mordadson twice, a sharp backhand blow to each side of the face.

This amused Twitchy Ziz greatly. 'Thwack! Thwack!' he exclaimed, flipping his head from side to side as if he, too, had been hit.

Mr Mordadson smiled at Naoutha. 'Thank you. Very refreshing. I feel much better now.'

Naoutha studied him for a moment, then struck him again, this time with a firm fist.

'Ooh!' said Twitchy Ziz, wincing delightedly.

Mr Mordadson swivelled his head back round to look at Naoutha. A line of blood started to ooze from the corner of his mouth.

'What a tease you are,' he said. 'All this caressing. When are you going to start hitting me properly?'

Before Naoutha could react, Wallimson stepped forward and slammed his fist straight into Mr Mordadson's swollen nose.

It was agony, like splinters of glass being driven into his sinuses, but Mr Mordadson refused to give anyone the satisfaction of knowing how much it hurt. Even as fresh blood began trickling from his nostrils, his smile became a grin.

'Such a lovely chat we're having, isn't it, Naoutha? The four of us, getting along so nicely. We must do this more often. You, me, the flight lieutenant, and that – that *pet* of yours there.'

Twitchy Ziz bristled. 'Pet!?' He stepped forward to take his turn hitting Mr Mordadson, but Naoutha stayed his arm.

'No, Ziz. He's goading us. He wants us to keep hitting him till he passes out from the pain, and then he won't be any use to us.'

'Curses, you've foiled my cunning plan,' said Mr Mordadson.

'I know this man, Naoutha,' said Wallimson. 'He won't cough up information willingly. Beating it out of him is the only way.'

'Depends,' said Mr Mordadson. 'What do you want to know? I'd be happy to tell you all about the flight lieutenant here, for instance. Couldn't handle someone else getting the captain's job when he felt it should have been his. That's all it took to drive him into the arms of our enemy – resentment because someone else got promoted over him. That's the type of man your new ally is, Naoutha. Pathetic, eh?'

'That's not the only reason I decided to throw my lot in with Naoutha,' Wallimson said, stiffly.

'No, I'm sure your personal dislike of Az was also a factor. Anything to get back at him. But you know what I think, above all, convinced you you wanted to be a pirate?'

Mr Mordadson left a pause, so that the flight lieutenant had no choice but to ask, 'What?'

'You're a freak. And look who you're with now. *Look* at them. Where would a freak like you feel more at home than in the company of other freaks?'

With a grunt of rage, Wallimson flew at Mr Mordadson and began pummelling him mercilessly. The helpless captive's head snapped from side to side as Wallimson punched him, right hand then left, over and over – mouth, nose, cheek, eyes. It took all of Naoutha's strength to pull him away.

'No!' she said. 'No. Don't let him get to you. There'll be plenty of time for that later.'

Wallimson struggled in her grasp. His cheeks were flushed with humiliation and spite. 'Bustard!' he yelled at Mr Mordadson. 'Call me a freak? You try going through life with one working wing. See how *you* like it.'

Mr Mordadson could feel the skin of his face tightening. Contusions were starting to form in all the places where he had been hit. His head throbbed all over, pulsing in time with his heartbeat. The pain of the wound in his arm added to his general agony. He felt near to vomiting.

Nevertheless he forced his mouth to bend once more into a

smile, or as close to a smile as his mashed and swollen lips could manage.

'You're enjoying this, aren't you, Wallimson? Settling scores with me. Getting your own back for what I did to you at Gyre. Well, make the most of it. I won't be tied to this chair for ever, and then I'll show you a thing or two about inflicting pain. That goes for you too, Naoutha.'

Wallimson made another lunge forward, but Naoutha swung him round and bundled him out of the cabin.

'Stay there,' she ordered. 'And you too, Ziz. Out.'

The skinny pirate whimpered pleadingly.

'No,' said Naoutha. 'I think I'll get better results on my own.'

Twitchy Ziz left the cabin with a sulky pout.

Slamming and locking the door, Naoutha turned back to Mr Mordadson. 'Now then. It's just you and me ...'

CHAPTER 90

Bait

'So this is what it's all about, eh?' Mr Mordadson said, clucking his tongue. 'You've a thing for older men. I knew it! And here's me without a bunch of flowers or a bottle of wine or anything.'

'That's enough cheap bravado, Mordadson,' said Naoutha. 'I'm not here to be impressed by how well you can withstand punishment. I'm here for facts, and I will get them.'

'Surely Wallimson's been an excellent source of intelligence already.'

'He has been helpful, yes, but there's still one or two things I need to clear up.'

'Well, seeing as it's just you and me, as you say, Naoutha, I'll do what I can.'

'Sarcasm,' Naoutha said with an audible sniff. 'Delightful. Now tell me, why is *Cerulean* persisting on chasing us?'

That explains why Behemoth*'s flying hard,* Mr Mordadson thought. *Az is behind her and he's not giving up. Good lad.*

He said, 'Maybe there's some irresistible attraction between *Cerulean* and *Behemoth*. Airship love! After all, *Cerulean*'s been one of a kind for so long. She must have got lonely. Horny, too. And then another airship comes along. Not much to look at, but beggars can't be choosers. And so —'

'Stop it,' said Naoutha. She was starting to sound annoyed, in spite of herself. 'I mean it. This is pointless. This whole situation is pointless. Don't you see? You can't win. You'll never be able to bring us down. However many Alar Patrollers you send, you'll never succeed. We'll always beat you, because we're younger and we're faster and most of all we have nothing to lose.'

'Now who's indulging in cheap bravado?'

'It isn't bravado if you believe in it.'

'So how come you're still fleeing from *Cerulean*? That would suggest your side didn't actually win the battle. I'm guessing you forced a standoff, using me as leverage, but even so *Cerulean*'s still on your tail and you can't shake her off.'

'Well deduced. And so nearly correct. You don't think we're genuinely *fleeing*, do you?' Naoutha had recovered her poise. From her tone of voice, it was easy to picture a triumphant sneer behind the mask and goggles.

'What would you rather I called it? "Tactical withdrawal"?'

'The commonest word for it is trap.'

'Trap,' Mr Mordadson echoed. His stomach felt as though someone had dropped a large stone inside it.

'We're leading *Cerulean* a dance,' Naoutha went on, 'and at a certain point we're going to dip into the clouds, lose her, and hide somewhere where she can't easily find us. And if she does eventually manage to find us, by then we'll have augmented our attack capability ... and that will be the end for your precious airship. Then there'll be nothing to prevent us from going about our business.' She straightened her shoulders, pleased with herself.

'You didn't really come here for information,' Mr Mordadson said, with cold certainty. 'You came here to gloat.'

'Guilty as charged. But in a way you *are* providing me with information, Mordadson. Your reaction speaks volumes. It says that you understand that you're the bait in the trap and that you think *Cerulean* won't be able to resist being lured. The Gabrielson boy won't abandon you, meaning he's going to play right into our hands.'

'No, no, Az will give me up if he has to. He's no fool. He'll realise I'm expendable. We're far out from the airlanes here, a long distance from the nearest refuelling stop. He'll soon take the decision to leave me and head for home.'

'Too late to bluff. You've already given away your true feelings. First responses never lie.' Naoutha rubbed her gloved hands together. 'A very satisfactory outcome. And I didn't have to resort to violence after all. All I did was use my wits. Maybe you could learn from that.'

Her captive barked a rancorous laugh. 'The day I've something to learn from *you*, Naoutha Nisrocsdaughter, is the day I die.'

'Let's not get too hasty here. No one said anything about dying – at least not just yet. Although I do have to ensure that you don't attempt anything tiresome, such as escaping. Those ropes are all well and fine, but even trussed up like a turkey you might find a way of slipping out of them. If I could only think of some means of rendering you helpless ...'

She pretended to rack her brains and come up with a solution. 'Ah! Of course.'

From her trouser pocket she took out an ampoule of clear liquid.

'Pterine,' said Mr Mordadson. 'Fine. Go ahead. Increase my strength and resilience. I'll stand a far better chance of freeing myself.'

'A single dose would certainly benefit you.' Naoutha produced two more ampoules. 'But a triple dose?'

Mr Mordadson's eyes went flinty hard.

'I'm sure you know what pterine in excess does to the human body,' she said. 'Too high a concentration in the bloodstream produces all sorts of nasty effects. Heart palpitations. Uncontrollable tremors. Loss of muscular control. In some extreme cases it can even lead to death. But let's hope that's not the case here. All I want is for you to be a gibbering, shuddering, incontinent wreck for the next few hours, nothing more spectacular than that.'

She bent down, rooted around on the cabin floor, and selected one of the used hypodermics. Breaking the caps on the three ampoules, she inserted the syringe needle into each one in turn and drew the contents into the tube using the plunger. Then she held the full syringe with its needle upwards and tapped the tube so that the tiny bubbles in the liquid rose to the top, forming an air pocket. She got rid of the air pocket by depressing the plunger gently till a droplet of pterine beaded at the needle's tip. She did all this slowly, in full view of Mr Mordadson, taking her time. She hummed a tune to herself throughout.

Finally she brought the syringe over and pricked the needle into his neck.

'There?' she wondered. 'Or the arm?'

'Just get on with it,' Mr Mordadson snapped.

'Patience. One mustn't rush these things. Yes, the neck. That way the drug'll reach your brain sooner.'

Mr Mordadson braced himself.

'Now, you may feel a slight scratch,' Naoutha said, and jammed the needle all the way in.

Seconds later, Mr Mordadson started to scream.

CHAPTER 91

Yes Or No

A long, long, lonnnng night. *Behemoth* always ahead, a blankness in the sky, a blot against the stars. *Cerulean* heaving and moaning, like an exhausted person eager for sleep, begging for rest. Az himself barely able to stay awake, eyelids drooping, head nodding. Somehow forcing himself not to succumb. Knowing that Mr Mordadson was counting on him. And all the while, the fuel gauges creeping down, heading for the red zone and E for Empty. And the bitter, knifing cold of the high altitude winds. And the no less icy fear inside – fear of failure, fear of disaster, fear of letting down a friend in his hour of need.

As a mental exercise to keep him from dozing off, Az picked out and named constellations, all the star shapes he knew, each representing a character or creature from Airborn mythology, each with its own story. He recalled doing this on his first ever visit to the Silver Sanctum, up in the Astral Dome, shortly before he gave his decision to Lady Aanfieldsdaughter on whether he would accept her assignment to travel to the ground. The immense changes that had taken place in his life since had all stemmed from that moment.

That moment . . .

It was late, time was short, and Lady Aanfieldsdaughter couldn't wait any longer. She needed an answer. 'Yes or no?'

Az said no, and from then on he was ordinary. A boy without wings, yes, but otherwise just a seventeen-year-old, leading a normal, average, humdrum seventeen-year-old Airborn's life. He never had to deal with Humanists who wanted to bring the sky-cities down. He didn't confront the mad Deacon Shatterlonger, who tried to strangle him. Nor was there any of this stuff now – pitched battles with pirates, death in the air, shooting a man with the bolas gun, pursuing *Behemoth* interminably through the dark. Az finished school. He found himself a job somewhere. He was just another citizen.

He said no, and Lady Aanfieldsdaughter nodded but she was clearly disappointed, and standing nearby in the Astral Dome was the Count of Gyre. The Count held up the strip of tickertape with Az's prophecy symbol on it. He pointed to the question mark in the centre of the double arrow.

'Up or down?' he said, peeling back his lips to reveal his yellowy clothes-peg teeth. 'Light or dark? Right or wrong? Yes or no?'

Az's decision remained firmly no, and he didn't go to combat lessons with Mr Mordadson and he never became captain of an airship and he stayed at home with his parents and he never learned of the term *extreme sanction*. He said no because that was the easier option, the answer which didn't scare him, the choice which brought the fewest unwelcome implications and complications. Why volunteer for danger? Why open yourself up to threat and misery and pain and death?

He said no, and the Count tore the bit of tickertape to shreds and bowed his head.

Mr Mordadson was in the Astral Dome too. He looked away, refusing to meet Az's gaze. Michael was ashamed of him. Aurora dipped her wings in regret.

Still Az said no, and there was no Cassie. There was never any Cassie. He never met her. She ceased to exist.

He wanted to be glad about that. He could think of her only with hurt feelings and a sense of dismay. Without her, wasn't his life cleaner and simpler? Wasn't he better off?

Yes.

No.

Az looked Lady Aanfieldsdaughter in the eye and gave her his final answer, the one he had known he was going to give all along, the one he was meant to give. With an emphatic nod of the head, he said —

'Sir? Captain? Did you hear me?'

Az snapped alert. Idiot! He *had* dozed off!

'Sir?'

'Yes, trim-master?'

'*Behemoth*'s going down.'

'Down?'

'Into the clouds, it looks like.'

The black shape ahead was indeed descending towards the moon-silvered cloud layer. Soon her propellers were whipping its upper tufts into vaporous whorls.

'Should we follow?'

Az thought hard. 'We follow her in there and we'll lose her for sure. That's what the pirates want. So instead we stay put and wait for them to come back up. Go into a holding pattern. Halt engines. Use them only if we start to stray from position. We stay here and we keep watch.'

The propellers stopped turning and *Cerulean* drifted.

Az peered down at the cloud cover as it parted silkily to let *Behemoth* in. All the once, the black airship was engulfed. The clouds closed over her. She was gone.

He was gambling on her resurfacing, as she would have to sooner or later. Was this the right thing to do?

He remembered the dream he had just had.

Decisions.

Yes or no.

In the end, that was all life was: an endless succession of alternatives. Do this or do that. You couldn't ever know which was the correct path, you could only trust your instincts and judgement and make a choice and hope that hindsight would prove you had chosen well. There was no going back once you'd settled on a course of action. There were no second chances.

In other words, if this gamble of his didn't pay off, Mr Mordadson was dead.

CHAPTER 92

The Razorweed Vortex

Daybreak greyed the world, and Den Grubdollar crawled out from under the rocky overhang beneath which he had hunkered for the past few hours, clutching his knees and shivering. The night-time cold had penetrated to his bones, and his body felt as stiff as sticks. He spent several minutes stretching and bending and massaging some life back into his muscles. He was hungry and thirsty, and during the small hours he had developed a racking cough which was chillingly reminiscent of his beloved Orla's final days. It didn't take much to bring on a case of rattle-lung. The disease was latent in most people and could emerge with very little provocation, when you were already ill with some other sickness, for instance, or when you had allowed your core temperature to drop low for a sustained period. The cough might be just a cough, of course, his lungs troubled after a night spent out in the open, nothing more sinister than that.

But wouldn't that take the biscuit, Den thought, to be lost in the Relentless Desert *and* come down with rattle-lung. Wouldn't that be the icing on the cake.

Biscuit and *cake* sparked an image in his mind's eye – a host of delicious, sugary teatime treats piled high on a table – and his stomach grumbled. He ordered himself not to think of food. Not to think about eating in any way. He mustn't torment himself with what he couldn't have.

A coughing fit overcame him, bending him double. He hawked up and spat out what felt like several lungfuls of phlegm.

Then, straightening up, Den started to walk.

It was hopeless, he knew. This was the Relentless Desert, one of the most inhospitable environments on earth, and he was in the middle of it without victuals, without transportation, without any means of protecting himself. He was as good as dead.

But he walked nonetheless, and vowed to keep walking till he couldn't go another step. Where the clouds were lightest at present, that was east. Therefore he knew roughly where north was, and he aimed his footsteps in that direction. He would continue going north, using the sun's position as a guide, because it was the only bearing worth following. North, ultimately, meant civilisation. Civilisation was impossibly far away. He would never reach it. But still, nonetheless, north.

Den had no idea how long he'd been walking when he first heard the strange sound. Nor did he have any idea how long it took him to arrive at the sound's source. He was already losing track of time. Seconds were footsteps. Minutes were the intervals between coughs.

The sound started as a faint rustling hiss and from there evolved into a deeper, skittering scurry, like fallen autumn leaves fluttering around in a breeze. Soon it had grown to a loud, resonant, strident crackle, which was reminiscent of the noise of a large bonfire but which could almost, almost, have been electrical in origin.

Den headed towards it with some eagerness, his pace quickening. If the sound was electrical, that meant machinery, and machinery meant the possible presence of people. But even if it wasn't machinery, he still had to know what was generating the sound. Hope and curiosity drove him to find out.

He came to the rim of a deep depression in the ground, a sloping-sided canyon shaped like an elongated horseshoe. Down in the rounded end of this rift, not far from where he was standing, was a throng of moving objects. At first Den took them to be animals of some kind, further examples of the bizarre types of wildlife that were unique to the Relentless Desert. They shifted around one another, climbed on top of each other, jostled for position, collided, bounced, tumbled, exactly in the manner of sentient creatures. Somehow they had become stuck up one end of the canyon and couldn't find a way out, and in their agitation they were rolling around and mauling one another and growing desperate.

On closer inspection, however, it became apparent that they weren't animals at all. They were balls of razorweed.

Den recalled Hardscree pointing some razorweed out to him a few days earlier. It was a scrubby, thorny shrub, and it propagated itself, the Deacon had said, by dying and letting the wind uproot it and bundle it into a ball, which would then roll across the desert, popping out seed pods along the way. Razorweed's thorns were huge and brutally sharp, hence the name. It was said that one clump, if you didn't get out of its way as it hurtled towards you, could fillet the flesh from your body.

Here, hundreds of razorweed balls had collected in the base of the canyon like litter in a dead-end alleyway. The same wind that had blown them there was now harassing them mercilessly, propelling them round in circles to create a whirling vortex of barbed brown vegetation. Now and then the wind would lift one of the razorweed balls up, bring it near the canyon rim, offer it a tantalising glimpse of liberty – only to let it fall back down again at the crucial moment and rejoin its companions below.

To Den, the razorweed vortex was a mesmerising sight, and also a discouraging one. It spoke of trappedness and futility.

It also spoke of death. Imagine if someone were to fall into that spinning soup of tangled branches with finger-long thorns ...

He shuddered. It didn't bear thinking about.

'Doesn't bear thinking about, does it?' said Deacon Hard-scree.

Den spun round.

Hardscree was standing a few metres away, poised on the canyon rim. The knife was in his hand. The hem of his robe was dusty and torn. He wasn't even looking at Den, just peering down at the endlessly swirling, circulating razorweed.

'You – you —'

'I've been following you, yes, Den. Tracked you all this way. Not difficult for an Uplander. I could track a mouse in this desert if I wanted to, so you were no challenge at all. Only thing that made it hard was my knee.' He moved a couple of paces closer to Den, demonstrating a severe limp. 'You made a serious mess there. Tore a ligament, I think. It hurts like a son of a bitch. Every step of the journey has been agony, and for that you're going to pay – dearly.'

The knife blade glinted.

'Prepare to Ascend, Den,' said Hardscree. 'No, why sugarcoat it? Prepare to *die*.'

CHAPTER 93

Brawl On The Canyon Rim

Briefly Den thought, *Ah well, the desert'll kill I anyway, may as well let Hardscree do the honours instead. Might even be quicker his way, you never knows.*

But no. He wasn't going to grant Hardscree the privilege of ending his life. At least, not without putting up a fight.

Hardscree came at him, knife raised. Thanks to his damaged knee, he wasn't as quick or as co-ordinated as before, and Den was able to intercept his knife-holding hand, grabbing it by the wrist. Hardscree bore down with the weapon. Den resisted. Seconds passed, the two men grappling next to the canyon. The knife was between them, its point quivering mere millimetres from Den's face.

Then Den kicked out, and the toecap of his boot made contact with Hardscree's bad knee. Hardscree shrieked and hopped backwards, but rapidly recovered and prowled towards Den once more, slashing the knife from side to side.

Den backed away from the scything swipes of the blade, and all at once he found himself teetering on the edge of the canyon. One foot was half on the ground, half not. His heel had nothing beneath it but space, and the earth under his instep was crumbling. His arms windmilled. Down below, the razorweed vortex revolved, sounding almost greedy in its crackling, like someone smacking their lips before a meal.

Then the crumbling earth gave way and Den's leg shot downwards. At that selfsame instant Hardscree lunged, aiming to stab him in the throat. Den slithered far enough down the canyon slope that the knife thrust passed harmlessly over his head. While Hardscree regained his balance, Den grabbed the ground with both hands, dug his fingers in and pushed with all his might, shoving himself up out of the canyon before he could slide any further in. Rolling away from the brink, he leapt to his feet, and scarcely had time to catch his breath before the Deacon's next assault. The knife slashed towards his belly but he managed to sidestep out of the way and the blade caught only his clothing. It lacerated his shirt but not him.

Hardscree, fiery hair flapping in the breeze, went onto the offensive yet again. Den, even as he continued to dodge and dive, felt a horrible sense of inevitability. Injured knee or not, Hardscree would not let up. He would keep on coming, keep on coming, until his knife finally found its target. Den didn't have the energy to fight him for ever.

Again he entertained the notion of simply letting the Deacon do his worst. Get it over with.

And again, he rejected such fatalism. Give in? Not while there was a breath left in his body.

Hardscree stabbed, and Den made a desperate grab for the knife. He wasn't quick enough. Hardscree yanked it back and Den's hand closed around the blade rather than the handle. A fierce pain lanced up his arm. He recoiled, hand bleeding. A glance showed him his palm had been opened up to the bone. He had no idea anything could hurt quite so much.

Hardscree paused for a moment to crow. Tossing the knife from hand to hand, he said, 'First blood to me. And if you think that's bad, just you wait. There's worse in store.'

Den glowered at him, the breath rasping through his lips.

'Oh, don't be like that,' Hardscree said. 'You didn't expect this little scuffle of ours was going to have any other outcome, did you? You surely didn't think you could *win*.'

Den cocked his head. He had just heard something above the massed susurration of the razorweed. The noise was familiar. Absurdly familiar. He knew it as well as he knew the sound of his own voice.

No, not possible. It couldn't be what he thought it was. He was imagining things. The pain was fuddling his senses.

'What?' Hardscree demanded, with a frown.

Den listened harder. The noise was definitely real. He just couldn't quite pinpoint where it was coming from.

'Why are you looking like that?'

Den turned his head, scanning the horizon.

'Answer me!'

Den's gaze alighted on a far-off shape. It was heading this way, growing bigger, getting rapidly nearer.

Hardscree, scowling, followed his line of vision.

'Know what, Deacon?' Den said. 'All of a sudden I reckon I *can* win after all.'

And he started to cackle.

Just like *Bertha* was cackling.

Trundling across the desert plain, her throttle wide, her tracks churning up rocks and sand.

Bearing down on Den and the Deacon.

Like some lumbering fifty-tonne mirage, a glorious, smoke-spewing vision of salvation . . .

The most wonderful thing Den Grubdollar had ever seen.

CHAPTER 94

A Predator At Bay

Den had every reason to think that Hardscree would now surrender. The Deacon seemed utterly flummoxed by *Bertha*'s appearance. The knife drooped in his hand. Surely he would have to admit defeat. Reinforcements had arrived. Somehow, in the vast, trackless wastes of the Relentless Desert, against all the odds, Den's family had found him. Hardscree must realise that now he was outnumbered and outflanked.

Which was true, and he did.

But he was also outraged. Den hadn't reckoned on how deep the Deacon's animosity towards him ran. When it finally dawned on Hardscree whose murk-comber this was and he understood that the balance of power had shifted decisively in his enemy's favour, he responded not with a sigh of surrender but with a surge of resentment. Hot on the heels of that came a resolve to finish what he had started, while he still could.

And so he rounded on Den once again.

And so he sealed his own fate.

Hobbling towards Den with his knife aloft, Hardscree looked a lot like a predator at bay, wounded, crazed, certain of nothing except the urge to lash out at those who had him cornered and harm as many of them as he could. His eyes bore a feral gleam and his red hair flamed wildly. The sophisticated, articulate Deacon he had been was very little in evidence now. He seemed to have reverted to a more primitive mode, his Uplander heritage showing through. Here was a man of the mountains, someone raised to stalk and catch and kill, someone who was close in temperament to the very beasts he routinely used to hunt.

Briefly, Den marvelled at how easily a man's civilised veneer could be stripped away. Then he stirred himself, summoning up the energy to repel yet another attack.

And then he didn't need to.

A javelin slammed into Hardscree from behind, skewering him through the shoulder, its tip emerging with a spurt of blood just above his collarbone. A perfect shot, hitting the Deacon where it would disable him but not cause a fatal injury.

Reeling under the impact, Hardscree dropped the knife and groped behind his back with both hands for the shaft of the javelin. He was so intent on pulling the weapon out that he wasn't looking where he was going. He staggered blindly towards the canyon edge. On impulse, Den yelled out a warning. He would never fully understand why he did this, why he tried to help somebody who just moments ago had been hell-bent on murdering him, but then that was what made him different from Hardscree – his humanity.

At any rate, Hardscree didn't hear the warning, or if he did, didn't heed it. He blundered straight over the rim of the canyon, still pawing desperately at the javelin's shaft as he fell.

The razorweed made short work of him. His screams lasted half a minute at most, as the wind-whirled thorns flayed him to ribbons.

When the screaming had stopped, Den took a reluctant peek into the canyon. One glimpse at the shuddering, bloody mess that had been Deacon Hardscree had him tottering away wishing he had never looked.

Bertha chuntered to a halt close by, and Den turned towards her. He tried to move his feet but all at once he felt drained, utterly depleted. Instead of rushing to meet his family, all he could do was sag to his knees.

He saw *Bertha's* loading bay hatch open and Cassie spring out. She launched herself towards him at a run. Fletcher and Robert were not far behind.

Then, for a while, Den saw nothing. He was blind; couldn't focus. His eyes were too full of tears.

CHAPTER 95

The Merits Of Collaboration
Over Confrontation

When Den had finished weeping, when his children had finished weeping too, when Cassie had treated the gash in his hand with disinfectant and bandaged it up, when Den had (with some puzzlement) greeted Colin Amblescrut and (with even more puzzlement) Michael and Aurora, when he had gulped down some water and found this eased his cough, when he had had something to eat, when he began to regain his strength – then came the time for explanations and justifications and, above all, for apologies. Endless, profuse apologies, which his children batted aside, saying it didn't matter, he had nothing to be sorry for, they didn't care about any of that, they had their da back, that was all they cared about.

'Him seemed to have the answers, that Deacon,' Den said. 'With he, everything seemed to make sense. Even Martin dying. Hardscree made I think I could turn that to the good, make it mean something. I were ... vulnerable, I suppose the word be. I were so desperate to feel optimistic about life again, to feel hope, that I stopped thinking straight. I fell for his lines, his Deaconly patter, even though it weren't all that different from the crap the Deacons used to spout in the old days. It were the same old sales pitch given a bit of a tart-up and a polish. That were how them used to get to we all, offering us promises of better things, better days ahead, and I always thought I were smarter than that. Always. And what should happen but, at a low point, I turned into a dumb old sucker like everyone else. Let my guard down for a moment, and that were that.'

'What did him offer you, Da?' Cassie asked. 'What was you chasing after all the way out here?'

'Illusions,' Den said bitterly, and told them about the cavern full of aircraft and then about the arrival of the roughnecks from Desolation Wells and how Hardscree chose to side with them because, never mind his big talk of raising Groundlings up, all he really wanted was to bring Airborn down. He was interested in creating equality but only the kind that came from confrontation rather than collaboration.

'Compare that with you lot and Michael and Aurora here,' Den said. 'From the sound of it, you all worked together and that'm how you found I.'

'That and pure dumb luck,' said Fletcher.

Colin nodded. 'Us was starting to lose hope, but Cassie insisted us keep at it.'

'Flogged we on like a slave-driver, she did,' said Robert. 'I don't think she'd ever have let we give up.'

'It weren't completely luck,' Cassie said. 'There were the message left at Desolation Wells. You left a hint about "a needle in a haystack" in your note to we, Da, and the message on the ground mentioned a needle too. It were a long shot but I reckoned it were worth taking. That'm why us came this way. And I were right. Your needle weren't just a figure of speech. It were this mesa you just told we about.'

'Nice piece of figuring-out, girl,' Den said, patting his daughter. 'I didn't leave that note as a clue, just as a way of letting you know I hadn't gone off my rocker. At least, not completely off my rocker. I'm glad I wrote what I did now, though. Straight up.'

He turned to the two Airborn. 'And congratulations be due, be'n't they? On you getting married. Sorry us couldn't make it to the wedding.'

'Think nothing of it,' said Michael.

'Didn't even get you a gift.'

'Knowing you're safe and well is gift enough.'

Den laughed for what felt like the first time in weeks. 'Well, I doesn't believe it for a moment, Michael, but it'm kind of you to say so. Now then.' He clapped his hands together, and instantly regretted it. 'Yeow. Won't do that again in a hurry. Now then,' he repeated, this time keeping his hands well apart, 'shall us get going? I'd like to be saying 'bye-bye to this desert, and I expect you lot would as well.'

'Erm, just one thing, Mr Grubdollar,' said Aurora.

'Call I Den, Aurora.'

'Den it is. You mentioned that these roughnecks plan on taking on the airship which destroyed their oil installation.'

'In the planes, yes.'

'In your view, do you think they stand a chance?'

'From what I saw, I'd have to say the answer be no. When I left, them was barely able to get those aircraft off the ground. I can't deny that them showed some guts in trying, and maybe guts will be enough. But even so . . . Oh. Ah. I think I see where you be going with this.'

'Let's say, for argument's sake,' said Aurora, 'that they become reasonably good at flying and then go after the airship. I know a bit about the people who are in that airship. Before the wedding, Lady Aanfielsdaughter told me about them, and since then, of course, we've witnessed ourselves how aggressive and ruthless they can be. The state of the installation is testimony to that. So, the roughnecks take them on, in vehicles they know next to nothing about, and . . .'

'A massacre,' said Michael, picking up her thread. 'But then that's what Az and Mr Mordadson and all those Patrollers are out here to deal with. They're hunting the Redspire airship, and we know she's in the area, so there's every chance they've already brought her down by now.'

'But what if they haven't?' said his wife. 'Worst-case scenario, the pirates go head-to-head with the roughnecks in the air. They'll surely win. That's thirty more Groundlings dead, to add to the death toll of who knows how many at Desolation Wells. And a whole lot more anti-Airborn resentment is created as a result.'

'This be another one of those dangerously escalating crises, be'n't it?' said Fletcher. 'It'm the Grimvale Chancel all over again.'

'I'm afraid that's how it's looking.'

'And you'm thinking us should get involved,' said Cassie. 'Again.'

'The way I see it,' said Aurora, 'the roughnecks could do with some help, and here we are, not that far away from them, with two people who happen to know their way around a plane.'

'One of them's a genius when it comes to aircraft, actually,' said Michael.

'Even if he does say so himself,' said his wife. 'Now, I'm suggesting this very tentatively. I don't want to put pressure on anyone. Least of all you, Den. You've been through so much. If it's your opinion that enough's enough and it's time to go home, fine by me. Then again, as you say, this could be a chance to demonstrate how collaboration is much better than confrontation. Airborn helping Groundling.'

'Even if it'm helping them against other Airborn?' queried Den.

'Against rogue Airborn. Dangerous Airborn. A mutual enemy. So, what do you think?'

Robert piped up. 'Nobody ever asks I my view,' he said, 'but I be with Aurora. It sounds like something us ought to do.'

Den appraised his youngest son. Boys his age were so gung-ho, so reckless when it came to answering the call to action. 'Well, that'm one firm vote in favour,' he said. 'Fletch?'

'Not sure, Da. I suppose us could at least drive Aurora and Michael to where these planes is and see how it goes from there.'

'That'm a yes then?'

'A qualified one.'

'Colin? Only fair to ask you too, since you's been a part of this from the start, as I gather.'

'Den,' said Colin, 'I be your pal and I be a pal to our Airborn chums here. My answer has to be a yes.'

'Cass?'

Cassie bit her lip. 'I be'n't sure either, Da.'

'What'm the matter?'

'Nothing. I just reckon Fletch has it right. Us could just drive them there, limit it to that. There be'n't much else us could do beyond that, anyway, being as none of we Groundlings knows the first thing about flying a plane.'

Den turned back to Aurora. 'There you has it. The Grubdollar/Amblescrut consensus appears to be: us'll help up to a point.' He shrugged. 'OK with you?'

Aurora gave a gracious bow. 'It's absolutely OK. It's plenty. I couldn't expect more.'

'Then let's get cracking,' Den said, clapping his hands together again. 'Agh! Yowch! *Got* to stop doing that.'

CHAPTER 96

A Future Lady Aurora Gabrielson?

As the Grubdollars and Colin scrambled to various positions within *Bertha*, Michael wrapped his arms around Aurora and planted a huge, proud kiss on her cheek.

'You can do better than that,' Aurora teased, and there followed several moments of passionate, lip-locked snogging. Wings splayed in shivery delight.

'Pretty pleased with yourself, aren't you?' Michael said, drawing back to look at her.

'As a matter of fact, I am.'

'And so you should be. You did some good leadership stuff there. Persuading others. Winning them over. You spoke like a true Silver Sanctumer.'

'I did, didn't I?'

'Am I looking at a future Lady Aurora Gabrielson?'

'You could well be.'

They both laughed. It seemed a fantastical prospect – Aurora one day joining the exalted ranks of the senior residents at the Sanctum – and yet at the same time, thanks to her confident, commanding performance just now, it seemed utterly plausible.

'And you,' Aurora said, 'are pretty excited at the thought of getting your hands on some vintage aircraft, aren't you?'

'Can't deny it. I can't imagine what's been stored down there in that cavern but I'm looking forward to finding out.'

'Then,' Aurora said, with a slight clearing of the throat, 'I suppose now would be as good a time as any to tell you that I think I'm pregnant.'

Michael: jaw open to the breastbone, eyes standing out on stalks, voicebox rendered incapable of speech.

Bertha: ignition, rumble, cackle.

CHAPTER 97

Little Miss Deadeye

Den occupied one of the front observation nacelles, and Cassie squeezed herself in behind him.

'What'm up, lass?' he enquired, as *Bertha* trundled southward, retracing roughly the same journey he had made coming the opposite way this morning and last night. Soon, surely, the needle mesa – that vast place-marker – would hove into view.

'Nothing, Da. Just wanted to be with you.' Cassie slipped an arm around his neck and Den patted her hand.

'But you'm troubled about something. Come on.'

She hesitated, then said, 'It be that Deacon. I didn't mean to kill he.'

'It were you that fired the javelin? I should have guessed. Little Miss Deadeye. That were fine aiming.'

'But I killed he all the same.'

'No, lass,' said her father, with finality. 'No, you didn't. You shot to wound, and if you hadn't done that him would've killed I for certain. Him would've gutted me open like a fresh-caught trout, quick as you please. You shot to wound and that means you did nothing wrong. Him's only dead because him fell into that razorweed. Don't even ask yourself twice about it. Your conscience be clean.'

'I – I saw he charging at you, and it were like Martin all over again. Somebody I love, fighting with a Deacon. Only, this time I could do something about it.'

'And you did.'

'I be guilty that him's dead but I be'n't sad. That make sense?'

'Does to me.'

'And ... and that has something to do with why I doesn't

313

want we to help Aurora. At least, not as much as us maybe could. Because, last time us helped Airborn, Martin ended up dead. And just now us so nearly lost you as well. I doesn't want to risk any of my family's lives ever again.'

'Understandable.' Den fixed his daughter with a gaze of stern fondness, or fond sternness. 'Let I tell you something, though, girl. You'm sensible and you'm responsible, and those be just two of the many, many things that I love about you and that make I so proud of you. But you also takes on too much responsibility sometimes. You can be too hard on yourself. I be'n't saying you should lighten up, just saying you might want to switch your priorities around a little. You always put others first, and that'm noble and laudable, but why not put *yourself* first for once? Accept that what *you* need be as important as what others need?'

'If I hadn't put you first, Da, us wouldn't be having this conversation now.'

'Agreed. That aside, though, there'm no shame in being selfish now and again. And if that means not volunteering to fight the good fight this time around, so be it.'

Cassie grinned with relief, and put her other arm around her father's neck and hugged him hard enough to choke him. When he pointed out that he was having a spot of bother with the whole inhaling, getting-oxygen-to-his-lungs process, she slackened her grip but didn't let go.

Nor did Den want her to let go. Not for a long time. Maybe not ever.

CHAPTER 98

Planespotter

It was well past midday by the time the needle mesa appeared on the horizon. Den had run and walked much further than he had thought. Such was the combined power of blind panic and blind faith.

Out of nowhere, a snub-nosed little plane appeared and buzzed *Bertha*. The plane shot past her on the right, its stubby wings seesawing in salutation.

'Pluck me gently!' exclaimed Michael. 'That's a Metatronco Condor. The most misnamed light aircraft in aviation history. Pathetic range, unlike a real condor. Pathetic fuel consumption too. The first production run was five hundred and they didn't manage to shift even half of those. There was this whole load of jokes about it, remember? The plane that nearly sank Metatronco. "What do you call a dustbin with wings?" "A Condor." "Name a bird that has to have a drink every half an hour" ...'

'Michael,' said Aurora, 'there's no point showing off. I already know what an aircraft nerd you are, and there's no one else around to be impressed.'

'Mike!' said Colin through the speaker tube system. 'Did you see that? That were amazing, that plane. Zoom! Whoosh! Went by so fast.'

'No one else around to be impressed, eh?' Michael said. He picked up the speaker tube. 'That was nothing, Colin. Just you wait. There's bound to be something better in that cavern. At least, I hope so. Otherwise, we're in for a big let-down.'

There *were* other planes, happily, and as far as Michael was concerned all of them compared favourably to the Condor, even the ones that were certifiable antiques. The sky around the needle mesa teemed with low-flying aircraft. None of the pilots appeared very confident, however. The planes bumbled along anxiously, and often strayed into one another's paths, resulting in some hair-raising midair near-misses.

For Colin's benefit, Michael identified each one they saw. That was an Aerodyne Striga II limo, with that pair of owlishly round viewing ports at the front. That was a Solarsoar C-class Cleaver (distinguishable from the B-Class model by the scalloping of its ailerons and the extra stabilising fins midway along the fuselage). That clattering antique rattletrap over there was a Blackbird ('Basically a box kite with a propeller attached,' Michael said). And that one there looked like an AtmoCorp 9-5, although someone had bolted the tail assembly from a Metatronco Shooting Star onto it.

Before *Bertha* even reached the cavern entrance, Colin had had a thorough grounding in the art of planespotting and was avid to learn more. Michael seemed to him just about the cleverest and most knowledgeable person alive, and if he loved aircraft, then Colin was resolved to love aircraft as well.

A small posse of roughnecks came out on foot to meet *Bertha*, with Magnus Clockweight at the fore. When Den emerged, shinning down the ladder from the driver's pod, Clockweight's expression went from wary to confused.

'Us thought you'd done a runner,' he said. 'You and the Deacon both. Only, where you'd have gone without taking a vehicle, that were a mystery to we all. And now you'm back in . . . a murk-comber? Where on earth did you get hold of that?'

'It'm a long story,' Den said, 'one for another time.'

'Be the Deacon with you?'

'Er, no. No, him and I got – ahem – separated. Cut off from one another, you might say. I doesn't expect to be seeing he again.'

'Oh.' Clockweight frowned, evidently sensing that he wasn't being told something; Den was leaving out some crucial detail. Clockweight, however, had other things on his mind, so he confined himself to saying, 'Pity. Him seemed a reasonable enough guy. For a Deacon and all.'

'Seemed,' said Den.

'And a useful ally, too.'

'You want useful allies?' Turning towards *Bertha*, Den put a thumb and forefinger in his mouth and whistled. 'I's got a pair of those for you.'

The roughnecks gasped as two Airborn stepped out from the loading bay. Several of them, still traumatised by their previous encounters with members of the winged race, raised the tools they were holding, ready to defend themselves.

'Now calm down,' Den said. 'These be friendly ones. Everyone, meet Michael and Aurora Gabrielson.'

The roughnecks gradually lowered their weapons.

'It'm obvious that you lot has found your feet, so to speak, with these here aircraft,' Den went on. 'But how much higher does you think you'll be able to fly with a couple of Airborn showing you the way? One of they is even a professional test pilot. How about that? How much of an advantage does you think *that'll* bring you?'

It was a rhetorical question. To Clockweight, the answer was abundantly clear: the advantage would be significant.

He had his misgivings, though. As with his men, his view of the Airborn had been coloured by recent events. Could he trust these two?

'I were under the impression you didn't approve of what us is up to, Den,' he said. 'Deacon Hardscree were all for it, and I got the distinct feeling you disagreed with he.'

'Him and I had our differences of opinion,' Den replied, 'but that'm in the past.'

'And you,' Clockweight said, addressing Michael and Aurora, 'you'm really willing to chip in and help?'

They nodded.

'Might I ask why?'

Aurora took the lead. She explained that she was a Silver Sanctum resident and therefore, in effect, an ambassador for the Airborn. She spoke with the authority of the Airborn race's ruling body and her view was that the Redspire pirates – whose airship *Behemoth* had inflicted such misery on Clockweight and his men – constituted a grave threat to the stability brought about by the Bilateral Covenant. They should be considered enemies of both races. Hence, it was her and her husband's moral duty to assist the roughnecks in their resistance against the black airship.

'Besides,' she added, 'by the looks of things, if some of you don't get proper flying instruction soon, there's going to be a nasty crash.'

'Us is doing OK,' said Clockweight defensively, but just then another of those close shaves occurred overhead as a puttering Wayfarer narrowly avoided ramming into a sleek Skylark side-ways on. Michael winced and clutched his face, appalled almost as much by the potential damage to the Skylark as by the potential loss of life. There could have been no more undig-nified fate for such a beautiful plane than to be T-boned by that which was the very definition of aeronautical mediocrity, the Metatronco Wayfarer.

'Wow, do you need me,' he said to Clockweight, pain in his eyes.

The roughnecks' toolpusher couldn't help but burst out laughing. 'Said with real feeling, that were.' He extended a roughened, grease-smeared hand to Michael. 'All right then. Seeing as you'm so keen to join in, it'd be foolish of I to refuse. Welcome to the team.'

Michael shook the proffered hand, without hesitation. He wasn't the slightest bit bothered by the grease that transferred itself from Clockweight's palm to his.

Getting his hands dirty – Michael had an inkling that there'd be plenty more of that to come.

CHAPTER 99

Developments

Michael worked with the roughnecks all afternoon. When he wasn't huddled with a group of them near the cavern mouth, peering under the engine cowling of a malfunctioning plane and offering repair tips, he was aloft in another plane, demonstrating to a passenger or passengers the basics of flying, then letting one of these amateur pilots take over and put into practice what he had just learned. This resulted in a few nerve-jangling moments, not least when one of his pupils stalled at a height of 800 metres and the plane went into a nosedive. Michael seized the controls and managed to re-start the engine and pull out of the dive, but with just seconds to spare.

Aurora also conducted lessons, about which Michael was less than happy. The revelation that she was pregnant hadn't fully sunk in yet, but it had sunk in far enough for him to realise that he wasn't comfortable with the idea of her going up in a plane with an untutored co-pilot. It wasn't only her life at stake, it was the life of their unborn child. He took her to one side and tried to explain this to her, but Aurora told him not to be silly. She said he couldn't treat her as though she needed to be wrapped in cotton wool, and if he insisted on trying to, their marriage would go down as one of the shortest on record. Besides, if it ever looked like she was in danger, she would simply eject herself from the plane and fly to safety under her own wingpower. Any poor Groundlings with her would have to fend for themselves, but that was their problem. She wasn't going to be *completely* reckless. She, too, understood the importance of the fact that she was carrying another life inside her.

'It's sweet of you to worry, Mike,' she said, 'but don't. I can take care of myself. Anyway, I think you need to worry more about the child you've already got.'

She was referring to the childlike Colin, who had decided that he wanted to fly planes too and went up with Michael at every opportunity, whenever there was a spare seat available. He drank in every word Michael said, soaked up every drop of information that fell from Michael's lips, absorbed the rudiments and refinements of aviation technique with sponge-like thirstiness and retentiveness, until finally he demanded to be allowed to have a go himself. Michael said no in a dozen different ways, but Colin persisted. Pestered. Badgered. And in the end, what else could Michael do but give in?

They went up together in the Skylark, which, of all the available planes, was the one Michael had not flown yet and the one he was itching to get his hands on. The last ever Skylark had rolled out of the factory gates four decades before he was born, and many of them remained in use even now, lovingly preserved by their owners. Occasionally he would glimpse one scudding along a sky-city thoroughfare, and he would stare in envious awe at its arched wings, its blue and silver bodywork, and its unique four-finned tail design. Although he was a helicopter man through and through, if he had to own a plane and money was no object, Michael would have had a Skylark.

This one, despite having fallen through the clouds and sat in a cavern for umpteen years, flew like a dream. The joystick had just the right level of responsiveness, the engine purred, and the plane as a whole had a kind of buoyancy, a lightness, as though exulting in every moment it spent in the air. While Colin crouched attentively in the passenger seat, Michael put the Skylark through its paces. He didn't want to hand over the controls. But eventually, with great reluctance, he did.

He feared that Colin would mishandle the Skylark and, through sheer clumsiness and inexperience, somehow mar the plane's perfection. Not by crashing it, simply by not flying it properly. He was regretting his eagerness now. He should have insisted that Colin have his first bash at being an aviator in another plane, any other plane. But Michael hadn't been able to wait for a spin in the Skylark any longer.

His fears proved unfounded. Colin was a natural. Almost as soon as he was in the pilot's seat he was guiding the Skylark along with ease, like a seasoned cockpit jockey. He was nervous to begin with, constantly seeking reassurance from his instructor, but in no time he had relaxed and was chatting casually, mentioning altitude and attitude readings, and commenting on geographical features below and the other planes that passed by.

Michael was forced to revise his opinion of Colin. Where he had once seen a good-natured but none-too-bright chap, lazy and fond of a fistfight, now he was looking at somebody with an enormous capacity and aptitude for learning who'd clearly had few chances to show off these attributes before. Within that dense-boned Amblescrut skull lurked a brain. It was the kind of brain which didn't respond well to schooling (assuming Colin had ever gone to school) but which grasped certain practical subjects instantly and intuitively. If something fascinated Colin, he would latch on to it and concentrate on it with remarkable focus and will. As he did with the Skylark.

He brought the plane smoothly back to earth, executing a soft, three-point touchdown that Michael himself would have been hard pushed to equal.

'Were that OK?' Colin asked, as he killed the Skylark's engine.

'Yeah, Colin,' said Michael, nodding, 'I think you could safely say that was OK.'

'Goody!' Colin leapt from the Skylark and ran over to *Bertha* to tell the Grubdollars about the flight. After that, like a contented puppy, he settled down inside the murk-comber for a nap.

Colin's desire to be a pilot was one reason the Grubdollars had delayed their departure. Their plan, of course, had been to drop Michael and Aurora off at the cavern and then be homeward bound. They'd stayed on, however, partly because Colin was so mad-keen on having a chance to fly. They'd stayed, also, because to turn and shoot off so abruptly struck them as somehow wrong. Now that Colin had fulfilled his wish and actually piloted a plane, strictly speaking there was no reason for them to linger. They could start *Bertha* up at any time, make their farewells and head north.

And yet they didn't.

For one thing, they had an obligation towards Michael and Aurora. How were the Airborn couple to return home without the Grubdollars' help? Maybe they would find a way. Possibly they could take one of the planes. But the only surefire, guaranteed, 100 per cent risk-free method of getting back up to the sky-cities was via the elevators at a Chancel, and to reach one of those, ground transport was required. There was a half-tarp van going begging, but it wasn't anywhere near as desert-capable as a murk-comber. Michael and Aurora's best bet – perhaps their only bet – was to travel with the Grubdollars.

So *Bertha* could not leave just yet.

And then there was Den, who found himself gravitating towards the roughnecks and the aircraft they were fixing, the planes which either no one had been able to start yet or had flown but come back down to earth spouting smoke or making some very disconcerting noises. The mechanic in him wouldn't allow him to stand idly by while others tinkered and mended and got smudged with grease and grime. Nor would it allow him to pass up the opportunity to inspect some exciting new machine technology. He sidled towards Clockweight, enquired airily if there was anything he might do, and in no time was up to his elbows in aircraft. Adjustable spanner in one hand, screwdriver in the other, he took engines apart component by component, identified the problem, and then put the engines back together so that they were as good as new.

Robert joined him in this. He said he wanted to show solidarity with the roughnecks, and Den agreed, saying he felt much the same way himself. He wanted to prove that he had come round to their way of thinking. The Airborn pirates *were* a threat that needed to be confronted. Before, he hadn't been in possession of the full facts, or at any rate his falling out with

Hardscree had prevented him from perceiving the full facts. He'd not been in a position to accept that the roughnecks had a case, that their grudge against the pirates was a valid argument for fighting back and their methods for doing so were appropriate. Now, thanks to Aurora, he saw matters in a fresh light.

Clockweight acknowledged Den's and Robert's contribution to the cause, understanding what it was intended to represent. He also was filled with admiration for the two Grubdollars' mechanic skills, Den's in particular. Here was a man with a clear affinity for machinery, a flair for finding out why it didn't work and making it work again, a talent that bordered on genius.

When he wasn't surveying Den's handiwork with professional approval, Clockweight was busy supervising his men both at the planes and elsewhere. A secondary effort was under way, just inside the cavern mouth. There, several of the roughnecks were piecing together their improvised weaponry.

Principally, they were building bombs, incendiary devices similar to the ones the pirates had dropped on Desolation Wells but portable. Scavenged glass bottles were pressed into service as casings and filled with petrol. For fuses, the men used twists of petrol-soaked rag, secured in place in the bottles' necks with plugs of dried mud. Nuts and bolts were taped to the exterior of the bombs to form makeshift shrapnel.

A few of the more enterprising roughnecks set about making catapults out of scrap metal and lengths of fan belt. They tested these outside, using the hubcaps from random broken-off sections of landing gear as projectiles. The hubcaps sliced keenly through the air, and their aerodynamicity was improved (and so was their lethal potential) by filing their rims to a blade-like sharpness.

Amid all this industrious activity, Cassie and Fletcher kept to themselves and minded their own business. They had no wish to participate. They'd done what they agreed to do, transport Michael and Aurora to the cavern, and from here on whatever happened was none of their concern.

Or so they told themselves. As the day wore on, however, both felt the tide of commitment growing stronger and becoming harder to resist. Colin had been up and down in planes all afternoon. Robert and their father were engineers at large. The involvement of Michael and Aurora was a given, but even so, it was slightly shaming to watch these two beavering away on the Groundlings' behalf while Cassie and Fletcher, Groundlings themselves, just moped around inside *Bertha* or sat on her tracks, looking on.

At last they both came to the conclusion that they were either going to stop feeling guilty that they were the only ones not making a positive contribution to the anti-pirate preparations, or they were going to make themselves useful.

As Fletcher put it, 'It'm time for we to poop or get off the pot.'

Cassie nodded but remained unsure. 'Da told I it were all right to be selfish sometimes. So how come it *don't* feel all right now? How come it seems childish?'

'Because us has got consciences,' said her brother.

'But this be'n't our fight.'

'Don't make any difference, ultimately. At some point, you always has to choose a side. Remember in the truck sheds at the CCC? When you talked I out of being a Humanist?'

Cassie did.

'It weren't really a choice at all,' Fletcher said. 'I knew that all along. I just couldn't see it till you showed I. Same here. Everybody be knuckling down, mucking in. Us has been watching from the sidelines, pretending us be'n't part of the deal, but deep down us knows us is. It'm just taken we a while to recognise it.'

'And now us has?'

'Now us has,' he confirmed. He stood up.

Cassie stood too. 'So what be on the agenda? Mechanic work, like Robert and Da?'

'Most likely. There be more than enough mechanics to go round but I guess two more won't hurt. Cass?'

'Yeah?'

Fletcher's tone of voice had suddenly changed, becoming low and slow. 'You know those floaty little specks you sometimes get in front of your eyes? Not sure what the proper name be for they, but you can get them when you'm tired or when you sort of half close your eyelids.'

'I know they. Why?'

Fletcher was staring out into the desert, squinting, his eyebrows knitted. 'Well, I's got one now. Only I don't think that'm what it actually be.'

'What do you mean?'

'Take a look. There.' He pointed into the distance. 'Tell me if you sees it too. If you does, then it'm no floaty speck.'

She followed the line of his finger.

Just above the seam where clouds met landscape, she made out a tiny dark dot.

She knew instantly, almost instinctively, what it was, and her stomach tightened into a knot.

'Fletch, go and tell Da and that Clockweight fellow.'

'Huh? Tell they what?'

'The black airship. *Behemoth*. It'm here. It'm coming this way. Go! Now!'

CHAPTER 100

Scramble!

While Fletcher ran towards the cavern entrance and the planes that were being serviced, Cassie sprinted in the opposite direction, towards the area where the airworthy planes were parked.

'Aurora!' she yelled. 'Michael! Everybody! The pirate airship! Over there!'

Shouts of alarm passed among the roughnecks. Heads turned and hands went to foreheads to shade eyes. Michael darted up into the air to get a better perspective and came down with grim confirmation on his face.

'It's *Behemoth* all right,' he said. 'At least, it isn't *Cerulean*, so it's got to be the other one.'

'How come them's coming here?' asked one of the roughnecks.

Michael shrugged. 'Your guess is as good as mine. Maybe they spotted us and want a closer look. Or maybe they're after spare parts. After all, the cavern's where got the airship from in the first place.'

Clockweight came charging over. 'What be you lot standing around scratching your behinds for?' he demanded of his men. 'This'm it. Let's get up there and attack.'

The roughnecks looked at Michael, who realised they were seeking his blessing. If he, the aviation expert, thought they were ready and skilled enough to take on *Behemoth* in the planes, then they were.

'Your boss is right,' Michael said. 'This is it. You may feel you could do with more training.' He himself certainly felt they could do with more training. At least a month's worth. 'But there isn't time. Think about it this way. The pirates aren't going to be expecting an attack, and they're certainly not going to be expecting an attack from a bunch of Groundlings in aircraft. So you may not have much flying experience but you do have the element of surprise, and that counts for a lot. Do what you can up there. But above all else, leave the way clear for me. Get that? I stand a far better chance of planting a bomb in the right place than any of you. You lot run interference, keep the pirates busy, attempt a hit if you can . . . but leave the fancy stuff to me.'

Clockweight glanced at Michael in surprise. Then he nodded to him, to show that he acknowledged and appreciated what Michael had just volunteered to do.

'Good strategy,' he said. He turned back to his men. 'There'm nothing more to be said. Hop to it. Scramble!'

The roughnecks let out a loud hurrah and ran for the planes. Other roughnecks came from the cavern clutching armfuls of bottle bombs and matches with which to light them. The catapults had already been mounted on the backs of some of the older aircraft, the ones that had uncovered cockpits and room for more than one person on board.

Men slid into pilot and passenger seats. Engines gunned. Propellers whirred.

Colin arrived at Michael's side, panting.

'Here I be, Mike,' he said. 'Which plane d'you think I should take?'

'What? What are you talking about?'

'I be going to go up and give those pirates a bloody nose, of course.'

'Colin, it's dangerous. You'll more than likely kill yourself.'

'Think I don't know that? But it'm what needs doing.'

'No,' said Michael. 'No, you're just not ready.'

'Neither's them oilmen,' Colin protested.

'They have a personal stake in this. They care more about getting their own back on the pirates than anything else.'

'But didn't I just hear you say you be flying with they?'

'Yes, but —'

'How about I join you then? As your co-pilot. You fly, I'll drop bombs.'

Michael could see some sense in this, not much but some, and he didn't want to stand around all day arguing.

'All right,' he sighed. 'Go and get into the Skylark.'

'Yippee!' yelled Colin. He dashed off towards the vintage silver-and-blue aircraft. One of the roughnecks was going in the same direction but Colin bumped him out of the way. 'That'm ours. Find your own plane.'

Michael was about to follow when a stern voice stopped him in his tracks.

'Hold on there, Mike Gabrielson,' it said. 'I heard what you just said to Colin. When did you agree to be a part of the attack? And at what point were you planning on telling me?'

'Aurora ...' Michael turned to his wife and flattened his wings to show resignation. 'I've got to help. These Groundlings haven't a prayer without me.'

'You're not even prepared to discuss this?' said Aurora.

'There isn't anything to discuss. You've seen how those men fly. This is a suicide mission for them. I can make the difference, maybe even save a few of them from getting themselves killed. I have to think about them.'

'You have others to think about too.' She touched her stomach, a coded gesture which only Michael could interpret.

'Listen,' he said, 'earlier today you told me you could fly yourself to safety if things got hairy. Well duh, so can I. Trust me, this is going to be fine.'

Aurora looked very doubtful but eventually she nodded, giving her consent. 'I love you,' she said.

'Likewise!' Michael shouted over his shoulder, as he took off and flew to the Skylark.

Cassie saw the concern on Aurora's face and the compassion in her eyes, and something clicked.

'Gabrielson boys,' she said. 'Them can be annoying, can't them?'

'*Really* annoying,' said Aurora. 'Impulsive. Wilful. Obstinate.

But they have a strong moral compass. They do what's right, and you have to admire them for that.'

'And forgive they too.'

'And make them forgive *you* if your moral compass points in a slightly different direction.' Aurora smiled briefly, ruefully. 'Cassie, we should have had this conversation days ago.'

'Days ago I wouldn't have been interested.'

'And now isn't the time, alas.'

'No, it be'n't,' Cassie said. 'Now'm the time for we to take refuge in *Bertha*. If us has to be bystanders, best do it somewhere safe.'

As they hurried towards *Bertha*, Aurora said, 'Just promise me one thing. When all this is over, you'll sit down with Az for a good long chat. Ask him and yourself a few honest questions.'

'Yeah. Yeah, I reckon us'll do that.'

'Good.'

One by one the planes taxied out into the open desert. Then, one after another, they rose to the skies. Some of the roughnecks managed the takeoff better than others. A few climbed at too steep an angle and nearly stalled. One scraped a wingtip on the ground just as his plane began to lift, although he recovered from this near-fatal mishap and still made it up into the air.

Eventually they were all aloft. They adjusted course till they were heading on the same bearing. The faster aircraft reduced their speed so that the slower aircraft could catch up.

A mismatched, maverick fleet assembled, and made its way in loose formation towards the oncoming black bulk of *Behemoth*.

The Skylark was among the last to get airborne. With Colin in the passenger seat beside him, Michael followed the roughnecks towards the airship, thinking that if any of those brave, foolish Groundlings made it back to earth safely, it would be nothing short of a miracle.

CHAPTER 101

Men Against Aircraft

Michael had predicted the pirates' reaction accurately. The last thing anyone aboard *Behemoth* expected was to see planes come swarming up from the ground and home in on the airship with obvious aggressive intent.

In the control gondola, amid various expressions of shock and amazement, Naoutha alone stayed silent. She was too outraged to speak. Those were *her* planes. She had returned to the cavern precisely in order to retrieve them and use them against *Cerulean*. She had boasted to Mr Mordadson about augmenting her pirates' attack capability, and these aircraft were it, her means of gaining an edge on the other airship – and now somebody else had got hold of them and was about to use them against *Behemoth*!

The pirates had had their hoard pirated. The raiders had been raided.

But Naoutha was in no mood to appreciate irony, and her sense of outrage only deepened when Flight Lieutenant Wallimson said, 'Are those pilots ... Groundlings?'

Everyone in the control gondola peered forward, and soon the conclusion was reached that yes, they were Groundlings all right.

'Groundlings flying? But ... that can't be,' said Wallimson. 'It's just not right.'

A dreadful, cracking noise filled the gondola, and everyone turned towards its source, Naoutha. She was grinding her teeth, so loudly that not even her mask could muffle it.

'They may be in planes,' she said, 'but can they truly fly? Do they have the instinct for it? I think not.'

'What do you want us to do, Naoutha?' asked one of her gang. It was Abuzaha Biletson, the mechanic largely responsible for the *Brightspans Empress*'s resurrection as *Behemoth*.

'What do you think? Go out there and fight them, of course.'

'But – but they're in planes. Men against aircraft? That's madness.'

Naoutha's arm flashed out, grabbed Biletson by the collar, and yanked him towards her.

'How dare you!' she shouted, shaking him. 'How dare you question my orders! Those are *Groundlings*. You are Airborn. You were born to fly. They weren't. You can run rings around them. Shoot the ones in planes with open cockpits. Otherwise, dodge around them, distract them, throw them off-course, do whatever you have to – just make sure those motherplucking aircraft don't get anywhere near *Behemoth*. Do I make myself clear?'

Meekly Biletson nodded.

'Good. Now go and tell the others.'

She shook Biletson once more then let go. He scurried aft to relay his leader's orders to the rest of the gang.

Moments later, pirates left *Behemoth* to confront the planes. They were armed with crossbows and fortified with shots of pterine.

They clustered at the front of the airship, matching their speed to its. As the planes neared they muttered among themselves, wondering if Naoutha really expected them to play chicken with aircraft travelling at around 100 knots. Then, as they watched, two of the planes veered towards each other, getting closer, closer, dangerously close, until abruptly they collided. In a tangle they spun out of the sky, tumbling to the desert earth, where they exploded in a mushrooming fireball.

Another of the Groundling pilots, observing this calamity, panicked and lost control of his aircraft. He went into a tailspin which he couldn't get out of. His plane, too, hit the ground and burst into flame.

'See that!' shouted Twitchy Ziz with a shrill chortle. 'They're useless! They really can't fly!'

The other pirates let out a jeering yell. All at once it was clear to them that they had the advantage. The Groundlings barely knew what they were doing.

They flew forward to meet the planes.

Naoutha looked on from the control gondola. Three of the aircraft were down already, and combat hadn't even begun. Even though those were her planes, she decided she didn't care if every last one of them was destroyed. No one had the right to steal from her. She'd found the cavern, she'd staked a claim on it, she was the rightful owner of everything in it – and she was damned if she was going to let these Groundling thieves take any of it away from her. If she couldn't have the planes, they certainly weren't going to.

The roughnecks saw the flock of pirates coming towards them. Half immediately took evasive action, peeling off from the formation. They were anxious enough as it was, simply being at the controls of a plane several hundred metres up in the sky. On top of that, having to try and dodge around living obstacles was too much.

The remaining roughnecks kept their nerve. Though inexpert aviators, they knew enough to realise that smashing your plane into a human-sized object in midair would be fatal for both parties. The pirates, though, surely wouldn't sacrifice themselves like that . . .

Would they?

Clockweight led by example. He was piloting the Metatronco Condor. For all that Michael despised it, Clockweight liked the Condor for its straightforwardness and the sturdy utility of its design. It looked like how a child might draw a flying machine, all squared-off edges and blunted ends, and it didn't ask for a fine touch at the controls. The opposite, in fact. You had to ram the joystick and throttle in their slots to get any response from either, and Clockweight found that comforting. The Condor was an uncompromising, no-nonsense aircraft – his kind of ride.

He aimed straight for the centre of the cluster of pirates. Behind, the half of his fleet that was still in formation followed.

The pirates loomed in the Condor's windshield, wings

flapping, wild-eyed. They scattered at the very last second, either darting into open space or seeking refuge in the shelter of *Behemoth*.

The planes passed over, under and alongside *Behemoth* in a wave. One of the roughnecks misjudged the gap between him and the airship. His port wing clipped *Behemoth's* rear starboard propeller, the one that Az had knocked out of commission. The wing crumpled and his plane went whirling through the air like a boomerang. It crashed into another plane, all but chopping off that aircraft's tail section. Momentum carried both of the stricken planes onward for a full minute, as each fell meteor-like in a long, graceful arc to its inevitable, punishing impact with the earth.

Meanwhile a roughneck, passing above *Behemoth*, managed to drop a bottle bomb on the airship. But the bomb simply bounced off the balloon canvas and fell, burning uselessly, dripping globs of fire into the air.

The roughnecks banked and turned, grouping for a second run at their target. They were joined by the stragglers who had balked at the start of the first run. Although they had taken casualties and *Behemoth* remained intact, the roughnecks had reason to feel encouraged. The pirates weren't going to be the formidable opposition they had feared.

The pirates felt encouraged too. It seemed that men *did* stand a chance against aircraft, especially when the pilots of the aircraft were so easy to spook.

Michael, in the Skylark, could see that the roughnecks had grown in confidence. He was holding off at the periphery of things, biding his time, waiting for an opportunity. As the ragtag roughneck fleet headed for *Behemoth* on a fresh sortie, he could tell they were keener than before. The planes drew tighter together. They upped their airspeed.

Now the pirates rushed to intercept, swooping at the planes with insane glee. The pterine was well and truly kicking in. The pirates' perceptions had become diamond sharp. Their brains bulged with the enormity of what they were capable of. They felt all-powerful. Nothing could harm them. The rest of the world, as far as they were concerned, was full of slow, stupid things that were easily evaded and bested.

Crossbow bolts were nocked. The pirates targeted the planes with open cockpits and fired as they zoomed past. Pterine improved their accuracy a hundredfold, and many of the bolts found their mark. All at once, several aircraft were zigzagging erratically or dipping towards the ground. In one case, a roughneck passenger had just lit the rag fuse of a bottle bomb when the pilot took a crossbow bolt in the throat. As the plane swerved out of control, burning petrol spilled everywhere. The plane was a streak of fire as it hit the desert.

Then Michael spied his chance. In the wake of the second run, the pirates regrouped at *Behemoth*'s nose-cone. Because Michael had held back, they hadn't spotted him. Now he steered the Skylark at the airship's stern.

'Colin,' he said, 'it's up to you. Don't miss.'

Colin grabbed a bottle bomb and lit the fuse. As the rag flared, he thrust open a small side window. A torrent of wind rushed in, like a hammer to his face.

'Wait,' said Michael. 'Waiiit . . .'

It took every scrap of willpower Colin had not to toss the bomb out immediately.

The Skylark overtook *Behemoth*'s skull-and-crossed-feather tailfins and Michael yelled, 'Now!'

Colin hurled the bottle bomb with all his might.

It was a dud. The fuse fizzled out before the bomb even reached the airship. The bomb rebounded off the balloon and tumbled from view.

On their third attack run, the roughnecks did their best to outmanoeuvre the pirates. They'd learned their lesson. Those crossbows were deadly. Now, in return, they brought the onboard catapults into play. Sharpened hubcaps zinged through space. Most went wide. The pterine-enhanced pirates saw them coming as if in slow motion and got out of the way. A few of the hubcaps did hit home, however. One beheaded a pirate cleanly. Another disembowelled its victim. He plummeted with his innards uncoiling and flailing bloodily around him.

This time, Clockweight in his Condor managed to score a direct hit with a bottle bomb. It exploded across the upper surface of *Behemoth*'s balloon in a burst of fluid fire. He really thought he had done it, and let out a whoop of triumph. The airship was doomed. Revenge was his.

But then, looking over his shoulder, Clockweight groaned. The fire failed to take hold. The flames dwindled and petered out. All that was left was a patch of grey charring on the canvas.

Clockweight had been afraid of this. The bottle bombs, even when they worked as they were supposed to, weren't enough. He circled the Condor round, avoiding a pirate who lunged recklessly close to the plane. His injuries throbbed and ached, and he wondered, miserably, just how in hell he and his men were going to bring down that airship. They were like mosquitoes buzzing around an elephant. They stood little chance of piercing its hide, let alone causing it a fatal injury.

Even with Michael Gabrielson assisting them, it seemed hopeless. Clockweight was close to despair.

Naoutha, on the other hand, felt elation as she surveyed the action from inside the control gondola. *Behemoth* had taken a couple of hits but was essentially undamaged. Her gang were repelling the attackers and thinning their numbers. If things went on like this, victory would soon be hers.

All at once Naoutha experienced a sharp pang, a sensation she knew only too well. It was mainly in her stomach but it affected the rest of her body too, a general, nervy ache, a system-wide yearning, like an all-over itch that must be scratched. How long had it been since her last pterine hit? Too long. Yesterday evening, it had been, shortly before she and her gang engaged with the Alar Patrollers.

She craved the drug. She longed for the alertness, the clarity, the invincibility it brought. Whenever its influence faded, the world seemed dull and slow and pointless. She needed more of it, always more. With it, she was Naoutha Nisrocsdaughter, pirate queen. Without it, she was nobody, nothing, a void.

But she was reluctant to leave the control gondola while the battle was still raging outside. Who could go and fetch her a syringe and an ampoule of pterine? Which of the gang members currently crewing the ship could be spared to run an errand?

'Wallimson ...' she said.

CHAPTER 102

Biting Wit

Wallimson traipsed along the keel catwalk, disgruntled. He didn't mind doing Naoutha a favour but he did mind the way she had asked for it. She'd spoken as though he was some sort of flunky, there just to do her bidding. *Get me pterine. You'll find some in my cabin.* Wasn't he her newfound friend? Hadn't he helped her in all sorts of ways? Yet he was beginning to feel that he meant nothing to her or to any of the pirates. They were treating him here much as he had been treated on *Cerulean*, as redundant, just so much lame-winged ballast.

A touch of ground-sickness was adding to Wallimson's bad temper. *Behemoth* remained quite high, not far below the clouds, so the symptoms could have been worse, but he nevertheless felt muzzy-headed and not-quite-all-there. Pterine would no doubt have helped, but he wasn't a drugs type of person. Never had been. Nasty stuff. Didn't do you any good in the long run.

Speaking of which ...

Wallimson reached the cabin where Mr Mordadson was being held. Pausing at the door, he listened out. Not a sound from within. Sometime during the small hours Mr Mordadson had stopped screaming, but his moans and the thumps of the chair legs on the floor had continued for a long time afterward, echoing along the catwalk. Now, those had stopped too. There was only silence.

Was he dead?

Wallimson hoped so, but also hoped not. While he wished only bad things for Mr Mordadson, he wanted him to remain alive at least long enough that he could have another crack at him. Last night Naoutha had intervened before he could really get started. He felt he still owed Mr Mordadson a lot of pain. Yes.

Wallimson reached for the cabin door.

This wasn't what Naoutha had sent him back for. Equally, the temptation was too great to resist. Just a brief detour from his journey. A couple of minutes alone with Mordadson. No one would mind. With all the fighting outside, no one would even know.

Wallimson turned the key in the lock and opened the door.

Mr Mordadson was sitting slumped. The ropes were the only thing holding him up. His head drooped, and his face, what Wallimson could see of it, was a mass of pulpy red flesh, barely recognisable. There was a circle of dried bloodstains around the base of the chair, like a dark spattery halo on the floor.

'Mordadson?' said Wallimson softly, with a singsong inflection. 'Mordadso-o-on?'

The head stirred. The eyes flickered between their swollen lids. The distended lips mumbled something unintelligible.

'How are you feeling?' Wallimson shut the door behind him. 'Pretty rotten by the looks of it. Have you heard what's going on outside? Another fight – this time against Groundlings, no less. Flying Groundlings! Wonders will never cease. Everyone else is busy with that, anyway, so I thought you and I might have some together time, just the two of us. Now, refresh my memory. Didn't you promise you'd show me a thing or two about inflicting pain? Did I remember that right? I'd love to know more. Do tell me.'

With a wicked grin, Wallimson moved closer to his helpless target.

Again, Mr Mordadson mumbled.

'I'm sorry, you'll have to speak up. I can't make out a word you're saying.'

Mr Mordadson tried to talk clearly but still all Wallimson could distinguish amid the string of burbled syllables was the phrase 'listen in' – although it might have been 'glistening'.

He leaned down, putting his ear next to Mr Mordadson's mouth. It wouldn't hurt, would it, to discover what his intended victim wished to say, before the savage beating commenced. Famous last words and all that.

'Come on, Mr Silver Sanctum Big Shot. What is it? Spit it out.'

Next thing Wallimson knew, his ear was clamped between Mr Mordadson's teeth. The whole ear, right to the root, and Mr Mordadson was biting, biting, and Wallimson was howling in agony and blood was pouring down his neck and he pummelled at Mr Mordadson, battered him with his fists, but he would not let go. The pain was excruciating. A shrilling sound filled Wallimson's head. He felt himself becoming faint. He couldn't even manage to hit Mr Mordadson any more. He just wanted the pain to stop. Stop. Stop. Please stop.

It didn't stop but it did lessen. Mr Mordadson relaxed his jaw-grip slightly, although his teeth continued to dig in.

Wallimson's thoughts cleared. He grabbed hold of Mr Mordadson's head to push it away. Immediately, the teeth sank deeper again.

The next time the pressure of the teeth abated and the pain dulled, Wallimson tried to wrench his own head away.

More agony. Fiery agony.

Finally it dawned on him: resistance only brought suffering. Compliance, however, had a more positive result.

'What – what do you want?' he stammered.

'Uh ooh ooh ink I onh?' Mr Mordadson said, his voice reverberating down Wallimson's ear canal with horrible vibrancy.

What do you think I want?

'You want me to untie you.'

'Eh-eh eh-oh.'

Clever fellow.

'But ...'

Pain, drilling into Wallimson's skull. Not as bad as before. Bad enough, though.

Obviously no *buts* were allowed.

'Naoutha will —'

Pain!

339

'I can't —'

Pain!

Wallimson realised, miserably, that objections were futile and he was likely to lose the ear if he carried on lodging them. He had no choice. He was going to have to do as Mr Mordadson asked.

He reached round the back of the chair for the first of the knots that secured Naoutha's prisoner.

Shortly they were undone and Mr Mordadson was free. He maintained his tooth-hold on Wallimson's ear right up until the last rope came loose. Then he opened wide and Wallimson staggered away, clutching the side of his head.

Mr Mordadson spat and spat till he had rid his mouth of Wallimson's blood and all that came out was pinkish saliva. Then he eased the cramps out of his wings and limbs. Then he strode towards Wallimson.

Cowering in a corner of the cabin, the flight lieutenant looked up as Mr Mordadson loomed over him.

'What are you going to do to me?' he moaned, still pressing his hand flat against his head. It numbed the pain a little. 'You can't just leave me here. The pirates will kill me if they find out I released you.'

Mr Mordadson's bruised, battered, bloodied face was inscrutable.

'Please. Please forgive me,' Wallimson begged. 'I never meant for any of this to happen.'

And implacable.

'I just needed to belong somewhere. I —'

Mr Mordadson cut him off. 'It's not what happens to you . . . that makes you who you are,' he said, shaping the words with great effort. 'It's how you . . . deal with it.'

'Yes. Yes!' said Wallimson, like a man in the throes of an epiphany, flooded with clear-sighted understanding. 'I've dealt with it badly. That's it. I accept that. I should have been better. I'll try to be better from now on. I'll try to be a good person.'

'No, you won't,' said Mr Mordadson, kneeling down. 'Believe me, I've . . . tried to be a good person too, and it . . . hasn't worked. Some have the capacity for it, others ... don't. I don't. I am ... what I am, and I've learned to deal with it ... and live with it.'

Wallimson looked deep into the other man's eyes, and what he saw there left him helpless with terror.

Mr Mordadson seized the flight lieutenant's head in both hands and slammed it against the bulkhead behind.

Slammed it and slammed it until Wallimson's body finally stopped twitching and shuddering and lay still.

Leap Into The Dark

Az's self-imposed time limit of twelve hours was up, and his gamble had not paid off. *Behemoth* had not resurfaced. Naoutha and co. were still down there below the cloud cover, somewhere, and Mr Mordadson with them.

Az was beyond exhaustion now. He'd entered a dreamlike state of suspension where everything seemed real but existed just out of his reach, as if behind an invisible wall; everything he did or said seemed to be someone else's deeds or words. He found himself, at one point in the middle of the morning, having a blazing row with Wing Commander Iaxson, and as soon as it was over he couldn't recall what it had been about. About Mr Mordadson, probably, and about heading home. All he knew was that he had won the argument. At least, he thought so, on the strength of the look Iaxson had given him as he left the control gondola – a steely glare that said, *If you were a grown-up, I'd have punched you.* Iaxson had agreed to his time limit? Probably. Reluctantly.

Az wasn't sure that he knew what he was doing any more. He was operating on automatic, with all his systems shut down but the essential ones. His inner reserves were as near-empty as *Cerulean*'s fuel tanks. Some dim, distant part of his brain was telling him the mission was over, it was a failure, *he* was a failure. He tried not to pay it any heed but it was hard to ignore. The truth was hard to ignore.

Cerulean was drifting. Had been for some while. Az had ordered the crew not to correct the drift, not to waste precious fuel trying to stay put. One of the less dynamic jet streams had the airship in its grasp and was nudging her gently but insistently – which way? Az could have checked the compass on the navigator's station. He could have found out her bearing. He just couldn't be bothered to. Some direction. Whatever. Didn't matter.

Now was the time. He knew it. Now he had to admit defeat, abandon all hope of rescuing Mr Mordadson, and make the run for Redspire. The four crew members, sleep-starved zombies, were waiting for him to give their command. *Let's go.* That was all he would have to say. Two words. Two simple syllables.

He tried. He couldn't.

Visions paraded through his brain. People he knew. People he loved. His parents. Michael. Lady Aanfieldsdaughter. The Grubdollars. Cassie. Dominating everything was the Ultimate Reckoner's prediction, the allegedly significant symbol. It hovered in his mind's eye like the afterimage of a glimpse of the sun. Wherever he looked, whatever he tried to think about, there it was, gibbous and ominous.

The Count of Gyre's voice echoed insinuatingly.

Up or down?

Right or wrong?

Light or dark?

Yes or no?

'Descend,' Az said abruptly.

The crew's heads turned. Their grey-ringed eyes blinked. Their brows furrowed.

'Sir?'

The question mark, poised between one thing and another, in that grey zone of uncertainty, pure quandary ...

'Descend. Go down. Lose height. Sink. How many ways can I put it?'

'Through the —?'

'Right through the clouds.'

'But —'

'An order. Do it.'

The crew eventually, and grudgingly, obeyed. *Cerulean's* rear propellers started to spin. Helium was vented to increase the rate of decline.

Az clambered up the ladder to the control gondola's ceiling hatch. He swung the hatch shut and turned the wheel that slid the locking bar into place. The hatch could not be opened from above. This was a security measure dating back to the airship's troop-carrier days, to seal off the gondola against enemy boarders and give the crew time to make a safe exit.

Moments later, Iaxson came storming along the keel catwalk, as Az had known he would. Finding his access to the gondola barred, the wing commander pounded angrily on the hatch.

'Gabrielson!' he roared. 'Open up! Let me in!'

'I can't do that,' Az replied evenly.

'You damn well can. Open up, or I'll force my way in.'

'Do what you have to. I have to see this through first.'

'This? See what through? Why are we descending? If we're going anywhere, it's to Redspire like we agreed. Exactly what are you up to here?'

'I'm answering the question,' Az said. It sounded ridiculous even to him, and yet it was the truth.

'Question? What question?'

The crew's faces were asking much the same thing.

'Just . . . the question,' Az said.

Cerulean was touching the cloud cover already. Tendrils of white vapour were snaking in through the broken windows.

'All right,' said Iaxson from above. 'That does it. I'm taking over this vessel. By the powers vested in me by the Alar Patrol Statutory Authority, I am relieving you of your command, Azrael Gabrielson, effective as of now.'

'Not without entering the control gondola you're not,' Az replied. 'It's . . . it's the Custom of the Skies. In order to revoke his command, you must formally confront a captain face to face.'

'Custom of the Skies? Never heard of it.'

Hardly surprising, since it was something Az had just invented. It was a blatant bluff, but he was hoping it would buy him time, both with Iaxson and with the crew. He could not expect the crewmen to be willing to defy the law the way he was, but if he could just keep them on his side long enough, and keep Iaxson at bay, everything might pan out the way he wanted it to.

'Stripping an airship captain of his rank must be done in person,' he said. 'Otherwise it's considered mutiny.'

'Oh really?' said Iaxson.

'Captain Qadoschson had to tell me in person that I was to take his place. He couldn't surrender his position by, for example, writing me a letter. It's standard practice on airships. Custom of the Skies.'

The crew were now sure that Az was talking nonsense, but their expressions said they weren't *completely* sure. Maybe Az knew something they didn't, some arcane piece of airship lore. For that reason, they were prepared to give him the benefit of the doubt, for now.

After a lengthy pause, Iaxson said, 'Fine. Then I'm coming in. If I can't break through the hatch, I'll exit the ship and get in via the windows.'

'Suit yourself,' said Az.

The control gondola was now flooded with whiteness, a whiteness so dense that the crew had to strain to see anything, even the gauges and instruments in front of them. *Cerulean* shuddered with a mild tremor of cloud cover turbulence, a taste of worse to come.

Az was counting on Iaxson being unwilling to fly outside *Cerulean* while she was in the clouds, and on the hatch proving difficult to bust open. Iaxson would find his way into the gondola eventually, of that there was no doubt. All Az wanted was to get below the clouds first. One glimpse of the ground, that was all he was after. One look, to see if this leap into the dark he was taking was a leap of faith, or a leap in logic.

CHAPTER 104

Skyjack

The pirate gang saw the Groundlings repeatedly fail to make any impression on the airship. Their bombs either didn't go off or, at best, merely scuffed the surface of *Behemoth*'s balloon. Any advantage their planes gave them was cancelled out by the ineptness with which they flew them.

Brimming with bravado and pterine, the pirates scaled greater and greater heights of mad daring. Twitchy Ziz led the way, by commandeering one of the enemy aircraft. It was an almost impossible feat which no sane person would have even dreamed of attempting, but then Twitchy Ziz was long past sane.

A roughneck made a bombing run at *Behemoth* but got it badly wrong. He hit the flaps too hard and his plane, the AtmoCorp 9-5 with the Shooting Star tail welded on, shot upwards in a sheer, near-perpendicular climb. Inevitably, he stalled. The 9-5 slowed as it reached the peak of its steep rising curve, and for a brief moment, the merest fraction of a second, came to a full stop.

By chance, Twitchy Ziz was just metres away when this happened. He spied his chance and lunged for the 9-5 as it began to descend, tail first. He latched onto the cockpit canopy and wrenched it open, one-handed.

Inside, the terrified roughneck was slamming the joystick around as if this might save him – as if he could somehow fight the pull of gravity by making the ailerons flap like a bird's wings. Twitchy Ziz reached in and hauled the man bodily out of his seat. Pterine-strong, he flung him aside and took his place at the controls.

Side by side the roughneck and the 9-5 fell. The roughneck

screamed and windmilled his arms. The 9-5 was silent and inert, just so much dead weight. Twitchy Ziz let the plane tip forward, the heaviness of its engine bringing its nose down. Then, as the 9-5 began to dive, he hit the ignition. The propeller screeched into life and the plane corkscrewed crazily, till Twitchy Ziz brought it under control. The 9-5 flew. Its erstwhile roughneck pilot continued to fall.

Twitchy Ziz giggled gibberingly as he swung the plane up and around. In no time he was gunning for the Groundling aircraft. He buzzed them and swerved at them. The roughneck pilots took drastic action in response. At the sight of the 9-5 rocketing towards them, they barrel-rolled out of the way, or nosedived. Most of the time they were able to correct and carry on flying, but now and then Twitchy Ziz got one of them to go into freefall. Then there was nothing the doomed pilot could do but watch the ground wheel closer and closer, and cover his face with his arms, and scream, and perish.

Inspired by Twitchy Ziz's example, other pirates tried to take over planes too. They weren't as successful. Twitchy Ziz had been able to skyjack the 9-5 only through a set of exceptional circumstances. The other pirates' attempts ended in gory disaster. After four of them would up mashed against windshields or mangled on propellers, the rest gave up. Even though each death also brought down one of the planes, it didn't seem a worthwhile price to pay.

They resumed using their crossbows, while Twitchy Ziz battled on with the 9-5, scattering the Groundling planes, creating havoc, an eagle amongst pigeons.

Until he came up against Michael.

CHAPTER 105

A Bonkers Plan

Michael watched the commandeered AtmoCorp 9-5 devastating the roughneck ranks. The pirates definitely had the upper hand now. Only he could even up the balance again.

'Colin,' he said.

'Yup?'

'That Nine-Five. The red plane with the yellow tail section. It's making a right mess of things.'

'I know. Somebody should do something about it.'

'Yes. Us.'

Briefly, Michael outlined what he had in mind.

'That be a bonkers plan!' Colin exclaimed.

'You have a better one?'

The big, spherical Amblescrut head rotated from side to side. 'Not as such. But you must admit it'm crazy.'

'Crazy as a headless hen. I reckon we've a one in ten chance of getting through it alive. But we can't let that pirate keep scaring the roughnecks out of the sky.'

Colin heaved a sigh. 'All right. But I be trusting you not to screw up.'

Michael half-laughed. 'I'll do my best.'

He spun the Skylark in a dizzying loop, then dived towards the 9-5.

Colin clamped a hand over his eyes. 'Can't look.'

They zoomed past the 9-5's nose, missing it by a whisker. The 9-5 shuddered in the Skylark's slipstream.

Michael peered upwards as he recovered the Skylark from its dive.

The 9-5 was coming round.

'That got your attention, didn't it?' Michael said to the pirate. He poured on speed. 'OK then, come and get us!'

CHAPTER 106

Only Flesh

Magnus Clockweight had come to a decision.

It was seeing the pirate in the red-and-yellow plane that did it. He recognised those green dreadlocks. He remembered all too well the man's demented laughter during the first attack on Desolation Wells. Now he was watching this same pirate cut a swathe through the roughneck fleet. The roughnecks were dropping like flies. Clockweight's workmates, his friends, the people who were his responsibility, were being killed mercilessly.

Too many of them had died already at the pirates' hands. Here, during this futile assault on *Behemoth*, and back at Desolation Wells. Too many.

Enough.

Clockweight knew what he had to do.

He banked and turned, moving away from the mêlée around the black airship. He felt suddenly, sublimely calm. The low pain from his injuries melted away. He looked down at his burned arm, and the blistering and scabs and redness meant nothing. It was only flesh, and flesh was just a temporary shell. It was the casing that your soul walked around in. The body had no value in itself. Its value lay in the things your mind could make it do – the deeds it could carry out, the purposes to which it could be put.

The sacrifices it could make.

When he was a couple of kilometres out from *Behemoth*, Clockweight turned the Condor again, through 180 degrees.

He lined the airship up in his windshield and throttled forward. The Condor gathered speed unenthusiastically, as though it knew what its pilot intended and wasn't at all pleased.

Then, one-handed, Clockweight lit the fuse of a bottle bomb and tossed it over his shoulder. With a *whoof*, flames flared behind him, and the cockpit rapidly began to fill with heat and smoke. Clockweight focused on nothing but the oval silhouette of *Behemoth* as it grew larger in his field of vision. The smoke thickened. Soon his eyes were streaming, and he was choking for breath. But he kept the plane steady.

In a way, it was a relief. Moments from now, everything would be over. Of course Clockweight was dreading death, but somehow it wasn't so bad, when his death would help save the lives of the remaining roughnecks and finally avenge those who'd been murdered.

He was the toolpusher. The boss. Head honcho at Westward Oil Enterprises extraction and refining installation number 137.

He had always done his job dutifully and to the best of his abilities.

This was his last ever task.

Fear and joy wrestled in Clockweight's heart as he aimed the burning Condor for the exact centre of *Behemoth*'s balloon.

CHAPTER 107

Precision Timing

Michael drew the 9-5 away from the fray, out into the open air. He wobbled the Skylark a few times, to give the pirate the impression that an untrained Groundling was at the controls, not an expert Airborn pilot. It would aid his plan if the pirate underestimated what he was up against.

Abruptly he flung the Skylark into a sharp turn, bringing it about to face the 9-5.

He lined up with the other plane and shot towards it on a direct collision course.

'Ready, Colin?'

'Nope, but let's do it anyway.'

The gap between the Skylark and the 9-5 narrowed at an astonishing rate. Colin groped for the door latch. Michael's bonkers plan required precision timing. Opening the door would create a sudden sideways drag and throw the Skylark off-kilter. Michael would factor that in to their line of approach, but even so, they could not bail out until they were close enough to the 9-5 to guarantee a direct hit.

'Wait for it,' Michael said, clenching his teeth. 'Only when I give the word.'

Colin knew he had to have perfect faith in Michael. There was no alternative. His life was now in his new friend's hands. That was scary but also oddly thrilling. Colin felt giddy.

The pirate, at least, seemed to be playing along. He kept the 9-5 on course, no doubt confident that in a test of nerves between him and a Groundling aviator, he stood to win.

Then . . .

'Dammit!' yelled Michael.

The 9-5 had swerved away. Far too soon.

'I didn't think him'd wimp out like that,' said Colin.

'Me neither. Not his style. Oh, I see.'

The pirate hadn't taken fright, although it looked like that at first. In fact he had spied another target, one that was of more pressing concern than the Skylark.

Clockweight's Condor, spewing smoke from its cockpit as it arrowed towards *Behemoth*.

Michael didn't hesitate. He understood at a glance what Clockweight was up to. He knew, too, that the pirate in the 9-5 recognised the threat to *Behemoth* and would stop the Condor by any means possible.

The bonkers plan was still in effect, although Michael reckoned the survival odds were now down to something like one in twenty.

He homed in on the 9-5, wringing every last scrap of speed he could out of the Skylark. Both were swift planes, but while the 9-5 was closer to the Condor, the Skylark had the lighter airframe.

Michael thought he could just reach the 9-5 – just – before it reached the Condor.

If he was lucky.

CHAPTER 108

Enlightenment

Twitchy Ziz shrieked at the Condor's pilot.

'No no no no no nonononono nooooo!!!'

He'd forgotten all about the Skylark. *That* little escapade was in the past. This other enemy, in his bumbling old clunker of a plane, was going to ram *Behemoth*. The Condor was alight. The Groundling pilot was on a suicide run.

Twitchy Ziz would not stand for that.

A ribbon of spittle froth snaked from his lips as he swooped to intercept the Condor. He didn't even check behind him once to see what had become of the Skylark. He continued to shriek in fury at the Groundling in the Condor, and the words merged together, becoming one long senseless howl.

In the seething turmoil that was his brain, Twitchy Ziz had devised a plan that was much the same as Michael's. Namely, fly at the enemy at top speed, bail out at the very last instant, and *blam*.

He nearly managed to pull it off, too.

He was metres away from the Condor. But just as he was starting to undo the cockpit canopy . . .

The Condor jerked upward, out of his direct line of sight.

Twitchy Ziz didn't hear the impact of the Skylark striking his plane. All he was aware of was a plunging sensation, his stomach slamming into his throat. The Condor and its streaking trail of smoke kept getting smaller and smaller, further and further away.

The 9-5 was shaking and rattling around him.

Cracks crazed the glass of the canopy.

Then, suddenly, Twitchy Ziz understood everything with

pin-sharp clarity. He was fully conscious of his predicament. He knew his aircraft had been hit and downed, he knew he was about to die, and he knew there was not a thing he could do about it.

During the final few seconds of Twitchy Ziz's existence, he was perhaps the sanest he had ever been.

All those birds he had tortured and killed as a boy.

He remembered every single one.

Now he knew how they had felt, what they had gone through, as he'd clasped them tight and wrenched off their wings and snapped their skinny little legs. The helplessness. The abject terror.

He could almost hear their shrill squeals and squawks, coming back to haunt him.

These, though, were the sounds of metal rending and tearing, an aircraft disintegrating, with Twitchy Ziz trapped inside.

And the sounds of Twitchy Ziz himself, in an agony of enlightenment, screaming.

CHAPTER 109

The Men Who Fell To Earth

'Now!'

Colin yanked down the latch and opened the door, swinging it outwards against the onrushing force of the Skylark's airspeed. It took all his considerable strength to keep the door from slamming shut in his face. Wind hammered into the cockpit and the plane lurched sickeningly, yawing and rolling at the same time. All at once the doorway framed a view of nothing but ground.

'Jump!' Michael shouted.

Colin hesitated.

Then a hand shoved him between the shoulder blades and he tumbled out.

Colin had vowed to himself that he wouldn't scream, but he did. He screamed like a girl. He knew Michael was right behind him. Or rather, he didn't know it but had to believe it. Michael had jettisoned himself out of the plane in Colin's wake. Any second now, Colin was going to feel Michael's hands grabbing him. That would happen.

Nevertheless Colin screamed. The desert below him seemed an awful lot nearer than it had any right to be. His eyes were screwed up, his vision a blur. All the same, it was plain to him that the rocks and scrub and sand were rushing up to meet him with terrifying speed.

There was a *boom* of impact from above. Colin had no idea if this was the Skylark colliding with the 9-5 or the 9-5 colliding with the Condor, and he didn't care.

Where was Michael?

Where . . .

Was . . .

Arms banded around Colin's chest. Legs fastened around his midriff. The breath was wrenched from his lungs as his freefall was halted with a powerful jerk.

Clinging to Colin, Michael beat his wings with all his might. The root muscles in his back groaned with the strain. The secondary flight muscles in his chest throbbed in protest too. He felt something tear – a sharp grind of pain low down in his spine. He'd never carried anything this heavy. Even Fletcher Grubdollar was a featherweight compared with Colin. The man was solid bone, it seemed.

Michael flapped and flapped, and the pain intensified, and he knew this wasn't going to be a flight; it was going to be a more or less controlled plummet. That was all he could manage. And he and Colin were going to . . .

. . . hit . . .

. . . the . . .

. . . ground . . .

. . . *hard*.

Dust blossomed in a cloud.

Both Michael and Colin lay still for a long while. They were dazed. They were tangled together so tightly, neither was sure whose limb belonged to whom. Each was scared to move, in case it hurt. Right now they were numb. There was no pain. It was weirdly comfortable to lie there in a heap while the dust cloud thinned and settled around them. If either of them moved, that was when they might find out if they were injured, and how badly.

At last Colin said, 'Mike?' His face was buried in the sand, his voice muffled.

'Yes?'

'Not that you weigh a lot or anything, but . . .'

'What?'

'Would you mind getting off I?'

'OK.'

'Just because, you know, it be'n't very dignified. Two grown men, all hugger-mugger together like this. If you know what I mean.'

'Yeah, I get you.'

Slowly, stiffly, carefully, Michael stirred himself and clambered off Colin. Colin, in turn, picked himself up off the ground, brushing dust from his clothes and spitting out grains of sand. Each checked himself for injury, but everything seemed in working order. Scrapes, bumps and bruises they had in quantity, but nothing more serious than that.

'Did us . . .?' Colin began.

'Get the Nine-Five? We did,' Michael replied.

'And did the Condor . . .?'

Michael peered upwards to find out.

CHAPTER 110

A Mortal Blow

Choking and spluttering, Clockweight steered his plane head-long into *Behemoth*.

The impact stove a hole in the balloon and sent a shock wave rippling out across the canvas. The Condor fragmented. Its engine was rammed through the dashboard and into Clockweight's torso, killing him instantly. The plane's wings folded backwards. Its fuselage crumpled concertina-fashion. The remaining bottle bombs in the cockpit shattered and petrol spurted everywhere. The fire Clockweight had started became a billowing inferno. Flames erupted in all directions, leaping onto the balloon canvas and also onto the walls of the gas cells which had been exposed when the Condor ploughed into the airship.

Behemoth shuddered from stem to stern and lumbered side-ways. She had been dealt a mortal blow. Her frame was bre-ached. Her structural integrity was fatally compromised. What the impact of the plane had started, the fire would finish.

From now on, the lifespan of the former *Brightspans Empress* could be measured in minutes.

CHAPTER III

Stowaway

Aurora and the Grubdollars watched the battle around *Behemoth* with their hearts in their mouths. From time to time Aurora spotted the Skylark at the fringes of the frenzied swirl of action, and she would let out a hiss of relief. There was dismay aboard *Bertha* too, as assault after assault on the airship met with failure and Groundlings fell from the sky. Cassie and Aurora were gripping each other's hands, and the longer the struggle went on, the tighter the knot of their fingers grew. *Behemoth* sailed on through the chaos surrounding her, apparently immune to harm. She seemed as relentless as the desert beneath her, a vast, indomitable, unstoppable thing.

No one in *Bertha* saw the Condor strike the airship. It happened on the far side of her balloon, out of their line of sight. Nor, for that matter, did they see the Skylark crash into the AtmoCorp 9-5, or Michael and Colin hurtling to the ground.

Immediately, though, they perceived that something significant had happened. Things had changed. All at once *Behemoth* was lurching rather than gliding. She rolled slightly, like a wounded whale. Then smoke appeared from behind the crown of her balloon, soon followed by fire, licking upwards, churning in coils and spirals. The blaze spread quickly, heading fore and aft. In no time the black outline of the airship had a corona of flame, like some elliptical solar eclipse.

Den led the cheers. 'Them did it!' he exclaimed. 'Bless my bum, I didn't rate their chances, but them did it!'

'I don't see Michael,' Aurora said softly, anxiously, scanning the sky through a porthole.

'Him's fine,' said Cassie. 'I be sure of it.'

360

Aurora said nothing.

Meanwhile, secreted in one of the murk-comber's crawl-ducts was a figure who should by rights have been dead and yet was still, miraculously, alive. A figure who was more a walking wound than a whole person. A figure sustained and animated by hatred alone.

Centimetre by suffering centimetre, Deacon Hardscree had hauled himself out of the razorweed canyon. He had wrenched the javelin out of his back and then tottered, hobbled, shuffled, often crawled across the desert, following the distinctive pattern of dual furrows churned into the ground by *Bertha*'s caterpillar tracks. Though in unimaginable agony, Hardscree had trailed the murk-comber all the way to the cavern and had slipped aboard, unseen, shortly before the air battle got under way. He'd hidden himself inside and lain still for a while, to recover from the ordeal of the journey. He was summoning his strength for a dying deed, a lethal swansong, one final outburst of violence.

Now, the vengeance-crazed stowaway stirred himself and began to slither out of the crawl-duct, knife gripped beneath his teeth.

Hardscree knew he didn't have long left to live. Minutes at most.

But in that time, while he was still capable of it, he vowed he would slaughter as many Grubdollars as he could.

Desperation + Lack Of Alternative = Extraordinary Feat

Turbulence subsided, cloud dispersed, and *Cerulean* was in clear air.

This coincided with Iaxson and several fellow-Patrollers finally making progress with the hatch. It had defied their best efforts during the journey down through the cloud cover. They had stamped on it and thumped it with the butts of their lances, gradually bending the locking bar and loosening the hinges. Still the hatch had stood firm. Now, at last, it budged. Suddenly it was hanging part-way out of its frame, twisted. It wouldn't hold out much longer.

While the barrage of blows continued overhead, the crew stared out through the windows, astonished.

'Planes?' said the trim-master. 'What are planes doing down here?'

'Never mind that,' said another crewman. 'Look over there. *Behemoth*. And she's on fire!'

The airship lay some five hundred metres off the port side. Everyone clocked her, then turned and stared at Az.

He was no less astonished than they were. How had he done it? How had he pulled off the extraordinary feat of bringing *Cerulean* down in exactly the right spot, getting her to exactly where she ought to be, and, it seemed, just in the nick of time?

He wasn't sure himself. He had obeyed an impulse, that was all. Desperation and a lack of alternative had played a part, but what it boiled down to was that he had surrendered to luck, fate, chance, whatever you cared to call it – all those things that the Count of Gyre claimed didn't exist. He had chosen without trying to make a choice. It had just ... *happened*.

He tried to fathom what this meant, and couldn't.

Then the hatch was finally bashed free from its frame and fell to the floor with a clang. Iaxson dropped down into the gondola. Without any further ado he pounced on Az, seizing him by the shoulder and swinging him round.

'Right, sonny. Enough's enough. *My* ship.'

'Erm, maybe you should take a peek out there, wing commander,' Az said, with a jerk of his thumb.

'Don't give me any more of your guano. There's nothing out there but ...'

The sentence tailed away as Iaxson realised that there was, in fact, an awful lot out there. Namely: a number of planes engaged in aerial combat with Naoutha's pirates, and a certain black airship whose balloon had a huge hole in the side and was on fire.

'Pluck me gently!' the stunned wing commander swore. 'How the —? What the —?' He peered at Az in frank disbelief.

'I've no idea myself,' Az said, 'but we have to get across to *Behemoth*. She's going down, and Mr Mordadson won't thank us if we just stand here and let him go down with her.'

'Men!' Iaxson called up through the hatchway. 'Down here. We're boarding *Behemoth*.'

'And I'm coming with you,' Az said.

'Don't be daft, kid.'

'Wing commander,' Az said, with steel in his voice, 'let's not waste time arguing. I'm coming with you.'

Iaxson looked Az up and down. He realised the boy wasn't going to take no for an answer. And Az had, somehow, given him a chance to rescue his old friend Mordadson. He owed him for that.

'All right. But don't expect me to nursemaid you. Once we're on that airship, you take your chances like the rest of us. You fend for yourself.'

Az nodded. 'Gotcha.'

'Then hold on tight,' Iaxson said, and he scooped Az up in his arms and launched himself out through the viewing windows. Patrollers, lances in hand, followed.

CHAPTER 113

Cheap Psychoanalysis

Mr Mordadson could barely think straight, but he knew two things for certain. One, *Behemoth* was in dire straits, and two, he wasn't leaving till he had dealt with Naoutha Nisrocsdaughter.

He had felt the airship rock just a couple of minutes ago as something smashed into it from the side.

Now, staggering along the keel catwalk, he could hear and smell *Behemoth* burning. Smoke was creeping down into the lower reaches of the balloon, and from above came shrieks of metal warping with heat and firecracker-like bangs as rivets popped from their sockets. In her distress *Behemoth* swayed and wallowed, and the catwalk kept canting at an angle, now one way, now the other. Mr Mordadson tottered from side to side, using his wings to prevent him from being thrown completely off-balance. He would have flown, except his brain was still reeling with the aftereffects of the triple dose of pterine and he was generally in too much pain. He could only just muster the wherewithal to walk.

And he thought he was in a fit state to tackle Naoutha?

He wasn't. But if there was one personal characteristic which Mr Mordadson prized above all others, it was his willingness to keep plugging away till the job was done. Whatever the cost to him, Naoutha would not survive to fight another day. Not if he had anything to say about it. And not if the contingency weapon in his coat pocket had anything to say about it either.

As he neared the entrance to the control gondola, there was a tremendous *crump* as one of the gas cells imploded, emptying itself flat in a second. *Behemoth* lurched downward, engines whining. Mr Mordadson thought she had embarked on a final, fatal, irrevocable plunge, and clung to the catwalk railing and braced himself. But somehow she stabilised and stayed afloat. Truly these troop-carriers were a hardy breed. They had their weaknesses but it took a lot to kill one.

Traversing the last few metres of catwalk, he readied himself to jump into the gondola. If Naoutha was down there, his one hope of defeating her lay in catching her by surprise. All he needed was to get in two or three good hits before she could retaliate, then he could finish her off with the contingency weapon while she was still reeling.

In the event, it was Mr Mordadson who was caught by surprise. A crushing weight struck him from above, sending him sprawling face-first onto the catwalk. He thought he had been hit by some chunk of falling debris, till he tried to rise and was knocked flat again.

Then a pair of leather-encased legs touched down in front of him, and the owner of the legs, in mocking tones, said, 'Well, I went aft to find you, Mordadson, and you've saved me the trouble. How obliging. Now I can kill you and have done with it, and still get off this ship with time to spare.'

'Glad I could ... help, Naoutha,' croaked Mr Mordadson.

He made a grab for her ankle, but she swatted his hand aside with a sweep of one wing.

'I take it old Wonky Wallimson is no longer with us,' she said.

'I talked him into ... setting me free. Bent his ear, in a ... manner of speaking, till he ... gave in.'

'No great loss. He was an idiot. I was going to get rid of him myself, when I had a moment. Again, you've been very obliging.'

She kicked Mr Mordadson in the temple, with casual malice, how you might kick a piece of furniture you'd just stubbed your toe on.

Mr Mordadson rolled with the impact, fetching up with his wings against the railing.

Naoutha squatted beside him, resting her forearms on her thighs. 'Do you ever wonder,' she asked, 'why you do all this? Why you fight and kill on behalf of the Silver Sanctum? I bet you do sometimes, maybe at night when you can't sleep. I bet you lie there in bed and think, *I'm just a paid thug. They don't care about me, those high-and-mighty Sanctum types. They use me to do their dirty work and they're polite to me, but deep down they despise me because my existence reminds them that their world isn't perfect. They'd like it to be perfect, but to achieve that they'll always need people like me, and they hate themselves because of that and hate me for making them hate themselves.'*

'Spare me the ... cheap psychoanalysis, Naoutha,' Mr Mordadson said. 'Your airship's doomed. Your little pirate game ... is over. Face it, you've lost.'

'*I've* lost? So says the man with the face like minced giblets and less than a minute to live.'

'Less ... than a minute? Better hurry ... up, then. I don't think your ... airship's got even ... that long.'

Naoutha bent her head sideways, acknowledging the point.

'Very well then. This may hurt.'

She grasped Mr Mordadson's head with both hands, planted the tips of her thumbs in the corners of his eyes, and got ready to dig them in.

CHAPTER 114

Under Threat

Den Grubdollar saw which way the stricken *Behemoth* was heading, extrapolated her trajectory, and announced to Fletcher, via speaker tube, that perhaps now might be a good time to start *Bertha* up and move her.

Or as he put it: 'That airship'm coming straight for we! Reckon us should shift our ruddy arses!'

Fletcher, seated up in the driver's pod, agreed. *Behemoth* was drawing near to the needle mesa. If she continued on the same course at the same rate of descent, she was going to plunge into the cavern mouth, and that meant she would come down close to, if not right on top of, *Bertha*. Fletcher started up the engine and engaged gear, and *Bertha* lumbered away from the cavern.

'Be that ... be that *Cerulean*?' said Robert, as *Bertha* slowly gathered speed. 'Just past *Behemoth*? Anyone else see that?'

The bright blue airship had appeared just above and behind the black one. It was like some strange optical illusion, *Cerulean* a ghostly double image, shimmering in the heat-haze generated by *Behemoth*'s flames.

Cassie pressed her face to the glass of a loading bay porthole. She could make out a column of winged figures moving across from *Cerulean* to *Behemoth*. One of them, the man in the lead, was carrying a non-winged figure in his arms.

'Az.'

Even as she whispered the name, Cassie felt a surge of fear and impotence.

Az had entered the fray, and was rushing headlong into danger. In a flash, Cassie regretted all the obstacles and mis-understandings and antagonism that the two of them had allowed to rise up between them and cloud their relationship, and she wanted nothing on earth so much as to have that talk with Az, the one Aurora had recommended; to have an opportunity for them to clear the air and start over. She feared she might never get it now.

The boarding party from *Cerulean* entered *Behemoth* at the rear and disappeared from view. The burning black airship continued her slow, inexorable downward progress. Streamers of smoke were billowing back from her nose-cone. Fully half of her balloon canvas was aflame.

Meanwhile, unbeknownst to anyone in *Bertha*, Deacon Hardscree was hauling himself forward through the crawl-ducts. His legs had ceased to work properly so he used his arms only. The razorweed had flensed the skin and meat from one of his elbows. Bare bone bonked every time he jabbed down the elbow and pushed off with it.

At last he made it to the end of the crawl-duct. It opened onto a small storage area which afforded access to the loading bay and also to the driver's pod. Hardscree slithered out. A glance up the shaft into the pod showed him there was just one person there. He could see boots, trouser legs, an arm. They belonged to a young man. Den Grubdollar's elder boy, he assumed. Fletcher was his name? Yes, Fletcher. As good a place as any to start his Grubdollar massacre.

Hardscree grasped the lowest of the rungs and heaved his body up the shaft bit by bit, till his head emerged into the pod. Hooking one arm over the top rung to anchor himself, he took the knife from his teeth with the free hand. He flipped it over, catching the tip in his fingers. The nape of Fletcher's neck was exposed between the back of the seat and the headrest. The range was a little over two metres. An easy throw. An easy kill.

Hardscree angled the knife so that the haft was beside his ear. The blade would enter between two vertebrae and its point would exit through the throat. Fletcher wouldn't feel a thing. He wouldn't even know he was dead.

Muscles contracted. Wrist flexed and straightened. The knife zinged through space.

CHAPTER 115

The First Rule Of Punching

'Spread out!' ordered Iaxson. 'Check every cabin and cranny within a hundred metres. We're here for one minute and not a second longer. If we don't find him within a minute, we bail out. No delaying. No heroics.'

The Alar Patrollers fanned out along the keel catwalk, darting down side-corridors and kicking open cabin doors. A pall of smoke hung in the air, thickening rapidly. Az felt his eyes start to water and his nostrils start to sting. It wouldn't be long before no one was able to breathe or see. Nevertheless he joined the Patrollers on their search. The airship was dying around them. Her groans of suffering merged with the roaring crackle of flames. A minute wasn't enough. There were so many places Mr Mordadson could be.

Soon, all too soon, Iaxson blew a long peep on his whistle, signalling a pull-out.

Ignoring the order, Az picked up his pace. He heard Iaxson shouting for him, and then telling him he was on his own. Fine by him. He plunged still further into *Behemoth*. He continued to try door after door along the catwalk, only to find empty cabin after empty cabin. He yelled out Mr Mordadson's name, but it came out more as a cough than speech. The smoke was becoming chokingly dense. Sparks and embers – scraps of burning canvas – had begun to drift down from above, like a glowing snow. They singed Az's hair. His eyes were streaming with the smoke. He was stumbling, half-blind.

Then, ahead, dimly through the haze, he glimpsed two figures. One was crouching over the other. Black wings. It could only be Naoutha, and by the looks of things she was about to sink her thumbs into Mr Mordadon's eyeballs.

Az didn't hesitate. He charged along the catwalk and ran full-tilt into Naoutha, barging her away from Mr Mordadson. He knocked her over but was going too fast to halt himself and went crashing down with her. Limbs tangled. Az managed to extricate an arm. He began raining punches on Naoutha. Instinct and combat training took over. Mr Mordadson had once urged him to memorise the first rule of punching: *hard to soft, soft to hard*. He couldn't impress on Az enough the importance of that. Unless you wanted to break your own knuckles, you should ease up when hitting an opponent's face or ribs. Anywhere else – stomach, neck, groin – you should feel free to hammer as violently as you liked.

Az hammered. But Naoutha's leatherwear absorbed much of the force of the blows. And Naoutha had wings.

One upward flex of her left wing, full in the face, sent Az reeling. He got to his feet, stunned and groggy, in time to see Naoutha lunging at him. He was able to get his forearms up in a standard block, but the collision was brutal. His forearms took the brunt of it but still he was slammed backwards against the catwalk railing.

'Little wingless brat,' Naoutha intoned. She grabbed him by the neck. 'You've been an absolute pain in the tailfeathers. I'm going to rip the heart from your chest.'

She meant it literally, as well. Az felt her fingers poke into his solar plexus. She fully intended to tear his ribcage open with her bare hands. And he was too dazed to prevent her.

He glimpsed movement over Naoutha's shoulder. A silhouette, rising. Mr Mordadson. Something in his fist. Small. Glinting. Sharp. A hypodermic syringe?

'A taste of ... your own ... medicine, Naoutha,' Mr Mordadson said, and jammed the syringe into her back and depressed the plunger.

And Naoutha ...

... *howled*.

And let go of Az and staggered backwards, tugging out the hypodermic.

And lurched towards the control gondola hatch.

And toppled over the edge and fell in.

And landed below with a thump, out of sight, still howling.

'What was in that syringe?' spluttered Az.

'Mega-dosage of pterine. Six times ... the usual,' said Mr Mordadson. 'Now let's get ... out of here.'

'Yes,' said Az. 'Exit strategy.'

'You have one?'

'You're it. But we have to go out that way.' Az pointed towards the control gondola. Somewhere down there, Naoutha continued to howl, as though her very soul was in torment. Her heels beat out a jagged rhythm on the floor. 'Quickest route. Back along the catwalk's too far.'

Mr Mordadson winced. 'I don't know ... if I can ... fly.'

Through the smoke, Az could see that Mr Mordadson was in dreadful shape. Injuries aside, it seemed that the simple act of standing upright was taking everything Mr Mordadson had. He looked ready to pass out at any moment.

From somewhere outside came a vast, thudding, grinding *boom*. The whole of *Behemoth* was racked with convulsions.

'Tough guano,' said Az, grabbing Mr Mordadson by the sleeve. 'Whether you like it or not, flying's our only hope.'

CHAPTER 116

Near-Miss

Behemoth had hit the needle mesa, just next to its 'eye'. She scraped her starboard flank along it, losing both propellers on that side. Balloon canvas peeled back in strips. The propeller mountings snapped off and tumbled down, ending up as twisted metal wreckage on the ground.

Behemoth carried on, her terminal plunge slowed but not arrested. Skewing sideways, she continued to fall at an acute angle towards the cavern entrance.

The mesa, however, came off rather worse. It shivered with the impact all the way down to its narrow base, and then, with epic slowness, began to topple. The 'eye' section fell first, and the rest of the mesa followed in layers, like the tiers of a tall cake that had been shoved sideways. Slab after immense slab sheared off and came thundering down.

Bertha was not directly in the path of the falling mesa but was close enough for Fletcher to feel the need to take evasive action. He jammed down on the left-hand control stick, and *Bertha* skidded to one side. The 'eye' of the mesa landed not far in front of her, striking the earth with enough force to make the murk-comber jolt. A huge cloud of dust was kicked up, swamping *Bertha*.

The sudden sharp turn saved Fletcher's life, for he performed it at the exact same moment that Hardscree launched the knife at his neck. Hardscree's aim had been true, but *Bertha*'s unexpected jerk to the left meant the knife thudded into the headrest rather than Fletcher's neck. Fletcher escaped death by a margin of three centimetres.

He felt the impact behind his head. Puzzled, he looked round.

And wished he hadn't.

The face that glowered up at him from the shaft was like something out of a nightmare. Torn, mangled, caked in dried blood – Fletcher had never seen anything so hideous, and the sight made every hair on his body stand on end and turned his guts to jelly. He lost his grip on the control sticks. *Bertha* started to decelerate and he didn't even notice. All he could do was stare in numb, abject horror at the head that had protruded into the driver's pod – the head attached to a body that, even as he watched, began to lug itself out of the shaft and pull itself with clawed fingers across the floor towards him. Every movement this *thing* made was shuddery and spasmodic and yet determined too. Grimly determined.

The clumps of red hair still clinging to the torn scalp, and the tatters of robe that wreathed the body, informed Fletcher that he was looking at his father's Deacon. But the man had been hit with a javelin and fallen into a canyon of razorweed. He ought to be dead. How could he still be alive? And how did he come to be here in *Bertha*?

As if from far-off, Fletcher heard his father's voice over the speaker tube, demanding to know why they had slowed down. They'd had a near-miss with the mesa but now they were closer than ever to the airship.

Fletcher could do nothing about that. He couldn't even move himself, let alone *Bertha*. The living ruin that had been Deacon Hardscree had reached his seat and was dragging itself up by the armrest and groping for the knife that protruded from the headrest. The stench of blood and death was awful. The half-dead abomination was almost, almost touching him. Fletcher longed to shrink away from it. But it was as if he was paralysed. His body would not obey the messages his brain was sending it. He could only sit, frozen with fear.

Now Cassie was calling up to him from the loading bay. He tried to answer but his throat was locked tight. He heard her start to climb up towards the pod. He tried to shout out a warning. He couldn't.

Hardscree yanked the knife out. He raised it above his head. Fletcher watched the blade tremble in the air. He knew he was about to die.

CHAPTER 117

Rendered (H)armless

Den Grubdollar scrambled along a crawl-duct from the rear observation nacelle to find out what was going on with Fletcher. The lad would get them all killed if he didn't buck up his ideas and give *Bertha* some juice.

Cassie, meanwhile, sprang up into the driver's pod just in time to catch Hardscree before he could bury his knife in Fletcher's chest. She didn't allow herself to wonder how the Deacon had got there, or to feel any squeamishness. She seized hold of his slashed-up forearm and wrenched it back. Hardscree fought her with maniacal strength, trying to bring the knife down and stab Fletcher. Cassie refused to let him. She would not permit another of her brothers to die. She had saved her father's life. She would save Fletcher's. With every erg of strength she possessed, she hauled back on Hardscree's arm. Her hands became slippery with his blood; it was dripping down her wrists. She clung on all the more tightly.

They were locked in struggle, stalemated, Hardscree trying to force the knife forward, Cassie forcing it back. This couldn't go on indefinitely. Something, Cassie knew, had to give.

Something did.

Hardscree's arm, to be precise.

To be absolutely precise, his shoulder joint.

The muscles surrounding the joint had had all they could take. Shredded, brutalised, under strain – suddenly, with supple slickness, they snapped. Tendons broke. The arm came free from its socket.

Cassie was flung backwards, still clutching the arm, which was still clutching the knife. Hardscree screamed and collapsed in the opposite direction, blood jetting from the ragged hole from which the limb had been uprooted. He landed on top of the access point in the floor of the pod. Cassie fetched up just behind the driver's seat.

She tossed the arm aside in a convulsion of disgust, then shouted at Fletcher: 'Him's lying on the access point! Hit the switch!'

Though her brother was still in a state of shock, he managed to galvanise himself into action. He slapped the switch on the dashboard. The triangular plates beneath Hardscree irised open, and the Deacon fell through.

But not without grabbing Cassie first. His one remaining arm reached out and seized a handful of her shirt. As he plunged through the hole, he dragged her with him. Fletcher made a bid to catch her. He got a hold of her blood-slicked wrist but she slid out of his grasp. Together, Hardscree and Cassie tumbled out of the driver's pod and onto the desert earth.

At that same moment, Den came scrambling up the shaft. He saw the detached arm, blood spray everywhere, Fletcher bending over the open access point. He took the situation in at a glance.

Then he saw *Behemoth* looming. The burning airship filled the windscreen.

Twenty seconds to impact.

CHAPTER 118

Twenty Seconds

20 . . .

The crew of *Behemoth* had sensibly abandoned ship several minutes earlier; they'd realised there was no hope of saving the airship. The control gondola was now empty except for Naoutha, who was howling and writhing on the floor in the throes of her extreme pterine overdose. Az and Mr Mordadson skirted around her thrashing form and made for the viewing windows, which the departing crew had bashed out in order to escape.

19 . . .

On the ground, Cassie lay on top of Hardscree. His body had absorbed the force of the fall, saving her from harm. His arm, however, was clamped around her like an iron band. She struggled but couldn't break free. She could feel his chest rising and falling and hear his breath coming in raspy wet heaves. He was on the brink of death – but he would not let her go.

18 . . .

Abruptly Mr Mordadson collapsed against the trim-master's station, where all of the dials and gauges were going wild. He looked at Az with eyes that were so bloodshot, their whites were crimson. It was almost as if he had his spectacles on again. 'I . . . can't,' he gasped to Az. 'You'll have to . . . jump. I just . . . can't.'

17 . . .

'One,' sighed Hardscree in Cassie's ear. 'Just one of you will do.' And then he let out a croak and his body stiffened beneath her. But his arm did not loosen. It locked her tight against him. A death grip.

16 . . .

'You fly or we both die,' Az said, pulling Mr Mordadson upright. 'Got it?' Feebly Mr Mordadson nodded, and together they staggered towards the windows, with Az supporting most of his friend's weight. And then, behind them, Naoutha's howling sharpened, becoming a keening shriek of fury.

15 ...

'Cass!' Fletcher yelled down from the driver's pod. 'Cass! Get up! Grab a hold on *Bertha*! Us has got to get out of here!' But Cassie shook her head forlornly. 'I can't break free,' she shouted back. 'Just drive, Fletch. Get everyone to safety.'

14 ...

Naoutha, standing tall, her wings out wide, snatched the mask and goggles from her face. What she exposed was not the vision of beauty Az had assumed lay behind her disguise. Far from it. The face might have been beautiful once, but now it was ravaged and half eaten with sores. In places the flesh had rotted away completely, revealing the bone beneath. The toll taken by prolonged use of pterine was terrible to behold, and Az, in spite of everything, was transfixed with horror.

13 ...

Fletcher was about to jump down to the ground, but his father stopped him. 'Drive, boy,' Den said, thrusting him towards the controls. Fletcher protested that they couldn't just leave Cassie lying there, but his father had already leapt down through the access point.

12 ...

Rage, as well as the pterine sores, disfigured Naoutha's features. She lurched towards Az and Mr Mordadson, fully resolved to stop them getting away. If she was going to go down with her airship, so were they.

11 ...

Landing next to his daughter, Den bent down and tried to prise her from Hardscree's clutches. The arm clung on with inhuman tenacity. Meanwhile, Fletcher brought *Bertha* back to life and shoved down hard on the right-hand control stick. Tears were pouring down his cheeks, but he knew his father was right. For Aurora's and Robert's sakes, he had to drive.

379

10 ...

Az went into a crouch. Naoutha took off and swooped at them. Az knew he had just one shot at this, one chance to get it right. His leg flashed out in a roundhouse kick. His foot slammed into Naoutha's midriff and she went hurtling backwards, crashing against the gondola's aft wall.

9 ...

Den grimaced with effort. He pulled. Cassie pushed. The arm bent, bent further ... Something creaked. Something cracked. Suddenly Cassie was free.

8 ...

Outside the viewing windows, the cavern entrance gaped like a dark, hungry maw. Az bundled Mr Mordadson over to the shattered frames. Pterine-crazed Naoutha was screaming senseless words of vengeance, flailing as she tried to get up.

7 ...

Bertha slewed to the right, her left rear track missing Den and Cassie by centimetres. Den grasped his daughter's wrist and dived for the back of the murk-comber.

6 ...

Az shoved himself and Mr Mordadson out of the gondola. His last glimpse of Naoutha showed her rising to her feet while burning debris began to pour down through the hatchway. She stood, a black silhouette against a backdrop of tumbling flames.

5 ...

Den latched on to a projecting piece of *Bertha*'s bodywork and clung on by his fingertips. With his other arm he swung Cassie round and up. She landed on the mudguard above the left rear track.

4 ...

For a second, it seemed to Az that he and Mr Mordadson were suspended in midair. They floated in space while *Behemoth* sailed above them, a vast blazing fireball, like the sun brought to earth.

3 ...

Den's grip slipped. Cassie viced a hand around his wrist before he could slide off *Bertha* onto the ground. Sprawled on the mudguard, she held him while Fletcher poured on the speed, trying to outrace *Behemoth*. The airship was so low that Cassie could feel the heat from its flames. The crackle of burning was deafeningly loud.

2 ...

'Fly!!!' Az yelled, and Mr Mordadson flapped his wings, weakly at first, but then with more force. Az clung on to his arm, as Mr Mordadson's wings carried both of them out from under the belly of *Behemoth*.

1 ...

Cassie looked up.

Az looked down.

Each saw the other lit up by the glare of the airborne inferno that was *Behemoth*. Illuminated.

Then ...

Crash.

CHAPTER 119

Simultaneous Burial And Cremation

Behemoth died amid fire and fury.

As she rammed head-first into the cavern, her fuel tanks ignited. The explosion cracked her apart in the middle, sending sheets of flame in all directions and shattering the rock around the cavern entrance. The roof of the cavern immediately began to crumble, coming away in boulder-size chunks. While the front portion of *Behemoth* rolled down the incline with a slow, elephantine grace, the rear portion was buried in a cascade of stone and stalactite. Framework was crushed, cables snapped, metal spars splintered, fins were flattened, all amidst bulging gouts of smoke and flame.

As the cave-in continued, gathering speed, the front portion of the airship rolled on, also gathering speed. Like some immense wheel of fire it hurtled through the subterranean darkness, following the course of the railway track, downward into the deeps of the earth where the aircraft mausoleum lay. It disintegrated as it went, shedding segments, losing shape, till by the time it reached the Deacons' depository of fallen planes it was more like an avalanche, a tidal wave of burning bits and pieces, a torrent of fiery fragments, which broke over the collected aircraft and parts of aircraft, and over the joists and the generator which the Deacons had installed, setting everything alight.

In short order, the dome-like chamber was ablaze. The place became one large conflagration which burned rapidly and steadily, destroying planes and infrastructure, laying waste to the handiwork of Airborn and Groundling alike.

Up above, the cavern mouth flattened with a titanic *boom*, sealing itself shut for ever.

The smoke and dust took an hour to disperse.

CHAPTER 120

The Talk

The Aerodyne Striga II rose till it scraped the base of the cloud cover. This was a safe, neutral zone, high enough for an Airborn not to get too ground-sick, low enough for a Groundling not to suffer altitude-related problems.

Michael put the Striga into a circling pattern, and for a while he and his two passengers, Az and Cassie, surveyed the scene on the ground.

Down there, the surviving roughnecks were gathered in a rapturous huddle, celebrating the demise of *Behemoth* and their part in her downfall. At the same time they mourned the death of their toolpusher, Magnus Clockweight. Their cheers were tinged with sorrow as they spoke of his heroic act of self-sacrifice, and the sacrifices of all their colleagues who hadn't made it safely back to ground.

Colin was in the midst of the roughnecks, and was enjoying the praise he got for his part in helping clear Clockweight's path to the airship. Michael didn't mind Colin taking the much of credit. The lad had done well. Besides, Michael would much rather be up here, scooting around in the Striga. It wasn't the Skylark, of course, but it was almost as good. And, being a limousine-class plane designed to be chauffeur-piloted, it had voluminous seats in the back and a partition that could be raised between cockpit and passenger section for privacy.

Cerulean hovered at a similar height to the plane. The Alar Patrollers had rounded up *Behemoth*'s crew and locked them in *Cerulean*'s cabins. Once the pirates had realised that *Behemoth* was doomed, the fight had gone out of them. They had nothing left to defend, the whole pirate escapade was over, and so they'd surrendered meekly to Wing Commander Iaxson. Iaxson wished that their ringleader, Naoutha, was in his custody as well, but he appreciated that that would never be. He and Mr Mordadson were both quite convinced that she had perished along with *Behemoth*. No one could have survived that explosion or the cave-in that came after.

Bertha was parked not far from the ruins of the cavern. She waited to take Cassie back to Grimvale. Michael and Aurora would be hitching a ride home with Az in *Cerulean*. The (now quite definitely) last surviving troop-carrier airship was due to depart within the hour. Rigz and Ra'asielson were showing signs of recovery and Aurora was attending to them. Their wounds remained a cause for concern, however, and getting them to a sky-city for proper medical attention was a high priority.

Az and Cassie did not, therefore, have long. But then, they were used to that.

Michael, with a sly smile, pressed the switch to raise the partition between him and them. The strained muscle in his lower back was hurting like crazy, but he wasn't going to let it stop him giving his brother and his brother's girlfriend this private time together.

The Striga completed another full circuit before either Az or Cassie could think what to say. Then they both blurted out something simultaneously.

'Cassie, I think I should —'

'Az, it'm probably —'

They stopped.

'You go ahead,' said Az.

'No, you.'

'No, *you.*'

'Don't be so damn polite.'

'Why not? I was brought up well.'

'What, and I weren't?'

'Don't get all snitty. I didn't mean it like that.'

Cassie relented. 'You'm right. Sorry. So, anyway. You got your bad guy, then.'

'I did. And so did you.'

'Yeah. Mine was a real creep.'

'Yeah, but mine was ugly.'

'Mine were pretty ugly too. Not to begin with, but him ended up a right old *urrghhh*.' She shuddered at the memory of the maimed and mutilated Hardscree.

'But mine had only half a face,' said Az.

'Yeah, but mine . . . Well, maybe us shouldn't get into a whose-bad-guy-were-uglier competition.'

'Agreed. On the plus side, you found your dad.'

'I did. And you found your pirate airship.'

'Which your side destroyed.'

'Which us'd wouldn't have managed if you hadn't chased her here.'

'Funny how we both wound up homing in on the same spot in this desert.'

'Yeah, funny.'

'Separate quests, same destination.'

'If you want to be all fanciful about it.'

'I can't help it. I'm feeling a bit odd and fanciful about the entire situation. Like there's something more to it all, something I can't easily explain.'

'Such as?'

Az frowned, searching inside himself for how he felt and a means of expressing it. 'When I came down through the cloud cover, I . . . I somehow knew that that was what I had to do. It was a statistical improbability that we'd end up almost on top of *Behemoth*. It was absurd, a million-to-one chance. I was winging it completely. But it makes you wonder, doesn't it?'

'It makes *I* think you were just phenomenally lucky.'

'Could be that's all there is to it,' Az conceded. But the faraway look in his eyes suggested he thought otherwise.

'Whereas I,' said Cassie, 'had to track down my da through detective work and sheer hard slog. Nothing more'n that. No luck involved. Well, not much.'

'Oh, you had it easy, definitely,' Az said with a laugh.

'Cheek!' Cassie gave him a playful punch on the arm.

'Traipsing halfway across the Westward Territories, getting caught up in a mob in Craterhome and nearly eaten by hackerjackals and nearly killed by a raving-mad Deacon – and you's the nerve to call that *easy*???' She hit him again, and then a third time, for good measure.

'Stop that!' Az said, rubbing his arm. 'You don't know your own strength.'

'You Airborn be soft, that'm the problem.'

'Soft? I'd punch you back, if you weren't a girl and I wasn't a gentleman.'

'Go ahead,' said Cassie teasingly.

'I'm trained in combat, you know.'

'Don't care.'

'I could kill you without meaning to.'

'You and whose army?'

'Just me. I'm a living weapon. You should have seen the kick I nailed Naoutha with.'

'Ooh, you're such a big hero.'

'I *am*, though.'

'Such a bighead too.'

'Hey!'

They both started laughing, and suddenly, in the middle of the laughter, they both caught themselves and halted. They looked at each other.

'This . . .' said Az. 'This feels good.'

Cassie nodded. 'I know.'

'This is us. This is how we are together. How we should be.'

She nodded again. 'Stuff got in the way, Az.' She laced her fingers into his. 'I shouldn't have let it but it did. You know how important family be to I. That'm my only excuse but I reckon it be a good one.'

'Family's important to me too, Cassie. But you didn't have to shut me out. I'd have helped. You know that. Right from the start. All you had to do was ask.'

'Next time I will.'

'And don't you get the impression that someone's trying to tell us something?'

'Huh? Who d'you mean?'

'Not a person. Just – I don't want to use the words fate or destiny, but look how all this turned out. Your and my paths got drawn together, despite us. It's like we couldn't do anything about it. Even though we had our differences, we still got pulled into the same adventure. Doesn't that tell you anything?'

'Only that you be reading too much into things. You see destiny working, I just see life doing what it does, which be flowing together sometimes, falling apart at other times, coming back together once more, and so on. Just the usual give-and-take, that'm all. You'm a hero all right, Az, I be'n't denying that. You's done good stuff. Old Mordy owes you his life. But little things, ordinary things, can make a hero as well. There don't have to be an airy-fairy something like destiny running the show. It'm *people* who run the show. You, me, everyone. And us can be heroes in all sorts of ways.'

'But there's a grand scheme, isn't there? A bigger picture?'

'If so, it'm made up of lots of people. Humans. Groundlings, Airborn, whatever. Just we, all interacting and clashing and working together. That be your bigger picture.'

'I . . .'

Cassie rapped him on the forehead, as if to knock all the difficult thoughts to the back of his brain. 'Az, time's short. Let's make the most of it.'

'Eh?'

'I said, shut up and snog I.'

The Striga circled and circled until the needle on the fuel gauge hovered near zero. Then Michael brought the plane down for a smooth, perfect landing. It and its occupants touched ground as though as light as a feather.

CHAPTER 121

First Epilogue:
Lady Aanfielsdaughter And Aurora

'I understand congratulations are in order,' said Lady Aanfielsdaughter. 'We're expecting to hear the flutter of tiny wings.'

'That's right,' said Aurora, with a slight blush. 'It's early days yet, but still ...'

'But still, thrilling news. Anyone in mind for godparents?' Lady Aanfielsdaughter gave her a significant look.

'Milady, you are top of the list. Of course, I shan't let the baby interfere with my work. I'd like to continue at the Sanctum full-time, or as close to full-time as I can manage.'

'We can't function without you, Aurora. You'll have your maternity leave, and then I'm sure we can work out amenable hours.'

'I've been talking to Michael about his moving here, so he can help out with the childcare.'

'Let me know if he agrees to it and I'll help you find a nice large apartment.'

'*When* he agrees to it, don't you mean?'

Lady Aanfielsdaughter smiled. 'My mistake. I wasn't taking into account your formidable powers of persuasion. Which reminds me. I've just received a letter from the WOE executives expressing gratitude for our assistance in halting the pirates. They've lost their installation, of course, and we're working on a reparations package of some kind. But there'd have been a lot less compliance from them and a whole lot more complaint, I'm sure, if it weren't for your decision to get involved and coax your husband and the Grubdollars into helping out the oil company employees. You judged it brilliantly. It was a wise move, both tactically and diplomatically. Well done.'

'Thank you, milady.'

'And now that you've been back at the Sanctum for a few days, may I ask you something?'

'Please do.'

Lady Aanfielsdaughter rose from her desk and went to the windows to take in the view. 'How are people reacting to this whole Redspire business, now that it's over? How well do they think I handled it? What's your opinion on the general mood here? Be candid.'

Aurora considered her answer. 'There's some concern still. Not about what we did but about what the long-term consequences of the pirate attacks might be. I understand there have been reports of unrest in several Groundling cities, and up here the Feather First!ers are becoming ever more vocal and gaining new recruits every day. Those are worrying developments. But on balance I think the mood at the Sanctum is favourable. We did what we did, and it worked out OK.'

'And me?' said Lady Aanfielsdaughter, still looking away so that Aurora could not see the troubled light in her eyes. 'What are they saying about me?'

'Milady . . .'

'Ah. That bad, is it?'

'You're still the most popular senior resident by far,' said Aurora. 'But I've heard grumbles here and there, people saying you should have cracked down harder and sooner on the pirates. Some are even saying you should have done something about Redspire long before the pirates reared their heads.'

'Hindsight is a wonderful thing. What, am I supposed to anticipate every crisis before it happens? Am I supposed to have precognitive powers? And if a place like Redspire misbehaves but doesn't actually break any laws, I'm still expected to send in the Patrollers? Isn't that a bit, well, draconian?'

'I wasn't saying the criticisms are fair, milady. And they're coming from a small minority. I'd ignore them, if I were you. They'll die down soon enough.'

'I only wish I *could* ignore them, Aurora, but a minority grumbling today can become a majority calling for my head tomorrow. I need to take these detractors seriously if I'm to stay in this job.'

What Lady Aanfielsdaughter left unsaid was that she wasn't sure how much longer she actually wished to stay in the job. Instead, she turned back to Aurora, looking as regal and in-control as she always did.

'But let's just bask for now in the glow of achievement,' she said. 'There could be trouble ahead, but for the moment we've won. Let's enjoy that. Moving on to more important matters ... Have you thought of names yet? If it's a girl, I think Serena has a nice ring. Don't you?'

CHAPTER 122

Second Epilogue:
The Grubdollars

Rubbing sleep-grit from his eyes and yawning, Robert shuffled downstairs to the courtyard. Someone on the other side of the solid, portcullis-style gate was pounding away, hard enough to rattle the hinges.

'Who'm there?' he called out. 'You know what time it be?'

'Grimvale constabulary. Open up.'

'What does you want?' Robert asked, suddenly alert and on edge.

'Open up,' came the curt reply, along with more pounding.

Robert obeyed, and found half a dozen policemen standing outside. Two of them he recognised – local coppers. The rest were unfamiliar, from out of town.

'Robert Grubdollar,' said one of the locals. 'These gents with I be from the Craterhome police department. Them's here in connection with an incident that occurred a fortnight ago, involving your murk-comber.'

'What?'

'Son, don't play games,' said one of the Craterhome police-man, a cynical-looking sergeant. 'Us has a large number of eyewitness and victims, all of whom has given sworn affidavits testifying to the fact that on the date in question a murk-comber caused widespread bodily harm to a number of Craterhome citizens. There'm also the small matter of damage done to a piece of civic statuary, repairing which be estimated to cost five thousand notes. It'm taken we a while to establish whom the murk-comber in question belonged to, but following extensive investigations, and with the assistance of our Grimvale brethren here, us has narrowed down the list of suspects to one. To wit, the murk-comber under the registered ownership of Dennis Grubdollar and family.'

'But – but – them was all in a mob around us' said Robert, wide-eyed. 'It were self-defence. And that statue – that were a total accident.'

'So you be'n't denying either of the incidents took place.'

'No. Yes. No, I be ...' Robert was flustered and didn't know what to say.

He was rescued by his father, who appeared in the courtyard, dressed in his pyjamas, with Cassie and Fletcher in tow.

'What'm all this about?' Den demanded. 'What be you lot doing here at crack of dawn? Be'n't decent folk allowed their kip?'

'Put plainly, Mr Grubdollar,' said the sergeant from Craterhome, 'you and your family's in deep, deep trouble. You may consider yourselves under house arrest for the time being, and us is impounding your murk-comber as evidence of a crime.'

'House arrest? Impounding *Bertha*?' Den spluttered.

'Now, I be sure you'm willing to do this quietly. No fuss and nonsense.'

'Da!' said Cassie. 'Them can't take *Bertha*. Us can't let they.'

Den looked at her, and at his sons, and then at *Bertha*, and finally back at the policemen. His shoulders rose and fell in a gesture of defeat.

'Actually, I don't know how us can stop they,' he said.

At an order from the sergeant, two of the Craterhome policemen moved towards *Bertha*. Cassie ran to prevent them getting aboard, but her father grabbed her and pulled her against him. She struggled but he wouldn't loosen his grip.

Dismayed, the Grubdollars watched the policemen enter *Bertha*, start her up (on the fifth attempt), and drive her out of the courtyard.

Cassie was in floods of tears as the murk-comber disappeared down the street. *Bertha* herself seemed unhappy about this turn of events. Her cackle held none of its usual glee.

'It'm just a misunderstanding, girl,' her father said softly. 'Us'll sort this out in no time.'

But his face told a different story.

CHAPTER 123

Third And Final Epilogue:
Lord Urironson And ???

The visitor came at the prearranged hour. It was long after nightfall and the Silver Sanctum was dark. Lord Urironson was waiting on the balcony outside his apartment, and no sooner had the visitor alighted than he ushered him hastily indoors, closing the windows behind him. For several moments the two of them stood in Lord Urironson's sitting room, saying nothing, while the mynah bird that occupied a cage in a corner eyed the new arrival warily, cocking its yellow-flashed head from side to side.

'You're here,' Lord Urironson said at last. 'You actually came. I must admit, your request for a meeting surprised me. Not so much the request itself, more the way it was phrased. The tone. It sounded almost conciliatory. As if you aren't here to upbraid me, or even – and I hope I'm right about this – hurt me.'

'Hurt me, *awrrk*,' croaked the mynah, accurately mimicking its owner's rich, fruity tones.

The visitor answered Lord Urironson with a curt nod, nothing more.

'In fact,' the senior Silver Sanctum resident continued, surer of himself now, 'although I have every reason to fear you, I suspect that you come in peace. Would I be correct in that surmise?'

'Correct in that surmise,' the mynah cawed.

Lord Urironson silenced the bird with an irritable gesture. The mynah, miffed, turned round on its perch and began to nibble at the underside of one wing.

The visitor nodded again.

'I thought as much,' his lordship said. 'You see, had your intent been hostile, you would not have requested a meeting at all, and your message certainly wouldn't have asked me to keep it a secret from your immediate superior. In the normal course of events I'd have consulted with Lady Aanfielsdaughter beforehand, as soon as you got in touch, to establish if you were acting on her behalf or independently. By telling me not to, you were letting me know that you are acting of your own volition. Which is interesting indeed. Am I detecting a schism? A breaking of the ranks? Is there a whiff of betrayal in the air?'

The visitor gave a calm, discreet smile.

'Then elucidate,' said the senior resident. 'Tell me what you want from me.'

With a slight bow and a small fluffing of the wings, the visitor did.

'Yes, I agree, Lady Aanfielsdaughter *is* a spent force,' said Lord Urironson when the visitor had finished outlining his motives and intentions. 'You're wise to be distancing yourself from her. But what about Az Gabrielson? How will your young protégé feel about this – this change of heart?'

'Az?' said the visitor. 'Az could be a problem. But he'll be *my* problem, and when the time comes . . .' The smile on the visitor's bruised, black-and-blue face widened, turning cruel. 'When the time comes, I will deal with him. You can count on that.'

'Then,' said Lord Urironson, extending a hand, 'let us shake on it. A new partnership. An alliance. A clandestine one for now, but not for long.'

'*Thweep*, a new partnership,' echoed the mynah softly, still with its back turned to the two humans.

'Indeed,' said Mr Mordadson, and he reached out and firmly shook Lord Urironson's hand.

The End